About t

Christopher Beanland is the author of the novels *The Wall in the Head* and *Spinning Out of Control*, and is currently writing a third work of fiction. He has also written the non-fiction book *Concrete Concept – Brutalist Buildings Around the World*, and contributed to and edited other books about architecture. He is working on several new non-fiction titles. He writes about culture for various newspapers, magazines and broadcasters around the world including the *Guardian*, the *Independent*, the *Telegraph*, the BBC and Euronews.

The Wall in the Head

The Wall in the Head

Christopher Beanland

unbound

This edition first published in 2019

Unbound
6th Floor Mutual House, 70 Conduit Street, London W1S 2GF
www.unbound.com
All rights reserved

ISBN (eBook): 978-1-78965-030-3
ISBN (Paperback): 978-1-78965-029-7

Cover design by Mecob

Printed and bound in Great Britain by Clays Ltd, Elcograf S.p.A.

These words would not have been written and this book would never have been published without Nicky Trup. Beginning, middle and end, this is for you, with all the love in my heart.

Super Patrons

David Baldwin
Carole Beanland
John Beanland
Michael Beanland
Akeela Bhattay
Richard Bratby
John Chapman
Monica Glasgow
Tracey Higginson
Dan Kieran
Andrea Klettner
John Mitchinson
Scott & Kate Moseley
Ronan O'Shea
Michael Paley
Justin Pollard
Nicky Trup

0

Fragments. Everything is fragmentary, everything is fleeting. Cracked little shards sometimes coalesce into stories. But stories never end neatly. Dramas happen, from time to time, in half-hour blocks – like cheap television programmes. Then it's back to a bleak routine. Why bother trying to arrange things? Why bother trying to jam the jigsaw pieces together?

1

1 September 2008. Monday. Belinda was gone. She'd been gone for weeks. So I tried to kill myself. And I meant it. God, I meant it. But something got in the way. I'm still not entirely sure what. Answers on a postcard?

The sky was burned out black. But the darkness couldn't stretch itself; there was too much light fighting its way in, too much of an iridescent glow blasting from the awful offices and the takeaways. Electric citrus, a fake nocturnal sunrise. The city refused to be cloaked. It screamed back. It yelled and it kicked out. The buildings, the lights, the people. They all attacked the night. The yelps from twenty-eight floors below. They put me off. People having fun? Wasted people. Drinkers. Revellers. Stag parties. Hen parties. Broad Street piss artists. I just wanted to be with her, to be away from here. I just wanted to hold her cheek in my hand again, to sit at the kitchen table watching her whisk batter again, to hear her speaking to me, for me, again. The smell of her hair and the touch of her skin. I can't bear not owning her anymore.

The wind whipped and curled and funnelled; the rain flecked on the roof like hammers on tin. The sky yelled. The ledge was narrow. Now. The horizon rose up and up and up as I tilted forward. Steel cut through the inertia. Possibility was pregnant. A lump in my throat. I couldn't swallow. My temples throbbing. Blood and bile and hope and sickness rising through my veins like poison taking hold. Wind and pressure and horror. Explosions and heat. My head is going to burst. Shrill traffic noises, beeping and revving. Something happening, something finally fucking happening. (For God's sake, don't see this as some kind of encouragement to jump off a building or I'll have blood on my bloody hands. I'm telling you this because we've already got something, haven't we? I'm addressing you. Everything I write is for someone, for someone's entertainment. I haven't got her anymore; at this second and for this ending, I've just got you. Whoever you are.) Liquid running down my cheeks, but what variety? A salty tang at the corners of my mouth. Birmingham's concrete forest blurred. The scene needed a cut. I said, 'I love you Belinda. I'm coming for you... *Ich liebe dich...*'

Finally, I fell. When that moment came, I didn't hesitate. Remember that. I didn't hesitate for a second. I stood on that ledge, and then I let myself fall forwards, slide right off it, hoping to go through an invisible portal, towards a place where everything was possible – because nothing was there. And it felt good. Yes, it was exciting. Truthfully. The power you feel for that second or two or three or four – the levers are yours again. Your hands back on the controls. Push and pull. Oh, it was like the best fairground ride. I think I was laughing. I know I was grinning. Faster, whizzing and whooshing towards the square below. Falling, falling, falling... then suddenly, not falling? What? An immense belch of wind crashed into me from below; my whole body shuddered. A deity's handprint? No. Just pure chance. It was unreal. The gust swirled and spiralled and magic-carpeted me upwards again.

Rising, rising, rising, rising, rising… how? Why? The spurt of wind flipped me up and over that ledge I'd just been standing on. A sack of bones and organs smashing into a tarmac roof, bouncing, skidding along until I came to a stop. I lay there, blinking, looking up at the angry sky. I pulled a cigarette out of my pocket and placed it between my lips, fingers quivering. Sparking the lighter over and over again. I mouthed, 'What the…?' as a pain like nails piercing fresh flesh spread along my back and legs in waves. Then I just started laughing as the pain grew more intense. Ripping. Rippling. Agony. A loud clanking noise, metal on concrete. Boots tramping along. A man in uniform, a beam of light attached to him, appeared from the darkness of the fire exit door. The door I'd walked out of. The door I hadn't intended to walk back in through. He cupped his hands round my cigarette, lit it, lit one for himself and crouched there in silence, smirking and staring out into the middle distance.

'This is going to be perfect in my next TV show,' I groaned, inhaling, cig between cracked lips, as a nicotine head rush blasted my brain. And by way of explanation, should it be needed: 'I write comedy.'

He raised his eyebrows, shook his head, and looked at his watch. I was blinking furiously – liquid stained my vision, emotion stained my mind. I looked at the guard. For a split second the guard had become a woman with blonde hair in a ponytail and a face that was free of make-up and expression. But the next time I blinked the guard was a man again. I lay back, head on hard something, eyes towards sky-something, feeling something – but what?

2

I yanked the fridge door and it opened with a surprised gasp. Inside, a fragile light flickered in the dark. The fridge was empty, wiped, it stank of surgery – I'd cleared it out this morning in anticipation of my death. I didn't want to seem like a monster – no one needs the spike of rotting food in their nostrils when they're clearing out a dead bloke's house.

I went upstairs to my desk, looked out of the window at the caramel street lights of Moseley, at the trees swaying back and forth in the high winds. I flicked on the computer and started writing about what I'd done tonight, but the words didn't come easily. Words hadn't come easily since Belinda had to ruin everything. When I could manage no more I lay down on the bed, staring at the ceiling. Sleep hadn't come easily either, but tonight it ate me up. The duvet enveloped me; my eyelids slid shut like they were greased. I succumbed to the darkness and the solitude it promised.

This is a dream:
   I can see. I'm part of the world I'm seeing – I'm participating,

not just observing. I look down and I see hands. I twist them around, tensing and flexing. I'm alive, alright. It's Birmingham. I'm watching a blonde-haired woman sleep. She's lying on a bed in the middle of a roundabout overlooked by two tower blocks. It's daytime but there's no one else around. Just her. She's dozing peacefully, curled into a ball, with golden locks falling across a face painted with a honey glow of serenity. I don't think it's Belinda. I think it's someone else. I'm not sure. I wouldn't put a bet on who it was – I can't see well enough. It's a dream; things are a bit fuzzy, misleading. It's like watching through cataracts. I turn around and I see a new scene. A skyscraper stretching upwards into the sky like a sentinel. It's made from concrete; its hue is deep grey, with jagged lines running up and down it, and different-sized blocks around the bottom. The Mids TV HQ. The studios and the bar at the bottom, the office tower stretching upwards. The office tower I just jumped off. Tension, fizzing, refracted sunlight, pickled emotions, streetscapes grey and green, no people, bridges red and brown, a heartbeat jumping, my heartbeat jumping. The same blonde woman is sleeping on the same bed below; she wakes and points up to the Mids TV Tower. Next scene. A thinner tower without windows – the BT Tower. The blonde woman is standing by it, wearing a knowing expression, looking a little like a witty English teacher? I turn a final time. One more scene. The same woman on a bed in the middle of an open-topped atrium space. There's nothing surrounding us at ground level apart from twelve slender pillars. Above about the third storey there are concrete sides of a box with windows facing inwards to create a courtyard – but the roof is open and sunlight falls in like it's being shovelled down onto us by a giant gardener. The woman wakes up, stretches her arms and sits up on the bed. She lights a fag. She turns and swings her legs down over the edge of the bed. Her face. A sudden crash-zoom in on her face. She looks at me, helplessly. She stares right into my eyes. Her mouth doesn't move – but this sound comes out of it: 'Donald.' There's a drummer in my chest, hitting so hard I can hardly concentrate.

TEN BRUTALIST BUILDINGS

By Belinda Schneider (Published 2002)

Chapter One

Birmingham Central Library

Use your eyes. Listen to your heart. Two things interest me most: what does a building look like? How does a place make you feel? That's it. That's the secret. Architecture is really about the art around us, the art you spend your life inside – or outside, looking in at – and it's about the things that happen there. Things that have happened to you. Things that have happened to all of us.

Life isn't just fragmentary, it isn't just fleeting. Put the little pieces together and mould them into a story. You can slot things together into a narrative jigsaw. Draw lines between feelings and meanings like art does, connect events and ideas like philosophy does. There is a purpose. Art explains the world. We as participants in art and in life can achieve something. And with these particular buildings, built at a particular time, we did try to achieve something – something for everyone. Something for everything. Perhaps brutalist buildings are the closest thing to a pure evocation of utopia that we ever achieved. Or tried to achieve, at least. These buildings, these places, were for the people and for the future. Public places where public lives were led, lives both sad and happy. That's why I love them.

The first time I saw my future husband was inside the courtyard in the middle of Birmingham Central Library. There was no roof and no stupid fast-food joints back then – they were moronically added later. There was just a huge open space with cliffs of pure white concrete surrounding a cool plaza. Sunlight streamed down; the splash of water fountains and the chatter of people filled the air. I liked Birmingham because it was a city defined by its architecture and by its hopes. By the future, not by the past. It still is. People think of it as a place filled with certain buildings, certain types of buildings. They probably don't like those buildings much. I do.

Important moments have to happen somewhere, and because they happen in a certain place or a certain building, then that place or that building is forever imbued with an importance that goes far beyond the structure, beyond bricks and beyond concrete. These places are the theatres where real-life dramas are played out. How many couples had their first lunch date here? How many couples had their first kiss here? How many couples had sex here? How many couples broke up while sitting on benches in these squares? You have to look around and feel these ghosts – the ghosts of the present, of the past, and of the future.

Here's my story. Donald was dressed as a chicken. He'll deny that, of course. But he definitely was. A human-sized chicken. He took his chicken head off and I stared at him for a while as I smoked a cigarette. He looked quite handsome, I thought. His mop of blonde hair was all scruffed up from being inside the chicken head, and his eyes squinted as they came to terms with the afternoon brightness. I liked him. He drank a can of soft drink, cola perhaps, put the chicken head back on and manoeuvred round so he was between me and the camera. He did this stupid little dance and handed out a few flyers to some passing office workers, then the director yelled, 'Cut!' A little later they filmed another segment, and after they'd done that Donald came over to me and asked me if I could do a Birmingham accent, and I tried but it was pretty laughable. I was glad he talked to me. I noticed he looked into my eyes for just a second too long while we chatted. It was a total giveaway. He came into the library a little later when I was studying, and we talked some more. I was sitting down at a desk and he was standing up. The recessed squares of the coffered ceiling framed his face beautifully; the scene was so symmetrical. I enjoyed the aesthetic perfection of it all. He thought I was rather too amused by him. I was.

Motion. Movement. Meaning. I watched people moving up and down the escalators in that library for hours. People moved smoothly and diagonally, like they were starring in a line graph. They were literally moving forward. We all were. 'Forward' is Birmingham's motto. That was before things changed and we lost faith in the power of the future, of modernism, of the state, of architects – in fact of anyone who told us to do anything and anyone who tried to make it better for us. We're all on our own now.

Now the way I felt about that building, the Central Library, will always be different to how Donald feels about it. Women feel buildings differently, just as women feel words differently. My words come from my body; they're born of me. They have some kind of inner meaning. Words can be female like buildings can be female. Birmingham Central Library is a woman. A grand dame, an Aztec goddess. All the librarians were women too. The architect of Birmingham Central Library was a man, of course. The architects of nearly all modernist buildings were men. But we can't blame the building for the fact that its designer had a dick. Half a century ago I'd have been typing the notes for some man in a suit – some functionary, rather than typing out my own thoughts and feelings like I'm doing now. Some things have changed for the better, then. But, crucially, these buildings were trying to break us all out of that staid age, to shoot us *into a technological future where women would have more value and people wouldn't be wage slaves anymore. And we'd all live in clean, planned cities packed with buildings that made you go 'Wow'.*

The storm had passed. Eyes full of sun. I yawned. A proper night's sleep – my first proper night's sleep without Belinda. A gnawing ache ground into my left hip. I heaved myself up, went to the kitchen and made myself a cup of tea – black; I had no milk, of course. Slippers on, out to the garden. I lit a cigarette in slow motion and looked down the garden, away from the house, towards the railway line. The line was tucked away beneath a steep slope behind the garden.

Should I restock the fridge, or should I kill myself?

I sucked on the death stick and sipped my tea. Smoke more? Smoke a hundred a day? My watch said 9:51 a.m. The time trembled on my wrist as the nicotine and caffeine acted like fiends, the numbers a blur. If a train came before 10 a.m. I'd finish the job tonight. Of course I knew there'd be a train just before ten, there always was (except on Sundays). I sat down on a low wall in the garden and stared at a bee dancing around a plant.

10:06 a.m. Engine noise. I rushed to the wooden fence at the back of the garden and peered through a hole in one of the slats. My nostrils started to fill with the faintest tang of diesel. A two-carriage train chuntered past, bound for Worcester Foregate Street. I only saw it for about fifteen seconds, a blur of blue-green metal, a haze and a stammer down in that deep wooded valley.

'Late. Fucking railways.' I turned towards the house. 'It should've come before ten. I'll do it anyway.' A snail slithered towards me over the paving stones, its movements taking an age, its antennae asking constant questions of the air in front of it. The futility of its journey bewitched me. So slow, so simple to pick off, so tasty, so easy to cycle over by mistake. Pathetic. Accommodating. I loved it. I bent down and stared.

TEN BRUTALIST BUILDINGS

By Belinda Schneider

Chapter Two

Priory Square

I'm not a Sturm und Drang *kind of girl – I believe in rationalism and modernity. But rationalism and emotion are not incompatible. Rationalism and fun can be cosy bedfellows. Things that make sense can also be beautiful and enjoyable. Places that make sense can be settings for beautiful and enjoyable experiences. To wit: dancing fills me with glee. Brutalist buildings aren't always thought of as gleeful locations, but this one is. Why can't somewhere that's thoughtful also be a place you can get enthusiastic about, even a place you can get exuberant about? Brutalist buildings aren't boring, and if they're cared for they're not depressing either. This building is called Priory Square, and it has rhythms – like the music you can hear inside. Levels on levels, sharp corners and stacked boxes. They call it a 'square' but it's more like a tiny town wedged into a hill as Birmingham city centre slopes from high ground to low, with shops on top, and below, this wonderful, huge covered den for drinking in live music. The outside of the music venue is just a cliff of concrete, uncompromising and stark and grey and ready to have any experience or any sound imprinted onto it. It's a blank sheet where you can draw your own*

11

fun. This is a building where fun triumphs. Sound, concrete and emo-tion conspire. It's neat.

Donald and I went to see The Rationalists play at Priory Square. They were astonishing. I think I fell in love with Donald that night. I thought he might become my husband. He did. We'd got drunk at the pub before the gig – me on gin and him on woeful English lager, which I think was to spite me in some way. He always shouted 'Prost!' before the first gulp as a satirical gesture. I asked him why his countrymen couldn't make beer – or, rather, why his countrymen insisted on drinking the worst of their brewed output while phasing out the breweries around Birmingham that could whip up the half-decent stuff. He always just shrugged his shoulders.

The gig was great. The Rationalists saved their best song, 'Eliza-beth Anderson', until the encore. Elizabeth Anderson was the name of the girlfriend of the band's singer, Charlie Sullivan. Ex-girlfriend. They broke up, and forever she'd be remembered by this song. And that song always made me think of that moment and this place. That song made shivers of pure electricity snake up and down my spine when I heard it performed live or listened to it through headphones or on the stereo.

It was such a lilting, beautiful song, so… strung out. Its power built and built from foundations that weren't so solid. In fact it was made of nothing; it would have probably floated away – that's how fragile it seemed when it started. So brittle and beautiful. But then as the song progressed it became more potent and more substantial. Those words and those guitar lines just dragged at your soul as you listened. They pulled you into the world that the band were inhab-iting, and it was so exciting and bewildering all at once. Tribal and yet gentle, so poignant it made you think of your own life and the important people in it. The best songs always make you think of people – of a person – like the best buildings do. They provoke you and they evoke things from the past at the same time. They tumble up your insides and change the way you feel. And if you don't feel anything, then something's wrong. Perhaps you're too old, because if you're young you'll feel things and they'll mean something to you because they're important, all this is important, songs are important, architecture is important, all art is important.

Donald pressed his hand into the small of my back as the song began, then he curled it round the top of my hip and squeezed me into him, my head coming to a soft rest on his chest, which moved up and down as he sang the words to the song. I sang them too. And as I sang them I looked around the room and marvelled at the right angles and the space above my head. I'd never been to see a band in a venue where the roof was so high above your head. The Rationalists were from Birmingham, and their songs were only about two things: architecture and love. That's why I adored them, I guess. My two favourite subjects as well. Why did Donald like them though? He was a cynic, but he had some blind spots.

Anguish growled at me. Pity was wired in from heart to brain; lolling sadness permeated body and mind. I couldn't concentrate on reading or writing. What I wrote was staccato. Disjointed. Small. Pieces. Of a bigger whole. A whole I could no longer comprehend, perhaps a whole I didn't ever comprehend, and perhaps there was no whole at all? There definitely wasn't a whole, I knew that. Just bits and pieces. Most of the time all I could do was watch – stupefied, petrified, paralysed, anaesthetised, deadened – as other events took place on a screen in front of me. When I got home last night and wrote about the evening's horribly failed suicide bid it was the first thing I'd written since Belinda went away. At least last night I began cataloguing what was happening to me. Still, what I've begun to document isn't what you might call a great story; it's not exactly a compelling narrative. It is a trove of one man's sadness. It's not good enough. My work has never been good enough. I'm a writer for regional TV. I need editing. Edit me. Edit this.

I could hardly speak: 218 missed calls on my mobile. I couldn't face the interrogations of others, however gentle and well-meaning they were.

There was one thing I needed to do. Do right. The pain was too much. I emailed Pete, a telephone engineer I'd been to school with in Moseley a very long time ago. He was kind and quiet, clever and polite. Though there was something behind his mask I could never work out. I bet he's a spy! Or in the special forces! It would be fine though. He replied immediately, agreeing to the plan. I had to lie and tell him that I needed his help scouting locations for a new TV programme I was writing for.

10 p.m. I glugged a double shot of whisky and caught a bus into town. I had to cross the city centre on foot to get to the place where we'd arranged to meet. But it didn't take long – Birmingham's core is disproportionately small for a city whose suburbs stretch for miles and miles and miles. I walked without thinking. It was unreal. What was I doing? Recently, I've found myself doing a lot of things that I'm not really sure about – which is strange, because, before all this stuff started happening, I always knew exactly what I was doing. Which was usually 'failing', but at least it was failing in a comprehensive, ordered and predictable manner.

So this was almost it. I stood at a crossroads. Not a metaphorical one – I knew exactly what was about to happen in the plot. No, I stood at an actual crossroads. I'd been walking up Newhall Street. Great Charles Street sliced across the road from left to right. I knew that, underneath me, a tunnel carried more traffic – I'd driven through it myself. Dignified Victorian buildings wearing three-piece suits of ornate decoration rose on two sides, 1960s and '70s office towers on the others. Offices for solicitors and property developers in the new buildings and the old ones. I wasn't sure exactly where Pete would be. I waited for the green man and crossed the road. A young couple – she in a dress, he in jacket and trousers – walked towards me, deep in conversation with each other, not noticing anything or anyone else. The night was crisp, the air had been paused. No weather, no wind. I pushed on for one more block and turned right into Lionel Street. A few paces down the road and I saw Pete leaning on a silver saloon car, smoking. He saw me and stuck his hand out.

'Hello, mate.'

'Hi, Pete. How the hell are you?'

'Yeah, good thanks. The wife probably thinks I'm having an affair, out at this time on a Tuesday. So we'd better be quick.' He looked me up and down. Perhaps I should have changed out of the green tracksuit I'd been wearing all day. 'I hope you don't mind me saying this, but you look like shit, mate. Everything OK?'

'Oh yeah, course it is. Just like to, you know, keep it casual sometimes.'

'There's casual and then there's the bloody charity shop.'

I laughed to lighten the mood. I felt like I'd swallowed barbed wire. One of the fears that paralysed me was that I'd break down in front of people. At home by myself it was fine, but I hated getting upset in public. These days I felt like I could go off at any minute. Just one trigger. One little trigger.

'I heard about Belinda…'

Her name. When I heard her name and we were together it summoned a cocktail of delicious Pavlovian responses: excitement, awe, pleasure, calm, lust, longing, delight. Now it's the

15

opposite. I felt as if I'd been slashed with a penknife every time I heard the word 'Belinda'. How many more cuts could I take?

'It's awful, really awful. If you ever want to get rat-arsed then you just pick up the phone, you hear me? Any time, Don. Actually, I wouldn't mind a night off the missus and the kids, so the offer's there.'

'Cheers, Pete, I appreciate that.' I swallowed hard.

'No problem. So let's get this sorted then,' he said, leading me towards the priapic tower. 'Can't stay long. You're sure you want to stop up there all night? It'll be sodding cold at the top, mate.'

'Yep,' I lied, 'that's what I need to do – to see the sun come up. We need a location for a sketch… in this new show I'm writing, and I need to make sure this is the right one.'

'Oh, so you'll be writing for the telly again? Brilliant. Always watched the shows you wrote, I did. Always. The one set in the planning department…'

'*Big Plans.*'

'That's it. That was pretty funny. You wouldn't have thought that a planning department could produce many laughs.'

'The TV critics agreed – they didn't think a planning department produced many laughs.'

Pete chuckled warmly at this.

'*Big Plans* was only ever shown on Mids TV. Never networked. Did you know that nothing I've ever written has been shown outside the region? Spectacular, isn't it?'

'Londoners don't know their arse from their elbow. You've got the knack, don't fret.'

'Thanks, pal.'

My career as a comedy writer was starting to get back on track, and I was just minutes away from death. The BT Tower loomed above us both. It glowered down at me, provocatively.

I bent myself backwards and strained my eyes to catch sight of the top. It looked like a hideously stretched, upended cardboard box which could have been stuffed with a billion sweets to make a rich child's Christmas present.

Pete rattled some chunky metal keys in the outer door and we were in. There was another locked door to the staircase; he opened it with ease. He flicked a switch and the staircase was illuminated by bare bulbs chucking light against naked concrete walls. Sometimes it stuck, sometimes not. I stared up through the murk.

'We're walking!' he said, beaming masochistically.

It was a pull. When we finally reached the top I was hopelessly out of breath; Pete was too. The pair of us stood there wheezing – two men in their forties who were utterly past it. Sweat dripped from Pete's greying hair and fell across a stretched face that was starting to wrinkle. Did I have wrinkles? I couldn't look in the mirror anymore.

'Ciggie?' Pete offered.

'Fuck it,' I said, taking one.

'Built in 1962, this was.' Pete exhaled. 'Tallest building in the city.'

We sat in silence, staring out at the twinkling lights of Birmingham – from this height it appeared as an ocean of warm neon contrasting sharply with the blackness. The amber light bobbled and jostled against itself. In the distance, to the north, a river of lights ran both ways the full length of the horizon. Pete must have clocked me looking puzzled.

'The M6.'

'Ah right. I was wondering.'

In the still of the windless night the city suddenly looked more relaxed, more sure of itself. We were surrounded at the top of the tower by a more chaotic scene: aerials, vast circular satellite dishes, boxes of equipment, coloured wires. Pete gently said his goodbyes and walked back down the steps. In my ears: his feet stomping against cold hard concrete, all the way to the bottom; echoes; the clanking of metal. I thought I'd give it half an hour first.

I was mesmerised by what lay before me. But it was nothing without her. I was scared by the depth of love I'd felt for her, the amount I missed her when she was away speaking at events or visiting buildings abroad, the daydreams about her I kept having when she was away. Now my love for her has unfolded, spread out into sticky desperation and boring grief that stretches beyond every horizon. Beyond Sutton Coldfield in one direction and the Lickey Hills in the other. That far. As far as I could see. So far. What was a tightly wound bundle of feelings we shared and nurtured is just a flat, featureless desert of memories and despair. No direction, no thought, no shape. I would give up everything to change things, to change the ending. Everything so futile. Liquid poured into my eyes, then out down my cheeks. The view became wobbly and ill-defined.

Calm descended after half an hour. I fudged the right arm of my shirt across my face to erase the tears and the snot, and I stood up by the ledge. I looked out across a tarmac-bottomed canyon. On my right a giant 'M' smiled out from the crown of the Mids TV Tower, the point I'd jumped from before. This would work out better. It was cleaner this time, more serious, less dramatic. I didn't hesitate.

I said, 'I'll be with you soon, darling. I love you.'

And I stepped off the top of the tower.

But here's the funny thing: I didn't feel myself falling. My eyes were screwed tightly shut as I realised that. So at first I couldn't confirm my sense that I wasn't falling. I opened them and saw Lionel Street thirty-one floors below. It was moving very gently forwards and backwards. Was I dead already? I turned round and immediately it became obvious that my belt had caught on an aerial and I was dangling over the edge.

'Jesus Christ,' I mumbled, scarcely able to believe it. And then, as I looked back to where my belt was caught, I felt a warm jet of liquid land on my left cheek and forehead. Confused, I made to wipe it with my hand. It was white, sticky. I saw an enormous shadowy bird swooping majestically above me, having just squeezed a piping-hot shot of ornithological effluent all over me. A peregrine falcon. I knew there was a pair living on top of the tower. It crowed and flapped away in triumph. A few minutes later it returned with its mate. They perched side by side on a satellite dish right above my head. I could hear their feathers ruffle as they shook their wings and folded them in.

Using my last reserves of strength, I hauled myself back up onto the balcony on which I'd just been sitting, careful not to let my belt snap. I sighed, crawled into a ball and drifted off.

At dawn I was woken by a light so blinding and a sunrise so brilliant that I thought I'd been born again. I squinted towards the east as the sun rose above the city. It was a cold morning, icy and full of promise. I don't know how the cold didn't wake me up. I felt bemused. Maybe it was time for the suicides to stop.

Pete arrived at 7 a.m. and let me out into the street. If I'd done it properly he'd just have found a stain on the pavement. And entrails in the canal. I promised I'd go for a drink with him soon. He didn't suspect a thing. I bought a cinnamon pastry and nibbled it very slowly as I walked back towards the bus stop on Moor Street. I concentrated on each sweet mouthful, but my chewing provoked only a feeling of ambivalence. I caught a bus home, and once inside I went straight up to my office on the first floor. I reached to take my diary off my desk but stumbled a little through tiredness. I knocked very gently into the bookcase, and it wobbled. A single photo fell from the top shelf and floated down to the floor in slow motion.

I picked the photo up and stared at it. The photo showed Belinda standing among a forest of grey pillars. I stared intently at her auburn hair and her blue eyes, at her cheekbones and her full, pink lips. She wore a short-sleeved top and a knee-length skirt. The palm of her left hand was resting on one of the pillars. She had a handbag slung over her shoulder and carried a bottle of water and a camera in her right hand. The location was the *Denkmal für die ermordeten Juden Europas* – the Holocaust Memorial in Berlin. The picture was taken in the afternoon, at about 3 p.m. You can make out bolshy sunlight, make out shadows cast by the pillars. The shot is almost perfectly framed, save for a blonde woman wearing sunglasses and standing in the background. I didn't remember her being there.

It was quite a day. Seven hours later, as we were finishing dinner at a restaurant in Hackescher Markt, I'd got down on one knee, pulled out a ring and asked Belinda to marry me. She said, 'I can't believe you're doing this. I'm in shock. Of course I'll marry you, Donald. I want to be with you forever.' We kissed and hugged, and the waitresses – seeing what was going on – began to clap. One waitress brought out schnapps, and even our shy fellow diners – strangers, Germans, tourists from Scandinavia and Britain – joined us in a toast. They yelled, '*Auf Euch*', and Belinda and I replied, '*Auf Uns!*' Sometimes, even though you're aware the earth is still spinning, it feels for a moment as if it's stopped for you, and you don't have to feel dizzy anymore. That's how I felt during that entire day.

The photo was one of my fondest memories of my and Belinda's life together. I delicately placed it on my pillow and lay on the bed next to her for an hour. Thoughts spun through my head: reminiscences, conversations, ideas, plans.

I went downstairs and fished around for a VHS tape in a cardboard box under the stairs. I went over to the VHS player and stuck it in. The machine swallowed the cassette greedily and a fuzzy picture emerged on the TV.

Welcome To The Masshouse. A light entertainment series – with jokes and comedy sketches that I wrote. The title? A wheeze that only Brummies would get – there is a small pie-slice of Birmingham city centre called Masshouse. The title of the show is a play on 'Madhouse' and cocks a snook at the 'craziness' of the planners who, in the 1960s, created a city some people felt was a place that could only have been built by the insane, for the insane – a place whose false monumentality would eventually drive all of us insane too. Masshouse was a fool's paradise of interlocking platforms, decks, dual carriageways and subways, which provoked a primal scream in people who got lost within the confines of its damp walls and blackened ceilings. I was shocked by it, drawn to it – and unable to figure out quite why. Like so much of my home city, this piece of a place doesn't exist anymore. The roundabout, the motorway, the slip roads, the subways: all wiped off the map. Now in their place: car parks, waste ground, some tall residential blocks for yuppies.

*

[Countdown clock]

[Title music – jaunty and insistent, like the soundtrack to a fair pulling into town. Scenes of Birmingham play out in the background, but they all look grotty to my cynical eyes – motorways, underpasses, tower blocks, concrete boxes. And between these shots are stabs from previous editions of Welcome To The Masshouse *depicting bizarre moving tableaux – lots of people dressed in chicken costumes,*

*custard pies being thrown, fat men appearing to be telling jokes –
though you can't tell what they're saying as they're mute, thank
God.]*

Title card – WELCOME TO THE MASSHOUSE

*Voiceover: 'Welcome to the Masshouse! This week we ask Brummies
whether [inaudible due to dodgy tape recording] really want to see
another [inaudible, screen goes fuzzy and the picture sort of drips
downwards, resolving into squiggles, then suddenly returns to nor-
mal] built? And, can foreign visitors to Birmingham do a little bit of
Brummie on camera for us? We'll see, bab!'*

*

Welcome To The Masshouse aired late on Friday nights in the so-
called 'post-pub' slot, but only on Mids TV, never networked.
I guess viewers in other regions wouldn't have got the punny
title. But I've no doubt they'd have immediately understood the
base humour of the show itself. Even a child could understand
that. I skipped through the video using the fast forward button
until I came to a part I wanted to watch.

*

*[Cut to a human-sized chicken asking foreign visitors – fuck knows
how we found any of those back then – if they could a) understand
a Brummie accent and b) replicate one. Concrete in the background
– definitely Birmingham Central Library. Which idiot is wearing
the chicken costume this time? Oh… it's me. Camera pans round to
reveal a woman with honey-coloured hair sitting on a bench, looking
right down the lens with the most intense stare. She's puffing away,
obviously. Pan left. An equally beautiful young woman with chest-*

22

nut hair and twinkling blue eyes, smoking with equal fervour; she's also staring at something. She has a book on her lap but I can't make out the title. Something about... the future?]

[The chicken asks the brunette – the one who we just glimpsed – if she can do a Brummie accent. She makes a good fist of saying 'Y'oright bab!' before collapsing into giggles. She has a thick German accent. The chicken asks her why she's in Birmingham, and she says she's an architecture student; she's also working as a barmaid at a pub in 'Moseley Willage.*']*

*

I paused the video and sat there for a while, transfixed by pixels on the flickering screen. The girl's smile was freeze-framed, as if the world had ended and all that remained was happiness and youth. A train came past just before 10 a.m.

All the time that Belinda was considering the sublimity, or not, of spaces and the man-made monuments of the next thousand years (or as it happened, rather fewer years), I was writing gags about fucking chickens crossing fucking roundabouts. Or about men in planning offices deciding where to put roundabouts – which was my highbrow period. Or else I was dressed in costume, harassing people in the middle of a roundabout in Birmingham city centre for a light entertainment programme on regional TV.

I spent the rest of the day lying on the couch, bumpy cushions underneath me, hard armrest against my head. Sometimes I thought about various odd concepts that had intrigued me for years, and sometimes my mind was as empty as my fridge. I rolled from side to side on occasions. The clatter of trains passing every few hours broke the day into sections. The noise they produced – the rumble and the growl of a diesel engine having power applied; sometimes a whistle too – gave me a fleeting feeling of well-being that few other things could provide right now. This behaviour was becoming habitual. Every day. Just lying, or sitting, just watching life pass me by. Frozen. Unable to relate, unable to understand, unable to function. I knew the world was continuing around me, but it seemed to be on pause here in the house. I seemed to be on pause. Even the few things I actually did seemed laboured – a trip to the kitchen or the bathroom. Both felt like they took an hour. I couldn't get excited about anything. I didn't want to see anyone – well, there was one person I wanted to see, but that was out of the question now. The emptiness is a blue whale that swallows you whole. When you're inside the creature's belly every sensation is muffled; taste and smell and sight and sound are dulled. It's impossible to get yourself back until the creature shits you out.

Night fell. I summoned up some courage to walk to the supermarket in the centre of Moseley. As usual, the lights were turned up to full. Bastards. Was I in heaven? No. The end was the end. With a head full of metaphysical conundrums I negotiated the crisps and dips. Though actually, what was Moseley if not a kind of earthly heaven? I used to love living here with Belinda, us sharing a house and a life in this cute Victorian village (which was actually just a 'suburb' with delusions of grandeur. It wasn't surrounded by fields as villages must always be). Belinda, of course, thought Moseley's architecture was too twee and too timid. But she bit her lip and indulged me. She liked the bohemian feel here at least, and the Middle Eastern deli where she could get Turkish spices that reminded her of the food she once enjoyed in Berlin's immigrant cafes. I think she'd secretly developed a crush on Moseley when she was a barmaid at the Bride of Bescot in her student days. The Bride was, coincidentally, also my local.

A four-pack of lagers and some triangular Mexican-style

crisps went sailing into a blue plastic basket. For about five minutes I dallied over whether to buy a jar of salsa too. Realising how trivial the internal discussion in my head was, I decided to beat myself once and for all. I extended my right arm and scooped every jar of salsa from the shoulder-height shelf into my basket. A woman standing near me, examining the ingredients of some breakfast cereal, turned and looked aghast. My right arm stretched painfully under the weight of a basket which now contained twenty-five jars of salsa – the shop's entire stock. The basket's handle bent.

Ayesha, the friendly checkout girl, looked me up and down briefly. 'That's a lot of salsa, Donald. Are you having a party?' A sly wink. A licked lip.

'I am, Ayesha,' I lied. 'Can you get me a bottle of single malt from up there too?'

'Of course,' she said, reaching, winking. 'If I'm invited...'

I paid up and walked home with the heavy load and a heavy heart. Once I was back and safely ensconced on the sofa, I started eating the spicy tomato salsa with a tablespoon, but two jars was enough. I felt sick. I drank three of the cans of lager, said, '*Prost!*' with guttural gusto, and wiped some tears away with my sleeve.

How can you describe what's not there? I guess it's my job as a writer to find a way, but it just doesn't seem possible right now. How can words do justice to emptiness, nothingness? Photos contain fragments of truths, pieces of memories. They show lives paused. They're more real than words because you can't edit them or misremember them. Videos are even better because the memories move; they're alive. Ultimately, everything that tries to capture a mood or a moment is an imperfect snapshot of a place, a time, an emotion. But if that's all we have…

Belinda will always live on inside these photos. I held one, staring at it, staring into Belinda's eyes, into her soul. And at her body, I must admit. Belinda is lying on her back on a Sardinian beach, her face turned towards the camera, her mouth open, her lips slicked and rouged. She's smiling. The frame crops out everything below her stomach. The sun is in her eyes and they're barely open. She's holding up a hand to shield them, her nails red, a ring on the third finger of her left hand – my ring. Her white bikini top strains. Greenery licks the back of the beach.

I put the photo down, went downstairs, swallowed a couple of painkillers and some whisky, and stuffed a handful of triangular Mexican-style crisps into my mouth, crunching down, my mouth filling with the disgusting tang of sweaty pseudo-cheese. I exhaled deeply and lay down on my back on the living room floor, blinking, thinking. I put my right arm up against my forehead. The small terraced house had felt like my castle keep. I wrote here when the studios became too boisterous. This was the place I could always retreat to; these were the walls that always seemed to deliver the jokes the script needed – however shit those jokes turned out to be in the final edit. Four walls. Two bedrooms. One living room. My office upstairs. A little garden and a railway line down beyond it. The front door was yellow, and the tiles on the hallway floor were exquisite Edwardian monochrome. And when Belinda moved in with me, the sun always shone through the windows set into the door, shone through coloured panes and projected a warm glow, shone into the hall, shone into the house, shone into my heart. And I found myself caring a little less about regional TV programmes and average-at-best jokes, and a little more about architecture and love, which were her two preoccupations. And to those preoccupations a third was eventually added: me. Feeling so treasured by someone was an addictive sensation, a rare sensation. And now I was having to go cold turkey in the most brutal way possible.

TEN BRUTALIST BUILDINGS

By Belinda Schneider

Chapter Three

St Agnes Kirche, Berlin

The happiest day of my life took place here in Berlin. My husband and I got married at St Agnes Kirche in Kreuzberg. Go and see this place for yourself. Touch its walls. Think about it.

I heard about it when I was a teenager. We smoked cigarettes in a park where there were bushes you could hide in. It was our space, one of the few private spaces we had in a society that watched everything you did. A boy told me about seeing this blank-faced church in Kreuzberg, near to his family's house. I can't remember exactly who it was, but he knew one of my friends. I was intrigued – by his discovery, and by him. His family lived in the west, and so when he crossed over to our side he must have been shocked by us, by everything. He didn't snarl like most boys I knew, I remember that. All the boys on our side were being prepped to join the army and kill 'fascists'. In West Berlin you didn't even have to do National Service; you could drop out and play in a band or do anything you wanted. He spoke softly and slowly. When he started talking about this strange thing, this weird building, it pushed a button somewhere inside me. I wanted to surround myself with art and explore the worlds that I couldn't explore. Me and my friends told each other stories; we asked each other about our fantasies. When our contemporaries from the west came – like this boy – it made the possibility of an escape one day seem possible. Sitting in those bushes, it was all so profound, being caught between childhood and adulthood. We talked about boys, of course. There weren't many I liked around Lichtenberg, just the ones who had some idea of a bigger world and a cultural life. Usually their parents were creatives. I didn't like the boys whose dads were one of Die Grünen – the Volkspolizei – I was scared to speak when they were around, lest things be reported.

There was so little real art in East Berlin, aside from the state galleries we'd be shepherded round, and the pointless cultural centres. Real creativity was stifled. We had to retreat into our minds. I wandered round by myself and felt spaces, explored spaces, believed in spaces. Whether it was a caged bridge over a road or that little shrubbery in the park where we smoked cigarettes and giggled about boys. My inner monologue tried to make those spaces bigger than they were so I had some room to move.

But we were Berliners – we were outcasts and we were dreamers, we were wanderers and we were wonderers. My mother told me about how Berlin had always been a refuge for free-thinkers, for subversives, for those who wanted to live outside the normal mores. She told me about the Jews who hid in the forest through the entire Second World War; she told me about our friends who tunnelled to the west to escape the stifling atmosphere and the fear, about the gays and the punks and the people who wanted to find their liberation in Berlin, about how Berlin began as an industrial city, about how people were offered their freedom here, about how a quest for enlightenment had defined the city throughout its whole history.

I wanted to grow, we all did. We talked about what we might do when we got older and what we might see, but we knew there'd be *trouble if we talked too much about that kind of thing:* Das war die DDR. *But no one could stop you talking about boys, blushing about boys. One day we played a game of listing all the things we thought our first boyfriend would have. I chose kindness, a handsome face, blonde hair, creativity – a boy who wanted to be an artist or perhaps a writer. My friends were perplexed by this.*

'Why would you want a boyfriend who writes? He'd be sitting on his own all the time, he wouldn't have time to take you out. How about one who makes things with his hands and works 8–4?'

It was a silly game because it wasn't even something any of us wanted then. We were just playing around with the notion of having a boyfriend – to look older than we were, to fantasise together about what it would be like when we were finally in control of our own lives.

'Yes,' *I said, smoking, waving my cigarette and fluttering my eyelashes.* 'A blonde boy who writes. I'd marry him at St Agnes Kirche. The wall will have come down by then.'

Gasps. 'You can't say that! It's an anti-fascist, counter-revolutionary protection barrier to guarantee our safety!'

'Bricks should be our salvation, not our imprisonment.' *It made me laugh. It also made me scared. I smoked more.* 'Definitely blonde.'

The first time I crossed into West Berlin – just after the wall fell – I didn't know where the hell I was. It was new territory. My mother told me to head past that hulking building that held the offices for the right-leaning newspapers of West Germany and eventually I'd find what I was looking for. And I did find it. I found the church – which, sadly, had rubbish bags strewn around it. St Agnes Kirche. It was plain, so plain that you could project your own thoughts onto the campanile just like a cinema projector shows a film against a white wall in a classroom. I ran my hands all over the porridgey exterior of the building and then I ran inside. The priest saw me and raised his eyebrows. He said he didn't know me, and I said, 'Of course, I'm an Ossie!' He said, 'Bless you, my child,' and fetched me a barley water and asked me how it felt to be here and did they let us pray and were the Stasi real and did they and really and how did we and why and… I looked at the ground as I confessed that I didn't believe in God but in people, though if one building could convince me to change my mind then this would be it. He laughed and said it wasn't a problem, I was welcome any time. The priest asked what I was going to do next, and I said I wanted to try a banana but I didn't have any Deutsche Marks. He went back to the rectory and brought out a banana. I said, 'Danke!' Peeling it seemed so odd, the custard-coloured flesh seemed so soft.

I felt drunk. It wasn't the barley water the priest gave me – I was drunk on hope, excitement. That day thousands of East Berliners just ran round West Berlin. I jogged to Potsdamer Platz and then across the Tiergarten. I actually jogged. Walking was not fast enough. I had sneakers on so it was OK, and that first banana – which tasted weird, but nice all the same – gave me more energy. But the day was warm. How did I find my way? On the maps we were given, Berlin didn't exist on the wrong side of the wall; it was just a blank, just cream space, just nothing. In reality the blank space more accurately reflected the real state of our side. I got to Interbau and I didn't know where to start. I'd read about it in my parents' books. I ran one way then the other, looking at the blocks of flats that the great architects had built for pure propaganda purposes to show that West Was Best. But they'd lied to us in the east and told us in the newspapers and on the state TV that Interbau was decadent and not Marxist; million-aires had moved in and spoiled the for-the-people rationale. Not true. But to me it was more socialist than the plattenbau blocks in Licht-enberg that we lived in. They were rows of emptiness. Prefabs. They would fall like a house of cards if you blew on them. At Interbau the blocks were strong and manly, like a built version of my blonde boy, the one I'd kiss one day. These blocks were handsome, and the gardens blended in so nicely with the strong architecture. The flats were homes for normal people, not millionaires – they were socialist. But they were beautiful. If only people could sieve out the plattenbau rubbish when they think of modern architecture and see the beauty of the bespoke buildings put up with such love. They might change their minds. I was so tired after running round the Interbau, so tired after St Agnes, so tired after weeks of hope and years of fear, so tired of chasing and hoping, so tired of everything, that I laid my head down in the Tiergarten. And I fell asleep. And I dreamed of England, because as much as I was free in my homeland, it was too small and too Teutonic for me. I needed to see something different. I would be going to England to study. To an England that even Englishmen don't go to – to the middle of England, to the best of England, to Birmingham. Not London. And perhaps because it rather reminded me of my home town, I felt happy there from almost the moment I arrived.

You probably don't know what's it like to lie prone in bed or on the sofa, morning after morning, afternoon after afternoon, doing nothing, just feeling the duvet or the cushions smudge against you – the only touch you're likely to get. Nothing. No movement, no contact, no progression. Or maybe you do?

Jowls squeezed against cushion, cheeks crushed against sheets, arms by sides, stomach so flat because I wasn't putting anything into it aside from booze and nicotine and snacks. Each blink lasted a minute, more time with eyelids shut than open. Breathing rate plummeted, I could hear and feel every long, drawn-out breath. A strange insensitivity – cut fingers and bleeding gums emitted the same dark fluid, but physical pain didn't turn up to the party.

Moving hands and digital displays marked time in an aggressive way, the ticks baying at me. The radio alarm clock on the bedside table seemed particularly malicious, with its red, robotic numerals. Me and that machine were at war. Ten minutes I'd say, fifteen minutes I'd say, then I'd get up. Then I'd be cured – for a little while. Ten more, five more. Sometimes the snooze button, sometimes the infernal beeps yelling at me to GET UP. I'd stare at the wall, at the ceiling, through the window at the sparrows and at next door's cat, who was also staring at the sparrows with a murderous glint in his eyes. Sometimes I'd smoke outside and contemplate clambering down onto the railway tracks. The gradient was almost vertical, the drop more than a two-storey house.

I wrinkled my nose; I frowned. Here's where Bel did Pilates. Here's where Bel wrote. Here's where we fucked. All in the past. It was a disconsolate soap opera with no resolution. I could write this up. Many Mids TV viewers must be sad or old. The majority of daytime viewers, surely? And if that was true then maybe there was a market for a soap opera where the characters just eke out a pathetic existence, where they succumb to pressure and just lie there doing precisely sod all. That could work. I'd suggest it to Bob next time I saw him. Something really sad, really pathetic. Oh, but it'd have to be sadder than the saddest thing you could think of. I hope you know that feeling. I hope you've known it at least once.

My eyes were drawn to our bookshelves. My novels, her books about the world. So many of my books were funny or sad (I thought that writers who could blend both together were really hitting the sweet spot). So many of Bel's books were about utopia and optimism, about how ideas could work and how people were ready to adapt to new worlds.

Belinda had thought I fostered a climate of cynicism which had led us to lose any belief in doing better by everyone, in thinking we could build nicer cities for all with incredible, ambitious buildings sitting at their heart. Sure, it was my job to take the piss out of people, out of the stupid things we saw every day. I told her satire was very different to blind cynicism. We had playful arguments. I told her that, today, people thought all authority was bullshit – whether it was benign leftist or malign rightist. Once when we were in London on a trip to see one of her beloved concrete monstrosities, I told her that people just wanted to do their own damn thing and that individualism wasn't necessarily part of the capitalist conspiracy, was it? It's just the counter-culture. Think of the freedom we have now: we don't have to live or love in any way we don't want to. All social barriers have come down. Grand narratives are for the past. We just do whatever we want in whatever city in whatever country we want, and we don't listen to anyone. We especially don't listen to anyone who thinks they can dictate our lives or rebuild our cities. And surely, as she came from a totalitarian state, she knew the importance of freedom? My job was to prick pomposity. My job was to take the piss. My job was to be against all authority in all of all authority's multifarious forms. This is what I said. She'd make her eyes expand as much as she could and call me a 'fucking anarchist' with a look of mock horror, then she'd crease up with laughter, take her top off in one motion, sidle over and kiss me.

TEN BRUTALIST BUILDINGS

By Belinda Schneider

Chapter Four

Eros House

We were in South London. I wanted Donald to kiss me up against Eros House. I wanted to feel his hands around my waist. I thought it would be funny. Actually it felt better than that. It was sensual to experience the concrete cheese-gratering up and down my back, to place my hands on that rough exterior, to feel hot breath on me and smell his sweat, the beer and the cigarettes and the lust when he half opened his mouth and looked down at me.

We went to the top of the Catford Centre car park afterwards and drank cans of cider. He thought it was a 'concrete monstrosity'. He was joking – mostly. There were all these French paperbacks lying around on the car park decks – books by Baudelaire, Camus, Houellebecq. It was very strange. These things don't happen by chance. Each end result is the end result of a complex chain of events. So what was going on here? Who had been here? What was the building trying to tell me? What was it trying to tell us all? I loved that place. It was no-nonsense. I got drunk pretty quickly. We started talking about politics and about comedy. About how attitudes in society shape attitudes to things, to art, to architecture, to TV. Donald said to me, 'People just want to do their own damn thing. Individualism isn't necessarily part of the capitalist conspiracy, is it?' I told him he was a fucking anarchist and I seduced him again.

Did you like that bit? I hope so. I'm trying to write something here that'll make you sit up and think. Call it criticism if you want

– maybe it is, maybe it isn't. Don't assume that all architectural criticism has to be as pointed as 'This is a good column' and 'That is a bad pediment'. Break through the walls of words and the words of walls. Examine and feel. Brutalist buildings are the ones that precisely lend themselves to this state of intimacy, an intimacy between space, people and words. They provoke. They provoke you. They provoke me. Prod them back. They're beasts, they can take it. Experience what's being meant by the building, however abstracted the thought might seem or the building might look. And when you've done that, for pity's sake just go and enjoy the damn place. What's wrong with going to a multi-storey car park and making art or getting drunk or holding a rave, or fucking, or reading French paperbacks? Nothing. It's your space – get out of the house more and use it. Buildings love to be loved, like people.

Another afternoon lying on the sofa. I felt myself drifting off. My heart tapped out the faintest tick-tock like a shy clock. My breathing was laboured like an old man's. So it's no wonder that I slipped into yet another make-believe world.

This is a dream:

I can see dead people. The people who used to live in buildings. And seeing dead people suddenly seems to bring these dead buildings back to life. I'm in a flat. They're everywhere. All the people that lived here. It's like being in some kind of computer game. They fuss around but they don't bump into each other. They don't even seem like they can see each other. Next I'm in Priory Square. Dead shoppers are milling around. A guy is walking round the roof. He pauses for a moment, looks down, then throws himself off. I wake up sweating; my stomach aches.

3

1988

'Thanks for a nice night, Donald.'

'My pleasure, Julie. Wanna do it again?'

'Absolutely.'

'Another Chinese?'

'Or… something else?'

'Anything.'

'Yeah, sure. Give me a ring. There's a phone in the corridor. I'm back most afternoons.'

A peck on the cheek. 'Bye.'

'Bye.'

Julie was a girl I'd been out with a few times. A psychology student at Aston University. I'd walked her back to the halls she lived in. The hall was actually a tower block, but the drugs consumed and the disturbances made in the tower were very middle-class variants of the type of disruption you read about in the *Evening Brummie,* the type concerning the crumbling council tower blocks that stood in less comfortable parts of the city.

I started walking back towards Digbeth, happy enough with the date, a little fretful. I saw Masshouse Circus looming up before me. It was characterised by light and dark, purporting – perhaps – to represent good and evil. The structure of the roundabout floated in the sky, eight entry and exit slip roads. The tangle was impossible to fully comprehend at night. As a pedestrian, you're funnelled down into the bowels of the interchange.

Henns Walk subway.

James Watt subway.

Chapel Street subway.

New Meeting subway.

Ryder subway.

Hospital subway.

All the roads are above you, held up by stacks of brick and concrete, heavy legs. You have to descend in the direction of your own grave and you must lump it.

The sonic deluge builds up and up as you penetrate into the junction, like a pressure cooker going full tilt. The echoing and booming and clattering of cars rumbling over tarmac makes your heart march at double time. I felt woozy and strange. Not in control of myself. This had happened down here before; in fact this sensation of being overcome had hit me in other subways too – Old Square, Colmore Circus, Bull Street, Hurst Street, Lancaster Circus, Holloway Circus, Paradise Circus, Hockley Circus, Five Ways. I'd ended up down in this liminal zone for hours. I was too puzzled and ashamed to admit that fact to anyone. I needed to know, for myself, what made the subways make me turn into Mr Hyde. I didn't know.

I reached a point where it felt natural to stand still and concentrate on the noise in my ears and the greasy tangerine glow from the street lights in my retinas. I remembered how much my mother hated this place, how terrified by it she would become. She said she felt trapped down here. She said she constantly worried that she was going to be attacked. It menaced her. It was a weird set-up, like no other junction in the city, like no other I'd seen. The main road ran at ground level with the roundabout above. A car park was inserted into the spare spaces. A fiendish plan. Hard to fathom. Impossible to escape easily.

A guy was here too – elderly, bearded, troubled, drinking a can of beer and having a smoke.

I said, 'Can I join you, pal?' He nodded, a little perplexed look dancing across his features, trying to suss me out. I sat down next to him. We sat there together in silence for what seemed like a long time. I offered him cigarettes, and he offered me a can of strong lager. The whoosh of cars shooting past over our heads every five seconds kept nerves sharpened like knives.

After about half an hour, the tramp shuffled over to me a bit. He looked straight into my eyes. 'You, sonny, you just… ah, what's the point?'

'What is it?'

He looked to his left, but at what? 'The factory… I used to. It was… we all did. No more. The bloody, the… bloody… shut, they… the…'

And then he folded himself back into himself, pressing his whole body towards the wall that kept all the hot metal and masonry above from crashing down onto us and snapping our necks. The subway rebelled: reeked of piss, was stained and dank, sucked at your soul. The walls were streaked with black shapes, Rorschach tests that would never end well. The space seemed to close in with every passing car. The strong lager made me feel sick. The cigarettes made me jittery. And yet… it was an island of sanctuary. Nobody would bother me here.

I had a companion. I had a place. Masshouse was a madhouse. Maybe the madhouse was where I belonged.

What would Julie's reaction be if she knew I was here, sitting on a step with a tramp, casting my eyes around the subterranean pathways, the red parked hatchbacks, regarding the bricks and the stains running down once-white walls, obsessing over the piles of grit and grime? Would it be enough of an excuse to say that I would one day write a sitcom about the insanity of the Birmingham city planners and this was (sort of) research? Would she agree that I was experiencing life to write about it better – or would she worry that something was wrong, really wrong?

4

2008

You know nothing much is going to happen, right? But that's honesty, that's reality. I'm not pretending to be someone I'm not; these words aren't pretending to be something they're not. How many times do you catch authentic representations of what grief looks like? Of what alienation looks like? Of what post-industrial cities in the English Midlands look like? The dullness and the sadness and the boredom of all of it? Well I can confirm, now I've been punched in the face by grief, that it doesn't look anything like it did on TV. It's even more prosaic. It's even more trying. Thanks for sticking with me this far.

When you lose someone, your mind is consumed by them. You might not have thought about this person very much when you saw them each and every day, but when they're not there your mind goes into overdrive. The brain reacts badly when deprived of its normal routines. You notice this if you have to get up early or go to bed late, if you're jetlagged from a long-haul flight, if you're suddenly made redundant, if you move to a house in a considerably noisier area, if you give up cigs. However, humans and their minds are actually surprisingly adaptable. But we need time. Within a few days, weeks or months, humans can adapt to a new situation and a new environment – that's what helped us to become masters of our universe. Pete told me that the brain is so good, it can adapt to the loss of the most important person in your entire life – eventually. He also warned me that it might take a while. I wonder what Bob would say?

I drove the car to town. Snow Hill car park. I screeched up the spiral ramp to the top floor of the multi-storey, parked at the front of the deck, switched the engine off and reclined the seat. I looked out over the city. And when I got peckish I snacked on crisps and salsa – I had enough of the bloody stuff to get through. I thought. There's no reason to the way things happen, of course. It's just bad luck, and sometimes there's good luck to balance it out.

I knew each of the skyscrapers. Mids TV Tower, BT Tower, Evening Brummie Tower, Bank Tower, Legal Tower, Local Government Tower. We'd filmed outside most of them, and inside some of them. One thing I always liked was the way puffs of steam strolled upwards from the tops of the roofs, from the vents, or wherever it was they came from. It made me think of Toytown, of a playful chocolate factory. I sometimes imagined that inside, rather than bored middle-aged Brummies pushing around meaningless pieces of paper, the priapic office buildings were instead full of dancing midgets causing a fucking hullabaloo as they sought to make sweets or toys or whatever, crashing into table legs and each other. In fact I wrote that very joke into an episode of *Welcome To The Masshouse*.

I lit a fag and wound down the window, but it was too stale even with a bit of breeze. I got out of the car and slammed the door. It was windy – trees and aerials slow-danced, leaves flew all over, even though no English trees grew this high. I wandered over to the edge of the rooftop. My original plan was to kill myself by jumping from this very spot – but I wasn't convinced it was quite high enough and decided on the Mids TV Tower instead. And then of course I also tried the BT Tower, which is higher still. I leaned over. The drop from the car park was ultimately unpromising – only five or six storeys, I guessed. Peering over the edge was still enough to give you that sensation that someone's reached right down your throat, dragged your stomach up and wobbled it around. Looking down towards the ground from here was like looking through the camera lens. Your view is sucked into one place by one point in the near distance which drags your eyes. There's nothing you can do about it. And around the edges of that view, the spaces close in. Like now – the parallel lines of the parking decks below me stacked until they smashed neatly into the street. A computer-game character walked along the street from left to right, a round head with two protruding stubby arms and two stubby legs. I tossed the cigarette and watched it whirl away from me, blown outwards from the car park decks by the wind. It dropped until it hit the street, making a Lilliputian firework display on impact, a tiny copper puff of sparks before it died.

I heard a train whistle. This car park sits above the tracks and platforms of Snow Hill railway station.

I felt hungry again. Strange. There was a Chinese food stand a few floors downstairs, in the upper concourse of the station. It had been a while since I'd been here.

'A pork bun please, Mrs Chu.'

'Mr Donald! Haven't seen you for ages.'

'I know. I'm back now though, aren't I? Couldn't live without your pork buns.'

Handing it over, along with a fortune cookie, Mrs Chu frowned and said, 'I can see your future, Mr Donald. Your phone is about to ring. They're going to invite you back in to work.'

My phone rang. Mrs Chu beamed and turned round to busy herself preparing some food.

'Donald, how are you holding up? I'm glad you answered.'

'Not bad, Bob. I'm just eating a pork bun.'

'Great news! I'm glad you're eating again.'

'I'm trying.'

'Listen, would you like to come back to work? It'd take your mind off things.'

'I'll think about it.'

'OK, no rush. You look after yourself. Either way, meet me for a cuppa? Or a beer. Friday? There's something I want to talk to you about. A programme. A film.'

'Sure. I can do that.'

'Great, see you soon. Chin up.'

Mrs Chu winked at me. 'You gonna go back?'

I shrugged.

'Mr Donald!' Mrs Chu called as I wandered away. 'A blonde woman.' I didn't know what she meant. 'She's... well, you find out soon enough.'

I squeezed the fortune cookie and it cracked under the strain, like a miraculously burst Brazil nut on Christmas morning. The unfurled slip of paper read: *You will be happy again*. I scoffed, shook my head. Smiled though. Just a tiny one.

5

1990

'I want you to write the script for a new game show we're going to do. About dogs.'

'About dogs? Are you pulling my fucking leg?'

'About dogs. It's going to be called... "*I Love My Dog!*"'

'I love my dog?'

'Yes, isn't that great?'

'Jesus.'

'Don't moan. If we don't get this off the ground the powers that be want to do some demented sport-themed game show in the National Indoor Arena, when that opens next year. People chasing each other about like fucking idiots, dressed in spandex.'

'Kill me now.'

'Exactly. I can't see it happening, don't worry. But even more reason to make this dogs thing work, right?'

6

2008

I went home and got down face first on the living room floor. I fumbled around with my right hand, fingering the hairy carpet in search of the remote control. I pressed the on button and then the channel up button over and over again: screen after screen of people arguing or food sizzling or animals or cricket or men in police uniforms or adverts for kitchen cleaners or people standing behind a podium with a number and a name on it or cartoon animals or more men in uniform or adverts for nappies or someone travelling on a train thirty years ago. My attention was finally caught by an attractive woman in front of a map of Britain. I rolled over. 'Millie?' She'd been in my English seminars at Leeds University. Now she was pointing towards the Hebrides and explaining something about strong winds. She flashed a pearly grin as she finished speaking. The forecast seemed to culminate and an advert for a personal finance product appeared.

I went next door to the cardboard box of unloved videos and found another VHS tape. I put it in the machine and pressed play. It was *I Love My Dog!* I groaned and, without thinking, said out loud, 'What were we…'

*

[Title music – absolutely horrendous computer-generated dog noises layered over some kind of pathetic synthesiser track which has been slowed down and manipulated to make it sound friendly to the ears of older viewers.]

Title card – I Love My Dog!

[Bob appears from the gap between two velvet curtains, spinning a huge bone-shaped slice of plastic about three feet long. He hands it to a woman wearing a sort of burlesque outfit, who curtsies and blows him a kiss. Bob winks at the camera. What the fuck is he doing? What the fuck was I doing? I wrote the line he speaks next.]

Bob: *'It's…* I Love My Dog! *I'm going to lead you up the garden path today with two local dogs who want to go from dogsbodies to champion hounds!'* *[Applause – but muted as there are only about thirty-five people, and when I say 'people' I do mean 'grandmas and granddads' – in the studio audience.]* *'In a minute, we'll have our first challenge – where we'll see which dog is…'* *[Bob widens his eyes and makes a 'come on then' gesture of desperate encouragement towards the audience, willing them, pleading with them to join in with the next line. They do, albeit without much fizz.]* *'…barking up the wrong tree!'*

[Burlesque woman wheels out a cardboard tree about twelve feet tall on a trolley. On the trunk it reads, 'THE WRONG TREE'.]

'So tonight we…'

*

Pause. *I Love My Dog!* lasted for four series. Four. Can you believe that? It was a game show for dogs and their owners, and I had to write the scripts for Bob. He horsed around and petted a poodle or whatever bloody dog it was on the show that week. There were always two dogs, and two owners.

'The things you do for money,' I groaned. No one was listening, of course. I opened a beer. I had to. Bob was a producer now. In fact, since everyone had fucked off or been fired from Mids, he'd also ended up as programme controller purely by dint of having been squatting there the longest. He'd left that presenting silliness behind him.

There was only one thing I wrote that I was actually happy with. Really happy with. And it wasn't even a comedy. *Hail To The Brummies*. It was a celebration of the city. I wrote the words, Baxter said them, and we got The Rationalists to do the music. This was something I was really proud of, a real celebration of life in Birmingham. No tapes of it remained. They'd all been wiped by some jobsworth at the studios. Maybe if I went back in to work I could also have a nose around and see if they'd left a copy under a filing cabinet somewhere. *Hail To The Brummies* wasn't a comedy, it was earnest. It was something proper. Deep down I sensed that writing serious stuff was somehow better, more worthy, more becoming. Seriousness was something to be proud of, comedy something to be embarrassed about at a later date.

Play.

*

Bob: '...have two dogs to meet. So let's meet tonight's first canine competitor. He's a beagle from right here in Birmingham called Breuer.' [Zoom in on my dog.] 'And here's Breuer's owner, please welcome the gorgeous... Belinda!' [Zoom in on my wife.]

7

1990

'How's the costume? Hot?'

I tried to make a joke. 'I think I'm sweating my organs out. Keep your eyes peeled for them.'

Her lips formed a pout. Her eyes narrowed inquisitively.

'How's yours?' I pointed at her dungarees. They looked a bit out of date.

'Fine, thanks. Practical. Why have you come in here?'

'You're very direct.'

'I'm very German.'

'Do you know where the, er, toilets are?'

'Yes, just over there.' While still looking at me she pointed towards a corner where two ribbed concrete walls met at a point.

'Over there?'

'What do you think?'

'I think you're leading me astray.'

'Would you like me to lead you astray?'

'Your English is good. I'm impressed.'

'My mother spoke English round the house. It was very easy to learn that way.'

'Was she English?'

'No, she was German.'

I sat down at the desk opposite, looked into her eyes. She blinked once and tilted her head. She hadn't taken her hands off the big book – the same big book she'd been holding outside a few minutes ago. I looked at the front cover. It read *Birmingham's Concrete Dreams*. The letters sat on top of a photo. A caterpillar straddling a canal seemed to be hiding in the photo. Or was it a motorway?

'Can I ask your name?'

'Belinda.'

'Hi, Belinda.'

'Hi.'

'Would you like to know my name?'

'Not particularly. But I'll listen if you want to tell me, if you want to get it off your chest.'

'It's Donald.'

'Now I know.'

'So you're studying architecture?'

'That's right.' She lifted the book up. 'I'm trying. It takes a long time. Years.'

'Do you like the architecture of this building? Not everyone does.'

'I do. It's mind-boggling. I think that eventually people will realise that. People might even get sentimental about the age it came from.'

'Brummies aren't very sentimental, I'm afraid.'

'That's a shame. Buildings are so important, so precious. They're the backdrops to our lives.'

'That's so true. Are you a romantic?'

'Yes. I'm Prussian. But also romantic. Are you, Donald?'

52

'Hmmm, am I? I've never really thought about it that way before.'

'Does the chicken costume make you feel romantic?' She raised an eyebrow. It sounded like a joke. I made laughter come out of my mouth on the off chance.

'Not really!'

'And how is that job – wearing a chicken costume? Does it pay well?'

'Not… egg-sactly…'

'Oh dear, oh dear. Was that a joke?'

'Maybe. You know my job isn't just to wear this costume? I'm doing it to help out on the shoot today. Our budgets aren't so huge.'

'I think the lady doth protest too much. It's fine that you're a professional chicken impersonator.' She seemed pleased with this line, and if she was happy, I was happy.

'It's the scripts that I do.'

'The scripts. You write what the chicken says?'

'I write what a lot of chickens, horses, dogs and even humans say. I'm a writer.'

'A writer. Have you written a book? Is it in here?'

'Unfortunately not. I write things that you watch on TV.'

'I don't watch TV.'

'One day I'll write other things too. Maybe. For now, scripts. And jokes. Lots of jokes about Birmingham, especially.'

'Well that sounds interesting. I'm getting fond of Birming-ham. Its weirdness is… creeping up on me?'

'Good! I'm a Brummie.'

'Wow, a real Brummie.'

'Do you live in Selly Oak?'

'I do. Do you?'

'No, in Moseley. That's where you said you worked, right? When we chatted outside just now.'

'Yes, in the Bride of Bescot. A few nights a week. Ever been in there?'

'Do you know what, I have. But I haven't ever seen you in there. I wish I had.'

'Maybe you will one day. Or if not, then in Selly Oak.'

'I'd like that. Do you think we could arrange something? Could I maybe… maybe take you for a drink one evening? In Moseley. Or Selly Oak. Or somewhere else.'

She drummed her fingers on the book cover and made a 'Hmmmm' noise.

'Or how about a glass of wine?' She looked confused when I said this. I looked confused. I'm not really sure why I said it or what I meant. Probably that wine wasn't a 'drink' in the sense that drinking pints of Birmingham Bitter was, that it was qualitatively different to going for a drink because it was much more than that – it was a chance to savour something classy rather than getting rat-arsed. It was a chance to impress her.

'How about you go to the toilet then come back? I'll think about it.'

'Sure.'

As I was walking back from the toilets I could already see the desk where Bel was just sitting had been vacated. I felt pretty empty. When I arrived I looked around a bit, but there was no sign of her hiding between the bookshelves. Instead I saw a piece of paper abandoned on the desk. I picked it up and unfolded it. It had an 021 telephone number written on it, followed by the letters 'B' and 'x'. I jumped up, punched the air and shouted, 'YES.' An elderly reader turned around and stared as if he'd just witnessed a crime. A young woman in an aqua wool jumper glared at me, looking askance at the poultry costume, at me talking.

'Bartholomew's,' I decided out loud. 'Sod the drink. I'll suggest dinner. A steak at Bartholomew's.'

An old lady wearing a plum cardigan and a kindly face sidled up to me and grinned. She beckoned me to come down closer, towards her face. She opened her mouth and whispered, 'We really don't care if you're going to a steakhouse or to the moon. Will you please just shut the fuck up? This is a library. I'm trying to learn about my family's links to the Quakers. Thanks.' Then she smiled again and sidled away at a snail's pace.

8

2008

I parked the car outside the studios. Grey clouds rolled overhead, setting a sombre tone. I sat there for about forty-five
minutes, surrounded by mid-range saloons which had been
spray-painted the same dour colour as today's sky by robots in
factories somewhere else. I sat there because I was summoning
up some courage. I wound the window down and smoked a
cigarette. The surfaces on the interior of the car were covered
in cheap, grotty plastic. The plastic seemed to attract dust and
grease. A car was ultimately just a machine for moving around
in, for snacking in, for smoking in, for dropping sweet wrap-
pers in. Brum. This is where cars were born in a previous age.
The perfect place to sire these no-nonsense boxes on wheels.
The place where the car was more intricately slotted into the
fabric of the city than anywhere else in Britain. The place
where buildings were designed to be like cars: machines that
just did the job in a modern, practical way. No glitz, no shit.
When I thrummed my fingers on the wheel the claustropho-
bia of being inside this tin can was amplified. The silence that

existed before and after the thrumming seemed to be turned up. Some cars were even quiet when you were doing 100 mph down the M40. You could fall asleep in them. Bel sometimes slept in the passenger seat as we drove home from a walk in the Malvern Hills or a trip to one of those enormous Scandinavian furniture stores laid out like mazes and which take a day to escape from. I got out of the car, leaned on the bonnet and smoked another. I felt as though I looked like a cop in the kind of shit drama show Mids TV made right here in the 1970s.

The studios looked sullen. I guess I'd never really examined them before. You don't, do you? Everyday life passes the everyday chap by. But let's look at them now. We often called the whole place, the whole of the Mids TV HQ, 'the studios', as in 'Meet you at the studios', but in fact the complex was split into distinct parts. There's a big box with curved sides that stretches down towards the canal. That's the studios themselves. The curvature isn't even; it's punctuated by protruding cubes and recessed squares along its length. The suspicion you get is that an ogre wearing a knuckleduster gave the building his best left hook. It's bashed in. And not just by design. When they used to run motor races around Brum's closed-off Inner Ring Road (perfect city for that caper, right?) a racing car once crashed into the studio complex. The commentators inside couldn't believe that they were describing a car crashing into a wall fifty feet away from them. The French driver who crashed escaped any injury, and, when he'd struggled out of the cockpit, nonchalantly lit a fag until the rescue teams arrived looking frantic. The exhaust pipe is still embedded into the outside of the studio. The programmes themselves were made in there: filmed and edited in there. There are no windows because you create unnatural light when you film. It could have been any time of day or night outside, but inside it was either pitch black when the studios were empty, or dazzlingly,

sickeningly bright when the cameras rolled. The lights gener-
ated so much heat that everyone appearing under them had to
wear make-up because sweat poured from you without your
say-so.

Round the other side of the studios, facing the library and
Paradise Circus, is a low boxy sort of building, not covered
in blackened concrete but instead glazed and grubby. At street
level a run of public spaces – shops and some cafes fronting
onto a square. Above those public areas, the bar and canteen
that all the workers and guests at Mids could use. The canteen
was always sparsely filled with people eating their joyless portions of fish with chips and peas, hamburgers and beans, or
roast pork and boiled potatoes. The smell that sat in the air
reminded me of washing that hadn't been aired properly,
musty and stale and disheartening. The bar was much, much
more fun. That smelled of cigs and bad cologne, of
pheromones and sweat and hunger. There were chairs around,
but no one was there to sit still. And then there was the office
tower – tall, 1970s vintage, brave, poised. The office tower
I jumped off. Belinda loved it all, of course. She cooed over
what a glamorous and utopian spirit it expressed. I took her to
the top of the tower, got the keys off the porter, and guided
her out to the roof – where you're not supposed to go. She
clung on tight to me as the wind whipped into us. Her cynicism melted. It was murder to light a cigarette up there. Her
world was academia and underpasses. I sold her cocktails and
skyline views, TV razzle-dazzle, glamour and art for the people. Everything's relative – in Brum, Mids TV seemed like the
last word in metropolitan glitz. If you were up from London,
it must all have looked as pathetic as the city it sat in. But to us,
it was cool. Decadent and disgusting at the same time – like a
prawn korma served with a Peshwari naan.

Inside the office block, everything looked the same as when

I was last here. The spiteful furniture and the tea stains and the dying ficuses. Up on the production office floor where my desk was, Baxter was polishing his glasses. He looked up but he didn't say anything. He never said anything until he was on camera. Only then would he let rip with a stream of poetic verbiage that dazzled me – and caused Midlands viewers to scratch their heads, reach for thesauri, or simply change channels.

I walked across the sticky grey ocean of carpet to Bob's office. He wasn't in. I tried to find Kate, production manager and drinking buddy; understander of me, somehow. I shuffled over to her desk, but there was just a volcano of paperwork slung all over it. I asked a girl I didn't recognise if she knew where Bob was.

Her reply? 'The bar.'

The Mids TV bar was where we'd written *Welcome To The Masshouse*, while shit-faced – on Wednesday and Thursday afternoons. I used to think it was glamorous, that we were warriors. When you're young things excite you; they seem important.

The walls were made of exposed concrete which looked like bowls of Weetabix had been slung sideways and eventually dried out. Red and black squares of paint appeared seemingly at random. A long, sleek, jet-coloured bar ran down one side; on the other were tall plate-glass windows with low tables and groups of easy chairs with exterior views. The bar was two floors up so you could look down on the street life. I walked out onto the bar's small al fresco terrace, which jutted out over the piazza. Bob was there, leaning back into a black faux-leather chair, fag in hand.

'The fucking wanderer returns.' He got up and gave me a chunky, fatherly hug.

'I enjoyed that.'

'Good.'

'Pint?' I offered.

'Yep.'

I came back with the beers.

'Have you been drinking with anyone?'

'Nope.' I hesitated. 'On my own. A bit.' A lot.

'Have you been out?'

'Not really... the shops?' I didn't mention the suicide attempts.

Bob's wrinkles stretched themselves. His big sallow jowls dangled. His eyes reflected my own unhappiness back at me. 'Come on, sport. Remember that song? The one that goes "Life is like a mountain railroad"? There'll be ups and downs. We all miss her terribly too. I'm here; you can come in every day and we can just get pissed. It'll get me out of whatever shit game show I'm supposed to be producing next.'

'At least you're not fucking presenting them anymore.'

'Oi. Don't take the piss out of my presenting skills. Granted, I'm better behind the camera – producing, organising, kicking arses – but so are you.'

The thing about friends – really good friends – is that you can be silent with them. So we just drank for a few minutes and looked out at the bored office workers in suits and the students and the mums down in the piazza. The sound of skateboards scraping and knocking into steps somewhere nearby soundtracked our little moment.

'I've had an idea.' Bob stubbed out his latest cig, brushed the ash off his white shirt and the blue jeans it was tucked into. 'I want to talk to you about it. We're going to make a posthumous version of *Ten Brutalist Buildings*. I want to make it as a tribute to Belinda. It's the right thing to do.'

I rubbed my face. 'It's not. It was her idea. It was going to be her programme.'

'I know. But I've been thinking – I reckon we should do it

anyway. I had to grind those bastards upstairs down enough to get the cash to make this. The readies are still on the table. Let's use them.' A well-placed pause in the drama. 'Have a ciggie.'

'You trying to charm me?'

Bob sparked up my fag. 'Come on, mate, think about it. We'll go to Leeds and London as well, we'll do it properly. But most of all we can film around the city – we can capture the buildings in Brum she loved before they pull them all down. You know how much it meant to Bel to document the city, these buildings, the whole Sixties and Seventies aesthetic.'

'You'd better be quick then.'

'Exactly. You see, that's it. We haven't got much time. Everything's on borrowed time – Bel's buildings, Mids TV, my ticker. We need to just go and do it while we've got the chance.'

'Bel was going to write and present the film. That's what you two organised, right?'

'Exactly. I wanted her to do it, mate. But this will still be hers. It'll be a way to remember her. Our way to remember her. And the buildings she loved. And fuck over the bosses. I don't want fucking Mackenzie getting his hands on the commissioning cash he's already signed off for this. Not that the budget he's deigned to give us is going to take us very far, but I'll find a way to fudge that. I always do. We'll shoot it cheap. Good but cheap. Cut down on tech and effects. Just keep it simple. Location shoots, no voiceovers.'

'What would Bel say?'

'She'd say: "Do it." You know she would. She said yes, she acted, she was a bloody doer.' Bob grabbed me by both arms. 'Will you write it, mate? Write the script for it. I want you doing it. You can write it. Baxter can say it.'

'Baxter? Does he have to?'

'Look, I know he's… trying, but let's just do it with him.

He's probably the man for the job. God, I wish Bel was here still so we could ditch him. I'll have to hook him up to life support to get any kind of human emotions out of him when he's doing his pieces to camera, but beggars can't be choosers. At least he's presented arts programmes before, architecture ones. It's a bit... niche.'

I walked over to the bannister at the edge of the terrace. It was flimsy; it warped in and out when you shoved it. I thought about Belinda walking and talking, enthusiastic. Academic yet sexy. A TV producer's dream. Why hadn't she done this before? She was made for presenting TV architecture documentaries. Any documentaries. She knew everything, she'd written the book, and she could talk too – all that lecturing had sharpened up her skills. And when she got her chance, finally...

'She'd have been a wet dream for the bastards upstairs. They'd have loved her.'

'They did love her. And if she'd made it onto the box they'd all be trying to shag your woman, Don. All over Brum, all sorts. But there's only one idiot she had eyes for... Lucky, wasn't it? I can't believe she... well... just before we were due to start filming. Literally weeks before.'

'Me neither.'

'And with you two so settled. Everything so perfect. It's tragic, really.'

I looked up at the sky and switched on my cerebral TV screen: Bel was on, standing still with a slight pout while the photographer took production stills to be circulated to the newspapers and magazines, who would undoubtedly give her five-star reviews. Bel on the front of the *Evening Brummie*. A famous wife. I'd have taken us on holiday to Sardinia again to celebrate. She loved it there. I walked over to the grubby windows and looked back into the bar. The barman seemed lost in his own world. Polishing glasses. I wondered what he was thinking about. To my right, buses swarmed along Broad Street.

'Cities are a work in progress – they're never finished and they're never started. Bel knew things always change. They always change, Bob.'

'People are a work in progress.' Bob's eyes looked apologetic. He squeezed my right arm. 'Not just cities. And yes, things change, and mostly we don't want them to. We want things to just stay the bloody same, because it's less of a faff that way. You'll get better, mate. We'll look after you. I'll look after you.'

'She made this city, and the squalor, so appealing. She made me see it differently, love it. Now every fucking building I look at, every stupid subway I walk through – it always reminds me of her.'

'Course it does. I know that. And that's a good thing. You shouldn't forget her. We'll all remember her. Let's do this. For Bel?'

I nodded.

'Now you need to read that book of hers again, and you need to magic me up the best bloody script you've ever pissed out. Bring that book to life. Bring Bel's thoughts to life, and we'll film it exactly how she wanted; you can say all those things she wanted to say – well, Baxter can if I can hotwire the fucker. But let's do it. I want you to have something to do. I want you to be busy. Don't brood. Promise me you'll do this? You won't just sit at home moping?'

'OK, Dad.'

He jostled me, good-naturedly pushing himself into my flank. 'That's the spirit. Aren't you glad you came in? Now I'm going to get Kate straight on to this. She can plan out all the shoots, organise the dates and the transport and whatever else. The archive footage. I'll get her to come and get a script off you in, say, a fortnight? And then I want you on all the shoots with me and Kate and that gothic tosspot who's presenting. You never know when it might need a rewrite, or he might need a kick up the arse, or I might need a drinking buddy.'

'You just want to keep your eye on me?'

Bob smirked. Of course he did. 'Nah, I just want my best people around me. Anyway, who knows when – or even if – we're ever going to get another crack at shooting something like this. Mids is going down the toilet. We're running out of time.'

'Alright.'

'Excellent. We'll do Bel proud. Oh, and another thing. I think we should get her onto *The Obituary Show*. You know, the one on the radio? I've got a mate in London; he'll have the producer's details so it'll be easy to sort out. She deserves it, Don. To be remembered all over the country, not just in the Midlands. You know it's the right thing to do. For her memory.'

'She never liked obituaries. I remember her saying they gave her the creeps. She thought she'd live forever.'

'No one likes obituaries. No one lives forever. She was an optimist though. She wasn't bitter like us. Even more reason why we need to do this for her, for her spirit to live on. To encourage all the other optimists not to lose faith. Now I'll make the calls; you don't have to worry about any of it. All I need you to do is read that book, write the script for *Ten Brutalist Buildings* and give it to Kate in a fortnight.'

'You're steamrollering me.'

'Someone has to.' Bob ruffled my hair. 'Now then, son. Another beer?'

9

1999

'Do you think you're funny?' Bel purred as she sparked up. It was a sticky summer afternoon. Heat dragged at her words and her movements. She seemed more feline in the summer; she melted in and out of scenes, appeared in front of objects and on top of furniture, luxuriated, took me by surprise. She stretched and stared and knew she was in charge. I was naked, lying on the bed, reading Bel's copy of *The Fountainhead*. The duvet clung to my back; a parched sensation gripped my throat. It cried out for an icy beer. She lay on her stomach, naked too, her head bobbing near my chest. I could feel her breath on me. She got up and started walking around, effortless, pausing by the window, entirely comfortable in her own skin. Endless bike rides had given her body a tautness that always thrilled me.

'Stop being so Teutonic,' I said, without looking up. I felt her smile without needing to see it. 'There's no room for originality in architecture. No one can ever improve on the buildings of the past. One can only copy them!'

'Good quote. True.' She chuckled. 'But do you? Do you think you are?'

'What?'

'Funny? Do you think you're funny?'

'Not really. Do you think I am? How do my jokes translate into *Deutsch*?'

'They're not really jokes, are they? They're more clever than that. I think you're funny. You make me laugh.'

'Satire is different to those shitty stand-up club jokes. Satire's what I really love. You're just ripping into what's given to you, looking at how stupid a thing is or how stupid people are, and mocking that.'

She stood by the open window, looking out down Leighton Road. 'Why are all the cars in our road red or white?'

'It's a law we have in this country. It's the 1990s, we like our cars red or white. We legislate.'

'Shut up!'

'OK, it's not a law, but I guarantee this – the shittier the car, the more likely it is to be red. Look. Seriously. It's just fashion. All cars will be, I don't know, silver in ten years' time. Slightly less shit ones are white. It's common knowledge. Tell me what colour the small cars are.'

'Red, you're right.' Bel chuckled. 'I think you're funny. But funnier on paper, funnier in what you write for the telly than in real life. But I wouldn't want to go out with a stand-up comic or someone like… that. They'd be on duty all day, you'd have to laugh all the time at what they said.' She paused. 'If you were like that I would have to kill you. I like what you say. And I like what you write, even the stuff that's shit, like the game show with dogs.'

'Even the stuff that's shit. Lovely.'

She chuckled again. 'I mean…'

'You won at that game show. Or don't you remember the

episode you and Breuer starred in? Our champion downstairs certainly does. He tells me about it all the time. He reckons he got a lot more attention from girl dogs down the park after his star turn.'

'What did we win again?'

'A very large bone made out of... plastic? Wood? And three hundred and sixty-five cans of dog food.'

'One a day. Very generous of Mids TV.'

'Got a deal from the pet food factory in Solihull actually.'

'So?'

'OK yeah... the thing about the planners, now that was funny. I think.'

'It was.'

'But I am rather ashamed that my entire fucking career has been spoiled on so many occasions by having to write all kinds of mainstream TV rubbish to pay the bills. If only I could have been one of those film auteurs who went decades between deals, only dedicating themselves to the very best and most important projects.'

'We all need to earn money. That's why I've done teaching. That's why I worked in a cafe when I was younger and pulled pints in the Bride. That's life. That's Western capitalism.'

'I love how it's "western".'

'Well it's not eastern, is it?' She planted a kiss on my cheek then retreated back to the window.

She thought I'd gone back to reading but I hadn't. I stared at her over the top of the book. She brandished her fag in one hand; the other was pressed on her hip. 'Do you think I'm too serious? Is my writing too serious?'

'It's romantic and it's passionate. It's perfect.'

'You're staring at me.' She turned. Her eyes on my eyes.

'Sue me.'

She looked away again. 'I like our road. I like the shape of it.

It's just the right length and width, and the houses just sit nicely against it. A row of happy houses like the ones kids draw.'

'It's too suburban for you, surely? Too twee. Too English?'

'I have time for some guilty pleasures too, you know that. A bit of twee, a bit of irony. And, as a matter of fact, I have rather a soft spot for England. For Englishmen. As long as they don't like football.'

'I don't.'

'I know. That's good.' She started forming her hair into a ponytail. 'There's Mrs Henderson, back from the supermarket.' She pulled the window further open, leaned out, still nude, and shouted, 'Mrs Henderson! How are you?'

I heard a muffled, 'Not bad, bab? How are you?' coming from our neighbour out on the street below.

Bel walked over to the stereo in the corner and began ferreting for something. 'Do you think it's naughty that I write about Brum so much but I'm not a native Brummie? I'm a foreigner. Worse – I'm the enemy.'

'Because you're not from here you can see things that the poorly educated locals like me can't see. You have perspective. Outsiders write the best stuff, I think. You can't be too close to the thing you're looking at, otherwise you pull punches.'

'That's what I hoped.'

'Anyway, you're very nearly a Brummie now. You married one, you live here. You could have lived anywhere.'

'I could have married anyone...'

She pressed the button that made the top-loading CD player door whoosh upwards. As it opened she smoothed her hair behind both ears. She reached up to the shelf and selected an album by The Rationalists, taking it daintily out of its case and popping it into the player. 'Yes,' she said, pressing play, 'this.'

Bel turned to face me, shut her eyes and started to dance. And do you know what? That was probably the best moment of my entire life. I knew that song only lasted a little under five minutes, but I wished it would go on forever, because that was as perfect as a piece of paused experience could get. Listening to that song while the only woman you'd ever loved danced naked in front of you like she'd come straight out of a fucking dream. I knew we were going to be together forever that day. That's what I told myself. I told myself: You and Bel will be together forever. Neither of you will ever die. Ever. Because you don't think that either of you will ever die, do you? If you did, everything would collapse in on itself. You just have to keep on believing, deluding yourself against the realities that stare back at you when you look in the mirror, the lines and wrinkles that grow as you get nearer to death. You ignore them.

10

———

What did I have in my satchel? Sweets, crisps and a glass bottle of pop. And my A–Z. When I'd turned ten everything changed. I was allowed to bike as far as I wanted. Well... OK, the rule was that I wasn't supposed to go further south than Kings Heath, further west than Cannon Hill Park, further east than Stratford Road or further north than the tram depot at Balsall Heath. In practice I learned that I could flout these rules with absolute impunity. As long as I was home by five on the dot, which I always was, I would get a kiss on the forehead, and fish with parsley sauce and peas, or sausages and chips, for tea. Really, the ruse now was stretching the forcefield to its outer limits, to see how far I could get before it snapped. This was, in effect, an ideal way to train a boy to be a spy. I was lying about where I'd been, deceiving my parents about where I was off to next. Along the way I was learning more skills in navigation, counter-espionage and observation than even the Cub Scouts was teaching me. It was enthralling to work these conundrums out. To play games with physical and mental spaces, spaces sometimes mapped in my mind and sometimes using the A–Z, complete with its jarring spelling mistakes – mistakes I could see even at a tender age. The game helped me to comprehend distances, time, the fabric of the city in three dimensions. I had to understand not just how far somewhere at the edge of my growing world was, not just how to get there, but exactly how long it would take to get there and, crucially, to get back in time for my fish-finger curfew.

Something had caught my eye in the *Evening Brummie* the day before. After Dad had read the paper, it was always avail- ' able for me to peruse at length. A new library was opening. I could have asked and I'd probably have been taken. It was a very innocent request, hard to argue with. But I craved something sweeter – doing it under my own steam. And so far the city centre had eluded me. I knew it would theoretically be fine. Not too far and not too long. Doable. Just. But the Middle Ring Road formed something of a barrier in my mind. I'd cycled up to the road – three times now in fact. But never crossed it. It scared me. The road itself was wide and disconcerting. The subways slung under it looked terrifying; the districts beyond it were filled with menacing blocks and dank-looking streets. I was particularly afraid of the tall flats in Highgate, on a hill, glowering down at me. I had an abnormal fear that someone was up in one of the blocks watching me. I'd seen curtains moving. Someone was there.

Twelfth of January. Saturday morning. I told my parents I was off for a bike ride and promised to be home by 5 p.m., as usual. I gave Ringo a big cuddle. He plodded all the way to the door when I left and seemed to sense tragedy. His eyes were more pleading than usual. I said, 'Bye, Ringo!' and he responded in his usual way, with a big, friendly bark. I cycled as fast as I could. North through Moseley, then the back roads through Balsall Heath I liked. There were fewer lorries and buses than the main road – I hated when either got too close to me and the parked cars. I reached the Middle Ring Road. It roared with traffic; at this precise point the road became something like a dragon, snaking down the hill. The cars were fire spewing out between its teeth, shooting past with deadly abandon. It took guts to go down into the subway beneath the road, and my heart raced as I strode into its dark maw. I saw some older boys approaching and thought I was going to cry. I held my nerve and walked past; they didn't even notice me. Each time a car thundered over the top of me I jumped. Once I was out the other side, I cycled as quick as possible through the council estate, dodging bollards, hexagonal planters and men in wheelchairs. I had a map in mind, imprinted. I followed it, up through Highgate, the gloomy back streets of Digbeth, through Chinatown, under another ring road – this time the Inner one. To cross that ring road, at Hurst Street, there was a large underground cavern beneath the four roads that met at the junction. The weird subterranean space had shops inside. And men shining shoes. Voices echoed. The smell was sweaty. I pushed up, skirting round New Street Station and onto Hill Street. I had to push the rest of the way as the incline was too steep. At the top, sweating, I saw a monster. I'd been in town before with Mum and Dad, but never here. Never to this.

The library looked like a spaceship, exactly how I imagined a spaceship would seem. I drank the pop and pushed through the crowd. I was just in time to hear a round of applause and see men in suits clapping and shaking hands. One of them cut a ribbon and – as the crowd cheered – held up the pipe he'd been smoking. I found a step in front of the building in Chamberlain Square and sat, facing the town hall, my back to the library. I just sat there quietly for an hour or so, shivering in the cold as the adrenaline inevitably dissipated. I wondered if it was going to snow soon. I opened my crisps and ate them, then started on the sweets. Then something strange happened. My stomach felt like it would burst. I sensed the building was talking to me. I imagined it had its left arm round me like my dad did when we sat on the sofa watching TV, and it – like him – wanted to say something important. I turned and stared at the building behind me. Its arm was curled. That's exactly what it looked like.

'What did you say, Mister?'

I heard the words: 'You need to get home for your tea, Don. Don't forget.'

I looked at my watch. 'Oh God! You're right.'

'I'm a library. I know a lot of things because of all the books inside me. You can trust me, Don. Go home to your mum and dad, but be careful on the big roads. Don't rush.'

I said thanks. I retraced my tracks and made it home by 4:20 p.m. Easy. Mum wondered why I was so red-faced. I said, 'It's been a hard day's cycling around Moseley!' I ate my chicken pie and mash so quickly I felt like I was going to be sick. Over tea, Dad muttered something odd about 'those tanks at Heathrow last week... It's a set-up. They're up to something – they're after Wilson,' but I didn't know who Wilson was or who the tanks belonged to. Dad said Wilson had opened the new library today, and I froze, thinking the game was up, but he didn't talk any more about the library. He just kept using the word 'conspiracy' and looking glum. He said he was worried about the IRA too and that I should tell him if I saw anything dodgy going on in Moseley. I nodded and promised I would, but I wasn't sure how dodgy the thing I saw would have to be for me to tell Dad about it. I ran upstairs after tea and immediately scanned the A–Z, tracing my route into town with my finger. I couldn't believe I'd made it. I really couldn't believe it. Neither could my stuffed dog, who I insisted we call Moseley. He was a Labrador. Just like Ringo. But not real. Moseley stared at the A–Z too, so in awe of my achievement that he could neither move nor speak a single word. But I could tell he was impressed – it was written all over his face.

11

___

I haven't ever really challenged myself. Belinda always set the bar high, always aspired, was confident, believed. Once she ran down Leighton Road and back, naked, when we were playing some stupid drinking game. I remember how her laughter filled the air, how the lights in the houses went on as she sprinted back up towards our house. How she couldn't stop giggling when I'd bolted the front door and refused to let her in, and Kate pleaded with me to open it. Belinda said I could write a novel. I probably could. But why don't I? Why haven't I? Can I bring characters on a page to life using only words? Only if it's a script. If I know they're going to end up on a TV screen it's child's play. But fleshing out real people on a page? It never seemed possible. It's so two-dimensional. People exist in three dimensions; they need to jump up and start living. But perhaps I should have tried anyway. I sat on the sofa and thought about *Ten Brutalist Buildings*. It was the book that made Belinda's name. It was one of the first attempts to reassess the style of architecture Belinda adored, the type of architecture she thought everyone should adore. She wrote it as a love letter, she felt that she was sticking up for the bullied kids at school, she felt like she was sticking up for ordinary people because she felt these were buildings for everybody. She wanted to change your way of seeing things in a fundamental way. She always challenged herself; she wanted to challenge everyone else too. The book had been intended as a small thing really, a toe dipped in the ocean. She was over the moon just to get published. She anticipated that a few lay readers would pick it up, but mostly it would be read by her peers in academia, in architecture, in planning and publishing.

I picked up the book and opened it. The printed dedication read:

For Donald

Underneath, in biro, she had added:

I fucking love you forever, D
Bxx

I had read the book when Bel had first written it. Now I read it again. It took two days. I went flat out.

Then I got my computer out and I started typing. And I didn't stop obsessing over the script until it was perfect. It took two weeks. I didn't leave the house. I lived on salsa. And crisps. And the odd vegetable thali delivered by a guy called Nikesh, who rode a moped whose waspish engine signalled the arrival of my daal, aloo saag, pilau rice, and chutneys. I had to get my vitamins somewhere. Bob came over once with one of those cardboard carriers that held ten small bottles of supermarket French beer in each hand. He got so drunk he had to call a taxi, and the neighbours complained the next day that he'd blocked them in with his beaten-up old car, which I knew for a fact he had deliberately parked in a peculiar way to be obstinate. Every day I wrote. My mind was always on that damn script. I rewarded myself for the number of words done – 250 for a cig, 500 for a cup of tea, 1,000 for some food. It wasn't always easy to steam through it. There were a lot of complicated portions of the book I didn't get, still don't get – Bel was trained in architecture whereas I'm a hobbyist with a vague interest in cities. Maybe that was for the best though – I was trying to make her words – her world – accessible. In fairness, her words were fairly accessible to start with. That was one reason why the book was so good. But I wanted the average TV viewer at home to really listen and think. There couldn't be too many words in the final film, just little snippets – like picture captions in a book. The images would do the talking as well as the words. Snippets. Like life. Just little pieces. I wrote these little pieces of talking that would bring the buildings alive, and I imagined the pictures running over the top of the words. I had to cut down loads of Bel's stuff and I had to write a few new lines of my own in other places. It was honestly more of an editing job than a creative writing one. I imagined Bel reading it all out; I imagined her standing in front of that camera, pushing her hair to the side of her face and behind her ear and smiling and explaining why concrete buildings were the most important things in the world. I did it all because I loved my wife. I'd always love my wife. I'll always love my wife.

12

Kate had arranged to meet me at the Bride of Bescot to pick up the script. I locked the house and walked straight down Tudor Road before turning left into Alcester Road, following it south, to the top of the hill. Then the hill fell away, and at the bottom, just before Moseley shaded into Kings Heath, was the Bride in all her dubious glory. Clouds bloomed like brooding cancer cells in the sky. I wanted to get away from them and was happy to heave open the maroon door that led to the saloon. It was late afternoon; there weren't many punters in. Most of the ones who were drank alone. I bought a pint and thudded the script down onto a small round table. The fireplace looked so homely, so welcoming. I wanted to throw a log on it and flame it up. I exhaled.

'You silly bastard,' I heard from across the room. Kate walking over. She wore tight black jeans and a Breton-striped top. 'What have you been up to? Why haven't you called me back?' I could smell her hair now. She threw her arms around me unflinchingly. I flinched, unused to touch for so long. 'Are you OK?'

'Well... I'm here, aren't I?'

'You silly bastard.' She grabbed my cheeks and looked straight into my eyes, then combed my hair using her right hand. 'What the fuck are we going to do with you, Donald?'

We sat and drank and talked until closing time. I told her I was sorry for not ringing, that I had looked for her that day I went back to the Mids offices to meet Bob. Kate listened with her heart, not her ears. Why hadn't I thought about calling her before? She was humane, a human antidepressant. I gave her the script as we staggered back up the hill towards Moseley, sheltering under a shared umbrella as the rain pelted down.

'What are you doing for dinner?'

'I haven't been eating much.'

'I can see. Why don't I buy you a balti? I want to tell you about a programme I'm doing – *50 years of Mids TV*. Been looking through the archive like nobody's business. I think there's some stuff you'll like in there, some stuff you've written!'

I scoffed. 'Really? Ah, I'd love to, but I need to sleep.'

'Fine, well I tried.'

'I want to see some of your archive finds soon though. Are you OK getting the bus back?'

'Of course I am. But I'm walking you home first. All sorts of nasty men round Moseley at this time of night, isn't there?'

At my door, Kate kissed me goodbye and walked off down Tudor Road, looking like Mary Poppins beneath the brolly. 'See you tomorrow. Bright and early. Baxter loves mornings!'

I thought I could hear a distant rumble of thunder. I fell on the sofa and passed out.

An hour later I was woken by a roar like a tramp clearing his throat. The storm was right over me. A crack of thunder. Black sky burned white in pulses, like paparazzi flashbulbs going crazy. Blinking, lights, bright, blinking, lights, bright. I went to the window and stared out at the garden. A huge explosion rocked the house. Thunder like mortars. I peered at the rain bucketing down, thrumming polluted water on the cold pane. The garden looked miserable. Another huge crack. Lightning flared up, illuminated the scene. For a split second I thought I saw the outline of a person in the garden. Startled, I pressed my nose against the glass. Another flash. Closer now, a blonde woman stood in the garden, motionless, staring at me. Flash. I swore, ran into the hallway to grab a coat and went out into the garden. No one there. Rain cascaded down on me from the broken gutter above the bathroom. The garden was dark between lightning flashes, overgrown and full of menace. Nevertheless I stood there for ten minutes looking at the spot where I'd seen her. She didn't return. My bike seemed to wink at me, goading me almost. I bent down, heaved up one of the loose paving slabs we'd been storing up in a heavy pile next to the point where the gutter outflow ran into the drain. I lifted the slab up to chest height, walked a few steps, and smashed it down onto the frame of the bike with a great guttural grunt of disgust. The paving slab bounced off the bike's metal. Angered now, I picked up the scratched bike, put it over my head and lobbed it towards the fence at the far end of the garden. It ricocheted off the wooden panels, which quivered and moaned. I paced to the carcass of the bike and stamped down hard on top of it. Thunder rumbled, but more quietly now, creeping away slowly, edging into the distance, ashamed and repentant.

I fell down on the ground without really wanting to. Who wants to lie on a wet patio in a storm? My body just gave up. I lay there, flat on my back, watching the fading flashes half-heartedly duel with the cloudy sky. My chest rose and fell with my breathing. I turned my head to the right and saw a friendly frog staring right into my eyes. I picked it up, and it bravely allowed me to hold it in my hand. Its slick skin meant it was as hard to grab as a bar of soap. I went upstairs and put the frog in a bath in case the neighbour's cat, Humphrey, was out with a thirst for blood and a psychopathic attitude whipped up by the thunderstorm. The frog kept trying to escape from the bath by climbing up the sides, but each time he tried, his efforts were totally frustrated and he slid back down to where he'd begun.

'I'll take you back out there in the morning, little man,' I whispered to him as I stroked the top of his head. 'Once that lazy fucking cat has gone to sleep. Then you can pop off back down to the railway line and find Mrs Frog. She's not going to be impressed about you staying out all night – take it from a man who knows.'

The frog replied with a single 'Rebbit', which amused me because I didn't realise frogs made that noise in real life, let alone that they could also understand English.

I went back outside to examine the remains of my bike. A frail voice fired over the fence. 'Is everything OK? I heard a commotion.' An old person. Busybodying. My neighbour.

'Yes, Mrs Henderson. Sorry about the noise. Just… fixing my bike.'

'Right you are.'

Up in my study, all seemed calm. There was nothing left to write; it'd been done. All I had to do now was keep an eye on the shoot and check that Baxter wasn't fucking up the words I'd penned. I'd written the *Ten Brutalist Buildings* script as a tribute to Bel. Thinking about her was the only way I could summon the wherewithal to put finger to keyboard. I had no more energy left for writing. It was all expended. What would I do when the film was finished? What then? I'd always fancied living in Berlin, but Bel wouldn't even countenance the concept of going back to her home town. I knew it was cheap. Maybe I could go and live in Berlin for a few months and just escape everything. Bel's mum, Frau Schneider, would cook me food with ridiculous names like *Knieperkohl* and *Hoppel Poppel*;

she'd give me big bottles of beer to drink and super-strong fags to smoke. It'd be simple, charming. I could look after her and she could look after me. Germany was relaxing. I always felt calm when I was there, though Bel found this impossible to understand – for her, Berlin had been a place of stresses and strains. Maybe I'd find some inspiration, inspiration to write something else, if I went there for a while – rented an apartment in Kreuzberg on the cheap, lived simply. Maybe I could write a sitcom set in East Berlin in the 1970s.

13

1990

'So this is where you work?' Bel's hair was permed. Her lips were provocatively slicked cherry; she kept licking them. She opened her mouth wide. She had a yellow jumpsuit on. She looked like she was a pop star who'd come to be interviewed on the daily lunchtime chat show Mids produced, the one which – inexplicably – always seemed to feature helicopters and parachutists. The lunchtime show's bookers would have to either hoodwink or blatantly bribe the 'showbiz' guests to come north up the M1, out of their comfort zones. They knew Birmingham smelled of shame in the capital's celebrity circles. And I think, sometimes, so did we.

Bel might have looked like a pop star today, but unlike one of them, one of those flash-in-the-pan beasts, she wasn't spilling fripperies about celebrities or herself or the cracked, quasi-glossy world of showbiz I knew to be a complete fucking sham of the highest order. She talked about architecture, about space, about ideas, about creating a world around us, about art, about making beautiful things.

'You know these studios shouldn't even be here? This was a second choice – you're a second choice, I'm afraid.' She stared at me then burst out laughing. We walked across carpets coloured chocolate, cream swirling patterns at irregular intervals. The carpets gave you static electrical shocks when you pressed the lift buttons.

'What should be here?'

'The plan was for an entire new district of the city. You know where the library is, right?'

'Of course.'

'And what it looks like?'

'How could I forget?'

'Well imagine that spread over the whole area, this whole area; strung out along Broad Street like a behemoth.' She looked dreamy. 'It would have been wonderful. The architect proposed so many exciting shapes and buildings. It would have looked like... a space station almost. The architect wanted to create a new civic centre for Birmingham, an expression of the pride of a city. Using buildings to say that Birmingham was heading to the future. Of course it was also to make the big-wigs feel more powerful, but that's men for you. And speaking of that, on this very spot, that's where there would have been a stupid priapic tower that would have shot up into the sky. That was a shit idea, obviously, but the rest would have looked great. They even wanted to build a monorail, but then didn't everyone?'

'Wow. They had some serious plans.'

Bel framed a face of agreement, eyes widened, a little half smile, turning away very slightly, nodding very slightly, to look clever and nonchalant all at once.

'So if they'd built that, no Mids TV HQ here?'

'Exactly. A convention centre, council offices, water gardens, maybe some flats for people to live in, a pointy tower, a monorail track above the roofs, big buildings and bridges, multiple levels. Lots of stuff, all going on together. Lots of people. Lots of life.'

'Instead, Brummies got an office block and some hefty studios where we make programmes that workers can wind down with after a day at the car plant.'

She giggled at this, lit a cigarette.

I pointed out the canteen, the bar, the offices. I said the studios were behind us and if nothing was filming we could go and look inside them.

'Do you fancy having dinner with me again? You liked Bartholomew's, didn't you? That Black Forest gateau must've reminded you of home?'

Bel laughed a little too much. Was that a good thing?

I continued. 'I heard about this little French place. Apparently they do a nice confit duck.' I was very pleased with this line. Scandalously, it was both pre-prepared and cynically intended to both make me look better than I really was, and to manipulate Bel into saying yes. I couldn't suggest a curry on Ladypool Road. And I wondered whether Bartholomew's had been a mistake. I thought my prawn cocktail and chicken Kiev were first rate, but she seemed more amused than romanced by the place. I remember her commenting on the fake brickwork and the waitresses' miniskirt uniforms. She said the place was only a decade old, but they'd tried to make it look as if it was approaching its 500th birthday. She told me it was postmodern, and that wasn't 'a good thing'. I had to impress her. She was sophisticated. She was foreign. The funny thing was, when I finally did take her for a curry, she said she preferred it to some of the fancy places I'd taken her because it was 'real', 'authentic'.

She snickered. 'Very sweet.' And lit a cigarette. 'Tell me, do you like the programmes you write? Do you like the words you put down on paper?'

'I like that question. The answer, Miss Schneider, is essentially: not always. Sometimes. Sometimes I like things I've written, and then other people don't. Sometimes I don't like things, and other people agree with me. It's funny that all these fictions come from your head, and land on a screen, on paper. These falsehoods that masquerade as truths.'

She stared out into the distance. 'I want to write. I want to write a book about brutalist buildings. I want to write about how they touch me, what they make me feel. What they are capable of making everybody feel. I want to find a new way of writing about architecture that hasn't been done before. You could help me.'

'I'm impressed by that. I think it's great that you want to write. And about something you're passionate about. And about Brum, right?'

'Of course! A love letter to Birmingham and its dreams of bigger things. Other cities too, but mostly, yep, Birmingham. So you'll help?'

'Could I help you? I don't know enough. I'm an interested observer of the urban landscape. Well, of the urban landscape of Birmingham, because Birmingham's TV station is the only one that will pay me, and Brum – like all people in the world, if we think of Brum as a person – only wants to hear stories about itself.' I paused. 'Sometimes, when I was little, I thought that buildings could talk to me.'

'Me too.'

We stood in silence for a few seconds.

'What was that show you mentioned? That sitcom? About the planners. That sounds fascinating. You do know! You know more than you let on.'

'*Big Plans*? Yes, that's going to be a sitcom set in the planners' office in the 1960s when they were transforming the city. I've started writing it. When they were thinking about building what you just talked about, huge civic centres and big malls. And all the other concrete monstr... I mean edifices.'

'Ha! There you go.' Suddenly she seemed to be listening to me more intently. I could feel her eyes on me. I warmed to it. Often I felt self-conscious discussing ideas. Writers who talk about their work and its transient power leave me cold. I want my work to do the talking. But I made an exception to try and impress Bel.

'I've got the two main characters in mind – Rocaster, the city architect, who's idealistic but exasperated. And his boss, Benedetti, the megalomaniac city planner who wants to craft Brum in his own image; he isn't afraid of knocking stuff down and ploughing motorways anywhere he wishes. What do you think?'

'I think it sounds fabulous. I'm going to watch every episode, and I'll know the writer of it. But it's going to be funny, right?'

'Everything I write – well, almost everything – is supposed to be funny. It's a satire, of course. It's going to mock them for thinking that they can do anything, that they were gods in their own city. Gentle mocking. It's important to keep the people in power in check.'

'People in power are the worst people. We should have artists running everything.'

We squeezed into a small silver lift and it jolted upwards as if it were tired, as if it'd made this journey one too many times for its own liking.

Bel greedily watched the numbers getting bigger on the screen – each number was cut from a little piece of metal and a white light went off behind it as we hit that floor, illuminating the number.

'You know, in Berlin, television was a political act. We had television wars. The east built a big transmitter to try and send signals to the west, propaganda. In fact that transmitter itself was a big piece of concrete propaganda. And if you were in East Germany you could receive the West German TV signals. Each station on each side had programmes which tried to rubbish the output of the other side. The only place you couldn't get the western signal was right in the very far east of the country, around Dresden. They called it the "Valley of Ignorance" because all those Saxons got was the official GDR state propaganda, no balance at all.'

'But if you pointed your aerial to the west, didn't you get in trouble?'

'Exactly. Hey, you know your stuff! The Stasi would immediately suspect you if your aerial pointed to the west, but then if your flat was to the east of the East German transmitter like ours was in Lichtenberg, what could you do? You had to point it west anyway. It was a pretty stupid situation, I guess. I'm just glad we… well my parents really, had something to keep them sane. To show them that it wasn't all some fucked-up dream they were trapped inside of. I really worried about my mum. I know how much pressure she felt to conform to what those bastards expected.'

The lift pinged. Top floor. The doors shot open. 'Wow! I've always wanted to come up here,' she said, her eyes as bright as a rabbit's.

'Just a few more steps first – if I can remember which direction. Hmmmm… yep, over here.'

We tiptoed gingerly up the steps. I pushed. A heavy steel door creaked open and clanked loudly as it banged on the side of the stairwell exit. We walked over to the edge. The city spread out before us. As the view came into focus, the background din of the traffic and the wind became noticeable in my ears. The roads formed patterns like ones you find in nature – curves and swirls of roundabouts and slip roads which looked like stalks or streams. Yellow steel cranes looked alive but temporarily paused, flower-like. Concrete blocks of different shapes and sizes jumped up and down at you as you looked at them – that was just your eyes adjusting to the sensations.

'This view is amazing.'

'We're right on top of the office tower. Above that silly giant "M". Everyone who runs Mids TV is below us.'

'You worked your way to the top!' She seemed to like this joke.

I demurred. 'The closest I'll ever be.'

Bel looked awestruck by the city that was opened out below us. I watched her watching. She kept smiling, shivering slightly but grinning through what chills she felt, fumbling with her hair to keep it out of her eyes as it blew around in the breeze. She eyed up different buildings and the same scene from different angles, as if painting pictures in her mind to remember what she was looking at. I was painting too. She was in my pictures.

'This is Paradise Circus,' she said, pointing down towards the library.

'I thought it was the library.'

She made a circular gesture with her arm. 'Yep, but the roundabout is called Paradise Circus. Isn't that amazing?'

'Ah, I did know that. Of course.'

'Paradise. What an incredible name for a place. Paradise!'

'Isn't it!'

Bel laughed. 'Yes, a few people probably hate it. But I love it. What a name, what an idea. That was the whole idea of architecture back then, of city planning. To create a paradise. And this paradise is called Paradise. It's so perfect. Why don't people use it in their stories? You could write something set here, Donald, something nice, something that ends in Paradise.'

'Perhaps we'll end there some time,' I said. 'We began there, didn't we?' But it sounded too cheesy and she just made a kind of 'Hmph' noise in response.

'You know I was there on the day the library opened?' I looked too pleased with myself.

'Gosh. You are old! I'm impressed by that though. You can definitely take away from tonight that you've impressed me.'

Bel looked in every direction as she inched along the roof, gently, imperceptibly away from me almost without me realising. She was her own anchor, and her anchor was something a lot more solid than my own, something that seemed to weigh her perfectly, so that she could do anything she wanted, but she'd always remain perfectly connected to the ground. She'd never fly away. She was at the other end of the roof now. She turned and looked at me, and spoke. I didn't pick it up.

'I can't hear you.'

She spoke again. I couldn't hear.

'I'm coming closer, it's too noisy. What was that?'

'I said, "You can kiss me now".' Her lips were parted, moistened, calling out to me. Her eyes were shut. For a split second I could roam over her face, enjoying all of her features – her cheeks, her eyebrows, her small chin, her dainty ears. I moved towards her. My right hand was shaking a little as I brought it up towards her left cheek. I parted my lips and slowly aimed for hers, my mouth tense and greedy.

'Too late now!' She pulled away and giggled. 'You missed your chance.'

14

'Elizabeth Anderson' by The Rationalists

Is it me?
That you see?
Is it me?
Is it me?

Is it me?
That you see?
Is it me?
Is it me?

Oh Lizzie please.
Lizzie please.
Is it me?
Is it me?

There's a place where I can see.
Oh Lizzie please.
Lizzie please.

There's a place where I can see.

The city breathe.
Oh Lizzie please.

Will you see?
Will you see?
What you've done to me?

Oh Lizzie please.
Lizzie please.

Will you see?
Will you see?
What you've done to me?

Oh Lizzie please.
Lizzie please.

Is it me?
That you see?
Is it me?
Is it me?

Is it me?
That you see?
Is it me?
Is it me?

Oh Lizzie please.
Lizzie please.
Is it me?
Is it me?

2008

Baxter looked like a French scarecrow. Terrifying, suave. He never seemed to inhale or exhale; I didn't see him take a breath. I never witnessed him eat or drink anything. He ran on some kind of unnamed, unknown impulses – electrical, perhaps; chemical, certainly. Perhaps he also fuelled up on the blood of children, the skin of toads, heavy-metal-tainted canal water. His favoured gothic black polo-neck-and-suit combo was disconcerting. I wondered whether Baxter realised there was a slightly sick joke at work on this spot: just a few yards from him, down among the cheap ironic clothing shops in Priory Square, Birmingham's angsty teenagers bought everything they could find in black too. This was where the alternative strata shopped: the goths, the metal fans. I'd shopped here for T-shirts when I was younger too. I was a swot, but inside my belly lay a grenade charged with equal parts hope and anger – just like today's kids that exist outside the mainstream. I threw mine, but all I wanted to do was demolish everything using jokes.

The first day of filming. This was how Belinda's book would come to life. This was what television people did to boot the ideas of a writer presented in paper form into a sixty-minute programme that you could watch on the sofa with a cup of tea in one hand and a biscuit in the other. What would happen during this shoot? Could we do justice to what Bel wanted, to what she'd said in *Ten Brutalist Buildings*? We all knew Birmingham; it was our home. But what would we find in Leeds, Sheffield, London and Berlin? The researchers checked the most important thing of all – were all the bloody buildings in all the other bloody places even still standing? Apparently, the answer was a reassuring, though at the same time slightly concerning, 'yes, mostly.' 'Mostly?' I preferred the 'yes' bit. One thing was for sure – if we waited much longer to film at, and to tell the stories of, those buildings in Brum that Bel had written about and loved, it would be too late. All of them seemed to be on the chopping block. The powers that be wanted to bulldoze both the Central Library and Priory Square, the complex I was looking at right now. I wondered what these dickheads would want to put up instead on the site of the places my wife loved the most. The word was that the vultures were also swarming round Mids TV's own headquarters. I wouldn't be in the slightest bit surprised if they knocked down our home too – these days it was almost empty and the atmosphere sour. Mids had had some fat years alright – mainly at the start, alas. The last few had been a disaster, and to me at least, the writing seemed to be on the wall. I was surprised that Bob had managed to get the cash signed off to make Bel's show. But now it was without its leading lady to write and present it. I looked at Bob. There was something deliciously shifty about him. He made things happen, but I sometimes wondered how, and at what cost. People would do anything for him. I include myself in that.

Baxter glanced at the script for a few minutes while he smoked a fag. He took the almost-finished fag from between greasy lips, set fire to the script and handed the flaming paper to Bob and then crunched up the cig between his palms. As it dropped to the floor, cinders and ash followed it, demonstrating how hot it still was. Bob whispered something in Baxter's ear as the script burned, and punched him on the right arm. Baxter stepped onto the small, wobbly platform of a bright lemon-coloured cherry picker. It curdled into life. BEEP BEEP BEEP BEEP BEEP BEEP BEEP went the godforsaken machine. Smoking mums pushing prams along Dale End paused to look. Baxter stiffened as the machine began to jolt up towards the sky. Legs apart, arms by his side. He just stood there, eyes pointed to the horizon as if they were about to emit laser beams, chest puffed up. The cherry picker juddered even further upwards, and after about five minutes Baxter was at roof level. Without looking down, without checking whether he was about to fall to earth and become human jam – the kind of jam I'd planned to be the other day – with a belly full of trust and a heart not (apparently) knowing fear, he simply sidestepped through the little gap in the rails, from the cherry picker's platform… and placed his feet down on the corner of the roof of the huge Priory Square complex. I could scarcely believe he had just stepped over a perilous gap without even checking his footing. Obviously the machine's operator, brandishing an oversized radio control panel on terra firma, had done a good job of manoeuvring the platform cheek by jowl to the corner of the roof. But still.

Baxter prepared for his piece to camera by coughing once, fist to mouth. We were still down at street level, eyes pointed up, faces painted with a mixture of abhorrence and a certain amount of perverse admiration. Bob shook his head, grabbed a megaphone – just like directors do when you see them in TV dramas or documentaries about TV or films – and angrily yelled, 'Action!'

TEN BRUTALIST BUILDINGS

By Belinda Schneider

Chapter Five

Mega-villages

I said to Donald, 'You already know more brutalist buildings than you think you do.'

He said, 'I know more than enough, thanks very much.'

I said, 'Shut up. Where did you go to university?'

He said, 'Leeds. You know that.'

I said, 'I know that. And did you know that all the time you spent in the library there, reading Nabokov, or Private Eye, that you were inside a brutalist building?'

He said, 'Actually, now I do remember that library. And you're right, it was.'

I said, 'And where did I go to university?'

He said, 'Birmingham.'

I said, 'Exactly. With all its beautiful brutalist towers. And your screenwriting course?'

He said, 'University of East Anglia. Ah ok, I see you what you're doing.'

I said, 'And where we met...?'

He said, 'Birmingham Central Library?'

I said, 'Yes, well done. And where have you spent half your life?'

He said, 'Mids TV HQ. But the other half was in a not very brutalist Edwardian house.'

I said, 'Correct. But the second part is only because you wouldn't let us move to the Barbican.'

He said, 'The Barbican's not in Brum. If it was I'd have moved there with you. Even if it is a bit… overwhelming.'

The brutalist mega-villages really take your breath away. I'm being contrary here and, for the sake of the Ten Brutalist Buildings of our title, for the sake of our survey being of a manageable 'ten' 'buildings', I'm saying that Leeds University, Thamesmead, and the Barbican all count as just one building each, when in fact they're all formed of many difficult, different shapes, all bundled together. In effect they're districts, cities within cities. Look at Birmingham University's 1960s campus extension and the whole of the University of East Anglia – both of which only narrowly missed my cut for the ten buildings I'd focus on, but they're still ones you should visit. All of the places I've just mentioned – and they are, genuinely, actual places with actual character and centres and a feel of their own in each case – they all overwhelm the visitor, as Don remarked. They supercharge, they plump up, they preen, they explode, they engorge: size, abstraction, horror and thrill. Public spaces, differences in height and vertical seg-regation, dominance over the landscape, urbanity, love of urbanity, excitement. They blow your mind wide open.

Brutalism was a breath of fresh air. It emerged at a time when everything was being challenged, when a new society was being birthed around the world, when new art and culture was emerging. Everything was changing. The New Wave of theatre, film, music, art was in step with the new society. And brutalism was its new archi-tecture. Funny then, that a lot of the people designing it were old fogies. And that it was never considered cool. Well, it wasn't – was it? Brutalism was seen as prosaic. People were into throwaway stuff, pop stuff, plug-in stuff, space-station stuff. But nowadays we see brutal-ism as being a symbol of a new era. (If we don't, we should.) Because it was. It is. If only we had such cultural vigour again in our life-time, in the 2000s. If only we had the guts, the balls to build these monoliths for the people. One of the main reasons I chose to lecture and write about architecture in books and magazines is that I knew from pretty early on that no one would ever let me build the kind of buildings I really loved. It wasn't even on the agenda. So, better to celebrate the best of what's been built, rather than adding more crap to the pile like so many of today's architects do.

Oh and, by the way, these monoliths for the people are also great places to walk your dog. I took Breuer, my beloved beagle, to all of them – and if he could have spoken, rather than slobbering and run-ning around with a goofy grin on his face (like my husband does sometimes, too) he'd have said that he loved playing in brutalist mega-villages even more than in the park.

And if you can't trust a dog, who can you trust?

15

My hand was tightly clasped around Belinda's. I liked the way it felt. I liked the touch of Bel's left hand – I enjoyed the feel of the firm, silky skin wrapped around it, but I also liked how holding hands made me feel in my heart. Comforted. Connected. I liked what it represented to cling on like this, to show that you were together; lovers in a private world, displaying a symbol of unity and intimacy in a public realm we all had to share. Lovers were never totally committed to that public world, just to their own bubble within it. We were cut off. And isn't this the trick of cities? To be a person (or a couple) who can function among millions – sometimes to engage with people, sometimes to float through scenes unnoticed, like a spectre. Life is just a series of seamless transitions between the world you spend time in alone and the one you spend time in with others. Sometimes the most alone you feel is surrounded by thousands, but the least alone you ever feel is holding someone else's hand when you're surrounded by those same thousands. That single connection of hands is a middle finger to the modern world; it proves to the world that you can't be atomised, at least not while there's someone else around.

Bel squeezed. I jumped from my thoughts to the real world. 'You're doing well. Look really hard. Look at the whole, look at the edges, look at the details. Look closely and look not so closely. Just relax and let your eyes enjoy the pleasure of it all.'

We both faced a painting. Standing side by side. There were a dozen or so other large paintings and photographs hung along one of the upper corridors of Birmingham Central Library.

'Do you notice how, if you actually concentrate really hard on looking, everything looks different?' I did. 'See how something you thought you knew takes on different... forms, different meanings – if you study it with your eyes. I'm not challenging you, by the way!' I felt her squeeze my arm. 'I'm challenging the art. If it's shit then it will never move you, but this is good, I think it's good, and so if you give it time you can get to understand it more. I think that if art is really good, if it's got a real meaning, if it's authentic, then it defies anyone taking the piss out of it, right?' It was a pointed question, or more accurately a pointed point.

'You think I'm a heathen.'

'I don't! I understand your job is to prick pomposity and bust egos. That's an important job. And most people need taking down a peg or two. But when something is just... when it's so good and so real, when it's been made with love and it's imbued with all these meanings – hidden and obvious – and when its meanings give you feelings, then I think it deserves honest and sincere appreciation.'

I was happy with Bel as my art history teacher for the day. I stared at the painting some more. The painting was based on a photograph, but the colours had been switched, like a negative of a photo. There were shades of colours you see in florists

– calming pastels. And the image was at odds with that; to me it was at odds with that because it showed a building that was large and seemed to have some swagger about it. A block of flats, I guess, receding at an odd angle. Something menacing shot out of the block, diagonally, in the direction of the top-left corner, like a gun barrel almost. But what was written on that protrusion was anything but aggressive. I read out the text to Bel. 'Clare Middleton… I love you will u marry me?'

'Exactly. That's good, isn't it? And it's real. It means something, anyway – because of the way the artist has made it. But it's real, too. A real place with a real message about real people and their real feelings. Just like us.' She squeezed. 'You and me, Donald. We're real people with real feelings – we're not fakes, we're not constructs, we're not characters, we're not fiction. And neither is our love.'

I turned to her. 'How can you be so sure?'

She smirked. Then tenderly pressed her mouth against my cheek, her lips hovering next to my skin even after she'd planted the kiss.

'I've enjoyed my lesson.'

'Good. All of these paintings, these photos, were inspired by brutalist buildings, and I think they're all – OK, not "all" but nearly all – done with panache. But this one, the I Love You bridge one, this is really my favourite. The artist who did it is very young. She's from Skopje – you know that city I visited in the Balkans that was flattened in an earthquake in 1963 and rebuilt? She's very talented. She even came to a book talk I did and I signed her copy. Lovely girl. And look at what she made.'

I looked back once more at the work. Bel was so sure, she understood, she was confident about what she found and what she felt and what she thought.

After a few minutes I glanced down at the card below the piece, which read:

Marija Trajkovski (Macedonia)
Clare Middleton I Love You Will U Marry Me (2004)

16

2008

It was early when I arrived at Birmingham Central Library. The freezing dawn nibbled at my cheeks. Day two of filming for *Ten Brutalist Buildings*. Bob already cradled a tea whose plumes of steam puffed up into the sky as he joked around with some of the crew. Baxter appeared suddenly, like a ghost, from behind one of the hidden doors that lead in and out of the rabbit warren of ghostly subterranean snickets the library sits on. It's hard to understand what's down there sometimes. Paradise Circus is too complicated to comprehend. Concrete stretches and distorts the horizon. Shapes and angles fistfight with each other. Some spaces seem to suck you in, some doors are bolted shut like a prison – but are you on the inside or the outside? The whole ground level is jacked up, leaving this weird netherworld underneath. Baxter seemed to levitate too, floating slowly across a wide, flat, tiled platform, coming to a stop just where we were all standing. But it must have been a trompe l'oeil. He looked into my eyes. He glowered. I gave him the script. He looked up at the sky, took the script and held it, then looked back at me, and for the briefest of moments his eyes softened and we seemed to share something very tiny. It was as if he wanted to confess something? Baxter silently retreated to a bench and read while the cameraman set up the shots on instructions from Bob.

Baxter's preparations to begin speaking were an elaborate routine, a baroque performance involving heavy breathing and quasi-yogic posing. I found it tiresome. Now standing, he clasped his hands together in front of his chest and seemed to be summoning up some kind of evil spirit from the paving stones below, from the earth itself. The ritual would last around ten minutes, and neither I nor any of the production team paid the slightest bit of notice to this nonsense anymore. It was only the revolving cast of interns who gawped in awe and bafflement at the spectacle unfolding in front of them. I wondered if I'd ever seen Baxter without his dark glasses? I certainly couldn't remember a time. Was Baxter born wearing shades? How could he have popped out of his mother in such a state?

It took about an hour for Baxter to complete his waspish pieces to camera. He walked as he talked. I wasn't excited about seeing this idiot on TV in the final cut; I was just excited about seeing Bel's beloved buildings and hearing about why they mattered. The camera panned up from Baxter to reveal what I knew were going to be some startling shapes on screen: avant-garde Tobleronic triangles that Brummies hadn't really seen for some time – hadn't noticed, at any rate. Brummies didn't see the baffling, enticing poses their city struck right in front of their eyes. They looked at the floor, at their phones, at the shop windows, at each other. I squinted up at the corner of the great library, the piece that prodded with expectation and courage out into clear sky, and then I looked at the stepped levels that slid themselves beneath this prow, shadow giving each a slightly different hue. Was I beginning see what Belinda saw?

Pieces of a puzzle sliding together ever so slowly. Maybe we could find some kind of whole. Beauty emerging. It was stark. I swallowed.

I left them to the filming and wandered about. A staircase presented itself to me like a gift. It wasn't a staircase I remembered seeing before. I looked both ways as if checking whether anyone was following me. No one was; no one cared. I stepped down, pulse racing. At the bottom of the stairs was another world, a secret world, a hidden world. A huge square underneath the platform which led to the western entrance of the library. Dingy, dismal, mean in its way yet disgusting and thrilling too. The spaces between buildings are the thing. I hated the undercrofts, the underground car parks, the dungeons. So why was I drawn to them like a moth to the flame? I couldn't stop myself. It was a macabre fascination, like an interest in crime and punishment, in horror movies, or diseases. I thought I knew Brum; this was my home. But this space under the library was new to me, a mystery I'd never discovered before. I tracked across the underground square. Something moved in my left-hand field of view. A fox pounced upwards onto a wall, plodded along and dropped over the other side into a bush. My eyeline was dragged down. A voice echoed, trembling and terrifying in the covered space.

'Spare… change, mate?' A talking sleeping bag resting on cardboard with multiple cans all around.

A human head popped out, a little like a tortoise, wary. We locked looks. For a split second it felt like we knew each other, but how could we?

He stared at me intently as if he knew me, mumbling something about a 'factory'.

'What?' I asked.

'Masshouse. Ma… You…'

'Yeah, that's the programme I wrote. You watched it?'

'Watch? No... TV.' Arms flailing. 'Masshouse. I... You... We... in Ma... they demol... so I... now here...'

'I'm sorry,' I said, and handed him a fifty-pence piece.

I penetrated further, into the eaves directly below the library building itself. How could this place, this space, exist in the middle of the city – right in the very eye of the storm, the dead centre of the city? It was dark and threatening inside the sub-terranean passageways. Two men with matted hair and faces drawn from despair squatted on a kerb, sharing a pipe which oozed noxious fumes. They looked up at me but said nothing as I passed by. Fours eyes, each one rattled. A broken-down car that must have been parked here for years. Bel never told me about this. Did she know? She must have. She was an expert, the expert. Did she like it? Was she ashamed by the sinister undertones of this place – did she think they detracted from the majesty of the building above? Or did she guiltily treasure such places, like me? A locked door; I was trapped. To my right I could see the outside world but it was barred and not available to me. There were trees swaying in the middle of Paradise Circus, on the island in the middle of a roundabout. That's where we were. The library was on an island in the middle of a roundabout. Of course... she told me, I knew that. I knew all of this. I just... forgot it? I held the bars and stared at the outside world, at the civilised town hall beyond the lanes of traffic. That was a straight rip-off of the Parthenon in Athens.

I looped back round and found another space on the northern side of this underworld, still underneath the library. Bricked-up shafts where stairs or escalators would have dropped down from above to this, the minus-one level, made me feel like I was a ghost, an optimistic stiff searching for a way back to the world of the living. Concrete boxes and shelters and benches appeared to me and seemed to suggest that this was supposed to be a bus station, but I've never heard of any bus departing or arriving from down here. Maybe it's a bus station for the dead, taking them to the city's cemeteries.

I heard some clattering. It made me think of the filming that was going on above me. I decided to slip away from this place and leave them to it. I burrowed back up to the surface on a service road and vaulted a fence. I ducked out from beneath the greedy shadow the library's podial superstructure cast and legged it across the road, dodging the roaring traffic of Paradise Circus Queensway. Escaping from the concrete island.

A feeling of calm returned momentarily as I meandered down Fleet Street, away from the traffic. My pace slackened; my breathing settled.

On my right was the old coffin factory on Fleet Street. Next I could see the base of the BT Tower, the second place where I'd tried and failed to shatter myself. It was rearing up on my left. The canal ran parallel to Fleet Street, down its northern side. What if, when I had jumped the other night, I had landed in the canal – which jammed itself right up against the tower – instead of hitting the street in rather more spectacular style? Would you live then? No, of course not. Falling onto water from a great height is just like falling onto concrete.

My body swerved left onto Newhall Street. I flashed past a Bangladeshi restaurant – though you'll (wrongly) think of them as 'Indian' restaurants – where I once took Belinda. I forked fluffy hillocks of biryani and oil slicks of ghee-laden lamb bhuna onto her tongue. She nodded approval, held up her right thumb, and sipped her pint of gassy, tasteless lager as if she'd been English all her life.

St Paul's Square seemed like an oil painting. Rusting leaves fell around me, their hearts fired up for one final performance. On the slabs of St Paul's churchyard the foliage accumulated, creating a greasy surface. It wasn't even my plan to arrive here.

At the north-western corner of the churchyard, a grave in

a prison. Iron bars sprouted on all sides to prevent the cadaver from going on midnight walks in the Jewellery Quarter – or beneath the Central Library. I saw something a minute ago, and now, moving closer, I can eye it up close. A cream belt from a woman's mackintosh, perfectly still on one corner of the grave, threaded gently and purposefully through the bars as if deposited deliberately. A totem. I rubbed the belt between my thumb and forefinger, and the friction produced the slightest feeling of heat, of life. A single strand of long, blonde hair was stuck on the belt. I yanked it off, held it up to the light to examine it. The bells of the church began to peal, throwing their clanks up towards the clouds, and I turned around to see two ushers had appeared at the door, ready to direct guests to their seats at the wedding inside. The ushers wore grey suits and big smiles and handed out orders of service to women wearing elaborate hats and looks of pure delight. One of the ushers took a call on his mobile phone and dashed off towards Newhall Street to deal with some unknown issue. Perhaps the bridal car needed to be shoved out of a pothole? I looked again. The church caught my eye this time, rather than the people milling outside and filing inside. Its windows glinting in the sun. What would Belinda have told me to note about this building – the hard stone walls shaped like a huge cardboard box that's been airlifted in, or the added-later spire that doesn't fit with the formal shape and yet somehow does add to the form as a whole? I knew Belinda liked St Paul's because she'd pointed it out and cooed after we went for that curry. Why did she like it? Perhaps because its stone exterior looked almost like concrete and its toughness was almost forgiving, almost modern, almost a place for the people. Maybe, at a push, she'd have got married to me here if Berlin had been off the cards. For a second I allowed my mind to drift, to imagine what it would have looked like. What if these ushers were my mates and the old women sporting odd millinery were Bel's aunts from Potsdam? What if we'd have emerged from St Paul's Church, into the light, as man and wife? Our wedding photos could have had the auburn leaves of the trees in the square as their background – and we could've had our reception in that same Bangladeshi place in Newhall Street that we rated so much. A chicken tandoori and Birmingham Bitter wedding breakfast. A wedding breakfast of champions. I wondered how many couples in total had married here, had their photos taken on this square – tens of thousands? And each couple wouldn't have given a second thought to any other couple – each couple would be totally obsessed with each other, with their day. The thought of marriage chilled me. The thought that I might have to do it again someday seemed so outrageous, so unexpected, so unappetising. I looked at my watch. It was time to head back to the library, to see if they'd finished shooting.

Bob was standing with the crew at the north-eastern corner of Paradise Circus, where the road leaps under the plaza like a four-lane bobsleigh run. He saw me crossing the carriageway and waved me down, then ran over like an excitable puppy and punched me in the gut.

'Where've you been, you truanting bastard?'

'Went for a walk over in the Jewellery Quarter.'

'Oh? Went for a walk over in the Jewellery Quarter? You don't have to act like a grumpy teenager by disappearing off if you're bored. Some of us have got to put up with managing this lot. I wish I could just piss off whenever I fancied.'

'Calm down.'

'I need a pint. Let's go to the pub. And give me a cigarette.' He turned towards the crew. 'Right, you lot, that's it for now. I need a break. You do too. Go and have some tea and I'll see you back here in two hours.'

115

Excitable noises emerged from the crew; they looked like school kids who'd just been told they were on a snow day.

Bob and I walked west. I lit a cigarette and handed it to him.

'Ah, that's better. There were times this morning when I wished I hadn't been able to screw the last lousy bit of budget out of the powers that be, and then at least we wouldn't have to face however many more days it is traipsing around the country with that clown. Don't get me wrong, I *want* to make this for Bel. I just forget how quickly I run out of patience with Baxter.'

'Traipsing round the rest of the country... and Berlin. Don't forget that.'

He puffed with comedy gusto. 'Berlin? Berlin? You're kidding, kiddo? I read that on the script as *Bromsgrove*. I thought we could all get the bloody bus.' Bob looked knowing. 'And now you tell me I've got to fly this lot out to Europe's clubbing—'

I guffawed.

'Yes, clubbing capital—'

'How do you know that?'

'My niece told me. I've got to get this bunch of chancers on a plane, off a plane, keep them out of the bloody discos, off the pills, and babysit that arsehole of a presenter as well?'

'Why did we pick him?'

'Because there's no one else. Belinda should have that job, obviously. And if not her, then who? I can't do it, I know jack shit about architecture. *You* can't fucking talk in front of a camera without stuttering or fluffing your lines. Who else are we gonna get? There's no one left. Ralph Marks who used to do *Bullseye* – he's been pushing up daisies in some churchyard in Warwickshire for a decade. Do you want one of the comics off

Welcome To The Masshouse to do it? You may as well ask Millie, the network weather woman.'

'I went to university with her.'

'Perfect. Give her a ring.' Bob made a phone shape with his hand and lifted it to his ear. 'Say, "Hi love, we know you're great at telling us when it's gonna rain, but how do you fancy presenting a very arty documentary about brutalist buildings? Mmm hmm? Yep. No, darling. No, love, I haven't got a fucking clue about concrete myself. But I know we absolutely must bloody 101 per cent do it because I made a promise to Belinda Schneider and I'm damn well going to keep that, even if it means we've got a weathergirl pointing at stuff she doesn't have a clue about. Oh right, you're busy anyway? OK, fine. Bugger you, Millie."'

'Millie's quite clever actually.'

'I'm sure she is. I'm sure she is.' Bob paused. 'Why the hell aren't we going to the Mids Bar? It's cheap. And it's over the road.'

'Variety.' We headed to a pub overlooking the canal called the Lasdun Arms. A brick building perched on the towpath – it looked like a quaint house that some kind of eccentric village baker or blacksmith would have lived in 200 years ago. The area around it was obviously rural when it was built; now the city had crept up on it. The city creeps up on us all eventually.

Bob sat down and I went to the bar. I heard him shout, 'Get me some crisps as well, son!' at the top of his voice. I came back with the beers and a bag of prawn cocktail.

'Prawn cocktail? Donald, Jesus, do you have any conception of taste, of fucking… flavour? You can't be trusted when it comes to food, you really can't.'

'More for me,' I reasoned aloud, ripping the bag, inhaling the noxious chemical scent, popping a plethora of the pink-stained crisps onto my tongue. They exploded in an acrid shower of not so much seafood as just a criminally acidic over-load. They beguiled me. I was only just beginning to take rudimentary enjoyment from eating again. I remember Kate saying that breaking up with her other half was the easiest way of losing weight she could have imagined, and I knew exactly what she meant.

'Honestly, I don't know how long I can put up with Baxter. I really don't.'

'You and me against him.' I managed to get out, my mouth full of crunched-up crisps.

Bob supped his pint, sucking through his moustache, on which some of the beer stuck. 'Now look, I don't want you getting too mournful while we're out shooting this film. We've got a lot more to do. Er, where are we going again? After we've done in Brum?'

'Leeds, Sheffield, London and… Berlin.'

'Berlin!' Bob spat out some beer for comedy effect. 'I read that on the script as *Balsall Heath*. I thought we could walk everyone down Digbeth High Street for that shoot. Now you're telling me we've got to go to bloody Berlin? You'll be the death of me, Don, the death of me. Remember when we were doing *I Love My Dog!* and you couldn't get the bloody jokes right some weeks? I ask you to do the easiest thing, to write me some material about dogs and leads and bones and all that kind of thing, and you just couldn't get the bloody laughs from those coffin-dodgers in the audience?' Remember that?'

'I do.'

'And what did I say?'

I put on a uninterested voice. 'You said, "This show is going to the dogs".'

Bob winked. 'Damn right I did. It was. Cheers!' He held up his pint. We chinked. 'Now I mean what I say. I don't want you… going to the dark side. Bel would have wanted us to do this film and she'd have wanted you to write the script and for this to get made. Because if it gets made then it becomes a permanent record of all those buildings she loved. And it might even save them.'

'It might.'

'Exactly. So chin up. This could be a difficult time, but I'll be here to box your bloody ears.'

This is a dream:

I can feel myself tossing and turning, searching for answers, perplexed. I'm trying to solve puzzles, find words. I can't get to where I'm going. A calm descends. A camera on a jib swoops down. Two actors are frozen to the floor; the pause button has been pushed on them. An old man in tweed and a younger one in a navy suit. Desks and drawing equipment lie all around. The flimsy studio backdrop has a big window and a fake view over Birmingham's 1960s skyline – a photograph, a cheat. I can't find the words, I can't find a script. A man wearing headphones comes running over and starts yelling at me, but I can't hear anything he says and the actors don't strain a sinew. They're still motionless. The man with headphones starts waving his clipboard in the air and opening his arms wide in a messianic, questioning gesture. I don't know where the bloody script is though, I just don't know. Where is it?

17

'...and cut! We're clear. Great show, cherubs. Loved the chicken costume business. More of that next week?' The floor manager looked pleased as punch.

'Praps.' Bob's face was harder to decipher.

I saw the studio director give us a thumbs-up gesture from behind the greasy glass of the gallery.

A few people in the audience started sparking up fags and putting the jackets of their shell suits on, cigs dangling from mouths, muttering. They didn't look elated, more exhausted. All I could think about was Belinda. I'd just seen her again on the big screen when they'd projected the VT of us pratting around outside the library the other day to the audience. And they – naturally enough, considering they were trollied – had thought it was all the height of comedy. This laughter is very important for a comedy writer because it shows that what you've written is, actually, funny. You sit typing away by yourself, thinking you might have concocted something amusing; you make yourself giggle the first time you come up with an idea, and when you read the stuff out to the crew they sometimes laugh too. But when you hear an audience really guffaw, even an audience that's been hard at the Birmingham Bitter or vodka sodas just before transmission, you know that the thing – the joke, the skit – is actually funny. It's proof of oneself, one's ability. People think we're cocky somehow, but I've yet to meet anyone in this business – any writer – who thinks what they're doing and who they are is enough. You're battling yourself. But maybe I didn't have to battle any longer. Belinda had agreed to go on a date with me.

'Oi!' Bob strolled over. 'I know what you're thinking about. Are you taking her out tonight then?'

'Tomorrow.'

'Well, well. She knows how famous you are, right? I hope you made sure she knows that bit. Where are you taking the poor lamb? Straight back to yours for a microwave lasagne?'

'Bartholomew's.'

'Bartholomew's!' Bob whistled. 'That'll cost a pretty penny. Don't forget your chequebook. Nice mixed grill they do though, went last year. Big portions. Nice chops. Chicken Kiev's alright too. Though if you're angling for a snog…'

'Not sure how much of anything I'll be able to eat. I'll need a few glasses of red wine first.'

'It's a pig driving home when you've had a few. Obviously three or four glasses sharpens your senses, you feel more in control. But six or seven…' Bob gurned like a Cumbrian farm-hand at a country fair. 'Fucking hell – you better watch for red lights. I've flown through a few of them after closing time! No fault of my own. Just the way it is driving home in Brum.' He slapped me on the back.

'The show seemed to go well. They were laughing.'

'That means you don't get sacked, sonny. Cos if they

weren't, you'd be down the job centre. And the queues down there aren't pretty these days.'

'So? Thoughts, dear leader?'

'They found the chicken bit funny, and they enjoyed that stand-up comic we had in, the one from the club.'

'He was awful. Hackneyed routine, fat bastard. From the past.'

'Hmmm. Well, he got the laughs.'

'Look at the crowd. We need a… more sophisticated audience, and some younger comics. This isn't the 1970s.'

We both looked up. A couple on the back row were engaging in heavy frottage; another guy was just collapsed in his seat, smoking. Everyone else had left. There were multiple empty crisp packets on the floor. 'Yeah, OK, point taken. I'll make some calls. Get a few students in the cheap seats next time. They'll do anything that's fucking free. And they'll laugh on cue. I think we need better sketches too. That's your job for next week – write me some funnier sketches.'

'What about?'

'I don't know what about – that's your job. Terrorists, footie, politicians, people off the telly. Who cares?' Bob turned and started walking away. 'See you in the bar in fifteen minutes.'

I walked over towards the rake of seats the audience had just been sitting on.

'Got a spare cigarette?' I asked the guy still sitting around smoking.

'Sure.' He handed me one. I lit it. What was I going to say to Belinda tomorrow? How was I going to convince her that she needed to give me a chance? I was going to have to write some material tonight, fold it up and put it inside my jacket. If I got stuck I could make my excuses and go to the toilet, then choose a pre-written line and get back on track. The cigarette calmed me. I looked around. The studio seemed bigger than normal today. Fat men dragged pieces of equipment out of it, their arses hanging out of their trousers. Every surface was brown or black. The kit went back into grubby boxes. The place was hot, the aroma… socks. A forklift truck drove in and picked up a Perspex tank stained with green gunge. It reversed back outside, beeping all the while.

'The glamour of TV.'

'Wass 'at pal?'

'Ah, nothing, ignore me.'

Kate sauntered over. She slid a pen bearing the Mids TV logo into the bun in her hair and winked at me, pushing her glasses up towards her face. 'That wasn't a bad show.' She smirked. 'It was an awful show.'

'You should be doing my job.'

'What job are you doing right now, exactly?'

'Very funny. You look nice.'

'Thanks. New shoes. I'm going out on Broad Street later.'

'Date?'

'Course not. With my housemates. On the pull. Not that there's much hope of scoring anyone interesting in Brum on a Saturday night. All bloody drunks or businessmen.'

'I've got no plans for tonight.'

'Well let's go for a drink now, then. Bob said he'd be in the bar. You've got me for…' Kate pressed the digital watch on her left wrist. '…45 minutes. After that I'm out and anyone's. Well, anyone that's showered, charming and well-endowed.'

'I think I tick one of those boxes.'

'I think I know which one.' Kate chuckled, for far too long and with far too much of a knowing look. I think I blushed.

The bar was absolutely heaving; the fug was disgusting. Almost everyone was smoking. I ordered a pint for me and a double gin and tonic for Kate. A fat man jumped onto the bar. 'Right, you bastards! Who just watched *Welcome To The*

Masshouse? And who thought it was the bloody bees knees, eh?'
Bob. The rabble groaned. A woman wearing a claret-and-blue
Aston Villa shirt yelled, 'Bugger off, I want me perry!'

Bob stamped along the bar. 'You boy,' he bellowed to me.
'Come with me.'

Bob jumped down, landed with a thud, and dragged me
over to the toilets. He slammed a cubicle door shut and pulled
out a small silver box. Inside was fine white powder.

'Jesus Christ, is that...?'

'It is. I got it last time I was down at HQ. Those bastards in
newspapers, those City bastards, those TV bastards, those business bastards, those lawyer bastards, those taxi-driving bastards,
those MP bastards – they're all at it down in London, believe
me. And believe me, it works. Just tried some before you got
here.' Bob racked up two fat lines.

'This is my first time.'

'First time's the best time.'

I hefted up the line. The powder stung my nostrils, then the
sensation of the drug going through my nasal passages made
me feel nauseous. It was like being sick backwards.

Thumping on the door.

'Fuck.'

'Ignore it,' said Bob. 'Fuck off.'

'POLICE.'

I turned to Bob. He didn't care.

Again. 'WEST MIDLANDS POLICE. OPEN UP.'

I opened the door gingerly, and saw Kate standing there,
winking at me. The drug banged into my synapses and I
started to cackle like an idiot.

'You cheeky cow.'

'Shut up, rack up,' she said in a deep voice.

Bob hoofed up his line and extravagantly started sniffing

upwards, nostril by nostril, his fingers on the opposite one, each in turn. 'Fancy seeing you in the gents,' said Bob.

'Shove over and give me a line of that,' said Kate.

I watched her red jumpsuit fold in two as she kneeled and bent over the cistern, Bob's rolled-up tenner in hand, ready to inhale. The pen fell out of her hair. She sniffed up the coke, and Bob started clapping his hands and dancing. 'I think we need to fucking go out on the town. John Bright Street. Let's get wasted.' His fists were clenched, his mouth pouting.

'Sorry, boys, I've got to meet my mates,' said Kate.

'Nonsense. You're coming with us.' Bob drained the pint glass he'd left by the sink and shouted 'Alright!' to some guy having a piss in the urinal.

'Bring your mates too,' I said, feeling like, now, I had all the answers a man could ever need.

The man urinating zipped up his fly and turned to face us.

'What are you lot up to? Twatting about as usual?'

'Fuck off, Ralph.'

Kate whispered in my ear, 'Is that Ralph Marks?' before collapsing into more giggles. I nodded.

'You can tell me to fuck off as many times as you want, Bob, but at least one of us is trying to make serious programmes for the network. Serious journalism.'

'It's boring, Ralph. No one cares about current affairs. And you don't even make it very well. They're not elegant like our programmes. Now we're off out. Joining us?'

'I'm driving back to Hagley.'

Bob pressed his face close to Ralph's. 'Hagley, Ralph? Or you stopping at the Spence Motel by the motorway in Quinton to shag your fancy man? What was his name again... Arthur, right? From accounts. Yeah, that's him. And while your poor wife's out at the Conservative Club, doing the teas...'

Ralph stormed out, muttering something under his breath about all of us being tossers.

'Wanker,' said Bob as he grabbed both our arms. 'You two are coming with me!'

We banged into the corridor and smashed out through the fire exit into the freezing cold, Bob yelling, 'Taxi!' despite us being in the pedestrianised plaza right outside the studios.

I said, 'John Bright Street's only over the road.'

Bob replied, 'I don't care. I want a taxi!'

Kate wiped tears of laughter away from rouged cheeks and shot me a glance which seemed to say a million things at once.

18

2007

'Who are the authority figures?'

'What do you mean – "Who are the authority figures?"'

'Who *are* the authority figures? You're always saying that your job is to satirise, that the highest art form of all is the art which takes the piss out of all the other art, out of art itself. Satire is the art which rumbles the bullshitters and the chancers and the authority figures. So who are they?'

'The planners, the architects, the councillors, the contractors, the politicians, the businessmen, the artists, the writers, everyone...'

'The writers?'

'Yes, even the writers.'

'What about the fucking old men who run Mids TV? What about the people who put all that sexist stuff on TV, all those girls being chased round parks in comedy sketches and prancing around in leotards on gameshows about dogs?'

'I love your *Berliner Schnauze*.'

'I love you. My *Berliner Schnauze*, as you always seem very happy to point out – my born and bred grumpiness that all Berliners, all *my* Berliners possess – is rightly directed at them. Those fuckwits. Those fucking men who run Mids TV, who run everything.'

'Rightly directed at them.'

'And you work for them.'

'I do.'

'So you are an authority figure too, right?'

'Well maybe. But I don't get to make any decisions.'

'But you get to set the tone of the culture.'

'Perhaps.'

'So why don't you stop all that sexist shit? It gets me down. Do something about it!'

'I tried. Anyway, on *Big Plans* there was none of that. I wrote female characters who swore and argued.'

'I should fucking hope so.'

'Very good. I do accept that *Welcome To The Masshouse* had pretty girls running around. And I also accept that *Welcome To The Masshouse* was a risible piece of low-budget entertainment.'

'Risible?'

'*Scheiße sein.*'

'*Ja.*'

'I've really got no time for those old dinosaurs. Especially the esteemed executives of the telly world. It's like the 1950s never ended with most of them. This is a new era. But anyone in power is always going to try and cling onto that power. Why would you not? Those architects and planners weren't, I don't think, as utopian as you think they were. I think they were trying to express themselves and their bold ideas for the future, but if they hadn't built those buildings they'd be nothing. They built to be powerful. They ejaculated concrete all over the city!'

'And how far have you ejaculated your comedy, your words, over the city, my darling?'

'A few miles.'

'A few miles? You can ejaculate your words a few miles?'

'More or less.' I paused. 'OK, look, we were bad. TV was bad. All that stuff with beauty contests and girls in bikinis was fucking shameful really. But architects haven't got the best track record. Have they? They're all blokes; they're all about the "grand vision" rather than collaboration – the typical male failure. Not asking anyone's opinion. And those subways weren't great for women with prams.'

'It was a different time. There should be more women architects, of course, and more buildings that aren't some kind of... priapic posturing.'

'I like that. It sounds good.'

'Thanks. Maybe though, maybe brutalist buildings were more female, more complex, more interesting, less of that cock-in-the-sky business. But you're right, it was the bigwigs in charge. It always is. But at least those bigwigs gave a shit. They wanted people to have something a bit nicer. What do today's bigwigs care about?'

'Just money?' I offered.

'Just money,' she said.

'But no one asked people if they wanted this stuff right? It was just, "you get what you're given." Maybe that's why people didn't respect those places, why they soiled their nests.'

'If you ask people what they want, they think they want a house a kid draws – with four walls and a triangle roof. But they only think they want that because they don't know anything else. When you're creating a new society you have to create things that haven't been there before. I think a lot of people really liked all these weird, modern buildings – once they understood them. And remember I'm talking about the

131

good ones here, not the system-built crap. You've got to push things forward otherwise what have you got?'

'Something simple.'

'Simple, yes, but boring. You can be boring, my love. You need to embrace the future!'

'I love how you believe everything, Bel. It's very attractive. I just never know somehow.'

'I believe in things. I think I'm right sometimes. I think people might be interested in what I have to say even? Television viewers in the Midlands maybe?'

Bel fluttered her eyelashes.

'Are you trying to tell me something?'

'Mids TV want me to make a television programme. About the book.'

'*Ten Brutalist Buildings*? On TV?'

'Exactly. Bob called me.'

'Bob called you? Wow. He didn't tell me. You're going to be a TV star! Men around the entire region are going to want to have sex with my wife.'

'They are.'

'Will you be wearing a bikini and running round a park very quickly while you talk about brutalism?'

'I will not.'

'I remember how good you were on that episode of *I Love My Dog!* You looked so... sexy doing all those challenges. Breuer was all over the place. But you did really well. And you were a great talker, a great onscreen presence.'

'Breuer was being very naughty that day. Beagles are.'

'I was being naughty that day. I'm sure it's against some law to have your own wife – and dog – on a game show you've written the script for. People might have thought it was a fix. The tabloids certainly would have.'

'Who cares? And anyway, how can you fix a series of canine

132

obstacle courses? Dogs are gonna do what dogs are gonna do. And that's make themselves look fucking stupid, mostly.'

'That really was funny. Breuer made me cry with laughter when he knocked into the table and mugs fell on him.'

'Sometimes I think he's a bit blind.'

'I know. But look, back to the point. This is amazing. I'm so proud of you.'

'I knew you would be. Let's go upstairs. I want to celebrate.'

'I'll open some wine.'

'Leave the wine. Just follow me.'

19

2008

Voiceover: 'It's the sixteenth of June, 2008. From the centre of the country, from the heart of your region... it's Bullseye! *Tonight... Birmingham looks to the future!'*

[Cut to footage of stained concrete buildings.] 'As plans are announced to demolish the city's failed 1960s buildings and replace them with much-needed and futuristic housing.'

[Cut to computer-generated views of shiny towers on sunny days and shadow people with no faces standing as still as sausages in front of the flats.] 'We'll be speaking to the property developers who will transform Brum.'

[Cut to video of a clean-shaven man in a suit and tie, complete with factory-fresh hard hat which clearly has never been used. Underneath his face, a mauve band topped with white text, which reads 'Alexander Newland' and 'Spokesperson – Aspiration Urban Existence Cocoons'.]

The man in the suit and hard hat: 'We all agree that Brum is looking tired. These three buildings we've bought – Birmingham Central Library, Mids TV HQ, and Priory Square – they no longer work. In fact they've never worked; they're failed architecture. Modernism, brutalism: these are failed styles from a failed past. They're built badly, and look at them – they are not fit for a modern European go-getting region like ours. So we're going to sympathetically de-build them using a light-touch technique. And once they've been sympathetically de-built, we are going to re-build fine new towers full of luxury apartments or, as we call them, chic cocoons, which will be attractive and provide chances for hard-working local people to buy their own home. And can I also add that this de-building and re-building will also empower hard-working local people with various employability opportunities. This is a chance to get rid of the bad old Brum and realise a renaissance, a vision for a glass-fronted regener…'

*

Bob said, 'You've got a day off from the shoot before we head to Yorkshire. Go and get yourself a kebab and then watch a film.'

I went to Cannon Hill Park, tracing the path me and Bel and Breuer used to take. I was going to watch a movie at the arts centre by the lake in Cannon Hill Park. Me and Bel had seen dozens of flicks there. Many foreign films – German, Danish, Czech, Spanish and Korean. Bel was addicted to foreign cinema; she loved to see how other cultures dealt with the universal human experience – happiness/sadness, love/loss. Today there was a British New Wave classic from the 1960s showing in matinee. It was set in Lancashire and written by an angry young man. I knew I didn't need to pre-buy a ticket.

There'd be a few bored mums with babies and some old people. What was conceived as a revolutionary snarl in black-and-white times had today become a gentle afternoon out. I hesitated at the box office and instead veered out into the park. The weather was warm and appealing, I wanted to be outside. As soon as I walked into the park I knew it was a mistake. I felt crushed. Belinda loved it here. We'd walk down with Breuer on each and every Sunday that we were in Birmingham together. We'd let him off his lead in the park. The three of us. And one day maybe there'd be four of us. But Breuer was enough of a kid, our kid. He knew instinctively where we were going when we left for our park walks and was as excited about it as a child on Christmas Day. It's funny how the excitement drains out of your life in adulthood – nothing really gets you fired up anymore, nothing moves you. Loss harms you, and loss becomes a constant as you get older. Life's pains and disappointments suck the enthusiasm away. But a dog, well… a fucking dog still gets excited the same amount; his frenzy never diminishes. He tugged that lead so hard as we walked up Salisbury Road, he was so bloody intoxicated by the prospect of a run, of chasing a stick and bringing it back. All he wanted to do was get into mischief. Bel loved Breuer – probably more than she loved me. The way she'd rumple his fur and kiss his slobbery mouth astonished me. It was endearing though. I miss him because thinking of him reminds me of her.

Remembering these things addled my mind. Too many memories. I couldn't compute the here and now. I propped myself up on one elbow and listened to The Rationalists through bad-quality headphones. I'd been meaning to buy some better ones. I suddenly felt very alone. The sun vanished without warning. The heavy sky above me seemed unusually ponderous. The bonds that appeared so strong had severed so easily, in the blink of an eye. My wife, once so real, so visceral, was now nothing but a memory. Did she ever exist at all? A German girl who ended up in Birmingham, a writer obsessed with a niche subject, a perfect mirror for me, who I adored and who, remarkably, adored me back. She seemed so implausible when I thought about it like this. A blade of grass between my fingers. I rubbed. I tugged it out and stared at it. How easily it would cleft in two if you pulled very gently. Two parts of what was once whole, split forever. Things you thought were permanent, things you assumed could never be moved – they weren't permanent, they could be moved. The trees that framed the edge of the park swayed with a solid grandeur, but one lightning bolt could split them down the middle too.

Fresh air was good – apparently. Exercise was good – apparently. Healthy eating and a reduction in smoking and drinking would also cure me of my ailment faster. My doctor had been very generous, very understanding. Doctors had always been so nice to me, so calm. My heart was actually hurting though; its sinews strained at every beat. No doctor could ever do anything about that. The pressure in my head. Steel pressing down on my shoulders. My legs like tungsten. Sometimes I couldn't move them. I had to lie down with my arms crossed over my chest. A beagle barked in the background. When I squinted, the scene turned sepia and the lines across my eyes became visions of wounds, oozing and seeping. With my eyelids closed I only saw Belinda smiling. 'Elizabeth Anderson' shot through the headphones and dripped its sombre, lilting pitter-patter of guitar and vocal into my ear canal and made my chest heave. Tears welled in my eyes, lakes with dams, dams were broken, liquid flowed, down my cheeks, first left then right. I sobbed as quietly as possible, muffled and serene. Everything was so slow, so lumbering. Everything had slowed down within me to match the way the city seemed to have slowed. My feet like lead. Rooted to the spot, one on top of the other, me lying on my side now. This was no way to live. My despair had a sensation, a sound, a taste. All of them repulsed me. And it was embarrassing. I couldn't bear the thought of people seeing me like this. I felt a hot, wet tongue slather across my right cheek. A friendly face appeared, a familiar-ish face coloured brown and black and white, covered in drool and with its tongue lolling out. Its ears were huge. It winked at me. Was it real?

'Buckley!' I heard. 'You naughty boy. Leave the poor man alone. Come back here!' And then a, 'I'm so sorry about that.' I couldn't say a word; I couldn't move. 'Are you... are you alright?'

'Yeah... just...' Wait for the worst to pass. Give it half an hour.

There was an ice cream van parked up. On the side of the van were painted the words *Chamberlin, Powell & Bon*, who must have been the owners of the ice cream company. The twinkle in a cartoon character's eye caught my attention. Maybe a 99 could be my salvation. The pressure had arrested slightly, the weight had lifted momentarily. I remembered how much I enjoyed these ice creams with a piece of fossilised chocolate sticking out of the top. It seemed right to order one, and I did. I dragged myself up and walked over to the ice cream van. The chocolate was frozen in the same way it had been the last time I licked one of these – which was a long time ago. The sugar gave me a brief burst of energy.

Guided by voices, led by urges. How refreshing to let the plot take you along. Where was it shoving me? I walked to town and found myself at New Street Station. I got on a Coventry stopping train and got off at Marston Green. I walked along the path that leads round, north-west, towards the end of Birmingham Airport's runway. Belinda had brought me to this unpromising spot once. Now, as then, the area was filled with caravans, scrap metal, cars, those portable offices that fit on trucks, banners and flags, footballs and horses. I loved it and ended up using it as a location in *Big Plans* – for a scene where the planners debate the merits of sacrificing the whole of Chelmsley Wood, that huge edge-of-town council estate, to double the size of the airport. Belinda thought there was a fierceness to this zone of industry and aircraft noise so near to the semi-detached houses of Marston Green which almost abut the runway itself. The sweaty reek of kerosene lifted my spirits, and when the planes started landing, roaring inches above my head on finals made treacherous by the crosswind, I watched them with awe. The runway wasn't flat. Instead you could see it bobble up and down like a crinkle-cut chip as it followed the contours of the heath it sat on. I thought seriously about jumping the fence and walking out onto it.

I bought a takeaway pizza on the way home, from a local vendor which shared its name with a US mafioso from the 1920s. By the time I slumped on the sofa, the fat from the cheese had started to ooze and attack the box's fabric. The food was tepid on my tongue; my mouth filled with the comforting sensation of salt and grease. I opened a beer and pressed the green button on my remote control. The TV fired up.

I went back under the stairs and swirled my arm into the box of Mids TV videos like the guests on the lunchtime show did when they were blindly selecting a competition-winning postcard, its owner to then be sent a toasted-sandwich maker or voucher for a free day out at the safari park near Kidderminster. I closed my eyes like they once did and revelled in the unholy sound of plastic bashing against plastic.

I picked a video out and went back to the living room, smashing it into the hole in the VHS machine with the same care that a postman puts a bill through your door in the morning.

Fuzziness, then the picture cleared up. I sat back and took a hearty sip of beer. A spinning 'M' greeted me.

*

[Title music – jaunty and insistent, like the soundtrack to a fair pulling into town. Scenes of Birmingham play out in the background, but they all look grotty – motorways, underpasses, tower blocks, concrete boxes.]

Title card – BIG PLANS

[The camera hovers over Victoria Square and then crash-zooms down to show two men in suits with drainpipe trouser bottoms strolling across the screen and into the Council House as the music fades out.]

[Two builders are playing football on the roof of Priory Square. Building machinery and rubble has been added by props department to make it seem like it's 1965 and the building is under construction. Because, remember, this is actually filmed in the 1990s.]

Seddon: *'Come on, 'Arris, your mam could do better than this!'*
    Harris: *'Me mam's in a bloody wheelchair.'*
    Seddon: *'Exactly.'*
    Harris: *'Roight. It's Villa vs Blues. FA Cup Final 1965...'*
    Seddon: *'I don't think that's likely, 'Arris.'*
    Harris: *'You can always dream! It's a penalty at Wembley. Villa's star striker Harris is up against that shite lad that Blues have got on loan. What's his name? Oh yeah – Seddon! He couldn't stop a ball for toffee. The crowd are going wild. It's this one for the match, this one for the cup. Harris steps up. Harris kicks it and...'*

[Seddon, the other builder, dives upwards but Harris has skied the ball. We see it fly through mid-air, out over the top of the car park, and then plummet to the ground…]

[Quick musical interlude; rapid montage of building-site views and girls in monochrome-patterned miniskirts walking through the Bull Ring Markets.]

[Two men in suits, one about fifty and one about thirty-five, are talking on a building site. We can't hear what they're saying. We just see a football drop onto the yellow hard hat of the older one then bounce off it and land in a pool of drying cement, where it lodges.]

[Shocked] Benedetti: 'What the…?'

[The other man stifles a giggle.]

Benedetti: 'What the hell was that, Rocaster?'
  Rocaster: 'It was a football, Mr Benedetti.'
  Benedetti: 'A blasted football?'
  Rocaster: 'I think so.'
  Benedetti: 'Well let's go and see where the hell it came from. This is ridiculous.'

[Music accompanies the two men striding purposefully up ten or so flights of steps. They arrive on the roof of Priory Square to find it deserted. A sign says: Coming soon! UTOPIA SQUARE.]

Benedetti: 'Whoever it was…'
  Rocaster: 'Probably a builder, Mr Benedetti.'
  Benedetti: 'Definitely a builder.'

[The pair of them stride over to the edge of the deck and peer out.

The view is masked by careful camera angles so as not to show any building from later than the mid 1960s.]

[The older man looks rueful.]

Benedetti: 'Does anyone in this city actually appreciate what we're doing for them, Rocaster? Do they share our goals? Do they desire a better environment for their children? Do they realise that order, progress and the segregation of different road users can create an urban utopia? An urban utopia like... like this one we're building – Utopia Square. Designed by you, Rocaster, and planned by me!'

Rocaster: 'I don't believe they do, Mr Benedetti.'

Benedetti: 'Your buildings, Rocaster, and my big plans. Together we'll build a new Birmingham. I've got no time for old ways or old buildings. Anyone – or anything – that isn't with me gets the chop.'

[Benedetti pulls out a pipe and starts to tamp it, his eyes looking warm and greedy.]

Benedetti: 'You see, Rocaster...'

[Rocaster rolls his eyes towards camera.]

Benedetti: '...planning and city-building – these aren't jobs for artists; they're jobs for engineers. What I learned at civil engineering school taught me much about how to build a proper city. You level it all out, sweep away the muck, install sewers and roads, zone it and neatly lay out blocks of flats or offices at nice right angles. Subways connect everything up. Utopia's not an abstract concern, is it? It can be planned and a correct end result established.'

[Rocaster rolls his eyes towards camera again.]

Rocaster: 'No, sir, not abstract.'

Benedetti: 'Exactly. Utopia is an achievable goal, the end result of hard work and lots of chaps looking at lots of plans and using lots of red pens and rulers to get that plan finalised. This is the rigorous, modern city of the future!'

[Benedetti notices something way down on the ground. Two men walk into shot. The two builders from earlier.]

Benedetti: 'Who's on site today, Rocaster?'

Rocaster: 'It's a day off, Mr Benedetti. Just the two overtimers, the union wouldn't let anyone else come on site.'

[Benedetti is getting increasingly irate.]

Benedetti: 'Just the two overtimers, eh? Not doing much for their extra shilling are they, the little buggers?'

[The 'Zzzzp' noise of a zip being undone.]

Rocaster: 'Mr Benedetti, are you…?'

Benedetti: 'Yes, I bloody well am.'

[Cut to the two builders at ground level, out of breath from running down the flights of stairs, chatting and giggling, but we can't hear about what.]

[Shocked] Harris: 'Bloody hell, Seddon, is it raining?'

[We see both builders assailed by a stream of hot liquid, golden in colour. They look up, mouths agape.]

Seddon: 'I don't think so! Ewww.'

144

[A gruff, indistinct voice yelling from the roof. Sounds like it must be Benedetti.]

'Get back to work, you lazy buggers!'

*

The words deposited themselves in my ears like tar. The jokes as welcome as a Christmas present from an unloved aunt. It wasn't that I thought *Big Plans* was shit, it was just that I knew someone had thought it was shit. Shit enough, in that particular someone's opinion, to ensure that people in other regions would never get the chance to watch it. Maybe if I'd just set it in London?

All the same, it amused me. I hated myself for the puerile pleasure I got from gags I'd written about pissing and wanking. This was stuff a ten-year-old lad would consider beneath him. I mean, this was satire. Light satire. But I couldn't resist my schoolboy urges – the occasional bit of scatology amused me. When I sat writing in my house or at Mids in some quiet corner, I used to think that if I could make myself laugh then that meant a few other people would be laughing too. You never really knew with a sitcom like this. In the studio, in front of an audience, you could see and hear them laughing along (or not) to the gags – whether they were watching the real thing or a VT. Like when we had the audiences in for *Welcome To The Masshouse* – they were so wound up by the warm-up guy and so pissed on their pints that they laughed at almost everything. As instructed. On cue. With programmes like this, I only knew it was funny – really funny – if I could see people sitting in front of their own tellies laughing at grown men urinating off the top of half-built buildings. And it was very seldom that I found myself in someone else's living room, watching them watching Mids TV. In fact, it was only at Christmas. When I took the kind of delight you reserve for visits to the zoo in watching this odd, greedy species in its natural habitat, arse on sofa, eyes on the bloody gogglebox, hand in a bag of crisps. Foul stench 'n' all. Same old story too: the more the creature has consumed from a cold can filled with frothy idiot-juice, the heartier the laughs. So was my writing making them laugh – or was their booze?

TEN BRUTALIST BUILDINGS

By Belinda Schneider

Introduction

A new way of seeing, a new way of thinking

Let me tell you about a new way of seeing, a new way of thinking. What if a building, like an idea or a book or a painting, wasn't easy to 'get'? What if it was dramatic and tumultuous, aggressive or pointed, exciting and unfamiliar? Brutalist buildings challenge us. But they're not ugly if you undo what you have in mind to be ugly. Why is concrete, sculpted and extravagant and spread over many levels, considered 'ugly' anyway? A place you can explore any time you want. A place that draws you in and makes you puzzle. A place with hidden depths and shapes that verge on sublime? That's beautiful, isn't it?

20

1992

'Well... thisss a... bloody party, ishn't it?' Bob was spreadea-gled on the floor. 'This... *is* a bloody party.' He stayed quiet for a minute. I bent down to see if he was still alive. I hoped he wasn't.

'Bob?'

'Fetch-a me a whisky. Go on, son.'

My body sprang up. Belinda was giggling. 'He needs some water. Shouldn't you be in that state by now?'

'Too professional, that's my problem.'

Some moaning noises came from Bob's mouth but I ignored them.

'Another white wine spritzer?'

'Why thank you, kind sir.'

'My pleasure.'

The barmaid was polishing a glass and regarding Bob with a sneer. 'I'll have to fowking kick him roight out if he doesn't gerris backside off that bloody carpet in five minutes flat. An another thing – he's gonna gerris wallet taxed. I can see it poking out of his arse pocket.' She scowled. 'Whatchavin'?'

'White wine spritzer and a pint of Birmingham Bitter, please.'

'Why are you lot 'ere? You're all from Mids TV, roight? Ain't there somewhere more glamorous you can go? Some wine bar?'

'It's plenty glamorous enough for me. It's the wrap party for my sitcom, *Big Plans*. I mean, I wrote it. Have you read about it? There was a quarter-page preview in the Midlands edition of *TV This Week* magazine this week.'

'Nope.'

'Ah well, OK. My boss…' I pointed towards Bob and he farted. Did he do that deliberately? 'Him. He said I could have four hundred quid behind any bar for the wrap party. So…'

'So you chose here. Verrry nice. More for your money than in town, eh? Don't get many celebrities in Moseley. Are any o' you lot celebrities?'

'Well…' I pointed to Bob again. Dribble had begun to run down his chin. A real river of saliva. 'Do you recognise the host of *I Love My Dog!*? And he's been in *Welcome To The Masshouse*. In fact, so have I.'

'Hmmm, really? Dunno either o' them. I watch repeats o' that one set in the 'otel but that's about it to be honest. Can they not stop the sodding sets wobbling though? We don't gerr earthquakes in Brum.' A pronounced sigh. 'Bloody 'ell. I'm in 'ere every night these days, no time to watch the box.'

'How much have we got left behind there before I've gotta get my coppers out?'

'Er, about fifty quid.'

'Thanks for the drinks.'

Silence.

I walked back over towards Bob and looked up to see Baxter

conversing with my girlfriend. As soon as I arrived he stopped talking and looked at me, directly into my eyes. It was harrowing. 'Don,' he said, before shuffling off elsewhere. I watched him walk away, and as soon as he reached the other side of the bar he paused and turned round, looking at Bel, thinking I wouldn't see. Staring at her. I should put him in the ground.

'He's a funny fish, isn't he? Cheeky sod's looking at you. If he keeps doing that...'

She seemed strangely unfazed by him. She didn't actually like him, did she? 'Clever but very odd. There's something a bit German about him. He's so serious. I knew a lot of people like that in Berlin. People who were a bit detached, a bit aloof. I like some of his arts programmes though. The ones he's presented about architecture aren't too bad actually.'

'Fucking awful guy,' I said, feeling more antagonistic towards him now, sipping my pint, checking what he was up to. He seemed to have joined a conversation, in the sense that he just stood there, next to a group of people, but not speaking. Just listening.

Bel chinked her glass against mine and planted a kiss on my cheek, changing the subject, winching me up from my grump. 'Well done. You made it. This is all for you!'

'Well if it's all for me, why don't you get back behind the bar? The service was so much friendlier when you used to work here. Do you know the barmaid who's here now?'

Bel looked over at her. 'God, no. Giving you hassle?'

'You could say. Why aren't there more barmaids that look like you working here now?'

'Oi.' She punched my right arm. I didn't flinch.

'I'm so glad you're here. I wanted to show you off.'

Bel adopted a tone of mock rage. 'I'm not a fucking doll. You can't parade me around.'

'Watch me.'

Bob made another moaning noise. The barmaid yelled out, 'Can someone gerrim of the fowkin' carpet, please? We can't have that sorrof thing in 'ere. What if the bloody council or the cops come in? We'll lose our sodding licence.'

Bel kneeled down. 'Are you OK, Bob?'

'I think... um... waaa... I am now I can see you, love. Stay here with an old man, will you?'

Bel patted him on the head as you would an attention-seeking golden retriever. She stood back up and spun round. She seemed to make eye contact with Baxter for a second. He was standing across the room, silent, looking at her. She inhaled and spoke dramatically, as if trying to distract me. 'Oh look, it's Kate over there. Let's go and say hi to her.' Bel waved to Kate, and then we walked over towards her. Kate was being chatted up by the actors who played Rocaster and Benedetti. The actors greeted us theatrically. It was strange to see them dressed down and camp. They started regaling us with stories from their time doing plays at Birmingham Rep. But I was distracted. It looked like the guy who played Seddon the builder was chancing his arm with the barmaid. He leaned over and blew cigarette smoke over her. She cackled.

I went outside to get some peace. The crisp night air pricked my cheeks. I stood on the pavement watching the traffic swarm down the hill from Moseley. The constant procession of high-powered beams gave me a headache. As each car or bus passed, it made its own unique whooshing sound.

I felt fingers creep around my face and cover my eyes, hot breath on my neck. 'Guess who?'

'Bob?'

'Shut up!' Bel ran her hands over my chest, proudly stroking. She clamped her hands together and squeezed. I could feel her head resting sideways against my back. She seemed content.

'Got a cigarette?'

'For the lady, of course.'

'When we've finished these shall we get out of here? I want you to myself.'

'I don't even have to think about that one.'

'Good. Let's go.'

'Good.'

'I love you, Donald.'

'I love you more.'

21

A yellow meniscus stretched several feet in every direction. The reason for this soon became clear. The studio floor was soaking with urine. I bent down and breathed in. The tang of urea shot straight up my nostrils. I heard some panting and felt a creature knocking into my arse.

'Bob?' I turned round.

A poodle was nuzzling me, its stupid tongue drooping out of its mouth like ham on a butcher's counter. I couldn't see into the creature's eyes because of all the fur crowding around them. It squawked a sort of 'Hello'. It was urinating as it stood there. I recognised the mutt from the episode we'd just filmed. Clouds of steam rose into the air as if from New York sidewalks.

'What do you want?'

It squawked again, concluded its business, and began dancing on its hind legs.

An attractive young woman with long legs and brown hair, wearing a burlesque costume and high heels, picked her way across the studio floor, between the puddles of piss. She walked towards the far wall of the studio. Pinned up on that wall was an oversized piece of cardboard shaped like a bone, and on that bone it said *I Love My Dog!*

'I wish animals had more dignity,' I said to the poodle. I bent down, parted the fur from its eyes and stared right into them. 'My dog's just like you. And the one we had when I was a kid was just the bloody same. Both of them, making a tit of themselves for one lousy corner of a bacon sandwich. Can't you… you… *people*, just for once be a bit aloof, a bit fucking standoffish?'

It squawked twice more, at a lower pitch and volume, as if agreeing with what I'd just said, perhaps even atoning for its brothers and sisters, for their simplicity; maybe even trying to say sorry.

'Rocaster! Rocaster!'

I sighed.

'Rocaster! Daddy's here.'

A chap wearing a brown corduroy blazer flounced towards me and the dog, feet slapping against the wet, black floor.

'Rocaster, my baby!'

Just before he arrived, his right foot completely missed its intended connection with the ground and he pancaked onto the studio floor with a dull thud. His momentum, allied to the newly slick floor, kept him sliding towards me. He ground to a halt a few inches short of me, like a human curling stone that had been delivered with aplomb.

He panted. The dog panted. It licked his face. He sat up and looked at me. 'Oh, I can't thank you enough for finding Rocaster. I thought I was going to have to go back to Worcester tonight without him.' The man looked genuinely pained. 'Do you work on the show? Thanks so much for having Rocaster on. He might not have won, but he'll treasure these memories forever. He can't wait to see himself on TV next month, can he? Can he?' The man made an extended 'Ooh' noise and played with the dog's salivary jowls.

I looked at the dog, then at its owner. 'So Rocaster – I thought he might be named... after someone?'

'Yes, look at me. Such a telly addict. *I Love My Dog!* is obviously my favourite programme on Mids, but my second favourite is *Big Plans.* I just can't get enough of Rocaster and Benedetti. I've got a collie at home called Benedetti.'

This made me smile. 'Have you now? And if you could meet the person who wrote that series, what would you say to him? Or her?'

'That they've written a great Midlands sitcom. That's what. A lovely great satire about Brum and its eccentricities. With two cheeky main characters. What would you say to them?'

'That he or she needs to write better... funnier jokes.'

'I think the jokes are, argh, quite good,' said the man, hauling himself up. 'I need to go and clean my trousers,' he bleated. 'Come on, Rocaster, come with Daddy to clean his pantaloons in the loos.' He looked up. 'Nice to meet you.'

'You too.'

Animal and human bumbled off out of the studio.

22

2008

We were due in Yorkshire to shoot more of *Ten Brutalist Buildings*. Leeds first, then down to Sheffield. I drove to the studios, where Kate had organised for some transport to pick us up. I was early so I went up to the production offices. It was empty. Apart from Kate. She was leaning out of the window, puffing on a fag.

'Where is everybody?'

'Lay-offs. We're all on borrowed time.'

Some shouting from... somewhere.

'What's happening?' I said, dropping my overnight bag on Kate's messy desk, sending papers and empty pre-packed falafel wrap cartons flying.

She motioned towards Bob's office. I could hear some muffled swearing, then a large clatter came a second after a black shadow shot across Bob's office window. More yelling. I peered inside and saw Baxter throw a chair across the room. Bob sidestepped the flying piece of furniture with the most casual nonchalance. It whizzed past his head and flew straight into a giant buzzer we'd used on *I Love My Dog!* It hit the big button, and a load of lights started flashing and high-volume barking noises began emanating from it. Bob exited the office and closed the door behind him. From behind the door the sound of frenzy continued – smashing and growling and banging and woofing and dinging noises. Baxter was going crazy like a caged bear.

'Don! How are you this fine morning?' Bob looked as carefree as if it were the first day of summer.

'How's Baxter?' I saw him smashing a chair against a giant fluffy dachshund.

'I just told him we're going to Yorkshire.'

'And?'

'He doesn't like Yorkshire.'

'Why not?'

'A woman.'

'Oh.'

Bob walked over to the window. Kate gave him a cigarette. He lit it, and the pair of them puffed away in silence, neither flinching nor even apparently noticing as the disconcerting clattering and crashing continued from inside Bob's bailey.

My mind wandered on the journey north. When I was a teenager I scanned through all the different frequencies late at night on the TV my parents had given me as a birthday present. This was before digital transmission, when you could search around manually to tune in and sometimes discover oddities – little fragments of programmes being broadcast by transmitters far away; tiny presents, miniature clues about what life was like in a different part of Britain. The delight I felt at finding a channel beamed out by a neighbouring regional TV station has stayed with me. One night I discovered the Northern TV region's signal. It was an interloper with no right to be on Midlands screens. It was fuzzy; the picture dipped in and out. You just got little portions of programming – if you were lucky. I was delighted by this find, obsessed, and went back time and again to find this ghost channel. The weather affected what I could see. I learned that when it was sunny and the sky was empty, the high pressure meant signals could travel further and I could see even more of this strange northern world. If it was cloudy and rainy, it wasn't worth bothering. Sometimes the picture was relatively clean and you could eat up the exotic opening titles of dramas, the baffling intro music for a different late-night local news bulletin, and Yorkshire accents. Thick, milky brogues with a mellifluousness and pride that seemed at odds with the rather more circumspect and comical Brummie twang – a twang I nevertheless secretly loved. At other times you couldn't pick the channel up at all. I was impressed with the mighty transmitter that sent the pictures our way too. I found out it was the Emley Moor transmitter, which looked like a concrete rocket in the photos I found of it in a book in the school library. It sat on top of a bleak Yorkshire moor and injected these flat-cap-and-whippet accents up into the sky. I was obsessed with how that channel came and went, a narrative you just dipped in and out of, pictures that were sometimes full and sometimes fuzzy. Life is just like that – action comes in pieces, not totalities. A buffet of experiences. Everything is ephemeral, everything is a canape. You think everything is solid but it isn't. Earthquakes can shake up even the firmest-feeling ground. The foundations shift all the time, the rules change all the time, the things you thought were so hard and permanent as rock can crumble to dust in the blink of an eye.

Kate and the others went for a coffee. I walked. I started by surveying the depressing liminal sprawl of petrol stations, warehouses and crass bungalows on Kirkstall Road. Bel and I had come for a weekend in Leeds a few years ago. I took her past my appalling old student digs in Hyde Park. We wandered down Cardigan Road, and at the bottom were presented with a view of the Aire Valley. My eye had to be trained, she said. Why not here? She weighed up the scene. She was especially taken by Kirkstall Viaduct, a railway bridge straddling the valley and curving towards Leeds city centre on the other side. It works like an arm, she told me, embracing the scene. Back here again, and sure enough I suddenly felt lifted looking at the viaduct's weight, bulk and embracing shape. The arches of the viaduct marched across the valley bottom like bored soldiers with broad shoulders. It trailed round to the left, pointing me towards the Yorkshire Gazette Building, leading me there like a clue to a treasure hunt. I followed where I was told, down Kirkstall Road, passing Northern TV – whose HQ didn't seem half as big or flashy as ours. This was where those weird programmes I found when I was a kid had originated. On a Leeds industrial estate, not even in the city centre.

Further. The Yorkshire Gazette Building, by the same architect as Birmingham Central Library. And my word, it reminded me of home. What a hulk. We'd film here tomorrow afternoon – after we'd done a shoot at Leeds University in the morning. I sat on a roundabout, under the huge flyover, and I stared. This newspaper office, Bel had told me, was a statement of provincial pride. It was a building as a boast, deliberately sited right next to the motorway that brought you into Yorkshire's swaggering metropolis, a city which didn't care about York and wanted to rival Manchester. Leeds dubbed itself the Motorway City of the Seventies. As well as bashing Manchester, it was also trying to outdo Brum, which was the real Motorway City of the Seventies – and the Sixties, and all the other 'ties. I watched the office workers, and the odd student, funnel past the great concrete ark of the YGB, but not one person looked up at it. It was invisible. But how could that be? It looked more striking than any other building in Leeds (apart from the campus of my alma mater, up the road). It was a supersized ark, a series of voids filled with concrete, a rockery surrounded by fractals, a growth, a sculpture. Bel encouraged me not to see what something was in plain terms – i.e. 'square' or 'tall' – but concentrate instead on what your mind thought it could be, what your heart felt it must be. I wondered whether, if everyone else could also start to see Bel's beloved brutalism like this, they might suddenly grow to like it rather more.

We were billeted that night in a place called Brutotel. It had only just opened. A great concrete slab that towered over City Square. It was kitsch, 1970s-themed, arty and full of people in their late twenties. It seemed beyond belief. But it looked completely familiar. Bel would have loved it. Maybe we passed by and she did love it? I couldn't remember. The lift doors popped open and I stepped out. The landing was totally devoid of natural light. The corridor stretched out in front of me. Regimented and regulated. I walked along the icy pathway, over clementine carpet and past scarlet walls, until I came to my room. A heavy door. The malevolent punch of air conditioning. A glass bottle of mineral water on a side table. A freshly made bed with all its components set at right angles. A vintage map of Leeds from the 1970s nailed to the wall above the bed. The outermost ring road preventing the city from escaping upwards and giving Leeds the unmistakeable shape of a brain. My eye was drawn towards the desk. Next to the Campari-coloured telephone and typewriter, a hardback book. It looked like it was for children, and featured retro fonts, crisp design, simple text and lavish hand-drawn pictures seemingly from days gone by. Except that it was a trick.

Welcome to Brutotel Leeds. This building used to be called Utopia Point. It was a block of council flats designed in the brutalist style. Brutalism comes from the French 'béton brut', meaning 'raw concrete'. The term was popularised by avant-garde architects in the 1960s and '70s to connote a stark, aggressive style of modern architecture and an honesty of materials – you could see the building was held up by the exposed concrete; you could see the marks showing where that concrete was poured. This tower block was home to 120 poor people, and was a tough place to live. In 2006, Brutotel Ltd bought it and refurbished it, opening it for a new generation of nomad aesthetes in 2008. Brutalism is back – and now it's COOL. Today, the building's funky, edgy glamour strikes a chord with our hip global guests, who value a well-designed hotel and want to make the most of the shopping, dining and hedonistic nocturnal options on offer in today's regenerated Leeds.

Brutotel prides itself on having recreated original 1970s touches throughout – so please feel free to smoke cigarillos and consume as much hard liquor as you wish in your room. Your fridge is stocked with sweet sherry, whisky, Advocaat and cigarettes. And if you need help operating the dial telephone, plug-in shaver, Teasmade, or soda fountain, just dial 1.

Downstairs in the John Madin Bar we offer retro cocktails, cheesy nibbles and sexual harassment from suited and booted bastards. Steak Diane is served nightly in our Rodney Gordon Restaurant.

After a brief shower and a change of clothes, I ventured downstairs, feeling refreshed and more relaxed. Photos in the hotel's lobby depicted the centre of Leeds 35 years ago. In the pictures, pedestrians scurried over walkways slung between office towers and over roads; walls looked grimy, fags were smoked. And really, even when I was studying here in the '80s it looked like that. If anything, it had deteriorated more. The whole of central Leeds' life seemed to be elevated – even if the way people were living wasn't. No one walked at street level in the photos, but I knew this was a fallacy. Obviously the pics were staged. People always found ways to avoid the steps or subways in Brum; they made like sprinters across busy roads and hurdled crash barriers. I'd done this myself on numerous occasions, often not even really knowing why. It was as much for the thrill of dicing with death as it was to save a couple of minutes. The roads in the photos were chocka with the smoky, boxy, British-made rust heaps of the era.

I met Kate in the bar on the first floor. The walls were bare concrete, the lighting very low, the carpets apricot, the furniture auburn. A photo of a man smoking a pipe behind a model that looked very much like Birmingham Central Library hung on one far wall.

'What are you having?'

'Another G&T. Double.'

I pointed at the barmaid; she nodded acknowledgement. 'And a pint of lager please.'

Kate had her hair up, some kind of make-up which made her eyes appear smoky and alluring. She'd ditched the glasses for contacts instead. She had a black dress on and looked more polished than usual.

'What's it like being back here then? Your old uni town.'

'That seems like a bloody age ago.' I paused. 'You have such a sense of being able to do anything you want when you're at that age, don't you? You just believe that you can do stuff, that we all can, that everything will be better somehow...' I paid for the drinks. 'You look great, by the way.'

'Thanks. Hot date with not one but two men? I've got to make an effort, right?'

'Got to.'

Kate snorted. 'I don't think I was ever like that, by the way.'

'Like what?'

'That thing you said about believing you can do stuff, feeling invincible. Not truly. I was always a cynic, even when I was younger. A happy cynic, but nevertheless…'

'A happy cynic. I like that. You're a happy cynic, and I am too.'

'Belinda wasn't a cynic though.'

'Nope. Bel could be grumpy – she was German! – but she was an optimist. She believed in people, in things, in ideas. Naively so, perhaps, but it was one of the traits I loved most about her.'

'I loved that about her too. I wished I felt that way sometimes.'

'Don't compare. You're you; that's incredible in itself.'

Kate giggled as she drank. 'I wish my ex-husband had agreed with that.'

'Now he is a dark sod. Jesus. I remember the first time we all got pissed together, I just thought, "This guy is trouble."'

'Well, he was.'

'When did you realise it wasn't right between you?'

'I sometimes wondered if I'd married the right person, I guess… all the time. Even the day I married the fucker. That "wondering" just kept growing. I don't think we had what you and Bel had. I was disgusted by him half the time. I made the wrong choice. What can you do? It was all completely pointless, a waste of time. When I divorced him I just thought, "This is it?"'

'I remember when you found out about him shagging that girl from the office. I hope you threw a chair at him.'

'I did.'

'What's he up to now? You never talk about him.'

'Oh he's still in Brum. I think he had a girlfriend on the go last time anyone mentioned him. Heard it was some Brummie barmaid from the Bride of Bescot, but that could have been –

and probably was – a wind up. Who knows? I used to fret so much about it, about him.' Kate took a long slug of the gin and rattled the ice around in the glass. 'I couldn't give a toss now. I just wish I hadn't screwed everything up, you know…? For myself. For the future. By leaving everything so late.'

'Is it too late?'

She looked up at me but didn't address that one directly. There was no need. 'Ciggie?'

I nodded. We went outside and smoked on the corner of City Square. There was less traffic here than I remembered; the council seemed to have partially pedestrianised some of the square. A lavishly clad hen-party group emerged from City Station, giggling, swigging pink liquid from plastic cups. They crossed over towards the hotel. One of the women, wearing some kind of sparkly minidress and a sash round her shoulder shouted, 'Oi oi, love! Bet you've got a massive dick, yeah?' at me, then blew me a kiss. Her friends were hysterical. She cackled and yelled, 'See you later, love!' as they wobbled down Boar Lane.

Kate guffawed.

'Unbelievable,' I offered, smirking.

Kate stared over towards the Old Post Office but didn't seem to really be looking at it. 'I want to talk to you about something that's been preying on my mind for ages.'

'What's that?'

'Well. I expect an expert viewpoint here. Isn't everything just… so fucking fake?'

I scoffed, surprised at her candour.

'I'm serious. How we experience the world – how you and I experience the world, or how anyone experiences the world – is unique to us. It's also so… potent and immediate; it's full of sensation and emotion. It's also messy and… I don't know… it doesn't always make sense, doesn't fit into holes and plans.

There's a lot of stuff going on, everywhere, so much stuff, all at the same time, and it's a big mess, basically. But every representation of life tries to make it all seem so polished – the way people speak and the things they do. The way people are presented, it's just not authentic. Life's not like that, you know that.'

I pondered what Kate was saying, looked into her eyes.

She was getting into her stride. 'It's a farce, a facade. The media isn't true to anything or anyone, and probably neither is architecture. Our TV programmes… I mean, it's just this formal way of presenting things and of behaving. It's a sort of a sham, right? It's not real, that's not how we behave. We don't speak like they do on soaps to each other – any more than we live how people want us to live in little boxes on council estates or wherever. People are unique and they just do things in their own awkward way. But no one ever shows that. The choppiness of it all, the half-heartedness of it all. People don't believe in big things anymore, we take the piss out of them – we rightly take the piss out of them. You and Bob took the piss out of everything and I loved that. I still love that. In programmes and in life. I hope this brutalist… monstrosities programme will have a bit of piss-taking in it too. Though Baxter will fuck up any joke you give him to read, of course.' She paused for breath. 'Don't believe any of the buggers that are in charge. Don't listen to them. Even the people you're fucking married to. There's no… anything. You've just got to feel around in the dark for yourself, just manage, just try.' Kate paused. 'There's a huge disconnect between the formal front people put on and what people actually think and say. Do you know what I mean, Don?'

'That we're all liars?'

Kate chuckled. 'Fucking hell, all men, you mean! Then yes. You bastards. We believe the shit you come out with. Women lie to themselves. They think, "Oh, this one's not like the others", but you're always like the fucking others.' She paused to smoke. 'But the one thing you can do well is to take the piss, to not listen to the lies, to show the grubby realities. That's what I mean about this fucking doc we're making. Seriously… oh God, maybe? No.'

'Go on, it's fine.'

'No… I… Oh, fuck it. I know it's for Bel and, God, I miss her, she was brilliant, but it's another bloody documentary. Baxter flounces around, using his long words…'

'Long words I wrote.'

'Yeah, OK.' Kate snorted. 'Pratting about here and there, and making everything seem like it's some kind of accepted order, some kind of mystical truth, something that's better and more clever than the viewers. And it's celebrating these bloody behemoths… I don't really see why Bel liked them so much. They look fucking oppressive to me, like they were built by a bloody dictator or something, and that's surely the last thing she wanted to be reminded of. And of course I respect her opinion – she knew more about it than me, and her passion was infectious. But ultimately we're celebrating yet another thing that was done to the people by… by these idiot men in suits, aren't we? The fuckers in charge, always the fuckers in charge. Seriously, aren't we? It's always men in suits that fuck you the most, the hardest. The same bastards who blacklisted the poor sods working on those buildings if they were in a union or something, the same bastards who wanted their monuments and their careers and their fees, the same bastards who wanted power and influence. That's why I liked *Big Plans*, because you were taking the piss out of those bastards. And that's why I loved *Hail To The Brummies*, because you were celebrating the ordinary people – it was their words, their lives.' Kate's eyes suddenly looked pleading. 'Don, you're not angry with me for saying this, are you? I don't know, it's just hard sometimes. Maybe I don't see it the same way you lot do. I'm just so sick of being on the receiving end of things, of everything.' She smoked. 'I've said too much, haven't I?'

'Of course you haven't said too much.' I put my arms round her and could feel her trembling. Maybe Kate was right. 'I know what you mean. You have to... ask questions. I think, anyway. Bel was just such an optimist, wasn't she? Beyond the normal boundaries of optimism. She believed that everything was being done for the right reasons, that everything was possible, that everyone was on the right track. That beauty was everywhere, even if no one else could see it. She trusted herself. Do we trust ourselves? Us two? Do we feel like that?'

'I don't, no.'

'You don't know?'

She giggled. 'I do know! I said "I don't, comma, no". I wish I did.'

'I wish I did too.'

'Do you think you and Bel were right for each other? Really? Did it always feel like it was as perfect as you remember? We romanticise the past sometimes. We remember the good and forget the bad.'

I pondered. 'I think we were right, I think things were right... but then how can you ever really understand another person? How can you ever know what they are thinking?'

'I remember times you'd tell me about things that seemed to get between you both... feelings and ideas. Bel loved you, don't get me wrong. But she was doing her own thing too, had her own path. I don't think I know if she was ever... I don't know... It didn't seem to me like she was ever as comfortable being married as you were.'

Maybe Kate had a point.

'Another drink?'

'Great idea. Doubles. Thank you, sir.'

After more drinks, we met Bob and walked up to a retro Italian on the Headrow that I distinctly remember going to on dates when I was at university. The trattoria was called Erno's. It was as scruffy as I remembered. The waiter brought us a bottle of Chianti encased in a wicker basket, and Bob, by now as tipsy as Kate and I after emptying his minibar of its five or six miniatures while he was upstairs sorting out some paperwork for the shoot, playfully yelled, 'You've got to be fucking joking!' when the bottle was placed on the table. The waiter looked incredulous.

I asked where Baxter was, and Bob replied, 'By himself, reading, having room service. Which isn't ideal for the budget, obviously, as we're massively over.'

'I hope he chokes on his club sandwich.'

'Yeah, exactly. I bet he's ordered some wine as well. Something expensive probably. Something… French.' Bob sighed. 'I don't even know how I got any cash for this. The bean counters must've felt sorry for us or something. They have done everything in their power to systematically strip out anything bloody good in entertainment, factual, comedy, drama and current affairs in the last ten years.' He paused. 'Actually, fuck current affairs. Who needs those arseholes?'

'There's always the game shows,' I offered, pouring the wine.

Kate snorted and glugged some of the red. 'Can't beat a good game show, can you? Maybe it's time to bring *I Love My Dog!* back.'

Bob looked grave. 'I'm serious about this. Don't tell any of the crew, but I've been summoned to HQ in London. They want a meeting. Pronto. I don't think it's going to be "Bob, we've got some good news for you – you've all done so well, so fucking bloody well, that everyone in Brum is getting a car and a holiday in the Seychelles; we've decided you all need a reward for that consistent great work you've been doing!"' He sniffed. 'Anyway, forget it. Let's get this film made. But first, let's get pissed. Though I realise we need to eat. So what's everyone having?'

I already knew. 'A Bo Bardi pizza, please – the one with all the meats. Oh, and with extra chilli.'

Bob looked at me slack-jawed. 'You are an animal.'

'What's wrong with that?'

Kate shook her head. As she lifted her wine glass to her lips I could see sadness in her eyes. And I think, at that moment, she could see the same feeling reflected in mine.

This place used to wrap me up. Leeds University Library was the safest place in the world. Surrounded by creamy concrete and desks and beautiful bookish girls wearing scruffy clothes, who chewed their pens and picked their noses when they thought no one was watching. To the young me, these girls represented perfection.

I chatted briefly to an elderly librarian, who gave me a visitor's pass and opened the electronic gate. Inside, it was as much of a cocoon as I remembered – so quiet, so warm and welcoming, the ceilings so low, the aromas of adhesives and plastics and ink and moistened paper and coffee. I went to the English Literature section in search of novelists and critics I'd studied, Marxist texts that fired me up. I ran my fingers over the dust-covered spines of the shelved books and landed on two that looked familiar. *A Dialectical Approach To The Ideas You Don't Yet Know.* And beside it: *Was That A Cough Or A Fit*

Of Genius: Reading Modernism In Literature Using Your Internal Eyes. I picked them both up and went over to a reading desk.

I glanced around, at the low lighting, the soundproof walls, the students snacking on chocolate biscuits – the knock-off brands sold by discount supermarkets. Someone had scrawled FUCK THE TORIES into the desk, but the graffiti looked very, very old. I ran my fingers over the indentation in the wood. I looked both ways then plucked my keys silently from my jeans pocket. I fumbled for the Swiss army knife on my keyring and whipped out the blade. I hunched over and began to carve into the desk. A big 'S' in front of the word 'TORIES'. I sniggered like a schoolboy. I rose and span round, to see the very same librarian who'd let me in standing in front of me. She was only five feet tall.

'I was just passing and I thought I'd see how you were doing,' she said.

I stuttered a little. 'Er…'

'Maybe it's time to leave.'

Upstairs was the Red Route, which sounds blue, but is in fact grey. The corridor stretches into the distance. Walking down it is like walking into your own future, and what is university really but a time machine? A machine that slows time to nothing, pickling the youth and optimism you came in with, the outside world sort of forgotten. It's just the most perfect way to fill your head, learn about life and romance, and use up three blissful years.

When we came to Leeds a few years ago on that romantic weekend trip, Bel told me that a sci-fi TV show was shot in this corridor, and I remembered the rumours going around about that nugget back when I was studying here. But in those days there were rumours about everything on campus, everything in Leeds; everyone was paranoid. There were tales about weird late-night practices involving dead bodies in the Worsley Medical Building, another concrete brute Bel had loved. There were stories about underground passageways – some blocked up and some top secret – stretching into the Merrion Centre (where defunct escalators descended into an open pit) and down, even, to City Square. There were fables about subterranean bunkers and secret rooms, about spies on campus paid by the security services to keep an eye on left-wingers and foreigners, particularly at the university's notoriously rabble-rousing sociology department. It was a strange and beautiful time.

I found myself lost in reminiscence. Who was that bookish boy obsessed by girls and indie music? Was he really me? Or was he an actor playing the young me, the me before I became an adult with a role and a soul? On our first date, I told Bel that I'd learned to become a *flâneur* here. It was a new word I'd learned from reading new books about new things in the new library. I didn't know about architecture. What I really wanted to learn about was words and how to use them. That was my job, it would always be my job – what I was training for. But exploring was a different feeling to writing. My greatest feeling of relaxation came from this simple act of wandering around, even as an untutored spectator who didn't really know what it was he was looking at. Birmingham's weird landscape had a profound impact on me. It trained me in exploring. But in Leeds I was a puppy on my first stroll without a lead. Why did no one else want to just blaze around Leeds like I did? Why did no one else take their A–Z and a coat and sometimes a mini Thermos of tea and make off for places that were simply letters arranged into words and printed onto streets and fields on a black-and-white page in a slim volume of maps? Meanwood and Weetwood and Woodhouse and Kirkstall; Moortown and Horsforth and Burley and Adel.

23

1983

I stubbed out the roll-up and closed my book. I could pass these exams. It would be fine. I fingered a bubbling spot under the crease of my neck. I was self-conscious about it. It was as red and angry as most of the students lolling around nearby. I wanted it gone in case I bumped into Millie, which I always did when I was looking under par. The weather was getting milder as the year stretched out. What drew me to walk? It was a pure desire to see. To explore my territory. I was washed up on an island and I wanted to go to its edges. I heaved myself up and rubbed my eyes. I surveyed the scene. The brutalist campus of Leeds University flowed away from me. A huge, wide wave of grey stairs took people down from the main university campus at the top of the hill to the pond outside the Roger Stevens Lecture Theatre at the bottom. Students walked in both directions. Most of them looked happy. This was Eden. I looked up at the social sciences building, a great concrete ogre looming over me. You had to walk between its legs to get past it. It was a petrified computer-game boss that had duelled with a pixellated superhero, been beaten, and just ended up lodged solid. I followed the path down those steps, past that pond, through the campus, out. Then I passed the Worsley Building, and after that the Inner Ring Road announced itself with a sooty roar, just like Brum's. I still didn't really know where I was going today. Towards the city – that's what it felt like. Just seeing where the desire took me. A friendly bakery jumped out at me on Park Lane – distinguished not so much by its visual contribution to the city (a red hand-painted sign on a white wall, a window full of loaves and buns) as by the enticing smells – of tepid shortcrust pastry and the raw sliced onions inevitably placed in the ham rolls they would sell. The old woman in the shop sold me a bottle of pop and a Cornish pasty. The sight of the pasty's golden crust made me salivate. I inhaled its buttery roof. I passed the angular Wellington Swimming Pool with its starry facade, and the Yorkshire Gazette Building. I traced a dead straight route down Wellington Street, finally coming to rest in City Square. I flopped on a bench with my back almost against the Post Office – and in front of me a looming council block of flats of the most austere design. From at least three of the windows, women were leaning out and smoking, a repetitive pattern. A couple of kids kicked a football against the outside of the tall block. A sign above the door read *Utopia Point (Leeds Corporation)*. I took my lunch out from my knapsack and laid it on the bench next to me. I popped the bottle and drew on the honey-sweet liquid. Then I carefully pulled the pasty from its white paper clothes, revelling again in the scent of the pastry. I took a huge bite, staring up at the tower block, at the women. My left arm hung over my head, shielding my eyes from the sun as I chomped. Shortcrust pastry fell luxuriantly across my T-shirt, which was emblazoned across its front with *The Rationalists*. I smelled my armpits. They were fusty. The shower in our despicable student house on Mayville Avenue was broken. I heard something.

'Donald? Hi, Donald, is that you? It is you!'

I mumbled, 'Shit,' under my breath and began to hastily brush the bakery detritus off my chest and legs. It was fruitless. There were crumbs everywhere.

'Donald, what on earth are you up to?' She regarded me, smirking. 'Is that… lunch?'

'Millie! Um, yes, just… been studying and then… walking and erm, pasty… a pasty.'

She twirled her hair, not listening to anything I was saying, pouting like a goddess, wearing a flimsy summer dress and chunky leather boots. 'Want some gum, Don?' A slight scowl. Her nose ring caught the sunlight and glinted. From this angle Millie was exactly as tall as Utopia Point. I was suddenly very conscious of the spot under my chin.

24

2008

The crew were setting up a shot. They were collected like low-ing cows at the bottom of the huge, wide wave of grey stairs that takes people down from the main university campus at the top of the hill to the pond outside the Roger Stevens Lecture Theatre at the bottom. For this shot, Baxter was going to speak as he descended the (many) steps.

What was he going to say? What I told him to. I'd noted Bel's interest in monumental scale in her book, and this bit was going to be about the XXL nature of Leeds University's campus (and of brutalism in general). The big stairs, the long corridors, the frankly frightening amount of open space. The industrial city aesthetic. The machine aesthetic. The bombastic aesthetic. The aesthetic of bigness. Baxter walked and talked when Bob called action, and it was done and dusted in a single take.

The crew packed the stuff up and we headed off without hesitation. And if you're thinking that it was a lot of stuff they had to pack up – you'd be wrong. Films use a ton of crew and equipment. We don't. We had a camera (operated by a man who kept himself to himself), a sound mic (operated by a man who kept himself to himself), a producer who was also a director (Bob), a make-up artist, a writer (me) and a production manager (Kate) smoothing out the inevitable creases that occur when you shoot on location. No lights, no effects – we had to do all this in the daylight. And pray it stayed sunny. We dragged ourselves upwards to the Red Route corridor, a covered skybridge that starts off at ground level at the top of the hill – but by the time it gets to here and the gradient has tumbled away, it flows along five storeys high in the air. Up there, Baxter would be doing another piece about rivers of people, and pathways and movement and motion – corridors, bridges, and how people are like salmon.

When we got up to the corridor in the sky, Baxter took a seat and, without a soupçon of anxiety or remorse or self-consciousness, took out a wrap of finely ground white powder and spilled a hillock of it onto a credit card. He moved it up towards his nasal canal – with the slight quiver of a hand that's been through this arcane routine a thousand times – and snorted it all up in two big heaves.

Bob turned to me. His eyes looking askance. A face painted with annoyance. Perhaps with jealousy too. He said nary a word, he didn't have to. He just looked at me. His eyes boiled and despaired and longed in the same moment.

Baxter clapped his hands, rubbed them together, and set off to take his mark a bit further down the corridor. As he walked away, he whistled. Bob looked like he was about to put his fist straight through a window.

After the uni shoot was done we had to pack up once more and get to the Yorkshire Gazette Building. The journey was rapid. We piled into a minibus and then it was straight down the Inner Ring Road. The YGB, as Bel referred to it, was right next to the road. From the flyover you could see it standing out like a horrible sore thumb. It was deliberately placed in view of the traffic, Bel told me; it was deliberately placed next to the motorway so the two pieces of concrete philosophy would work together as a duo, each riffing off the other. Like the drummer and bass player in a band. An unapologetic rhythm section. Or two comics. A comedy double act no one was laughing at anymore. But maybe we should be? This was what I'd paraphrased in the script I'd written for Baxter to speak. Bel's ideas, my take. She had an incredible knack for bringing buildings to life. I just made it all translate onto TV. I was really a translator on this job – words on paper arriving from Bel, words for the screen departing for Baxter. A conduit. Hopefully the sense wasn't lost.

Bob wanted to do a shot where Baxter would be saying his piece (even though it was my piece, and really, of course, it was actually Bel's piece) while standing at the front of the YGB with his back to it. The camera – trained on him throughout– would travel over the flyover on top of the van and capture Baxter from a disconcerting moving position. It took a dozen takes and a lot of faffing to get this one right. Every time it wasn't perfect, the van had to drive down to the Armley Gyratory, come back, shoot past us, then double back at the Park Lane junction to get back in the right starting position to do the shot once more. I watched the finished rush once we'd nailed it, and it was impressive. Bob was a little too pleased with himself when he saw how good the final product looked. We huddled around the little screen in the back of the van to see what we'd just captured on camera, happy that we'd created something which looked attractive, something that did justice to the point we wanted to make. It was the first time it felt like we might be making a good television programme.

TV might look glamorous, but let me tell you about the reality. Me, Bob, and Kate were squeezed into a minibus. Shazia was quiet – there to do Baxter's make-up. There was the cameraman and sound man, who worked with us as freelancers and whose names no one ever stopped to ask. They played around on each other's phones and bullshitted about football. Kate had found a couple of Polish guys somewhere – I got the feeling they were both heinously overqualified and rather embarrassed to be slumming it with us. One was driving us, the other was driving a bastardised version of our minibus which was the same shape and volume but had no windows and was thus a 'van'. All the cameras and technical equipment were in there, along with the luggage – and by default Baxter's array of *pharmaceuticals, both legal and prohibited.*

A road journey was much less classy than a train journey – you couldn't piss when you wanted and you had to drink whatever was available, and that meant anything brightcoloured, laced with sugar and contained in a cardboard box or oversized plastic bottle. The bumps of the road travelled up through my spine; the low-intensity conflict of boredom precipitated by the motorway against us all was felt keenly, especially when it got dark. The Polish drivers played a little game of constantly overtaking each other, making funny faces at each other as the vans raced, the clanking and clattering inside our van almost unbearable when it was going flat out, careering south. I knew it wasn't far down the M1 to Sheffield. The signs counted down the miles as if they were marking the city they mentioned with a diminishing score. Sheffield 37. Sheffield 31. Sheffield 28. I liked how the signposts also told us we were heading towards *The South* (which was full of wankers) and *The Midlands* (which was home).

'Why don't we stop soon?' I asked Bob, who was riding shotgun.

He looked at his watch. 'Yeah, we can do in... twenty minutes? Next services, Janusz. Fag and a hot dog, yeah?'

Janusz said, 'Fuck yeah.'

Bob turned to the rest of us. 'Have they opened any fucking pubs at motorway service stations yet? A beer's just what I could do with. Just a cheeky one.'

'I think that would be asking for trouble,' said Shazia. 'Drinking and driving?'

'Well anyway, we can get a burger.' Bob reached into his wallet and fanned out three fivers. 'I'm buying!'

The car park at Cribdon motorway services. 'Is desolate.' Janusz said everything that needed to be said. He wrinkled his nose, locked the van and then vanished like a ghost into the bland concrete pavilion of the service station, a hexagon that seemed like it should be slotted next to a few more of its mates. A fierce wind whipped in across the Pennines. I couldn't see any trees. Instead of trees, purple bins and white posts carrying flags and petrol branding appeared. The flags clanked against the posts.

'You need to be tough to live up here, don't you?' said Kate, as we walked to the hexagon. 'I hope uni toughened you up. No heating and all that.' She shivered, slotted her arm through mine. 'Bloody hell. I need a holiday after this. Somewhere warm.'

I held the door open for her and we went in. Bob took our orders for burgers, and I walked up the steps to the bridge chucked up over the motorway and connected to an identical hexagon on the other side. It featured the same small, all-purpose shop selling bananas and colouring books and chocolate bars and newspapers, but was topped off with a fried chicken outlet instead of a burger bar. I sat down at a table on the bridge. Cars thundered beneath us. The view was intoxicating. Traffic pouncing towards me without end. Dangerous and unchecked. Lunacy. It was hypnotic. Whoosh. Whoosh. Whoosh. A lorry: whoooooosh. It was hardly decadent; it was primal, disgusting, exhilarating. There weren't many other diners. Noise echoed around. The smell of deep-fat frying tiptoed up from both ends.

'I've been thinking a lot about the future.' Kate took a seat and stared out of the window at the booming traffic below. 'Because Belinda was obviously drawn to how people in the 1960s saw the future, how they were trying to create the space age.' She cast her eyes around this sad dining area, then turned to see me sniggering. 'But it just turned out a bit shit.' Now she cracked a smile. 'Didn't it?'

'Yep. Life never keeps its promises. I guess all we can do is try to see what people were trying to get right – before it went wrong.'

'Right, where the hell are the rest of them?' Bob breathed out as he sat and immediately unloaded a tray of burgers wrapped in greaseproof paper and fries in cardboard containers. The packaging said *Paul Rudolph's Burgers*. The scent of salt and fat and sugar trounced my nostrils.

Janusz sat down and started talking Polish with his mate, who'd just arrived in the 'technical vehicle' – that is, the one without windows. His mate produced a medium-sized bottle from his pocket.

'Vodka?'

I nodded. I turned to see we were all nodding, and Janusz's mate poured a generous double measure of vodka into the soft drinks and coffees we had lined up between us. Suddenly we were all cheeky schoolkids on a study trip to the Lake District again.

We ate the burgers and fries with the levels of enthusiasm you reserve for visits to the dentist.

Baxter looked particularly miffed about the meal. He lowered his head to look closely at his triple-layered burger like a dog with full bowels inspecting a forest clearing. The flabby bread barely rested on the greasy patties; limp green pseudo-lettuce poked from the side like infectious pus from a wound. Baxter removed the top of the bap and sniffed at the ochre burger sauce. I chewed as I watched, savouring the way melted cheese and ground beef mixes in your mouth, caressing your tongue with a light touch of grease, making you feel horrified and elated at once. Disgusting. Bob rubbed his eyes and looked like a dad with an uncommonly weird brood.

After the meal, me and Kate shared a cigarette outside the hexagonal pavilion. Bob stomped past on his way to the car park. 'No sleep 'til Sheffield! Let's get the hell out of this shithole.'

Back in the van. The air had begun to deteriorate. As we jolted over a speed bump and accelerated back towards the motorway a sign read *Thanks For Visiting Cribdon Services. Have A Safe Journey & Enjoy Yorkshire!*

Most of us fell asleep as the saturated fat hit our stomachs and caused a kind of food lag, a sensation that whatever time it was, it was actually time for a post-prandial nap.

TEN BRUTALIST BUILDINGS

By Belinda Schneider

Chapter Six

Park Hill, Sheffield

Where did it all go so right? Not everything we tried was as much of a failure as the media would have you believe. I say 'we' because 'we' was the spirit of the times – different times, times that we were all in together. It's not the spirit of these times, where we've become atomised individuals competing with each other for scant resources, to see who can earn most, buy most, show off most. Back then we were in awe, of worlds and the future, of our own futures. Today we live in a present which is mostly just a series of 'sorrys' and suggestions, an expectation of averages, a certainty that we can't do better, that we just do our best. 'Our best' is a cop-out, a realisation that we have nothing firm to offer history.

Brutalism is cheap. It's not the cheapest – the cheapest was system building, and sometimes people conflate brutalism and system building, wrongly. System building was a bit of a scam – mass-produce crappy pieces in a factory and throw up rows of identikit towers. The building companies were the ones making money out of that ruse. And the government, in Britain at least, encouraged them. Political parties fought to see who could build the most houses. At least their hearts were in the right place. When, of course, the politicians weren't in corrupt league with the building companies. And yes, those blocks could be bloody awful – they fell apart and they made people's lives miserable. But that story has been repeated so often, you could believe that was the only story. But it wasn't. Not everything conforms to

184

the official narrative; concrete didn't always come before 'jungle' or 'wasteland' or 'monstrosity' or 'hell'. It's startling to see how much the language has changed, how much hope was present back in that time after the war, and how little hope we have now. What do we seek to change now? Nothing. But the things we did seek to change – well, sometimes we got those things right. The answer to the problem could be a correct one; it didn't always have to be wrong.

Park Hill was built as a one-of-a-kind place. It's finished decently and it stands for something. It literally stands above Sheffield. Now I'm not trying to sweep history under the carpet – there were problems here too. But of course you're going to get problems if housing officials put too many problem families in one place or if councils are forced to skimp on maintenance and let things fall down because central government slashes their grants. But there's also more power and prestige in cutting a ribbon with big scissors than with funding all the expensive care and attention that buildings need: the workers to look after them, the cleaners to clean them, the painters to paint them, the upgrades and refurbishments of homes, the new play equipment, the replacement lifts. Maintenance isn't sexy, is it? And as soon as you start to let a place go to the dogs – well, people stop caring so much; they stop doing their bit too. People would fall apart if we didn't have the NHS. Everything needs to be cared for, especially as it gets older. The men in suits should have splashed more cash on all our brutalist buildings to keep them looking good, to stop them going off. Buildings need love too.

Yet love permeates from the pores of Park Hill itself. A love for people – for all people – is what made the place get built in the first place. This estate worked. It housed folk. It was socialist in intention. Give people the best housing. No more slums. A future of positives and possibilities. In a bold building. And people fell in love here in

The Wall in the Head

Sheffield. I can't get the image of the graffiti up on a balcony at Park Hill out of my mind. It reads:

Clare Middleton I Love You Will U Marry Me

'Clare Middleton I Love You Will U Marry Me.' Kate slowly and gently read out the words that had been daubed up on the highwalk that separated one block from another. This time she said them more theatrically: 'Clare Middleton... I Love You! Will You Marry Me!' She paused and turned to me, her hands on my chest, almost curtseying. 'Will you, Clare? Oh, will you!' Now switching to an approximation of a Tyke: 'Go on, love, you know you want ter. Go on.'

'That's how it should be said, I reckon. Reet Yorkshire.'

'Exactly. You know the story?'

I did. 'I do. Belinda told me the tale. It's a sad one. Clare and this guy called Jason, her paramour, were in love. He wanted to get married to her. He proposed by spray-painting this... declaration, and taking her to the Odeon cinema over there...' I pointed across the valley to where I assumed it was. I'd never been to Sheffield before. The wind howled in at us on this exposed hill above the railway station. 'He took her out on the cinema's balcony and showed her this; she could see it across the valley from there. Apparently she was slightly embarrassed by it.'

'You would be.'

'Well, exactly. She said yes though.'

'So they got married?'

'No, they never got to the aisle. They broke up. And Clare, sadly, has died.'

'Oh my God. Wasn't she young, though?'

'She was. Belinda read everything she could about them.

This was a really big obsession in her mind, this connection between buildings and lives. Especially *this* connection. Real stories playing out in real places, real people that architecture books never mentioned, walls hearing things, reliquaries and stuff like that. People were just… well, stick men I guess, for most writers, most architects, most planners. No one cared about thoughts or feelings. She did.'

'But people aren't just stick men, are they? They're real.' Kate pressed towards me and urged us both onwards.

'Right. We don't behave as they want us to behave, do we?'

'Bob doesn't behave as we want him to behave.'

'Neither does Baxter.'

Kate looked around. 'What do you think to this place? Honestly? Doesn't it scare the shit out of you – a little bit? There's something a bit like a castle about it. Like a compound. I don't know – some of the things Bel loved, obviously the intent was always right, but the execution? I'm not so sure. These guys in suits, do they really know what's best for mums with prams? My friend in Brum, Emaline, I remember her talking to me about this. She made me laugh. She was drunk this one time and just going off on one about how it was men that'd fucked up the city, men that'd knocked everything down, and men that'd invented the subway – and that you'd have had to be out of your mind to invent something so stupid and stick them all over, literally all over, the city centre. Women push prams and wear heels and…'

'Very feminist of you.'

'Shut up, it's her point, not mine – OK, some of the time women do. Anyway a subway is the most idiotic and useless concept if you think about either of those things.'

'Brum's nearly got rid of them all now.'

'Thank fuck. They were horrible at night. Grimy and scary. What are you supposed to do if you see dodgy-looking lads just hanging around down there in the middle of the night? I know it's a cliché but I really did see some disgusting old man pissing in the underpass at Five Ways, and that's a nice area of the city. God knows what the ones in… Aston or somewhere are like.'

'Sometimes I don't know if you're a real city girl.'

'Of course I'm a city girl. I've always lived in Brum and I always will… unless I meet a rich Australian guy with a passion for surfing on the side, in which case I'm on the next flight out – in business class. But no, I couldn't live in the country. It's too boring.'

'Our parents all wanted to though, didn't they? Even a lot of people our age. They hated Brum. They hated the city – like you.'

'I don't hate the city, you dickhead. I hate the bits of it that are scary and dirty and shit-looking and annoying. And Brum can be a bit rubbish sometimes, a bit boring sometimes, and my God there's enough weirdos there, aren't there? But I'm not like all those people – they thought escaping the city was the only answer, that the countryside was their salvation. They thought only the desperate would still live in cities. But hang on a minute, wasn't it architects who all moved out to the bloody country too? Or at least to the green suburbs, to Edgbaston, or to the nice villages by the motorway like Lapworth. I remember Bel telling me that. She wasn't impressed about it.'

'No, she wasn't. I think even Moseley seemed a bit "boho" for her.'

'I don't quite have Bel's love for the whole… shall we say… "weird and wonderful" world of concrete. Don't get me wrong, I love the library, and…' Kate turned and glanced up and around at our surroundings, at the austere lines of concrete running along the blocks, at the angles the creased-up building made when parts of it hit other parts of it. '…I could probably love this place too. After a while. But I'd prefer a nice little terraced house in Moseley, like you. Doesn't everyone? A house with a garden, not too big, just nice. A family home, not too many noisy neighbours, not having to worry too much about being robbed or anything.'

'Not everyone can afford those things.'

'No, well that's the problem, isn't it? Bloody male politicians or male bankers spending all our hard-earned money on whatever crap it is they do spend money on.'

Kate and I heaved ourselves up a staircase and mooched along the long corridor on the top deck of the building. I thought about Clare Middleton a lot as the wind and our footsteps echoed around the street in the sky. I thought about the people who had lived here, the people who still lived here. I stared at each heavy door and wondered what went on behind each one, how happy or sad the inhabitants of each flat were. The air was melancholy, but I knew it wasn't always this way, and it didn't have to be. You couldn't blow these bloody flats up; they were like rock. They'd last a thousand years. All you needed to do was spruce everything up, clean the concrete.

'They used to have a milk float run up and down here, didn't they?' Kate turned to me, wide-eyed, looking for praise. 'On the walkways.'

'Someone's been looking through archive footage.'

She laughed. 'I saw it. I remember seeing it. A bloody milk float, depositing milk bottles full of milk and picking...'

'Or orange juice.'

'Orange juice?'

'Yep, that too. Don't you remember?'

'I don't remember milkmen bringing orange juice to our house.'

'I think they did.'

We stopped and leaned over a balcony.

'You know Mackenzie was born here?' said Kate, looking wistfully into the sky.

'Mackenzie as in "The Bastard"? That Mackenzie? Born in Park Hill?'

'Yep, The Bastard. Our esteemed CEO was born right here, apparently. It's in the newspaper cuttings I checked out. Self-made man. Millionaire.'

'I never knew that. Just goes to show – social mobility used to happen.'

'I can't see that happening today. Can you? Can you see one of these kids going on to manage a media conglomerate?'

'Not really.' I paused. 'I think this was a happy building. I think this was a place that was built with the right intentions, and I think that...'

'What?'

'I don't know.'

'Inspired speech, big boy.'

'Thanks.'

Me and Kate walked down the steps to the ground floor. The sound of our stomping echoed around the stairwell. It sometimes seemed to me that buildings were alive, especially when they heaved and sighed like this one. Bel would have liked that; she believed that these things were organisms in some sense, not just inanimate objects we can treat like shit. We walked out towards the edge of the ridge where the hill fell away down to the railway tracks in the canyon, Sheffield city centre on the other side. We turned round and looked back at the building.

'Look up there,' said Kate, gesturing to the roof of the flats above the I Love You bridge.

'What the fuck is he up to?'

'Beats me, but he's going to get himself killed if he gets it wrong.'

Baxter was limbering up for something.

Bob sauntered over. 'You've got to see this. He's lost his fucking marbles this time.'

Baxter stretched and twisted then went off like a gun. He ran at full pelt along the roof line, then somehow span himself round and began to perform a series of repeated backwards somersaults across the top of the flats. He must have done about twenty in a row. He finished the demented routine with an elaborate double flip of the kind you'd see in the Olympics – at this point he was only about eight feet shy of a very long drop indeed.

'He wants to die?' said Janusz, matter-of-factly.

'He does, but... why?' asked Shazia.

Janusz shrugged his shoulders.

'Jesus wept,' said Bob.

Kate scowled at Bob.

'What? I'm just saying what we're all thinking. Why did I sign him up for this? I should've known better. Even Ralph fucking Marks would've been less annoying.' Bob sighed. 'And he's long gone too!'

Kate's face turned beetroot, looked like it was about to explode. 'Will you shut up?'

'Sorry.' Bob looked at his shoes. 'Right, let's get this pissing shoot set up so we can go and get some fish 'n' chips.'

'I'll have a battered sausage,' I added.

'You disgust me.' He turned to Kate. 'Are you sure those kids aren't going to nick anything?'

'Not with me around they're not,' she said. She strolled over to where a gaggle of estate kids had assembled with bicycles and began talking to them like a teacher would. The kids smiled, harmless, excited.

'Is this working?' I asked Bob. 'Really?'

He didn't reply. He just cast his eye over the castellated skyline of Sheffield.

'It's just… well, we both know… adapting books for the screen. Sometimes it turns into a dog's dinner. Books are meant to be read, and scripts are written to be filmed.'

'I know. It'll be alright. I think. Trust me.'

This is a dream:

Belinda is dancing. She sways and ducks and shimmies for me and me and me, just me. A summer dress floats around her lithe body. Her lips are bursting, rose-tinted. Her eyes are half-closed to defend against the brightness. We're by the sea wall at Alghero. The light is fierce and the sun bakes the scene. She grabs a lamppost and twirls around it, then hauls herself up onto the wall itself and dances along the length of it. She puts her arms out and I help her down, supporting her; I can't feel a thing, she's weightless. She dances round a trebuchet that had been left on the piazza in front of the sea wall by a giant who'd finished playing his war games for the day. My Steadicam eyes follow her round to the left, and she grabs a waiter who's standing by the door of a restaurant, trying to encourage tourists inside. She dances with him. He jigs along in good spirits. Then she turns and fixes her missile lock on me. She dramatically slides over like a ballroom dancer – first one foot then the other, until she's right in front of my face. She's open and blinking, smiling and perfect. Willing me to kiss her.

TEN BRUTALIST BUILDINGS

By Belinda Schneider

Chapter Seven

On building

Do you know what we forget about? We forget about the builders. Buildings aren't built by machines; they're built by humans. Buildings aren't designed by machines either; they're designed by the hand of a person.

The words associated with building flit around my head. 'Sites' and 'plant' and 'plans' and 'spirit levels'. They are evocative; they speak of more than just blind bricks and dead mortar. When you build brutalist buildings, men must mix concrete. They drive it to the building site. They pour it and they shape it. Concrete is basically a huge chemical reaction, yet it's something more primal than that too. The immense natural forces that form rocks and rivers are invoked when we pour concrete. The power we unleash is beyond our comprehension. Concrete freezes or sets or sticks or hardens or however you like to think of it. It's our answer to stone, our answer to the very part of the earth we stand on. The concrete we pour stays in place forever if we want it to be there for that long. And those men that do it are like so many ants in a colony. You watch them work, each doing a job, each one (perversely) invisible in their high-visibility jackets and hard hats. Hidden in plain sight. Pushing and pulling, heaving and lumping and smashing and smoking and hitting and measuring and cursing and believing in the rightness of the job they're doing. The job. These are some of the real heroes of our story. And yet who gives them a second thought? No book of architecture mentions the builders. Least of all by their names. But how can I even know their names? Architects are often illusions once their buildings go up; builders are scarcely even an idea. We can't even trust ourselves to say we really saw them, because we turn the other way, we put boards up around building sites, we pretend towers just rise and concrete just flows. In hot, dusty, dangerous emerging new cities where European rules of fair play don't apply, we close our eyes as men fall like ragdolls and splat like flies. They die for our architecture and we don't even know their names. What are their names? Without them we'd be nothing. We'd have nothing. Our cities are made by people. And then they are made once more by the people who populate them, who create their lives in the cities and inside our brutalist buildings. Hearts and minds are inside, hidden mostly. Maybe architects should be immured in their own buildings, set in their own concrete; maybe they should infect a building with their own spirit as a nod to the builders who've done the leg work and the arm work. Why don't we fill brutalist buildings with people, have them as 3D graveyards? I'd be happy to be interred inside my favourite building when I'm gone. Rather that than in the creepy churchyard or the deserted cemetery. You'd never be lonely, and the building would come alive with even more humanity.

25

2005

'Welcome, ladies and gentlemen, to this Birmingham University event. Tonight we have five speakers putting the case for different styles of architecture – each has picked one as their favourite, and we'll see who wins at the end of the night. The styles that will be duking it out tonight are Georgian, classical, post-modern, Gothic and brutalist. So, first on stage, I'd like to introduce Belinda Schneider, who'll be arguing the case for brutalism.'

I thought architecture was supposed to be dynamic. This lot looked like they'd been wheeled in from the hospital round the corner. A trickle of applause reached a damp crescendo, then subsided. Lots of coughing followed. Two women in their eighties, who were seated next to me, rummaged in a handbag – I presumed one of them owned it – and relieved it of a pack of the type of disgusting sugary boiled sweets that are fit only for the glovebox of an old car. They loudly unwrapped the sweets and muttered something about them 'getting smaller' as Bel took the stage.

She said, 'Hello,' then pressed a button. The screen behind her read *GLOBAL PROGRESSIVENESS*.

She continued. 'What if, instead of "brutalism", the most exciting type of architecture we've had for 200 years was known as *global progressiveness*? It's progressive – in moral character and in its sheer artistic bravado, its bold, bulky bravery. And it's global. Just an idea. Maybe you've got a better one. Really, "brutalism" could be called anything. Brutalism was a word that ended up being pejorative. Though today, perhaps we can see that it's been reclaimed as a positive thing. Anyway. Let's look at some unrepentant buildings.'

She pressed the button again – and then again after each slide had depicted the building she mentioned. Clicks. After. Each. Paragraph.

'Skopje, Macedonia. The Central Post Office.'

'Scarborough, Canada. A university.'

'Lyon, France. Couvent de la Tourette.'

'Buffalo, USA. Courthouse.'

'Marseille, France. Unité d'Habitation apartments.'

'Vienna, Austria. Wotruba Church.'

She ran her eyes over the audience. 'Look how inventive these buildings are, how sculptural. Yet they're just lumps of concrete!'

'Freiburg, Germany. An office block.'

'Poplar, Britain. A housing estate. Several, actually, next to each other.'

'Sao Paulo, Brazil. The MASP art gallery.'

'Gateshead, Britain. A car park and rooftop cafe on top of a shopping centre.'

'Sydney, Australia. University campus.'

'Chandigarh, India. A whole city.'

'Tokyo, Japan. Rissho University.'

'Brutalism was globalised, and it was exciting. It was the

196

future. Brutalism was honest, raw, avant-garde, a cry for more and a call to arms. Was it inhuman? In scale – perhaps; in looks – possibly. It was often provocative and it was often overwhelming. And sometimes we want an architecture that doesn't play nice, doesn't kowtow. But what people forget is how nurturing it could be too. Look inside those buildings and see how warm and inviting they can be, how they can be like cocoons protecting you from the world. There are so many plazas and cosy libraries and cafes and seating areas that we forget about. A true style for our times. A modern modernism. A style which wanted to be utopian, not dystopian – because the architects felt that what went before had let people and cities down. This new style would match up to the new way we were going to live our lives. Harmoniously. Purposefully. Peacefully. With technology as our servant.'

Bel looked down, paused, then flashed a wide smile at the audience. Some muttering wafted from around me. People seemed perplexed. Intrigued. 'I had another thought on the way here today. Do you want to hear it?'

A man in the audience piped up. 'Of course!' Some others giggled. The mood was instantly leavened.

'OK, so I was thinking about ageing. Bet a few of you lot know about that!' More laughter. I was spellbound by how Bel was working the room like a stand-up comic, like a… TV presenter. Fuck. Maybe she was going to end up on Mids TV one day, talking about this stuff. It would make a welcome change from Baxter. I'd prefer to hear my wife on TV, to show her off to the whole region too. I could even write a bloody show for her.

'I was thinking about how age affects our view of architecture, just as age affects our view of… well, human-tecture.' Some more laughs. Bel winked. 'We love babies; they are so magical.' She paused for a split second. I knew how much she wanted children. How we might not be able to have them. It's not as easy as you're led to believe. There are little hiccups along the way that you'd never dream of. 'We love babies and we love new buildings – even the shit ones. Well, a new building is so shiny and fresh, how could you not love it? But then buildings in their teens and twenties, they're not really appreciated. Teenagers, young people – they're annoying, aren't they? Self-centred, desperate to change the world, angst-ridden, try-hards, not really knowing their place. Same with buildings. People in middle age, they mellow. They're parents, they're artists and writers and thinkers and doers, they're calm and caring. They're attractive. Same with buildings – give them fifty years and suddenly we see their appealing side, the way they've adapted to their world, to their surroundings. Except so many of these great buildings aren't even given until their fiftieth birthday – they're snuffed out in their prime. Before we can come to some accommodation with them.' She paused. 'Think about colour. What colour are the buildings we're in?'

A student piped up. 'Red?' (It was said with a rising inflection? You know how all young people speak now?)

'Red, exactly. These buildings are a deep, controversial red. Sexual, I'd say. Gosh. Forthright, certainly. Loads of buildings in Birmingham are red. The colour, the way the bricks or the tiles are fired, it doesn't wear away. It's strident. People hated that red. Now we think it's quaint. How can the colour of fire and anger be quaint? But that's the way we see it now. Arts and Crafts niceness. Well, grey – concrete's colour – people have despised that. But why? Again it's just a point in time. Give it a hundred years, everything might be… stupidly, garishly coloured like a Tokyo crossroads, like a shopping centre, like a funfair. Maybe then that sombre, sober grey will suddenly seem so reserved and civilised. Buildings live in a time. But if they're lucky, if we do things right, they should live through many times – times that might eventually end up being kind – kinder – to them.'

Even I was becoming convinced. Georgian architecture won on the night, of course. There were a lot of old folk here – set in their ways; respectable, conformist, non-boat rocking types clad in cardies. But with her superior argument, her sultry and informal presentation and an air of total belief in what she was saying – bordering on devotion – Bel and her brutalism came in a very respectable second place. Partly because she was the most charming and least soporific speaker – not soporific at all in fact. When I heard Bel speak I wanted to listen. I wasn't the only one.

26

2008

Janusz looked like he was on his way to dreamland. His head kept lolling to the side, then abruptly snapping back to rigid as he tried to jolt himself awake. We'd been driving for over an hour, maybe two. The van was calm and quiet, the radio off. Everyone seemed to be dozing. From my seat next to the left side window I could read each road sign – each instruction, each letter-shaped white island floating on a light-blue sea, each huge signboard illuminated by a fading fuchsia sky, each advertisement aimed at another cluster of humans just like us. The sun was beginning its daily death. Each mile down equalled a mile nearer to home and a mile nearer to darkness. We came off the M42 onto one of those extended, brusque slip roads that connects one motorway with another. This slip road ran through fields and acted like it owned the landscape, carving its way right through farmland, going wherever it sodding well wanted. Tower blocks surprised me on the horizon, suddenly rearing up right in front of us, and we motored straight for them. Then, at the last minute, we curved up to the right and joined the M6. The countryside was over. Now the tower blocks had appeared on my left, hard on the left, right on the left, right there – right outside the window, right up against us. An aggressive move. They wanted to be seen, to start a fight perhaps. 'Come on then!' they seemed to shout. One vanished, then another appeared, and another, and another. Castle Bromwich. The tower blocks kept appearing. They were coloured-in as the 1970s was coloured-in: beige, brown, grey, black. Dusk did them no favours. They wore windows and balconies, placed so regularly that everything about them seemed unnaturally managed – mismanaged? I'd seen them before, driving into Birmingham on this route, but I'd never had a chance to really stare at them before. I saw a man standing on a balcony three floors down from the summit of one of the blocks. He was motionless, just staring out into space, perhaps staring at the waning sun. Perhaps just having a fag. He could have been a statue. Still more of them kept appearing, a real army now. Dozens in total; I lost count. Sunlight glinted off them. The streetlights at the side of the road broke each scene down into one-second frames as we passed each pole – cut, cut, cut, cut, cut. We seemed to be floating; it all looked like an apparition. But it wasn't, it was just the impression you got when you saw them from a moving vehicle. And maybe those tower blocks had been designed to be seen like this. To be floated past in the middle lane of the M6 at 65 miles per hour. Maybe that's what Birmingham wanted everyone to see. To see its proud flats from the window of the car. We passed the last block. The road we were on was high up now. From the top of the viaduct you could see the city skyline, tantalising and distant, just out of reach. Growing imperceptibly. I was aware of a jolt every time we passed over joins in the carriageway – bang... bang... bang...

The sign said *Birmingham Central*. Janusz steered the

minibus off the motorway. This was the best way to enter
Brum. We swooped high in the air, like a bird of prey,
over the tangle of Spaghetti Junction slip roads, but these
slip roads were narrow and short; the effect was like riding a rollercoaster. We crested, then fell forwards, down,
faster. A churning in my stomach, a grin on my face.
Onto the Aston Expressway. Over on the right I caught
sight of traffic thundering towards us. There's no barrier
down the middle of the carriageway. It's visceral to be on
Brum's wide roads – the thrill, the speed, the notion of
death round the next corner, the city unfolding itself but
never revealing everything. Just glimpses. Now we were
in a cutting, the skyline playing hide and seek. Then out
as quick as a flash. All the biggest buildings right next to
the road – where they can be seen. Everything designed
for the driver. Occasional pedestrians up on bridges or
emerging from subways, forlorn wanderers with strained
orange or white supermarket carrier bags weighing their
arms down. The best bit of all now. Approaching the city
centre. In other cities the Expressway would have termi-
nated and you'd be coughed out onto older, slower streets.
Not Brum. It keeps going. Still double lanes. The road
jumps up over Lancaster Circus. It's like you're flying.
(This very point, right here, right over the very middle
of Lancaster Circus, fascinated me. Julie – that short-lived
girlfriend from many years ago. In halls at Aston University. Another type of tower block, 'a better class of people',
they said. Not much more than 500 yards away. When I
showered in her stale, communal bathroom on the twen-
tieth floor, I could see right across and down to this precise point, to this flyover. I could watch the cars flying
through the air from right to left, a careless stream, a cease-
less conveyor belt. As I was washing my hair and soaping

my body. It was an electrifying sight watching this fly-over flurry bubbling through that little corner of window. Everything moving, everyone moving, nothing stopping. Where were they going? From her kitchen window on the opposite side of the block I could see down to Masshouse Circus – the place where I was drawn on strange days and nights without really knowing why, drawn to sit with those tramps, necking high-alcohol cider and smoking fake cigarettes bought in Eastern Europe. Especially after Bel's accident. I went down there a lot in those few weeks. I wasn't afraid of the traffic, the traffic that robbed me of happiness. I wanted to be near it, to understand it.)

Round a curve. Now the road heads down again, under St Chad's Circus, with its mean Z-bend that tested a tired Janusz's resolve. But he got us through it. Out the other side, and I could see the BT Tower looming on my right, a huge monster. I wanted so desperately to go through the tunnel with the sign that reads *QUEENSWAY* above the portal, but Janusz steered us left, up the hill of Great Charles Street, towards Paradise Circus. The library rose on my left, looking so glum yet so convincing, sober and absolutely ideally placed above a bloody road. We plunged underneath it. I loved the Birmingham City Council-branded stripes of red and blue inside this tunnel beneath the library. Sharp right. Mids TV ahead. Sharp left. A little further, another left, into the car park. Janusz parked and switched off the engine. He yawned extravagantly. No one in any hurry to move. Kate made a face like a contented child and squeezed my leg tenderly. 'Come on then, mis-ter.' The grind of the sliding door opening. I felt dizzy and apprehensive out on the tarmac, outside the hermetic world of the minibus. Cold air pricked my cheeks, woke me up. The sun had disappeared behind the Repertory

Theatre. The city seemed empty, it felt mournful. All those people travelling through, around, under, over. No one pausing, no one relaxing. I needed to go home. A shuffle over towards my car – silver, nondescript – and a button depressed on the keyring. The car greeted me in its own language with a 'Wheek wheek' and a wink of its indicator lights.

27

2007

'I think this is the most normal place we've ever been to together.'

Bel laughed. 'I'm sorry if our – if *my* – urban… wanderings get a bit much for you.'

I leaned over and kissed her.

'It's nice to be somewhere that's… objectively beautiful. No concrete.' She shoved me. I went back to my book, and a short while later a dog barking in Italian distracted me. I looked up and saw Bel was staring at me now.

'*Sì?*'

She pressed her warmth into me. I ran my right palm over her hips, her skin oily from suntan lotion. My hand filled the gap in her back where it arched inwards. Her head was on my chest now. I stroked her hair with my right hand and held my book aloft with my left. I saw her right hand pop out from beneath her like a spring-loaded clown toy. She reached round the back of herself and pinged the clasp on her white bikini top free. Muffled laughter came from the direction of my chest. She sat up and her top stayed resting on my chest.

'What do you reckon?' she said, looking down at herself, smiling to herself, then looking back at me, winking.

I said, 'Wow,' and then after a pause to take it all in, 'The teenage boy inside me is very grateful.'

She laughed. 'I hope I make a good holiday buddy. Come for a swim? It's so hot.'

'Absolutely.'

I put the book down and ran after her towards the shore.

As we splashed into the water, I asked her, 'Are there jellyfish in Sardinia, do you think?'

'I don't care!' was her response. 'Let them sting us.' She plunged straight up to her neck and started swimming away, yelling, 'Catch me!'

I replied, 'Oh, I'll catch you!' and she screamed. I caught up with Bel and threw my arms around her. She locked her thighs round me and we bobbed in the water. The sunlight dappled on the water, refracted in a million different ways. I sank my head beneath the surface, and the sound in my ears changed from the squall of birds and children to a dull, muted gloop of comings and goings as gentle waves washed across us.

The sea here was an unusually bright colour, the kind of azure you see in holiday brochures but seldom in real life. The waters were calm. The whole bay was a geographical anomaly.

'Look at the tower!' said Bel.

My eyes were drawn across the horizon to a ruined brown fort on a little sandy spit.

'It's called the Hairy Tower,' I said.

She sniggered, wiping saltwater from her eyes with her hand, squinting in defiance of the sun. 'What?'

'Seriously. You don't believe me? You can look in the guidebook back in the hotel room. I read it on the balcony after breakfast.'

'I don't believe you,' she purred in my ear, running her left hand slowly across my jaw, seeming to savour it, to be making a mental mould of it.

'I'll show you.'

She swam in front of me.

'Look at me,' she ordered, sternly.

'I'm always looking at you.'

'I want you to look at me. Whatever I'm doing. I want your eyes on me. Always. Mine will be on you.' Her mock serious-ness broke into laughter.

'I can do that.' I stared into Bel's eyes.

She paused. Everything seemed so still and calm; everything was so well balanced. It was a mirage. The world is tilted, the universe so big we can only know the most minuscule fraction of what's out there. Horrors are everywhere; disasters come from nowhere, sneak up on you. But sometimes you can be tricked into thinking that, for a few ticks on the second hand, there is no more terror, there is no more anxiety. The equilib-rium can be so perfect for such a short period that it blinds you; it hypnotises you. Chance can seem like fate, a bit of good luck like a masterplan successfully implemented. We bobbed in the water. I felt no steel on my shoulders, no tungsten in my knees, no lead in my ankles. Just floating. Just living. Life. A pure evo-cation of life. A scene someone would write in a novel.

'I want to eat clams and spaghetti tonight,' Bel said, her face painted with excitement. 'And I want to drink Asti.' She ran her hands through wet hair. 'Do you want to join me, my love?'

28

The empty studio was eerie. It was tricksy with space. Was it really a cube that could contain thousands of people stacked on top of each other? When Kate walked in I wondered if perspective was about to play a joke on me. Would she be towering over me, then pick me up in her hand?

I saw something on the other side of the studio; it must have wanted to be seen. It looked like a giant… bone? I walked over to the corner of the cavernous room and tried to yank the bone out. It was actually flat and seemingly made from some kind of wood, like pine?

'Kate!' Kate was standing by the studio doors, holding a clipboard and writing something. 'Kate!'

'What do you want? I've got to do some paperwork. And there's some videos I want to show you.'

'Come and give us a hand. I saw this from over there. I want to…'

'What is it?'

'I don't know. Help me get it out from behind here, will you?'

'God, it'll tear my blouse.'

'Pull it.'

'I am.'

'Harder.'

I yanked the bone until I heard a monstrous tearing noise. I fell on my back, and tears of laughter erupted from Kate's eyes. I looked at the giant bone.

Kate read aloud from the two lines of text: '"I Lo My D." I lo my d? What the fuck does that mean?'

I realised. '*I Love My Dog!* I wish I hadn't seen the damn thing.'

A pause. A crack. A pain emanating from the crown of my head. Something had just smashed down onto it. A twelve-foot-long arboreal approximation – and written on the side of it were the words 'The Wrong Tree'.

I dusted myself down and threw the stupid props to one side.

'Edit suite?'

'Yup.'

The edit suite was a vomitorium of yellows and beige. All shades were represented, from citrine to camel. The flimsiness of the whole set-up never ceased to amaze me. The exterior of the studios was so tough, so rugged. Inside, however, everything was clad in crappy half-finished padding and botched paint. It was as if we were being constantly reminded that we were just here for a while, that we could be kicked out at any moment; further, that everything which went on here and the stuff we made, the programmes we produced, were forgettable, temporary pieces that weren't anchored to anything, that didn't matter to anyone.

A row of shelves along one wall was labelled with things like 'PV' and 'TX' and 'Cam 1, 2, 3, 4, 5'. Above the shelves was a clear light, and imprinted in red capital letters on the front of it was the word *BOMB*. I pointed up at it.

'Don't you remember the 1970s?' said Kate. 'You know… all the fucking bombs and stuff?'

'Yeah but I've never seen that sign before,' I said.

'Well let's hope we never have to see it again.'

Computers did the work today, but there were still old editing machines and video players scattered around, cables trailing out of them like they were on a drip in an intensive care ward.

Kate sat at a desk, her face cradled by both palms. She pressed a couple of buttons to rewind what she was watching.

'Look at this.'

The tape whirred and the picture jumped around on the screen.

'Old Mids TV idents.'

'Oh yeah?'

'From the 1970s.'

'Ah, right!'

*

[A pushy voice argues from the speakers.]

'This is Mids!'

[A backing track twinkles; fingers run over all the keys of a piano; a jazzy drum and trumpet double act pipe up. A montage of pictures begins. A crash-zoom from the top of the Rotunda down onto two girls in their twenties walking along New Street; a crash-zoom into a group of four girls in a nightclub, giggling away and drinking Martinis (factually inaccurate – it would have been sherry or a snowball); a crash-zoom into a row of girls in bikinis standing (and smiling) under a sign reading MISS MIDS TV 1974; a crash-zoom into

eight girls frolicking in bikinis by a swimming pool. At least it looks like a swimming pool, but there's something big and concrete and angular right behind them. They're not in Sardinia.]

*

Kate looked over her shoulder at me and raised her left eyebrow at this point.

*

[A crash-zoom into a single stripper wearing a fur coat and some knickers, gyrating on a podium at a club somewhere on Broad Street. Then a spinning M appears, and the angry sod doing the voiceover returns.]

'Television… that's also… for HER!'

*

I guffawed.

'Do you see what women in this region used to have to put up with?' Kate grumbled.

'There were girls wearing bikinis in *I Love My Dog!*' I confessed. 'I'm as bad as the rest of them.'

Kate looked drained. 'Almost.'

'That is truly awful. Are there any more?'

'I've been through the looking glass. Dozens.'

'And *Miss Mids TV 1974*?'

'That got your attention, didn't it?'

'I'm fucking appalled, OK. Is that what you want to hear? I want to be scandalised.'

'Do you want to see it?'

'Go on then.'

Kate got up and fetched a battered video.

*

[Some footage of Birmingham at night, trying to set the scene for glamour.]

A camp feather duster of a voiceover intones: 'Direct from the centre of fabulous Birmingham… it's Miss Mids TV 1974*!'*

[A title track begins. It sounds like it should be the music to open a programme of live horse racing. There's a clomping rhythm and some jaunty synthesisers. The pictures accompanying it are of the contestants in daily life – a girl on a supermarket checkout, another cutting hair, someone acting up for the cameras as a secretary in an office, another girl in a stewardess uniform walking through the doors leading out from Birmingham Airport. Now the programme begins, and the building they're filming it in suddenly becomes all too familiar.]

The soppy voiceover again: 'Ladies and gentlemen, this year's Miss Mids comes live from Birmingham's brand new Central Library. Where, for today's girls, it's not the words that matter, but the figures! So join us as we find out which of our region's most beautiful lovelies will triumph, to be crowned… Miss Mids 1974!'

[Now more shots of the girls standing by that pool outside the library, wearing bikinis, under the MISS MIDS TV 1974 *sign; then the girls walking around among the shelves and ostentatiously picking books up. One of the girls, wearing a navy ballgown and a sash which says* MISS COVENTRY, *picks up a tome, on the cover of which is an elevated motorway cocking its slip road leg against the ground. The words on the front read* Birmingham's Concrete

215

Dreams. *She flicks through it in ten seconds then puts her right index finger up to her lips and makes an astonished face.]*

*

'Fast forward it,' I said to Kate.
    'My pleasure.'

*

'...*think it's a case of dialectics or just the subjectivity of the human experience, the...*'

*

'Fucking hell... is that? It can't be.'
    Kate stared at the screen. 'Baxter. Exactly.'
    'Well I'll be...'
    'Why in the name of God is Baxter presenting *Miss Mids 1974?*'
    'Why is Baxter wearing a shirt with a huge collar and frilly front?'

*

'...*individual at the centre of things, the individual experience trumping the objective, the collective...?*'

Miss Coventry, now in a canary-yellow one-piece swimsuit, and with a hugely bouffant and impeccably blow-dried hairstyle, flashes a huge grin. 'Well, bab, we certainly don't have many customers in the bakery by the Lady Godiva statue talking much about dialectical materialism when they come in for their cob at lunchtime and have to choose between cheese or 'am – I think it's just a case of "what-

216

ever you fancy at the time", to be honest. But I've been learning about Marx's writings in my social sciences course at Essex University, and I'd be happy to teach you anything you wanted to know about the ins and outs of political philosophy. Just say the word.'

[Baxter is stunned into an awkward silence.]

*

'Good on you, girl!' yelled Kate. I nodded agreement. 'That's enough of that,' she said, reaching for the stop button.

'Why have you been looking at this disastrous tripe?'

'The *50 Years of Mids TV* special. Didn't I tell you?'

'Maybe. Will it be good?'

'It will be good, because we'll make it good. And if I'm honest I'll quite enjoy telling the story of this TV station. Though, as you've seen, it was a fucking risible place for women to work for most of its existence, an existence when it was churning out mostly very, very bad programming. We'll have to point that out in the doc.'

'Good old Mids.'

'Good old Mids.' Kate picked up a phone. The wire hung loose from the handset; it had been sliced clean through. 'This place is falling apart. Nothing works and everything's old.' She paused. 'Like you. We're still working on bloody VHS. If they shut us down, this *50 Years of Mids* film will be the only memory people have left of us.'

I bit my fingernails and hummed. 'Show me another ident.'

'Do we have to?'

'Go on.'

Kate sighed. 'This one's creepy.'

*

[The same pushy voice argues from the speakers.]

'This is Mids!'

[A different backing track, more dreamy. Keyboards dance and I sense a flute about to drop in. A flute drops in. A montage of pictures begins. Dawn. The sun is rising. A scene showing two tower blocks framing a roundabout. A crash-zoom in on a blonde woman sleeping on a bed in the centre of the roundabout. A fisheye lens pans from ground level, past the same blonde woman sleeping on a bed in the middle of a jagged white concrete plaza, then heads up, up, up, scanning an enquiring eye over the totality of a craggy collection of buildings: it's the Mids TV HQ. Next: a tower, skinnier than Mids. It's the BT Tower. The camera pans down, this time from top to bottom, and the blonde woman stands at ground level. Now an empty plaza, again with a bed in the middle of it and the same blonde woman lying on it. The camera pans up to show two cliff walls of concrete and windows converging on a point. Now the view is of the same place from above. A square is marked out by the sides of the Central Library. The white bed is in the centre of the square. A spinning M appears perfectly centred on the square. Another voiceover.]

'It's a new day… and a new era!'

*

It was eerily familiar. 'I've been dreaming about the idents.'

'You're in a worse place than I thought.'

'Seriously. That blonde woman is in my dreams. Constantly.'

'The one from the idents?'

'Yes! I've seen her in photos too. What the hell is happening?

'Shut up, you're imagining it.'

'Maybe. Who is she?'

'Some woman… some model?'

Kate went back to looking for pieces of film she could use.

I spied the tapes lined up on a shelf along one of the side walls of the room. They were marked with sticky labels, titles written in capitals in felt tip pen.

'This place is about as low-tech as you can imagine,' I said, ostensibly to myself. 'The public probably think there are hundreds of people working here, shiny offices, computers everywhere, glamour. It's a fucking joke.' I scanned along the titles. 'This one looks good.'

'What's that?' Kate looked up.

I pulled the tape down and gave it to Kate. She read aloud from the sticky label. *'HOW DO YOU MAKE A TV STATION? THE SETTING UP OF MIDS TV.'*

'Bang it on.'

'Give me a ciggie, I will.'

I pulled out a pack. Kate daintily removed a fag, sparked it, put the tape in and pressed play.

*

[The colours in the film are saturated, as if they've been turned up too high. Tracking shot along a brightly lit corridor. Quite skilful camera work. Elegant. A plummy voice appears from nowhere.]

'1968. Britain is changing. The Midlands is changing more than any other part of it.'

[Now an aerial shot of Birmingham, dwelling on cranes and roads and office buildings. A lingering overhead of the Bull Ring, which looks like a kind of child's toy set. Blocky and overblown. Fat and

symmetrical. Cars circle round and through the complex like ants, moving slowly, smoothly, steadily. Next is an overhead shot of Paradise Circus. The middle of the roundabout is a huge mass of building materials and construction machines. Now the camera lingers on the Mids TV HQ. The whole thing appears blindingly white, freshly finished.]

'A dynamic region needs a dynamic television station. Mids is that. Years in the planning and now ready to open, Mids Television will revolutionise the way the Midlands and its go-ahead residents get their media.'

[Men in suits in a boardroom, talking and smoking. Fat men.]

'Various panels and government meetings in the 1960s. The conclusion? Something had to be done. The Midlands needed its own television station. Step forward a progressive bunch of true visionaries who would make it happen. These men knew what it took to bring television to the Midland masses. They certainly weren't doing it for the money. They were doing it because it was a vocation. Visionary men like these needed practical men who could make things happen on the ground.'

[An unpromising, windy hillside. Trees being chopped down. A zoom towards the skyline of Birmingham in the distance. Workers filling a hole with concrete. Then a lot of metal arrives on trucks and slowly the shape of a transmitter begins to rise into the sky.]

'The Lickey Hills, south of Birmingham. It was decided to raise a transmitter here on this lofty perch, where the Mids signal could reach right out to Shropshire, Worcestershire, Staffordshire, Warwickshire

– *and the West Midlands conurbation. Builders worked tirelessly to sink concrete foundations and erect a proud, hard aerial that no one could miss! Now there was a transmitter, programmes had to be made that could be broadcast from it.'*

[Back to central Birmingham. Looking along Broad Street a few years previously, the scruffy site where the Mids TV HQ and studios were about to be built.]

'*After much studying of suitable sites, Broad Street in Birmingham was decided upon as the location for the new Mids Television Centre. It has easy access to the soon-to-be-completed Queensway Inner Ring Road – and the building itself will have underground and surface car parking for 400 vehicles. This was a former industrial area, near to the Gas Street Canal Basin. A part of Birmingham that seemed unpromising in previous eras. But in the forward-looking 1960s, anything is possible! The site was full of dirt and grime; the memory of a former Birmingham was alive – a Birmingham where people toiled in factories and on canal barges. But those dark days of heavy manufacturing are almost over, and so they should be. The future is about technology and leisure! There's talk of ridding all of central Birmingham of these grubby Victorian warehouses and wharves, even concreting over the canals and turning them into motorways – wouldn't that be something?'*

[Builders swarming over scaffolding.]

'*Construction of the Mids Television complex has been completed in lightning-quick time – two years flat. And anyone that says you can't rush these things better think again. The architect reckons – and who are we to question him – that this lot* can stand for a thousand years. So let's look around. The site is split into three. The studio block where the programmes will be shot and edited – the stores, dressing rooms and other assorted technical tricks of the trade are in here. A different block containing the canteen and bar, reception and other public areas. Then, thirdly, the office tower, reaching high into the sky above the city and containing space for the programme makers; the advertising, administrative and accounts departments; and also management, who have the highest offices of all with sweeping views out towards the countryside – well, you can't run a tight ship without having some of your top men at the top, can you?'

[Inside the same corridor as earlier, tracking along.]

'So why don't we stop talking about the abstract and instead meet two of the men who'll be bringing television in the Midlands to life, when Mids TV goes live to air.'

[Zoom in to a figure standing in the Mids TV HQ car park. A man in a sharp suit, handsome and with hair slicked back. He takes off his glasses. He looks like he's in his mid twenties.]

'Meet Mr Ralph Marks. Marks is in his twenties. Married, he commutes by car into the studios every day from his house near Kidderminster. Mr Marks used to be the news editor on Birmingham's local newspaper, the Evening Brummie. But now he's got a new role and a new life – as a television presenter. Specifically, Mr Marks will be presenting Bullseye, the weekly current affairs programme, which will cast a glance at everything from industrial relations to consumer issues. Mr Marks votes Conservative and says his favourite tipple is a Campari on the rocks. Mr Marks smokes cigarillos.'

[Zoom in to another figure standing in the Mids TV HQ car park. A man in a suit again. It's not as chic as the previous suit, cheaper – obviously. The man is smoking a cigarette. His tie is loose. He's handsome but his hair is rather scruffy-looking. He also looks the same age – mid twenties.]

'Meet Mr Bob [inaudible]. He is in his twenties. Single, he commutes into the studios from his flat in Bearwood, Birmingham. Mr [tape skips] studied English at Birmingham University and has done work for theatre groups and small "underground" magazines in the Midlands. He also organised one of the country's first so-called "stand-up comedy" nights at Birmingham's Student Guild. He will be embracing his position as one of the troupe of multifunctioning writer-performers on Mids TV's flagship light entertainment Saturday-night spectacle Welcome To The Masshouse. The programme will feature satirical skits, comedic sketches, a sideways look at the week's news, games and the like. The title – in case you're wondering, and I know I was – is a pun of course on Masshouse, that infamous district of central Birmingham, which is now the site for a traffic roundabout super-interchange. Do you get it? I know I do now. Comedy will be a big part of the station's remit. Television is a new medium, and Mids is committed to challenging the status quo and pushing accepted boundaries to deliver the most revolutionary light entertainment programmes to its viewers. It is almost the 1970s, after all. Oh, and Mr [inaudible] votes Labour and says his favourite tipple is a pint of Birmingham Bitter. He smokes Gent Cigarettes.'

[A prototype version of the Mids logo – a spinning 'M' that's not been quite properly drawn. It looks half-finished compared to today's

version. It spins awkwardly in white against a drab black back-ground.]

'And what's this? Well, it's our logo. Mids Television will be rep-resented by the letter 'M'. The 'M' signifying, of course, Mids and thence Midlands, which is where Mids got its name from. Glad we cleared that up. And is there anything else we need to show you? I quite fancy a trip to the bar. Don't you?'

[A glamorous woman with a large cleavage and tight red dress sits on a stool at the bar, sipping fizz from a retro champagne glass. She holds up the glass to toast the camera and flashes a set of pearly choppers.]

'My, my. There's one good reason to visit the Mids Television bar. Or two good reasons! The Mids Television bar is the place to see stars and let your hair down after a long day at the office. It is already Birmingham's most glamorous after-dark lounge, with a range of cocktails you can enjoy while sitting on fine leather seats. You'll be able to sip wine and smoke a cigar in the company of the most excit-ing people of today.'

[On to shots of a canteen, which is painted bright white. Cherry-coloured hexagonal islands sit in the middle of the room, piled high with cold food. A line of hot dishes in shallow metallic vats are down one side of the room, and sets of chairs and tables are on the other side of the room.]

'Mids is a thoroughly modern enterprise which caters well to its workers' needs. There's a canteen with all kinds of foods served in a progressive style – that means, for cold grub, you can locate the food island you need easily: if you fancy an egg salad or some straw–

berry jelly, for example. Or if it's hot food you're after, like beef stew and dumplings or sausage and chips, head over to the heated stations where chefs dish up the piping-hot goodies. The canteen is just one example of where Mids Television is innovating. The architect of the building went to America, where he researched the way offices and television studios worked, in order to better understand what staff needed and what made a really great television complex, and I think you'll agree that the end results we can see here in Birmingham are truly second to none.'

[A montage: engineers coiling up cables in a studio, lights being wheeled across the floor. Outside broadcast vans – with the giant 'M' logo on the side – piling out of the car park onto Broad Street. Secretaries typing away; a man in a suit comes over and hands one of them a document, and she smiles. A security guard in the gate lodge and another guard out in the car park pick up walkie-talkies to chat to each other. Pan shot showing sweeping views from the top of the Mids TV Tower, looking down on the traffic and the cranes in Birmingham. Two cool-looking 20-somethings dressed in flower prints sit down in oversized yellow plastic pod chairs in a white, minimally decorated flat and begin to watch a TV. The spinning 'M' logo appears on the screen, and the couple bob their heads as if they're listening to some kind of funky song.]

'So this then is Mids Television. A new television station for a new era. A new television station for a region that's going places. A new television station for a new you! Enjoy the show.'

*

TEN BRUTALIST BUILDINGS

By Belinda Schneider

Chapter Eight

Mids TV HQ – why are people killing themselves?

The most depressing thing about modern life is the way it alienates people. But are people sad because of the physical world we've created, or are they sad because of the materialistic society we've fostered? I don't think brutalist architecture makes you feel sad. I think it's the pressures and stresses that go along with being poor or being troubled or just, maybe, being modern. Money, sex, conformity, relationships – all these things can blister you. Capitalism chips away at your heart. In recent years the talk has swung to how buildings can cause this feeling of anomie. But I'd counter that it's not that physical built world we have a problem with; it's the modern society we've created, the consumer society, that is specifically designed to make you unhappy. So you buy your way out of the morass.

The unfortunate truth has been that people in cities not only kill themselves, but kill themselves by jumping off modern buildings, off modernist buildings, off brutalist buildings. Is it because they're the tallest ones around? Or because they represent some of the hurt people feel? If you think I'm going to talk about TV when I talk about the Mids studios, I'm not. I'm going to talk about suicide. Many people have jumped to their deaths from the top of the office tower at the Mids TV HQ. Too many people. I find this fact profoundly depressing. We need to help people who feel this way. People who want to kill themselves. It's not just the studios either – all around Birmingham there are places where vulnerable people go to end their lives.

This is the sad secret of the city. And Birmingham is just one city. Tower blocks, office towers, car parks. People jump off these buildings to escape from their demons. I wish people wanted to live. I wish they saw these buildings as places they could go to think, to play, to enjoy. But they're too often places they go because they've reached the end of their tether. We can't ignore these things. But we should also try to see that just because these are places of death, the architecture doesn't have to represent death.

Of all the thinking about architecture I've done, this is the thing that troubles me the most. I don't understand it. I'm not a philosopher or a psychologist. I wonder what's really going on in people's minds. I wonder why this happens and what it says about us. I wish brutalism could be all about happiness and possibility, I really do. I've tried to show how I think it is and it can be. But I have to show this side as well, this tragic side. And if you're reading this and thinking about doing anything stupid, for God's sake please don't. You're loved. You're always loved by someone, usually by many people. They can't live without you. You'll break their hearts. Seek them out. Know there's someone there for you. Don't make yourself another one of those horrific statistics. Wherever you are in the world. Just stop and think. Please. When you die, however you die, you wreck everything. You wreck everything for other people. Your death ruins their lives.

29

2000

'I enjoyed *Big Plans*, I thought it was fu—'

'It wasn't, but go on.'

'It was funny, but—'

'It wasn't.'

'It was!'

'OK, maybe in places.'

'Exactly. But it nurtured a kind of attitude. All those films shot in the 1960s and '70s, they presented brutalist buildings as dystopias... or jokes.'

'They did, that's a good point. But to my eye they made it all look sort of glamorous and sexy sometimes. Strange, yes, but I don't know... intriguing?'

'To your eye. But sex and glamour to you is aggression and threat and sleaze to someone else.'

'With that show I was really mocking – apart from the idiots in power who are always idiots and always all-powerful – that feeling of being talked down to. You know, the public information films and the council documentaries that found their way onto Mids TV. Everything was rosy. Mums with prams, and flowerbeds everywhere. The future will be perfect if you TRUST US to lead you there. I bet you saw loads of those films on East German TV. Well, fuck them.'

'Everything was rosy – sometimes. It could really have been like that for all time. It almost was. They were building a new Jerusalem for all the people. The future was exciting; the buildings were exciting. The politicians messed everything up – they always do, wherever they are. But the architects were on to something.'

'People felt they were sold a pup though.'

I lit two cigarettes, passed one to her.

'You're attracted to failure. You can smell it.'

'Why would you say that?'

'You're attracted to a failed writer and failed buildings.'

'Other people might think they've failed, but I don't.' She inhaled, looked pleased with herself.

'Seriously, I've been thinking about it. I reckon it's got something to do with your caring side. You want to rescue things, to nurse them.'

'I'm a very caring person. I used to help animals I found outside the block of flats who had injuries.' She leaned in and squeezed me.

'I knew it!'

'So now you're happy that your fucking theory is correct, Dr Donald?'

'Very happy.'

'I'm happy about that.'

I picked up my newspaper.

'I'm very proud of you. You're famous in Birmingham. People at that steak house always recognise your name. Bartholomew's. Maybe it's because you go there too much though?'

'They recognised my name from the end titles of *I Love My Dog!* They said it was their favourite programme.'

'There's no accounting for taste.'

'That sounds like another sitcom I could write. *There's No Accounting For Taste*. Set in an accountant's office.'

Bel groaned.

We sat in silence.

'You know I love you no matter what, whether you're a success or a failure, though in my eyes it will always be success. And you'll love me no matter what too.'

'No matter what.'

'Do you want to possess me? Love is like possession, I guess. Men want to possess women like a car or something. I'd never change my name.'

'Keep your name. No one can possess you. You're a free spirit. I can borrow you, like a book from a library. That's all.'

She laughed. 'Like my students. They can borrow me for a term and then they have to put me back.'

'Exactly.'

'I'll get fined for keeping you out too long...'

30

[*Title music – jaunty and insistent, like the soundtrack to a fair pulling into town. Scenes of Birmingham play out in the background, but they all look grotty – motorways, underpasses, tower blocks, concrete boxes.*]

Title card – BIG PLANS

[*The camera hovers over Victoria Square and then crash-zooms down to show two men in suits with drainpipe trouser bottoms strolling across the screen and into the Council House as the music fades out. Benedetti and Rocaster.*]

[*Establishing shot of a deserted piece of waste ground, a grand old factory building behind it looking mournful.*]

Benedetti: 'Put that shovel down, Seddon, and come over here!'
　　Seddon: 'Yes, sir. What's up?'
　　Benedetti: 'The clock is frantically counting down until the arrival of the Minister. I want these explosives laid, charged and checked. And no monkey business. This is a big day. I want that custard

factory demolished with the minimum of fuss. When the Minister presses the button – one blast, all gone.'

Seddon: 'Whatever you say.' [Cut to Seddon's face. He silently mouths mock words, impersonating Benedetti. Benedetti turns round and catches him at it.]

Benedetti: 'And Seddon… what are you playing at? Stop larking around and get on it with it.'

Seddon: 'What's going in the gap once the Minister's blown it up?'

Benedetti: 'I'm glad you're taking an interest. First time for everything. A mixed-use development, Seddon. Library, school, flats, shops, offices, car park and a slip road connection up to the dual carriageway. All finished in fresh, raw, delicious, naked concrete – of course.'

Seddon: 'Blimey. Big plans.'

Benedetti: 'Blimey indeed, Seddon. Blimey indeed.'

*

[Cut to later in the day. A huge crowd of dignitaries has gathered a hundred yards from the exclusion zone in front of the huge old factory. Women in their finery, a few looking foxy in miniskirts. Men in suits, smoking cigars. Workmen in overalls milling around. Rocaster and Benedetti stand in front of a table at the front of the crowd, under an awning. A comical red plunger sits on the table. A workman appears, yawns and seems about to lean on it. It's Seddon.]

Benedetti: 'Seddon! What the hell do you think you're doing?'

[Seddon recoils at the last second then rolls his eyes out of Benedetti's view.]

Seddon: 'Sorry, sir.'

Benedetti: 'Right, Rocaster, everything's set?'

Rocaster: 'I believe it is. We've got the charges primed, the crowd moved back, the plans for the new development are propped up on a frame over there.'

Benedetti: 'Refreshments?'

Rocaster: 'Tea, coffee, a few bottles of that sweet German wine. What else? Oh, Mrs Pershore made a few rounds of ham sandwiches, two Dundee cakes and an apple pie.'

Benedetti: 'Ham finger rolls, Dundee cake and a fruit pie. It's not exactly what they served when they opened the great campanile at Siena is it? But it'll have to do, I suppose. Now, Seddon. Come over here, lad.'

Seddon: 'Sir?'

Benedetti: 'Now, Seddon. I'm only going to ask you this once. You and Harris absolutely, definitely cleared ALL of the custard powder out from the factory? Is this correct?'

[Seddon scratches his head.]

Seddon: 'Absolutely, sir.'

[Flashback to Harris and Seddon inside the factory. Harris kicks a football, which clanks into an industrial-sized tin of custard powder, jolts it, and causes yellowy soup to leap out.]

Harris: 'The rainwater's turned the powder to bloody custard!'

[They both chortle.]

Benedetti: 'Seddon…'

Seddon: 'Not to worry at all, Mr Benedetti. No custard. Not a drop.'

*

[Cut to half an hour later. The Minister and his entourage have arrived in a black car. The Minister greets the council dignitaries. He views the plans for the new development and then walks over to the table with the plunger on it. Mrs Pershore hands out bowls of apple pie to everyone standing around. Benedetti stands at the mic next to the table, tamping his pipe and wearing a face like a proud father on his daughter's wedding day.]

Benedetti: 'It gives me great pleasure, as chief planning officer of Birmingham, to welcome the Minister to our progressive and civilised city – a city which we are civilising…'

[Seddon and Harris walk in front of the table, conversing; Harris is carrying some wood, and Seddon a tin of paint. Seddon: '…and then she showed me it.' Harris: 'No bloody way!']

[Benedetti looks pained and clears his throat]

Benedetti: '…a city we are working very hard to civilise and progress… ivise. And so, without further ado, I'd like to invite the Minister to press the plunger, which will signal the end of the old era of industrial Birmingham and the beginning of the new Birmingham, by removing the eyesore of this old custard factory. And while the Minister gets his plunging hand ready, I'd like to thank Mrs Pershore for baking this exquisite apple pie. And can I remind you that you won't have to forgo your custard – it will be made in a new purpose-built, automated plant, which will be opening at Dawley New Town next year.'

The Minister: 'Thank you Mr Bemeletti, for the invitation. This government is committed to progress, and measurable progress at that, and today we progress on the issue of custard manufacture. *Today is a big day, and I'd like to announce that when we remove this dirty old Victorian factory using dynamite, this government will have been responsible for blowing up a thousand buildings since the start of office, a quite exemplary number I think you'll all agree. Britain today is about moving. Moving forwards. Moving upwards. Moving things out of the way, so we can move other things… into the… way. And that's just what Birmingham is doing under the exemplary tutelage of Mr Remejetti here. Now… I'd like you to all move forwards with us, move forwards as a Britain united, move forwards as a Midlands united, and move forwards to a better era – with better custard. And I for one am going to enjoy getting my chops around Mrs Pershore's sweet pie very much.'*

[Tittering from guests and a gentle volley of applause. The Minister smiles and pauses with his hands on the plunger while the photographer from the Evening Brummie newspaper captures the moment for posterity. Smiling, the Minister pushes down on the plunger and picks up his bowl of pie. After a delay of about three seconds, the factory explodes in spectacular style; it sounds like a bomb has gone off. The explosion takes everyone by surprise. Benedetti looks shocked. Some women let out screams. People look at each other to check everything's alright. The ground begins to vibrate and a cloud of dust starts to coat the scene.]

Benedetti: *'What the blazes…?'*
    Rocaster: *'I think that was a bit too much dynamite, Mr Benedetti. Just a little on the high side perhaps.'*

[The sky turns faded-citrus pale as a storm of gloopy custard suddenly begins to pelt down.]

Benedetti: 'Rocaster, what the hell is that yellow…? Those imbeciles!'

Rocaster: 'Er… That's custard, Mr Benedetti.'

[Rocaster holds out his right index finger. A yellow dollop lands on the finger. He sticks his finger in his mouth and sucks the yellow gloop down. His face remains expressionless.]

Rocaster: 'Definitely custard.'

[The custard begins to fall with vigour now on the assembled guests, covering heads, bodies and clothes in lemon-coloured gunk. A massive custard missile hits Benedetti so hard he falls to the floor. Women scream; men curse. Mrs Pershore is visibly on the verge of tears. The Minister looks aghast, but soon we can't see his face as his head becomes enveloped in a giant globule of yellow dessert. The custard slides down his face and falls into the bowl of apple pie he is holding daintily at chest level. The Minister scoops up a spoonful, puts it into his mouth and swallows. Benedetti scrambles up to his feet but is now coated from head to toe in yellow sauce.]

Benedetti: 'SEDDDDDDDDDON.'

[Crash-zoom on Seddon, who's laughing hysterically and wiping tears away from his eyes.]

Seddon: 'Bostin!'

*

2008

I stood in the bar and watched him sitting in silence; he was oblivious to anything. He just stared through the window at the world outside our strange cocoon. He seemed to be entranced by a particular spot on the ground a few feet away from the Mids TV Tower. Why was he looking at this spot, this piece of plaza? Did it mean something to him? I noticed how pale his complexion was today.

Baxter was a writer who came via academia, came via books, came up a path paved with knowledge. He deigned to do telly, but of course he hated it; he hated the people watching all the more. He hated the audience, hated Brummies, hated people who liked any of the shows Bob and I made. He played with the viewers; he wrote private jokes everywhere. In his defence he burned with a ferocity of spirit I couldn't match, a hot fiery envelope of flesh surrounding a brain which begged for attention. He was an arch modernist who took risks and provoked, believed in the future, believed in the cerebral, made programmes that didn't make compromises. Belinda liked his programmes. I sometimes think she liked him. What future was there left, though? High-minded discourse in mass media had been binned. Belinda said things like that. She was right. We'd have to travel backwards to the past to see any kind of future, any kind of... something clever on Mids TV.

Baxter became the leading artistic light of the Midlands, presenting many of the cultural documentaries that Mids TV made. And like me, his fame never spread down the M1 to London and thence around the UK, and thus you probably won't have heard of him.

Baxter's flame did not burn for long. Although he could still muster the spirit and bravado to present on TV, to say things

239

with meaning and conviction, to speak like an actor should (even though he was a writer, an academic), he was a writer long past his days of being able to write anything worthwhile himself. Bob reckoned it was the drugs – they'd fucked him, he'd fucked himself. I'd have to write for him now.

Unseen, I left him to it and walked upstairs to the production office. Not a single person was in, not even Bob or Kate. I walked into Bob's office. There was a giant *Welcome To The Masshouse* poster on the far wall. It was obviously pinched from a bus shelter. The poster was abstracted and very colourful, and at the bottom a line of text read, *Coming to Mids TV, every Friday at 10:30 p.m., this autumn.*

On Bob's desk there was a hardback copy of Baxter's debut novel, *Going Round And Round And Round In Circles Until You Die.* It was obviously a crutch for Baxter to have this document near him constantly, a reminder that he was capable of something – a concrete reminder of that fact. His skin was thin. Why was it in Bob's office though? Maybe Baxter had brought it in to use as a weapon during one of their regular 'brainstorming' sessions. I strained to lift the tome, flopping it down on my lap and opening it at the beginning.

Awake. Become. Come. Defenestrate. End. Fenestrate. Gouge. Hurt. I. Jay. Kinetogenic. Litmus. Meander. Northwards. Or. Perish. Query. Register. Sate. Tumble. Uniformed. Veranda. Wayzgoose. Xenodochium. Yttriferous. Zenzizenzizenzic.

I play literary tricks. On my readers. On my readers' eyes. On my readers' T's.

I.

Play.

Tri.cks

I'm talking to you! I'm fucking talking to you! I'M FUCKING

TALKING TO YOU. I am a writer, riter, righter; esconced on top of bus, on bus bus bus. Daily I write words in the fish n chip stink of this top deck, in the beer stink of this top deck, in the fags sink of this top deck. I am causing all the stinks, for I am eating pie n chips, eating beer, eating fags. I am an unhappy writer stuck up here and the only way to escape is to use my jaculiferous words as weapons. It's a case of writing as vaccimulgence. One day these words will be my cure, they will cause decrudescence of the mind and body.

For now, round and round and round me goes on this Godforsaken bus – this diesel-powered ekka – with people poking questions in me ears and poking their looks in me eyes. And you, you're the worst. You prurient bastard, thinking like that as you read these pages, thinking about me me me.

But really, what can literature…

It goes on in this vein for rather a long time.

The book was conceived and written in the suburbs of Birmingham while Baxter was recovering from the emotional trauma of the end of a romantic relationship. A secondary-school English teacher from Bradford, a woman he'd first met at uni, had cheated on him with a crisp-factory foreman from her hometown, and Baxter had discovered the betrayal. He retreated to the number 11 bus, circumnavigating Birmingham on a daily basis, chain-smoking and imbibing Birmingham Bitter from a can on the top deck, writing in hefty notebooks. His own loneliness gave him the fuel he needed, and the *flânerie* gave his writing the fire. His novel was an artefact of complete discontent, of powerful dislocation, of profound loss. The novel's protagonist, 'The Narrator', was, of course, a disconsolate writer who was travelling Birmingham's suburbs by bus. And as you've seen, he was addicted to addressing the reader at every possible opportunity. Can you work out why he'd do this? You, yes, you. What do you reckon? Because to me it seems like a cheap device. And another thing – why would Baxter set a novel in Birmingham? Ask yourself that. This must have been one reason why he hasn't skipped town to a literary life in London. I can't imagine the sales figures for this tome were exactly stellar. I had to set TV shows in Brum, write about Brum – because that's what regional TV is. It's close to home. But with a bloody book, you could set it anywhere. Why Brum? For one thing, you're immediately destroying any potential American market, as they think there's only one Birmingham – it's theirs and it isn't in the middle of the English Midlands, it's in the middle of the American South.

The outline of (English) Brum on a map is the shape of an Abominable Snowman creeping from left to right. Its head is Sutton Coldfield (the posh bit), its heart, of course, the city centre. And then there's all this body: all these arms and legs dangling down, all this flappy skin, all these southern suburbs, all these dual carriageways and all these cul-de-sacs, all these roundabouts and all these supermarkets. Trees fight with factories, railway yards scrap with canals, gardens have a punch up with motorway flyovers, and pubs play fisticuffs with gyratory junctions and DIY-outlet big boxes. No wonder Baxter lost his marbles going round on that bus all day every day.

TEN BRUTALIST BUILDINGS

By Belinda Schneider

Chapter Nine

Nowheresville, built by nobodies

Brutalist buildings, and especially brutalist mega-villages with multiple levels and multiple uses, are enigmatic beasts. Many of them were never written about by the architecture press in the 1960s and '70s; many were never visited by people from capital cities. You stumble on a building here or a planned development there and you wonder what it's about. You wonder who designed it – half the time you can't find that out. You wonder what people thought of it when it opened – maybe a local paper would have asked them; mostly it wouldn't have. There are some famous buildings and some famous architects, but not very many. Brutalism is really a story of nobodies building in nowheresville. Small cities around the world, provincial architects just doing a job or two. The architects who did New Street Station signal box in Birmingham are no superstars. They just plodded away. These were buildings by architects who weren't famous, in cities that weren't glamorous. But those architects believed in something, and they believed in themselves – in their own ability to construct something exciting and utopian. But it was always an anonymous utopia. A painter's paintings have a nametag next to them and a signature on them; a book has the writer's name on the cover. Ninety-nine-point-nine per cent of buildings have no nameplate; no one knows or cares who built them. Our brutalist buildings – the ones I (and I suspect you, if you're reading this) love – are only recognisable to a few people who know what they're looking at. Even

243

worse, sometimes the real designer of the building is erased from history completely and the boss takes the credit. I draw your attention here to the silver plaque on the side of Eros House. The bloody boss has taken the credit there – if you want to know the name of the real genius who designed it, well, it's not on that plaque. I'll happily tell you who it is after class. That's architecture. The reason I'm not banging on about the superstar starchitects of the 1960s and '70s (or even the ones with not-so-starring roles) in this book is that, to me, it seems like they want to be enigmatic; they want their buildings to be as well. That it's sort of ordained to have this mystery surrounding buildings and who authored them.

At least Eros House is still there. A present-day architect talked to me recently about designing a replacement for one of the many brutalist buildings we've decided to tear down. He said he liked what was being demolished, and he liked brutalism. He seemed sheepish. He guffed out the right buzzwords but didn't believe in himself or in his work or in the world that we live in today. He was embarrassed. His designs were appalling. I think he knew it.

Still no one in the production office. Mids TV was becoming a ghost town. I went back to look at the *Welcome To The Masshouse* poster. There I was, about two inches tall, in the background. Dressed in stereotypical Victorian prison uniform – black and white stripes, ball and chain attached to my leg. My acting career was very short-lived. I wrote a sketch for *Welcome To The Masshouse*, the premise of which was that a poor writer had come up with an idea – to get locked up and sent to prison as the perfect fillip to finish a book. The idea had come from watching a kid's cartoon at Christmas where the main character – some kind of anthropomorphised mammal – was too poor to afford any Christmas luxuries, and too cold to bear the whole frosty festive farrago. So he'd deliberately committed a crime so the police would lock him away somewhere warm where the grub was free.

In the *Welcome To The Masshouse* version I was made up to look like I was starving and diseased. I slashed the tyres on a panda car (in front of a policeman) so I would be sent to jail. I then explained, from my prison cell, that it was indeed the perfect place to write. You didn't have to pay for rent, you didn't have to pay for food, and there were few outside distractions, like, well – anything at all apart from lifting weights. All great for the novel. The screws even helped out with a touch of on-the-fly lit crit. I was terrible in the sketch: hammy and sweaty and stiff. Bob and I joked about it, but he was quite firm that I'd be behind the camera from then on. One acting career: over. Cut. I was happy – who wants to be a performer?

It sometimes struck me when I was listening to other people read out my lines that they weren't funny at all. Had they ever been? When I had an idea and it made me chuckle it felt good, fresh. But after I'd written, edited, read that idea, heard other people speaking it over and over again – well, then it hardly ever seemed funny at all. Was I even a comedy writer? Had I ever been? Bob had me penning scripts for any old shit that Mids was producing. Light entertainment, quizzes, documentaries. Funniness, such as you have it, drains away with age too. You get less funny as you age. It just vanishes with time. But then what was the value in funniness? Was something funny less valuable than something serious? Bel liked it when I wrote things that attacked people in power, but she didn't like it when I took the piss out of things that were rather closer to her heart. She believed in sincerity of purpose and result. Well, that made sense. Some of the 'serious' stuff I wrote was shite because I tossed it off, didn't put any effort in. Knew that I had to pen a thousand words by the end of the evening and just typed away frantically like a newspaper journalist on deadline. Some of it, like *Hail To The Brummies*, was carefully considered and sincere and written with affection. Audiences could tell, couldn't they?

It was good to do different jobs, to write different things. You need to move on in life. Bob could have been a comic, an actor and a performer forever. But he moved on. He did different things. I don't think that becoming a game show presenter was really the natural career choice for him – being pissed on and barked at. And that was just the human competitors on *I Love My Dog!* But it paid the bills and kept him busy. I think it's good that he's behind the camera now, pulling the levers, giving the directions, producing, running the show. No one would have believed that he'd end up as programme director and ultimately, de facto, the most senior member of the team in Birmingham, but then no one would have thought that Mids, that broadcasting behemoth, would have ended up with a team so decimated that a pisshead like Bob would emerge as the only passable candidate to lead this ragtag bunch from the pub to the studio and back again.

I knew I had to do different things; I was happy I'd written different kinds of TV programmes. But that's only one kind of writing. Could I ever break out of this self-imposed creative ghetto? Did I even want to? Would anyone in the Midlands miss my shit jokes, or would they be so distracted by the adverts that they wouldn't even notice? I fashioned a week's worth of *Evening Brummies* into a pillow and went to the sofa in the corner for a lie-down. It was hot in the office. Stuffy. I…

This is a dream:

Druids Heath. I'd recognise it anywhere. (There have been one too many instances of me waking up here. It sounds improbable, I know, but the estate is right on the very edge of the city, and if you fall asleep on the number 50 bus to Moseley and, well, go past Moseley, this is where you end up. And it's not, alas, somewhere you would particularly want to end up at 2 a.m. It's not 2 a.m. now though; it's more like 2 p.m.)

Two men are walking over. One in a tweed suit, and one in trousers and a shirt. The tweed suit speaks first.

'I say, you're here as well, Donald.'

'I don't know if he recognises you, Mr Benedetti.'

'Of course he does.'

'Rocaster and Benedetti. What are you two doing here?'

'We've been thinking about madness, Donald,' said Rocaster, rolling his shirt sleeves up. It was warm. Benedetti pulled out a pipe and began stuffing it. 'Madness. Lot of it here in Brum.'

'I never was sure about that pipe,' I said. 'Too much of an affectation, I reckon.'

Rocaster said, 'I agree.'

Benedetti looked stung. 'Hand me a lighter.' Rocaster did.

Benedetti puffed and spoke. 'Walk with us, Donald.'

Sunlight refracted, a surreal haze, a toasty glow, a starling staring. I looked at the bird. It opened its beak and chirruped, 'Hi there!'

Benedetti, Rocaster and muggins set off across the field, blistering yellow with buttercups. The starling fluttered behind us. Then we crossed into one white with daisies; next, one painted pea green with grass. No crops grew here – the heath was badly drained.

'I'm sure you know Druids Heath,' said Rocaster. I could make out the serpentine line of the edge of the houses and flats, where they merged into the bucolic beauty of the countryside. The estate boundary ran hard up against the city council's boundary, a wonky wall of development at the very edge of the city limits, the very arse of Birmingham.

'What is sanity?' Benedetti turned to me. 'Well? What is it? A day in the country probably, some fishing or sailing perhaps, a picnic, a beach, oaks and lakes, and spits and cliffs...'

'...a pub lunch, a cricket match, a burn up on the A34!' offered Rocaster.

'And where does madness come from? Madness comes from an urban environment you have to tame. I pull the lead tight...' Benedetti made an aggressive yanking gesture as if tugging a wayward setter.

'And I send the city in the right direction,' added Rocaster.

Benedetti swept his hand towards the fourteen slate-grey tower blocks rising from the heathside. 'I'm very proud of planning estates like these, of changing good old Brummagem for the better. However, the point can't be ignored – seeing as we're here to speak frankly to you, Donald, rather than being on the telly – that we are driving people... crackers. I certainly never meant to. But all you have to do is look at the evidence. Look at this block up here – a young mother hurled self and babe in arms to a double death. Several more the same at Castle Bromwich, Chelmsley Wood, Newtown. Not what I expected. Not what I expected at all. But maybe I should have expected it. Madness all over the city, suicides all over the city. High buildings, towers, car parks – being used as... killing platforms. Yes... maybe I should have expected it. I'm only human though.'

'Ah, you're not really you. I created you. You're played by an actor.'

'I'm not played by an actor now, Donald; at this point I'm speaking as myself. No one's written my lines for me. You've not written these lines for me to speak them, have you?'

'Someone's written your lines. You can't just speak by yourself.'

Benedetti's eyes bulged. 'Well... now, maybe you have a point there. Someone probably *has* written my lines. A writer who's outside of this little *tête-à-tête*. And that same writer has probably written your lines as well, Donald. You think you're speaking your own lines, but you're simply not. Think about it. How could you be? How could any of us be? Who writes you, Donald – who writes *your* part?'

'No one is controlling me.'

'Everyone's controlled in some way, Donald. I'm afraid to have to tell you that you're just a character in... I'd say, a novel.'

I scoffed. 'Not me! No novel here, this is real.'

'And everyone in the city, for instance, is a character in... what's essentially *my* novel, in my plan, in my city. In my city plan.'

'In your fictional city and your fictional plan, because you're not real. Unlike me.'

'Come, come. Fictional maybe, but this scene is real enough to you now.'

Benedetti pinched my arm.

'Ow!'

'Forget the hand of the writer controlling you for a minute, forget that young chap trying to write his novel, forget that chap sat at home in his cold room bashing out words on his typewriter, forget that elaborate double reality we exist in. My point, if you'll let me get it out, is that I've planned everything and perhaps I can see now that I've over-planned everything. Perhaps I've created a world where people behave strangely because they're... becoming atomised.'

'I don't believe it. We're creating... a brave new world.'

Rocaster seemed hurt. 'All these homes for people. The very best… for everyone. This is the welfare state, right here.'

Benedetti made like a batsman at the crease, sweeping Rocaster's reasoning behind for a boundary. 'Our cricket fan doesn't believe it. But I'll say he's wrong. Grids of streets, mass clearances, underpasses, remapping, rethinking, rebuilding, pouring, bricking up, bricking in, grassing over, concreting over, levels and piazzas, stairwells and towers, floors gone wrong, walls that aren't straight, flimsy pieces of a strange whole. I wonder sometimes. I really wonder. Of course, these are very personal concerns. I feel the city squeezing in on me. I think I hate the city, Donald. I need the country. The city is sick, a sick child. I operate on it, but it's so sick. I think the city has done something to me. I don't know. Do you know? Do you feel this? I saw you trying to kill yourself, Donald. I saw you try to jump off the Mids TV Tower and then the BT Tower. You wanted to die. You must be a victim too?'

'I have had moments of… well, let's say, feeling detached.'

'I knew you must have. Rocaster has too, haven't you, Rocaster? Remember when I found you up that crane? In your underpants?'

'I remember, Mr Benedetti. That was most embarrassing.'

I laughed.

'Something funny, Donald?'

'Well, I wrote that. I remember that episode of *Big Plans*. Maybe it *was* funny, after all. I've been too hard on myself.'

'Now you come to mention it, I remember that episode too. That was the one when I ended up having a Jimmy Riddle on those blasted builders, wasn't it? Good work, Donald; that was a well written slice of slapstick.' Benedetti turned and stared at me. 'But Donald, I think you need to really get your satirical juices going now. I think you need to show what a madhouse we've built. I think we need to do something about it. Something big.'

'One minute,' I said. I spied a red hoarding above a plate-glass window and a door – it said *Chu Chinese*. The rest of the shops in the row seemed empty or closed.

'What are you up to?' huffed Benedetti.

'I need to do something.' I walked over to the Chinese restaurant and pushed the door. I turned round as I entered to see Benedetti and Rocaster bundling in after me, and I sighed.

'Pork chow mein for me, please!' said Rocaster. 'And some special fried rice.'

'Nothing for me,' sneered Benedetti.

The old woman serving at the counter looked familiar.

'Mrs Chu. I didn't know you had a place here as well. I thought it was just in Snow Hill Station?'

'Yes, we have two outlets.'

'I wanted to ask you... about the blonde woman. From my dreams.'

'I know. You find her in Berlin.' Mrs Chu paused for a second then ducked back into the kitchen.

'Thanks, Mrs Chu.' I was glad to have this titbit. I turned to the other two, who were eyeing up the paper lanterns hanging from the ceiling. 'We're done now, thanks.'

Rocaster looked crestfallen. 'I thought we were getting some food? I'll just buy a couple of lagers then.' Rocaster took some beers from the fridge and left a crisp note on the counter.

We exited the shop and the three of us strode across a bleak square, towards one of the tower blocks. The two of them seemed to be shepherding me towards this particular building. It leered at me.

'Let's go inside,' said Rocaster.

'I agree,' said Benedetti.

I wasn't convinced. We entered one of the tower blocks and waited for a lift.

'System built,' said Rocaster, smashing his arm against a wall. His elbow went clean into the plasterboard and he had to yank it out. 'Pile of shit really. Poured-on-site concrete gets such a bad name from this kind of tat. Now that was really the stuff. It's so bloody solid. How a building should be. Jowly, fisty. What was it they started calling *those* kinds of buildings? Brutalist. Wonderful.'

'But this is cheap rubbish, isn't it?' agreed Benedetti. 'We had to get the maximum number of homes built. Tough choices.'

The lift pinged as it reached the ground floor. We squeezed into the silver sarcophagus. It smelled acrid and sweaty. The lift jolted and rose slowly. No one spoke. Benedetti removed his pipe and tobacco from his trouser pocket and commenced tamping.

The lift doors opened at the top floor and we walked up a flight of fire escape steps to the roof. There was no wind, just sun and a view of meadows, houses and tower blocks spread in front of me. 'Do you want to jump off this building and kill yourself, Donald?' said Benedetti. 'Your chance to be with your wife. I hear she liked our programme. She was a *Big Plans* fan, wasn't she? Seem to remember meeting her once. At a pub.'

'She was.'

'And then the buggers upstairs at your television station had to axe us. I wasn't enamoured by that carry-on, let me tell you.'

'What can you do?'

'They're swine. The bosses of Mids TV don't know their arses from their elbows. How dare they cancel us? That Mackenzie – absolute rotter. Mids TV is a rotters' club.'

Rocaster produced a beer from a pocket. 'Dutch courage?'

I shook my head. I took a walk to the edge of the concrete cliff and peered over. My stomach felt weak; my legs jellied up under me. It didn't look at all appealing. Not like before. I didn't want to die anymore.

'Donald, old chap…'

I turned round. Rocaster swigged the beer. Benedetti advanced towards me, pipe dangling from the left side of his closed mouth. The next second was a blur. I felt his hands shove me in the chest. I fell backwards off the edge of the building and began plummeting to the ground. I woke at the split second that I pancaked into the…

Still no one in the office when I woke up. I dragged myself up from the sofa, logged in to my computer, my eyes bleary and crusty. Emails ordinarily leave me cold. And for the past few months I've scarcely been bothered with the small talk and the tiny acts of grace that glue us together. But today was different. Today there was an email at the top of my inbox from Charlie Sullivan.

FROM: Charlie Sullivan
TO: Donald

Hi Don

Hope you don't mind me getting in touch again.

I heard on the grapevine yesterday about Belinda. I'm so sorry. It's awful. I also heard yesterday about the programme you guys are making in her memory. I think it sounds just perfect. We'd be happy to let you have any songs for it, or even write a new one – if you needed any. I know how much 'Elizabeth Anderson' meant to Bel, so if you want it it's yours, of course.

I also had this thought about writing a song about the Central Library in Brum. I wondered what the place might sound like, how you could bring it alive in music. Well, it's just an idea! Tell me what you reckon, pal?

We're going to be on tour in the UK. I'll be back from LA for a week if you fancy a pint in the Bride of Bescot? Save me from drinking all that piss-weak beer they have out here. Let me know when's good, Don.

Cheers mate
Charlie

31

2001

'What time are they on?'

'Nine.'

'I'm so excited!'

'Me too.'

'And it's here, in this building. In Priory Square. This might be the best concert of my life.'

'You sound like a teenage girl.'

'That's exactly how I feel. I can't believe you managed to get us backstage passes too.'

'I try.'

'Was it Bob?'

'It was Bob. He knows everyone in Birmingham. He got friendly with Charlie when they did the songs on *Hail To The Brummies*. It's funny; even though I remember the songs being amazing, I don't remember talking to the band very much when we were working on that. I think I was too caught up in writing that script.'

'It was good. Your best.' Bel hugged me tight. 'I cried.'

'I love to make you cry. It's a change from making you laugh. Something rare.'

'Maybe we could become friends with The Rationalists now too? Like Bob. Is he here?'

'He is. Somewhere. We'll meet up with him later. He's just got a mobile phone. Now we can always find him, wherever the hell he's disappeared off to. In theory.'

'But you haven't got a mobile yet?'

'No, maybe I should. I could call you all the time.'

'Wow! A man with a car AND a mobile phone. That would be something.'

Bel sipped her gin and tonic and seemed lost in thought. The room was like an oven; the sweat and breath and pheromones of the crowd created an artificial rainforest of damp, Brazilian heat. The chittering of a thousand people pecked at my ears. The crowd was a swollen mass, a lump of love, a group of people who all felt and thought the same thing. It was reassuring to be part of a clan, to be here to share an experience. The thought of hearing the songs I loved, played loudly, here, in person, made my spine tingle. I'm sure the same was true of everyone. I looked up at the black stage. What would it feel like to stand up there, in this venue, in front of all these people, them listening to your music?

'Why do we love music so fucking much?' I said in Bel's ear.

She snickered like a teenager. 'Music takes you to a place immediately; it's an instant hit. You hear that song and it's... bang, like a drug. I sometimes wondered when I was younger why people didn't give a shit about architecture, even about art. But they all loved music. Everyone loves music. It's because music has that instant power. You don't need to think about it or study it. A song is three minutes and it gets you. Under your skin. In your heart. And you experience it in this communal way, even if you're home alone, listening to a record;

you know there are other people around the world doing the same thing. But when you hear it live – a band or a DJ, right up there – it's magical. Art and architecture and literature take longer to fire up your synapses, but music is a rocket.'

'You're right. But my God, it can make you sad too, can't it? It can take you back in time.'

'My little Donald! What music makes you sad? What makes you think of all those girls you lusted after who wouldn't kiss you? Is it The Rationalists? I bet it is. All those girls at university… no handjobs for poor Donald.'

I shook my head in mock annoyance. She continued, 'You're right though. Wow, some songs… it's like you're being murdered slowly and gently, isn't it? You hear those chords and, that's it, you're in that sad place too.'

A snippet of electronic music began, like the sound of computers larking around together in a playground. The Rationalists' intro track. Images started to bubble on a screen behind the stage. Views of Birmingham, projected, sepia, nostalgic. Modern buildings. Roundabouts. Squares. Landmarks. Places we all knew intimately. Places where we'd all got pissed and some of us had kissed others of us. Brummies United. The crowd started to cheer wildly. We all cheered. Even me.

'I'm excited!' I could feel Bel's tongue tickling my ear.

'Me too.'

She gripped my arm very tightly and began to jump up and down on the spot.

32

2008

Catford. A bit of a shithole to be honest, but Belinda fell in love with some of the buildings round here. Eros House was her favourite, and on that point I was, perhaps, finally beginning to see what she had appreciated. It was an incredible hulk, even more domineering than I remembered – but strangely handsome. I'd kissed Bel here, in the rain, in the smog, in the fading dusk, among the traffic fumes, among the fag fumes, between tossing ten-pence pieces to beggars; a little perplexed as always about 'why' and 'where', but always ready to be led by her, to respond to her desires. After this, she'd begged me to take her up to the Catford Centre car park, and on the roof we found a corner and we had sex and then drank cider from cans. Someone was living one floor down, between a car and a rubbish skip. I wondered if it would be me one day. These odd spaces that are the preserve of people with no place felt like home. The guy residing in this car park had his books to keep him company. There were paperbacks everywhere. Not like Brum's subway-dwellers. The molemen of Paradise and Masshouse Circuses weren't such big readers.

The Catford Centre today was as maze-like as I remembered it. I'd arranged to meet Kate here. She'd texted me something cryptic earlier, alluding to a party. We'd got the train down to London together and checked in at the same cheap hotel in Holborn called the Gibberd, which must have felt rather fancy when it opened in the 1960s but was badly in need of redecoration today. I'd gone for a lie-down in my fusty room, and Kate had come down here to sort some stuff out for the shoot tomorrow. She reckoned she'd found some useful contacts – artists. There was a party and we were meeting them there.

The Catford Centre seemed grotty when Belinda had dragged me here. The grit appealed to me, the dream to her. These superstructures were like castles really – multiple levels, brooding, impenetrable, off-putting, bolshy, defensive, confusing. Me and Kate found a way up through some kind of staircase. An insistent thudding got louder as we climbed; it echoed around the bare concrete stairwell. We climbed up through the car park. That homeless guy was nowhere to be seen (had he ever existed?) and instead on floors five and six there were sculptures made from plastic, daubed in various primary colours, each one an abstracted shape it was hard to instantly comprehend. Video art was projected onto some of the walls. We reached the roof. A rave. Some kind of wooden pavilion had gone up, the type that were – apparently – colonising these now cool parts of London's crumbling concrete skyline. There was a bar, some tables and chairs scattered under an awning, some toilets and barbecues. Hundreds of people milled around, some dancing. Pairs of friends were bent over the tables in hushed reflection, credit cards waving around. Others huddled in groups, one person holding their palm out, others inserting dirty fingers first into a plastic bag in the middle of the palm and then into a mouth. Bottles of beer were clinked; the delicious waft of singed tobacco thrust up my nostrils.

Kate unwrapped a small square of paper and poked a finger towards a pile of greasy, grey crystals. She gave the paper a fingerprint, as if she was arresting herself. She drew the stimulant-loaded finger upwards.

'Open wide.'

I shook my head and made my most unimpressed face but ultimately did as instructed, and she used her little finger to spoon a hit of the MDMA onto my tongue. The acrid tang was foul, the chemical taste of stimulants crushed by sweaty feet in Holland. How could something which prompted elation taste so bitter?

'I need a beer,' I coughed. Kate produced one from thin air and I drank.

'This is a rare treat these days,' I said.

Kate raised an eyebrow. 'Belinda would have fucking loved this.' She lit a cigarette. 'Kids using brutalist buildings, people loving the city, being at one with it.'

'People getting smashed.'

Kate laughed. An hour later I was.

Me and Kate danced like idiots, me flailing around, her doing a sort of flamenco routine which erred more on the side of sweet than sexy. We found the artists Kate had been in contact with – they were friendly and we chatted easily. I offered to buy some drinks. Their eyes lit up. Kate shooed me away. While I stood waiting at the bar for the tepid bottles of lager to be dispensed, I heard a voice in my left ear say the word 'Donald'. This was unexpected.

'Millie!' I said with far too much enthusiasm. 'Wow... I... Fancy seeing you here!'

'I could say the same thing. How are you?' She regarded my pupils closely, squinting. 'How fucked are you?'

'Very?' I offered.

'Me too.' Her teeth were so white and perfect.

About an hour later, I was sitting on a wall on the top deck of a car park snogging a girl – well, a *woman* – I hadn't seen since 1984. My fantasy woman of 1984. And 1983. And 1982. The problem was, though, that as right as they were, Millie's lips and tongue and neck were wrong. They weren't Bel's. I had learned Bel like you learn English. I was proficient in her, an expert on her. This was a new language that I didn't understand, and one that felt wrong. I was uncertain. Despite me explaining everything to Millie about Bel and about the film, she didn't hesitate. It seemed right enough to her. Which is funny because it's an idea she would never have dreamed of back when we were both students. As we mixed saliva and I stroked Millie's hair, I suddenly felt a surge of guilt for not being here with Bel, for cheating on her in one of her favourite places. I broke off.

'That was nice,' purred Millie, fixing her hair and licking her lips. 'Feeling alright?'

'I feel bad. This is... I mean... maybe it's too soon? It is too soon.'

'Don't beat yourself up, Donald. You're not doing anything wrong.' Millie ran her hand along my leg but it only made me feel more empty and detached. I looked over towards Eros House, which blinked at me in the sooty sky.

'Eros.'

'What?'

'Nothing. Let's have a little walk.' We strolled over to the other end of the parking deck, then round a corner, where it was almost deserted and the music was less thundering.

Millie said, 'Want to come back to mine?'

I swallowed and she giggled. It's strange when something

that you thought you wanted turns out not to be what you wanted at all. Nevertheless...

I drank some beer. 'I do... but I'm not sure if...' I hesitated.

'Oh God, ignore me. I'm just being silly. But, look, let's go back to mine anyway and just... see? I'm tired. These people are young.'

'They are.' But were they? Half of the people here looked almost my age. People were partying well into middle age these days, if not further. 'But look,' I said, 'we can't go without Kate. We're a team. Let's get her.'

I found Kate but I needn't have worried. Her lips were locked around the mouth of one of the artists, who was maybe twenty years younger than her. I shouted the plan into her ear: that we would go back to Millie's for a coffee and some weed perhaps. Kate replied with this line: 'Fuck off and get yourself laid.' I stepped back, and she stuck two fingers up towards me as she continued kissing the artist, as his floppy hair was repeatedly molested by Kate's nicotine-stained fingers.

In the taxi back to Millie's flat all I could think about was what had gone before. When you're young each new experience is untainted and innocent. But when you age, you're forever going over old ground; joy seeps out of experience. It's always a retread. It never works as well. I was in a crappy black people carrier listening to deadening 1980s soft rock as we seemed to pass by multiple high-security prisons, multiple supermarkets, multiple fast-food drive-thrus, looking at a woman I was going to have sex with who wasn't my wife. But I didn't want to depress Millie by vocalising these thoughts.

'Don't you care about being spotted?' I wondered aloud instead.

'Not a jot.' Millie turned and looked at me. 'Do you know why? The people we were up there with tonight – do you think any of them watch TV anymore? The times I get recognised are in a furniture shop, or at the doctor's. We're done, Donald. No one cares about TV anymore. In ten years it'll all be over completely. Then we'll just have the Internet instead. Videos. People filming themselves.'

This is a dream:
Purple and black mist is swirling everywhere. People are turning into buildings and buildings are turning into people. I have no idea who or what I am. It's fucking frightening.

Lunchtime. I woke up with a start, wondering where I was. Sweating. There was a woman next to me, but it wasn't Belinda. I squashed my face into my palms, closed my eyes, looked again. It still wasn't Belinda. Why couldn't it be her? I got up, stretched and coughed. My mouth felt covered in a nondescript fuzz; my brain ached. I felt helpless and lonely – the telltale after-effects of MDMA consumption. I stood, pulled the curtains apart, and was taken aback by the view from the window. Dozens of tower blocks in serried ranks; courts and walkways; and all of it finished in various shades of grey. The buildings sat beneath a huge and brooding sky. The land was flat and strange. I saw plumes of smoke in the distance.

Millie yawned and stretched. I turned. She sat up in bed; the duvet fell beneath her breasts and I swallowed like a bashful schoolboy. 'Like the view?' I wasn't sure which she meant.

'It's austere. Where are we?'

'Thamesmead, of course.'

'Thamesmead? Belinda loved Thamesmead. She would have lived here. But I'm... I'm sorry Millie, I just don't under—'

'You don't understand why I live here? Why not? It's beautiful in its own crazy way.'

'Do you like the architecture?'

264

'I don't really know much about architecture, but I like the rigour of it I guess, the straight lines and the purpose.'

'I always seem to find myself in places like this.'

'Do you now?'

I hummed. 'Why did you move here? I pictured you more in…'

'Wandsworth? Kentish Town? Clapham? Perhaps. I've lived all over London. It's all so predictable. This is not a predictable place. If I'm entirely honest, it was an incredible fucking bargain too. After my marriage broke up I needed somewhere quite cheap that I could move to very soon.'

'So you came here. Wow. If only Bel could see. It's not what I expected at all.'

'It's good to do the unexpected… sometimes. We all conform so much. We're all so bland. What about being unpredictable? Remember uni? I remember you agreeing with me when I said in that seminar that my problem with fiction, well, the shitty fiction we studied – we *had* to study – was that it was just all so predictable.'

'I think I agreed because I wanted to sleep with you.'

'And now you have! I hope it was worth the wait. But my point remains: why conform? Why do writers conform? I like that you rejected all that London bullshit, all those publishers and all that national exposure, all those lunches and all those awards and national TV… and Hollywood. I like that you said "Bugger that." You chose to stay in Birmingham and write things that were important to you and make things that people loved to watch. It's fantastic. I just can't face anything to do with books anymore, to be honest.'

I shrugged. 'I don't see it in exactly those terms…'

'You should. That's what happened.'

I winced a little and decided to change the subject. 'So how did you become a weather forecaster?' I asked, wondering why I'd never asked this before.

'Well, you know I was a journalist to start with, and then a TV reporter. But it's all so blimming boring; the stories are all the same. It's pathetic. I ended up doing the weather and they liked me, and I liked it, and now I do it for the whole country. And because I'm such a contrary bitch I rather enjoyed the idea of doing something people wouldn't expect, something unpredictable. And now, I turn up, do a few computer models, write a little script and stand in front of a screen, pointing at a map. It's money for old rope. The rest of my time is mine. I like to watch films. Do you watch films, Don?'

'Often.' I stared out of the window, focussing on a mother guiding a double pushchair across a dual carriageway.

'Do you still fancy me, Don?'

I lied. I had to. 'Of course.'

'Why don't you come back over here then?'

An hour later, Millie made me a runny boiled egg, toast and a cup of tea. And after that I awkwardly bid her goodbye and promised to be in touch again soon. Millie stood on the balcony waving down to me in her dressing gown, the white billowing fabric juxtaposed with the monumental greyness of the huge slab block she lived halfway up. She'd given me directions to the train station at Abbey Wood, but I was immediately flummoxed by Thamesmead.

This had been a favourite of Bel's, though of all the places she'd taken me this was perhaps the one that I found hardest to get on with. In parts it was as serene as those Barbican water gardens. Along the lakeside – that's where it felt bucolic – the mix of nature and concrete was really pleasing. I imagined living happily here. Millie certainly seemed happy in her way. But south of the main road, Yarnton Way, things took on a more disturbing tone.

I climbed up onto a superstructure that ran the whole length of the road. I think it was the same road I'd seen the mother and the pushchair struggling to deal with. I went through a gap into the interior courtyard of the superstructure, but perhaps 'courtyard' is not the right word. It was a complex that stretched in all directions, as far as the eye could see. Great heaving stair towers jostled with stubby blocks of flats. Diagonal walkways ran up and down, connecting the levels, giving it a disorienting feeling. Some of the high-level walkways ran into black holes and some were blocked off with security doors. Down at the lowest level, light didn't penetrate, and the whole thing looked murky and sinister. I felt claustrophobic, trapped. The comedown from the MDMA was intensifying at the worst possible time. I felt sweat suddenly pour from my brow, my hands were clammy, my eyes sore and squinting. I was thoroughly lost. Suddenly some teenage lads appeared from nowhere, chanting and kicking a football around. A ghostly old woman dragging one of those wheeled tartan shopping trolleys crossed my path from left to right. Things came into shot and then evaporated. More people appeared momentarily on walkways and then disappeared. I tried to get through one of the security gates but as soon as I pulled it, a huge dog started barking at me.

Finally I found the correct walkway to descend from the complex's highwalks to ground level. But even here the torment wasn't over. Every turn seemed like it would lead to a dead end. The light was thin and ineffective. Rubbish bins were right next to me at every step, cars blocking pavements. Eventually I turned right and emerged through a passageway which led me out from the complex and into the blinking sunlight. My heart slowed and I exhaled. And on a grass verge, standing right in front of me, was a single white horse. The animal eyed me with benign interest. I walked over, keeping eye contact, and began to rub its nose. Its nostrils were hot and wet. The animal made a whinnying noise and I wished I had some food for it. It flicked its tail and looked towards the complex I'd just come from. A sign fixed to a tree, right next to the animal, read *NO HORSES ALLOWED*.

My phone rang. 'Where are you?' Kate.

'Where are you?'

'You first!'

'I'm standing next to a horse in Thamesmead.' Silence.

'You're still high. Why the hell are you in Thamesmead?'

'That's where Millie lives.'

'Oh… right. I thought she'd be taking you back somewhere a little bit more chi-chi to ravish you. Anyway, I'm pleased you survived.'

'I survived.'

'And you haven't forgotten what to do?'

'It's like the hokey-cokey. You put your left leg in, your left leg out.'

'If you're putting your fucking left leg in then you really have forgotten what you're doing. Now I need you to come and get me. I'm with the artists. They've got a lot of weed; it'll be worth your while.'

'Where are you?'

Kate shouted away from the phone. 'Where are we, Marija? How does Donald get here?' I heard a soft Slavic voice explain, and then Kate expressed surprise with an 'Oh!' 'It turns out we're in Eros House. Would you believe it? I must have been too fucked to recognise it when we came in. Well it'll be handy for filming later at least. We only have to go downstairs. So, Don, you know how to…'

'Yep, I've been before. Right in the middle of Catford.'

'Exactly, I'm looking out of the window, and I can, um…

yes! I can see the car park where we were, erm, dancing last night.'

'I'll be there in half an hour.'

'Oh, and Donald…'

'Yep?'

'Could you bring some milk for the teas? This lot live like bloody animals. Gone-off milk might suit some palates, but even the thought of it right now is making me gag. Don?'

When I was back at Eros House I ran my hand over the silver plaque at the foot of the stairwell, just as Belinda had done when we were here. She read out the name of the firm, of the architect, mentioned that the plaque boasted about the former but didn't acknowledge the latter – the name of the man who actually designed this building wasn't on the plaque, but it was always on her tongue. He was a bit of a hero to her. Personally, I thought the whole thing reinforced my theory that Bel was attracted to noble failure. That architect has had almost all of his buildings knocked down, and never became as famous as Bel and many of her peers assumed he would be. Like a middling TV writer, his work mostly went out in the provinces; hardly any of his buildings were in London. I ran my hand over the smoked glass and the rough concrete of the stair tower. I buzzed up to the flat, climbed the stairs and waited for the door to open. A beautiful girl with brown hair and dainty features greeted me. Enormous round earrings hung from her ears. They were canary yellow. I wanted to get in them and swing back and forth. 'Hi, you must be Donald.'

'Nice to meet you. I believe you have my colleague hostage in there?'

She laughed. 'We do. We won't kill her. My name is Marija.' We shook hands and she looked shyly towards the ground, as did I.

'I don't remember you from last night,' she said.

269

'I don't remember anything from last night.' I adjusted my eyes to the darkness of the flat's interior. 'Quite a place you've got here.'

'For us, it's perfect. We all studied art at college nearby.'

'Where are you from, Marija? Not London I think.'

'From Skopje, in Macedonia.'

I raised my eyebrows. 'That is interesting. My wife… she… she went to Skopje, and she also brought me here. She was a fan of brutalist architecture. Well, it was her obsession really.'

'Oh?' Marija stopped in her tracks, staring right into my eyes. 'Mine too.'

'That's incredible, isn't it? My wife wrote a book.'

'What was this book?'

'*Ten Brutalist Buildings*.'

Marija's mouth widened into a grin; her eyes brightened. She skipped off down the corridor like a caged songbird that had just been released. I heard some clattering and then she returned, grinning. She held a book aloft and opened the front cover. The signature of my dead wife appeared right in front of my eyes.

'Isn't this amazing? I went to see your wife speak and, after that, bought a copy of her book and she signed it. She was very charming. I'd love to meet her again.'

My face fell. 'Me too.'

Marija looked confused.

Silence.

'She died,' I said.

Marija looked stunned. 'I… Oh, I'm so sorry. I can't believe it. What happened?'

'She was riding her bike, and a lorry…'

Marija looked horrified, hands raised to mouth. 'Oh God…' Marija raised her hands up over her face, defensively, and began to cry.

'Really, it's OK. You don't have to.' I offered her a tissue. She mopped her eyes.

'I really was inspired by Belinda. I felt her work was important. You know? It meant something. It meant something... to me.'

'I'm glad.'

'Please, I'd like to show you something.' Marija gently took my hand and led me down the corridor, her manner of movement this time less like a freed songbird and more like a sad crow sloping across a lawn. Inside her bedroom, on the walls, were Marija's paintings and photographs. I ran my eyes over the images. They showed people inside rooms, and the rooms were always like boxes: haunted perhaps, but somehow homely. The people were looking directly into my eyes. The images also showed people outside the kind of buildings Bel loved. The people were still looking directly into my eyes. Some of Marija's paintings were in black and white, some in pastel shades of magenta or lavender.

'Wow.'

'You like them? My entire practice, it's inspired by the buildings Belinda loved. She made me see them in a way which... allowed me to make art about them.'

Marija guided my eye across the room. 'Look at this one.'

'Sheffield.'

'Exactly.'

A bridge painted with graffiti. *Clare Middleton I Love You Will U Marry Me.*

The power of the image hit me, almost physically. 'I know this one,' I admitted.

Marija said, 'Wow, you know it? Really?' She kneeled down and pulled out a canvas as large as a coffee table, straining to lift it. 'What about this one?' I helped and we placed it on the bed. She pulled tissue paper away to reveal the image.

271

'Birmingham Central Library. My favourite building. My muse!' She giggled.

'Belinda's too.' It was a sort of pop-art re-imaging of the library, arch pencil and ink lines jutting in and out, squaring off with each other, looking jagged and aggressive. A hypnotic whole when you stood back, almost enough to make you go cross-eyed. 'It's very good. We saw your work displayed inside this building, inside the Central Library.'

'That's amazing. And I'm so glad you like them.' She turned to me. 'You know, a lot of young artists are inspired by this stuff. Belinda's name, and her book, they were both well known in art college. I, well, I grew up with this kind of architecture around me. My friends, my family, they were not... impressed by it. But to me it spoke. It sang! Skopje is a strange place. Belinda mentioned in the book she went there once.'

'She did go. I remember she was taken with it. I didn't even really know where it was, Marija, I'm sorry.'

'No one does. My hope is that Skopje will be known for its architecture and its art. Maybe I can help that. I think there are so many underdogs, they deserve to be celebrated. That's what I want my art to do. To take the invisible or the... misunderstood. To make people look at it in different ways. I only wish Belinda was here to look at it too.'

'She loved your work too, Marija. She made me stare at your paintings and taught me about how to see.'

'I should be so happy about knowing that fact, but all I can feel is sad.' Marija sighed, head bowed; a long and pitiful sound squeezed from the back of her throat. A sigh which said there was some tragedy, something hidden in her own past perhaps. She moved closer and spontaneously hugged me. That hug provoked a strange feeling of both warmth and dislocation. She backed away and looked up at me, puppy-dog-eyed. 'A drink for the guest?' She looked bashful. 'Tea?'

'Love one.'

The beeping horn of a van suddenly filled the air. It was incessant. I went over to the window and looked down to see Janusz hitting the steering wheel and laughing, and Bob waving up to me. Baxter stood on the pavement, stationary, smoking. It took me a good five minutes to work out how to open Marija's bedroom window.

Bob yelled up, 'What the fuck have you been up to for the last 24 hours?'

'Scouting!' I replied, half-heartedly.

He shook his head. 'Well are we going to film this bit or not?'

A voice behind me. 'Who's that?' I turned to see Marija carrying two steaming mugs back into the bedroom.

'My television colleagues,' I offered. And after a pause, 'My friends. Did I mention we're making a film? About Bel's books, about Bel's buildings.'

Marija's sadness evaporated like water on a scorching day. 'Here? Wow.'

I'd received an email from one of the programmers at the Barbican. They were running an event celebrating brutalist architecture. They'd heard about us making the *Ten Brutalist Buildings* film for Mids TV. Would I come and talk? If things weren't too raw – and they completely understood if they were. After thinking it over I decided to do it. Bel would have loved the thought of me speaking about this stuff. It would have made her giggle. Some more information was supplied to me in advance of the evening. The programmer would meet me out in the gardens and take me through to the theatre where the event was to happen.

I walked round the Barbican, which was impressively clean

and modern, not a crime-ridden estate of the type you read about in the papers, but that's probably because so many rich people live here. It didn't test me like Thamesmead. Which was good as I still felt jittery from the previous night's antics. In a corner a young artist was growing herbs and asked me if I'd like a herbal tea. She was about twenty or twenty-five maybe, and her smile was so wide and innocent. I watched her picking herbs and brewing teas for people and suddenly I realised that she'd only been going round to ask those she considered to be old folk. I held up my hands and stared at the wrinkles that were becoming more pronounced with every passing year. The skin losing its elasticity and wobbling like tripe. I plucked at the skin on my hand and watched with horror as this human jelly rippled. I drank a lemon thyme tea overlooking the water gardens. It was serene.

'Donald?' A woman in her fifties wearing a kind face and a floral dress approached me.

She introduced herself as Eleanor, and told me that she had organised this event, that we'd been emailing. She chirruped that the theatre had sold out and she was very much looking forward to things. We walked through to the theatre, and I was fitted with a microphone by a guy with long, greasy hair and a black polo shirt on. Eleanor told me that there were two other speakers – an architect and a novelist. My role was simply to talk about Bel and her legacy, and to let the audience know about the documentary we were making, which, 'A lot of our audience will be very excited about, me included!'

As Eleanor chatted, I nodded and sipped a glass of white wine that had been handed to me, while not making it too obvious that it was very necessary for me to finish the wine to ameliorate my frayed nerves before the event began.

A crowd of 200 people filed into the theatre, observing the

group of us on stage. I finished the wine, the final gulp a greedy one.

The lights went up and the evening began.

'Good evening. My name's Eleanor and I work here at the Barbican. Thank you all for coming. Tonight we'll be exploring the world of brutalist architecture. And of course, we think this is not a bad place to do that.'

The audience tittered.

'Tonight we are very lucky to have three excellent speakers in conversation. Djende Mariosco is an architect who both refurbishes brutalist buildings to protect their legacy, and designs new buildings which evoke that brutalist spirit of excitement and utopia which I know we all love so much. And Aliana Wills is a young writer who has written a new novel which will be published by Discrepancy Publishing later this year and whose main theme is brutalism – and as far as I know, that's a first! And perhaps – who knows – a last!' Some mild laughter from the cheap seats. 'Both Aliana and Djende were huge fans of Belinda Schneider and her amazing book *Ten Brutalist Buildings* – a book I loved and I'm sure you all did too. The news of Belinda's death hit a lot of us very hard and it's an incredible shame that she's not here tonight. We are very lucky, though, to have Belinda's husband, Donald, with us, and I really can't say how happy we all are to have you along, Donald, to keep Belinda's spirit alive. Now not all of you will know this, but Donald is actually in London filming a documentary about Belinda's book – which will be transmitted in the next few months. So you'll all be able to watch it. It really—'

'If you live in the Midlands.'

'Sorry, Donald, what was that?'

'You'll only be able to watch it if you live in the Midlands. It's only on Mids TV, not any of the other regional channels.'

'Well, that really is a shame. It should be on everywhere. I guess maybe it'll be online later… or else we'll all need to book train tickets to Birmingham to watch it when we find out—'

'Northampton. You only need to go as far as Northampton; you can watch it from there.'

'That's very helpful of you to point out, Donald, thanks.'

'Or Leamington Spa.'

'Thanks… thanks so much again for being here. So I'd like to ask you to start, if that's OK? Just by speaking about Belinda really, and what she hoped to achieve. Was she trying to… almost change the world? And do you think that the film – the documentary you're making, that is – will help us to remember some of the things she did in her life and in her work… her work advocating that we save and love these buildings?'

My heart began to race. I was nervous about speaking. It was the audience. The racks of seats ran up high above my normal field of vision. Almost all were occupied. A person sat in nearly every one, each with feelings, each made of tissue and hot blood. What did they think of me? The scene was a mass of blurring shapes, but if you sat still and stared, the lines arranged themselves into forms, and the forms arranged themselves into intricate faces, each completely unique, with their own sets of twitching features. There were old ladies with white hair, teenagers chewing gum, thirty-something men in round-framed glasses clutching their programmes to their chests.

'Donald…?'

A great cluster of people of people of people of people, a mass of humanity. I stroked my palms with my fingers. They were clammy. Did I mention my acting career was short-liv—

'Donald…?'

Right at the back. What the fuck? I squinted upwards. Right at the back. Two men stared down at me. One was old, the other middle-aged. The old one yelled.

'Come on, old chap! We'll be here all night.'

'Mr Benedetti, I don't think there's any need for that. He'll speak in his own time.'

I was aware of some mumbling coming from the front rows of the crowd.

I looked around the crowd again for some comfort. I coughed. I saw a blonde woman take a seat in one of the rows on the extreme right. She looked familiar.

'Donald…?'

The novelist, Aliana, put her hand on my knee and looked softly into my eyes. She mouthed, 'Are you alright?' The architect, Djende, shot me a puzzled glance.

The doors to the theatre creaked open and two women walked in. One middle-aged, one much younger. They looked familiar. They both waved. The older one of them mimed 'Hi' and blew me a kiss. Kate and Marija. They hustled along a row near the back and found a pair of seats together. I stared at Kate. That calmed me. I cleared my throat, took a swig of water from a tumbler placed on the table in front of us, and began to speak about Belinda. The tension in the room started to lift; the pressure slowly exited like a balloon that had just been deflated. People listened. Kate gave me a thumbs-up gesture.

After the event, the audience filed out. I went straight down to the press bar and poured as much white wine as I could fit into a glass – much to the bafflement and slight consternation of the barman, who told me, 'It's free, sir. Just ask and I'll pour it.' I exhaled, a great heaving, heavy sigh, and glugged the wine down in three desperate gasps. The alcohol hit me like a train and I felt woozy, hot and cold at the same time, calmed yet perky.

'Donald.' A voice behind me, approaching. 'That was a very impressive bit of speaking.' Only now did I notice just how beautiful Aliana was. She had a dusky skin tone and over-pronounced each word; each syllable was spoken with the utmost care. I was a lazy orator in comparison, oafish.

'Thanks. Would you like a drink?'

'That would be delightful, thank you.'

I winked at the barman and he poured us two glasses of wine. I sipped in a civilised manner this time.

'Belinda's work… Belinda's book. It touched me. It made me want to write. I just wanted to say how much her work meant to me, how much her writing meant to me. She'll be very sadly missed.'

Djende appeared too. He caught the end of what Aliana was saying and added, 'I completely agree. Belinda's book energised me too. It galvanised what I wanted to build, to design. My aim has always been to do justice to that wave of brutalism. To try and design buildings which had the same rigorous ethics and aesthetics as those 1960s brutalist buildings. I always knew I liked them, but I couldn't find a way to say why I did. To justify what I felt, and I felt that there was something special there that most people didn't or couldn't understand. But Belinda, she expressed everything so perfectly. She was inspirational.'

Aliana was nodding and smiling. 'Djende put it so perfectly. She was inspiring. She saw something, and her work was so much about… feelings. It seemed impossible to me that you could mix this rationality: the cold, hard, rigour of concrete and brick and drawings on a board, with love and loss and human interaction with a space. But she did that. People say these places and these buildings are dehumanising, but Belinda was the lone voice saying "That's not true". Saying these are places where life flourishes, where people flourish. I never dreamed that I could write a novel where all the locations would be brutalist buildings and the characters would discuss the philosophies of architecture and love together! But

Belinda's book made it all seem possible. Belinda helped me to understand my place, my history too. My family lived in Chandigarh when I was young. My father was a civil servant with the regional government; my mother was a charity co-ordinator. The place was a mystery to me but also a fascination. You know it?'

'I remember Bel talked about wanting to go, but she never made it. It's in India, right? In the north?'

'Exactly. In the Punjab. Between Delhi and Amritsar. It's cold sometimes! Not how one imagines India. And the city is not how one imagines an Indian city either. Concrete palaces for the people, straight streets and brutalist blocks of flats. The most striking aspect is the public art everywhere – the giant open-palmed hands set into heavy, hard bases. They are a potent symbol of a city, I think. The districts of the city don't have names like "Stoke Newington" or "Dalston"; they're called Sector 8 or Sector 15. Very sci-fi in a way. I had to make sense of that, and even though Belinda didn't mention Chandigarh specifically in her book, the ideas she talked about resonated with me once I'd moved back to Britain. I could imagine her writing about the place.'

'I'm glad you liked it. I'm glad you both liked it.'

'She must have been a wonderful person,' said Djende, before smiling and slipping off to talk to a journalist who was standing nearby, holding a tape recorder.

'Perhaps we could... talk more?' said Aliana, leaving a gap which filled me with an odd mixture of emotions. Was I right to reply, after a pause, 'I'd like that,' and to watch Aliana's eyes as they opened just a fraction more than they had before? It was hard to know the rules of this odd new game I was reluctantly playing.

Aliana reached into her handbag, pulled out a card. It said:

Aliana Wills
Author
07690_____
a.wills@_____

'Why don't you drop me a line and we could meet... for a coffee?'

I considered for a moment. 'I... will.'

'Perfect.' Aliana beamed. 'Please excuse me, I must be going. I have to finish a book review for this weekend's paper; it's due in tomorrow. Might be a rather long night at the typewriter. It was lovely to meet you, Donald.'

'You too. And I completely understand. I have to get up early to get the train back to Birmingham, and then we're off to Berlin the following day to film the last part of *Ten Brutalist Buildings*.'

'I hope it goes well.'

I kissed her on the cheek. Her skin felt cool on my lips. 'Thanks.'

When I got off the train at New Street Station I felt like someone had tapped me on the shoulder. I turned round to see New Street signal box. It looked like a crinkle-cut concrete chip. It made me remember Bel, made me remember her pointing it out to me when we were waiting to take our first train together from Brum to London. A text arrived at that moment from Aliana Wills. The signal box's tinted windows winked at me, egging me on to read it. I didn't though. Not yet.

33

I was woken by the shrill nagging of the alarm clock. I showered and put on cords, a shirt and a V-neck jumper. My stomach bulged inside the jumper. I possessed an old man's paunch despite not eating properly for ages. How could that be? Beer perhaps? Outside, the air was frosty, and I didn't know if I was shaking with the chill or with apprehension. I deliberately sat in silence in the back seat of the taxi, not making any eye contact as the driver threaded a back way through Tyseley then Yardley then on through Sheldon. He had his foot to the floor as if there was some kind of prize going for the first taxi to make it to the airport today. We took off as we crossed the railway tracks on the humpback bridge at Spring Road. Were we in a rally where I just couldn't see the other competitors? My heart was in my mouth, but my mouth was closed. I wanted the driver to concentrate on the bloody road. I also didn't want a conversation that went like this:

Driver: 'Off anywhere nice?'

Me: 'Actually my wife's just died and I tried to kill myself twice recently because I'm so broken about losing her. Now I'm going to Berlin for my job – we're filming some of a forthcoming TV programme there – but in truth I also see it as some kind of macabre pilgrimage, because that's where I proposed to her and that's where I married her. I have no idea what I'll do or what I'll find there.'

Driver: 'Oh.'

I bought a coffee and stumbled into that weird no-man's land between the two terminals. I went right up to the window that looks out onto the apron. The heat from the coffee steamed up the glass and blocked my view out towards the runway. Memories of Mum and Dad bringing me to the old terminal – which still sits over on the opposite side of the runway, a fat squatting duck of a building – as a kid to watch the planes taking off. Dad bought me a small model of a BAC 1-11 airliner from the little shop that day in 1974, and it was a toy that I treasured and treated with uncommon amounts of respect. Which made matters all the more unpleasant when the family Labrador, Ringo, choked to death on it almost exactly ten years later on 4 April 1984, the day this very building – Birmingham's new airport terminal – opened. I was away at uni in Leeds, and my mum phoned to tell me the bad news. Ringo's last day was also the first day of one of Belinda's favourite novels – *Nineteen Eighty-Four*.

Places are often just pictures, points on maps, words, abstract ideas. You only make it to a fraction of them. You understand even fewer – maybe a maximum of ten in a lifetime. Even in today's globalised world many people still live their whole lives in one city. People like me. Civilised people who nonetheless spend their days and nights in the same place, the same comfortable town. But while you're curled up on the sofa watching TV with a mug of cocoa and a slice of cake, events are happening elsewhere. They happen in places you've never been to, places you can't comprehend. Places you don't know. Places with mysterious names. Because you can't empathise with these events and these places, you ignore them. But when you do finally choose to venture to other places, the airport is the place that allows you to make this leap. It's nothing less than a secret trapdoor between cities, between countries, between worlds. You walk in through an automatic door in Birmingham and you walk out through an automatic door in Berlin. Airports have this unnatural quality. It's intoxicating. Airports are ethereal, tantalising. They offer the chance of escape, the dream of the 'other'. Brum's airport is like this. Mostly. The departures screens were like adverts for mysterious products that you could buy by simply getting on a plane. Or else these single words were coded messages that only made sense to a few people in the know. After security I headed to the departures lounge. The word *Ashgabat* turned from white to red and started flashing on all the screens. A man in a suit got up from the seat opposite, folding his paper, grabbing his briefcase and finishing his beer in one gulp. Was he a spy? He looked Russian. He was the exception though. I wished he was a spy. He looked glamorous, unknowable. I quickly surveyed the scene. Almost everyone else was schlepping around with rolling luggage and bright yellow shopping bags; they had bare legs, baggy clothes and tabloid newspapers. They were destined for the Midlands-on-Sea. Spain.

In the newsagents I spun a cylindrical display of books around. It wheeled towards me, offering up a selection of appalling mass-market paperbacks: travel guides, novels about vampires or murders, memoirs penned by reality TV stars. The contraption slowed its spinning until one book arrived right in front of me. Baxter was staring into my eyes. It was a copy of *Going Round And Round And Round In Circles Until You Die*. Discounted in the sale to 99p. And against all publishing convention it featured a photograph of a blacked-up Baxter on the cover. And when I say blacked-up, I don't just mean his usual sartorial selection of all-black suit and polo neck; his face was also smeared in a crude tar make-up. Only his pinprick little eyes, those shifty little windows into his mind, were visible. And they were looking straight into my own soul.

GOING ROUND AND ROUND AND ROUND IN CIRCLES UNTIL YOU DIE

By Baxter Turncastle

Chapter 9. The unending purgatory of the No. 11C Bus: Dying for something different

Still round; still round. Still round. Still. Round. Still going round. Still cuckolded. Sat there thinking, even the seat seemed to be arguing with me – with my arse at least. That bench so hard with its padding so inconsequential.

Some young women boarded, got upstairs, passed by. Walking past. I can't believe it! Flirting with me like that so openly by brazenly walking past! Maybe it needs to be skoptsy for me. Cachinnation. At the expense of The Narrator, no doubt. Screaming. A frog jumpy jumpy along the floor and up onto my knee. I yelled at the creature, 'I'm no batrachophagous. Scarper!' It replied, 'Rebbit!' then 'Fuck you!' and eventually... hoppy up and out through window.

She was watching me. Oh yeah, she bloody sees me on this bus. She has a periscope in Bradford. She sees The Narrator's bloody anger. Can't contain it much longer. Defenestrate my arm up to the wrist but no further. Screaming and giggling from them females at the back.

Bus driver pops his head upstairs. 'What the bloody 'ell's goin' on here? Y'oroight, mate?' I tell him to piss off and ask who be drive bussy when it still wheels along carriageway without HIM at the controls.

'Ow shit,' comes the response. While he ducks back down it's floc-cinaucinihilipilification for me, looking at the bus map and wonder-ing which part of fucking Brum we're in, which part we're going to. Will this circular journey be my first and last?

A bang, bus wobbles, hearse been hit, coffin slides out, stiff slides out, crunched-up bones and human, red paste go up and all over win-dows. Fucking girls at the back REALLY screaming now, yelling: 'Oh my God!!!' 'The blood!!!' 'Why couldn't we have waited for the next bus!!!', rushing downstairs to see what be happening, one of them I hear vomiting all over the stairs. THAT's an accident waiting to happen.

I STEW. God, I stew. And in writing this encounter up, I wonder. Is it all just a fat case of adoxography?

'Oi.'

I jumped. Bob strode over, proud as pie, brandishing a box in a sealed bag, a bottle of cola and two empty polystyrene cups. 'Whatcha up to? Not in the mood for perfume shopping?'

I raised an eyebrow.

'Are you reading… Baxter's book?' Bob puffed out his cheeks. 'I don't know what to make of this. Not at all. Are you secretly a fan?'

'Fuck off.'

'No, you *are* secretly a fan. Hmmm.' Bob stared at my fore-head. 'What the fuck is going on in there? Do you want Baxter to *like* your writing? Do you want him to acknowledge you as an… artist or something? You want him to recognise that you're as good as… no, a better writer than him, don't you?'

'I do not.'

'Come on then.'

We walked over to some seats by the window and fell into them.

He ripped open the bag, groped at the box like a hungry fox and upended it. A bottle of Scotch slid out like a rat begging to be batted at a church fete. He poured generous measures into each cup and sighed contentedly. Then he sloshed cola into them both and slid one across the low plastic table between the seats. I took a sip, called him a heathen, and told him, 'You're not allowed to open bottles from the shop until you land.'

'Do I look like I give a fuck?' he said, without even looking at me.

We drank, staring out across the tarmac, our eyes drawn to the planes moving outside.

'Do you remember when we came to film a sketch here for *Welcome To The Masshouse*, a few years after the airport had opened?'

'I've tried to forget most of them.'

'You remember! It was something about a Brummie airline – about how the plane just taxied down the M5… and how they had a new destination for the summer – Weston-super-Mare.'

'Brum by the sea.'

'Exactly.'

'It was shit though, wasn't it? The show.'

'Complete shit. Well…? I mean there were… that one time. Well, OK, mostly. At least we had the dosh to make it though. Back then – ooh, 1980s, early '90s – even then things were getting tight. It's really a joke today. Do we make anything?

Mids TV have been cutting the budgets every single year. The things we used to do – the dramas, the live dramas!'

'Christ.'

'Yep, the live dramas always went wrong. Um… the comedies, everything. The serious stuff – current affairs. Arts. Incredible.'

Bob emptied the whisky and cola and poured a refill. 'You know they're bulldozing the studios?'

'Why?' I suddenly felt angry.

'Money. They're building offices and some flats for Brum's cool new urban hipsters.'

'Where's Mids going then? Are we out on our ears?'

'They can't get rid of us that easily. They'll have to rent some offices for us somewhere. We'll just have to borrow other people's studio space when we need it. God knows where though – I'm not even sure if there are any other studios left in Brum. The lunchtime chat show's been axed too. But we'll stick it out. I'll give 'em what for when I go down to HQ for this meeting.'

I drank. 'I don't know, Bob, all this fucking nostalgia. Was it ever any good? Was it ever any good at the time – the TV or the buildings? I've been spending far too much time looking backwards. I sometimes think it's all rose-tinted glasses and forgetting the bad stuff. At least we're honest these days; there's no rules, no rulers, no ideas.' I drank. 'Just cash, sex, fun… for some.'

'It was always shit. There's just more varieties of shit on the multimedia buffet these days to keep everyone nice 'n' happy. More shit, more shopping, more booze. It's all bollocks, always was. Everything.' He smirked. 'Bottoms up.'

TEN BRUTALIST BUILDINGS

By Belinda Schneider

Chapter Ten

The death and dismemberment plan

So it's almost the end of our story. All these concrete behemoths are being torn apart. Well, maybe they had it coming to them – something else had to die for them to live during the white heat of the 1960s and the fading light of the 1970s. Now death is the answer, death is the end. Death is the end for all of us. I just find it so strange to think that I'll outlast them all. That when I'm an old woman, with my kids and my grandkids, there won't be anything left that means anything.

Why do we accept this? Why don't we care? All those films and TV shows that were shot there – up on the walkways or down in the undercrofts – were priming us for this moment. They were depicting dystopia, when the intention of the original designers was the exact opposite. These artists and architects and planners wanted to create perfect futures. The imperfect present caught up with that task. I wish someone would shoot a rom-com around Birmingham Central Library, rather than a spy thriller or a gangland noir or a kitchen-sink drama or a sci-fi adventure. I wish someone would film a couple meeting and a couple kissing. I wish someone would film a girl reading, and a guy in a chicken costume catching her eye. I wish we could see the avant-garde and the urban as romantic, and not just the classical or the bucolic.

So many people use these places and these spaces to have fun. Yes, just to have fun. People eating their lunch or drinking a beer, smoking

288

*a cigarette or chatting to friends, playing football or chasing around.
Skaters and free runners have colonised these spaces. They see them
as playgrounds. They love the different levels and the ramps and the
steps. If it wasn't for these guys on their skateboards, brutalist com-
plexes would seem a bit quiet, a bit dead. But they go and bring
them to life. Why can't we encourage everyone to go and play, to
go and kiss, to go and eat and smoke? Who cares about the noise?
Let's just bring it all to life, bring people in. People are the users of
a building and of a space. Without them it's nothing. Most airports
are pretty lousy buildings, but those flows of people, those constant
streams, those constant waves – they are exciting. They make a place
exciting. Let's do that with our brutalist buildings – let's put people
in them and bring them to life.*

What do you reckon?

Could it be that Belinda was trying to tell me something from
beyond the grave, I wondered, as I spiked a chunk of sausage
slathered in a spicy sauce and finished off with an unapologetic dusting of paprika. I picked up the piece of currywurst
and watched it. I blew on it and ate it whole. It tasted hellish at
first bite – acrid and acidic, the sauces and spices assaulting the
tongue. But then the greasiness and the warm, soft meat that
came in the second part of the bite – they were comforting.
Could it be that Bel was telling me to eat, to not die? I think
that if Belinda was trying to tell me anything, it was to try and
live as normal a life as possible. Rather than getting a taxi to
the hotel with Bob when we landed at Tegel Airport, I turned
right and came to this S-Bahn-themed currywurst stand. Bob
said he'd meet me later.

Those five-foot-tall barrel tables they only seem to have in
Germany almost lend themselves to pop psychology. There's

something odd about casually leaning over on one, your weight sort of half suspended. They seem designed to make you spill out your fears as you pump sausage and beer back into your gob. They lull you into a false sense of security. There were three of these high table things parked outside the fake S-Bahn carriage, two businessmen at the others – German, I presume – and me. Each of us looking lost in our own world as we ate this children's food while time was marked by the roars of roguish accelerating engines attached to Airbuses taking off on the runway beyond us every three minutes.

I pushed the final fat disc of sausage around the paper plate to mop up the last of the curry sauce and popped it into my mouth. I twisted round a bit and caught my own reflection in the window of the S-Bahn carriage. I was still as tall as before – 6 foot 2 and hunched over a little, as was usual. I looked drawn, defeated. Like a boxer about to be out for the count. We'd been notching up too many miles doing this shoot. Not enough sleep, not enough vitamins. Too much drinking, especially in London. And I was still heartbroken. This last one was the most problematic of all – when would it end? When would I stop feeling lonely; when would the nightly sadness subside? I needed a haircut as well. Blonde hair was growing down over my ears, down my neck. My cheeks looked a little sallow, and my eyes were pale. Still that bloody pot belly though.

If Belinda *was* telling me to eat, then who was I to argue? I love the way German words get glued together to make longer German words. The menu was full of them. What should I choose? I played it safe and ordered some fries. I poured ketchup all over them and munched my way through the lot.

I picked up my bag and caught the canary-yellow bus to Alexanderplatz, then switched to the S-Bahn and got off at Warschauer Strasse. I asked a friendly looking man reading an English magazine for directions and he told me straight away.

Ten minutes later I was checked in at Hotel Bohm and lying alone on top of the bed in my room, twiddling my thumbs and wondering whether this was such a good idea at all.

I switched on the TV. I couldn't believe my eyes when the contraption fired up. There was a man in a chicken suit haranguing members of the public in a big square. If it wasn't for the massive sign reading *GALERIA KAUFHOF* behind the chicken's right wing, I'd have sworn it was the same trick that we pulled on *Welcome To The Masshouse* all those years ago. Either way I made a mental note to call my lawyer on Monday. Not that I had a lawyer, of course, but it felt like the kind of thing someone like me should do at this particular time. It was the correct reaction.

I switched the TV off and pondered. I went to my bag and pulled out a photo of Belinda, sat on the bed and stared at it. I suddenly felt very alone – in the room, in the city, in this world. I felt tears beginning to form in the corners of my eyes. I let a few roll out, just to go through the motions.

I put the photo down, washed my face, put on a clean(ish) shirt and left the hotel. I felt better the second I was outside and the breeze pricked my cheeks. I bought some cigarettes and smoked one extravagantly as I walked back up to Warschauer Strasse Station. I caught a beige-and-red S-Bahn train to Hackescher Markt and headed straight for the restaurant where I'd proposed to Belinda. I stood outside looking at the table on the square where we had sat, where she said yes. After fifteen minutes of staring I headed off to where we got married.

St Agnes Kirche rose up menacingly, partly shaded by trees which had grown up in front of it substantially since the last time I was here. Some blue bins were lined up outside; they leaned against the tough structure, rubbish spilling from them.

A group of people were standing around speaking English. I knew them well. 'I get sick of a shoot after about four days now,' said Bob, blowing a cumulus cloud of smoke over me. 'But then this isn't the kind of pissing about we used to get up to, is it? This is serious. And by God I'm gonna make sure the end result is something Bel would be proud of.' Bob turned to look at Baxter, who sat cross-legged on the ground, apparently lost in some kind of yogic trance. 'I only wish we had your gorgeous wife doing the pieces to camera rather than this fucking garden gnome.' Bob yelled at Baxter, 'ARE YOU DONE YET, MATE?' and shook his head in my direction, giving me a knowing look. Then he wandered off towards a pile of cables.

'You OK being back here?' asked Kate, rubbing my arm, regarding the church with a suspicious eye. 'It's a funny place though, isn't it?' She looked up at the tower, clutching the clipboard to her chest. 'Bel's choice, I take it?'

'Absolutely. She loved it. She said she'd always wanted to come here when she was a teenager but it was on the wrong side of the wall.'

'It's also on the wrong side of the North Sea!' Kate made a snuffling sound with her nose. 'That chapter of her book has cost us about twenty grand, as Bob keeps reminding me. If only she'd stuck to places in Britain we could get to in a minibus.'

I stared at the building.

'Are you going inside?'

'No, I don't think so. Maybe...'

'What was it like when you got married here?'

'There were less trees for one thing. Berlin seems like some kind of overgrown city to me. Nature just trying to reclaim everything.'

'What were her family like? And her friends? Did they throw a good party?'

'It was a piss-up. There was so much beer afterwards and so much cake. And cheap Sekt.'

'Excuse me!'

'Sekt. It's like champagne but cheaper. And shitter.'

'Ha.'

'You're going to see Bel's family while we're here, right?'

'Exactly. When you guys go home tomorrow – assuming that clown can get his lines out by the end of the day so we can pack up – I'm going to stay on for a couple of extra days to see Frau Schneider and just, well, see some other stuff too.'

'And I'll see you when you get back home? I'll come over and cook.'

'Of course.'

'Won't do anything silly while you're here?'

'I'll be a good boy, I promise.'

'Good.'

Kate kissed me on the left cheek and walked off to organise some more of the shoot. Baxter stood up, performed his ridiculous breathing ritual, stretched his arms. He reached into his pocket, pulled out some kind of pink pill – no doubt obtained from a guy in a leather jacket hanging around outside one of Berlin's myriad nocturnal dens of iniquity – and swallowed it.

Bob cleared the stragglers away and shouted for the filming to begin. Baxter opened his mouth and said...

34

The waters of the Rummelsburger See looked like a bowl of delicious broth. I wanted to dive in. Sunlight danced on the solid surface, which was only broken by ducks bobbing around.

Belinda rested her head on my lap and gently drifted off to sleep. I continued drinking cold pilsner from an oversized bottle and stroked her hair. It was perfect.

2008

The waters of the Rummelsburger See looked like an oil slick. I wanted to run away. Puffy clouds lingered overhead. No waterfowl lingered today.

I remembered this place, that time. It drained me to be constantly reminded of perfection, of a perfection you could never recreate. I didn't feel alone on that bench though. It wasn't exactly that Bel was... there with me, but there was something odd. Some kind of *something*. Some kind of presence. I drank the last of my pilsner and lobbed the bottle in like a true English hooligan.

It didn't take long to arrive at Frau Schneider's house in Lichtenberg. I hadn't seen her or talked to her since the day of Bel's funeral. As I climbed the steps of the drab grey apartment block, I suddenly felt very guilty for shutting her out.

'Ah, Donald, come here.' She crept over and threw her arms around me without shame. I could smell cabbage and potatoes and pork. The flat was as hot and wet as a kettle. 'It's so good to see you.' I saw Bel's facial features in her mother; I saw that kindness in her eyes, the cheeky grin too. I mustn't cry, I thought. I really mustn't. Not here.

'How was your trip? You could have stayed here. How is your hotel?'

'It's fine, thanks. You're very kind. Listen, I'm really sorry for not being in touch more, but I… I just…'

'I understand, Donald. You don't need to explain.' Frau Schneider paused very briefly before she spoke each soft sentence, eager to express herself correctly and precisely. 'You just need to know that I'm always here. That's all. Now let's get you a drink.'

While Frau Schneider fixed me a drink, I browsed the novels on her shelves, and below those, neatly arranged, the non-fiction catalogue – many, many art and architecture books. Books Bel would have been brought up on. Frau Schneider was a translator; her English was perfect. Which was very helpful as my German was limited.

We drank.

'Do you remember when your dog, Breuer, died?' An unexpected question.

'Of course.'

'I don't think Bel had had much experience of grief before

that. I remember her calling me in tears. She was so traumatised by it. She couldn't believe such a bad thing would happen.'

'I remember.'

'And she asked me, "Mutti, Don won't die, will he? I can't imagine that? Promise me Don won't ever leave me on my own. I couldn't cope." It was very sad.'

'I...'

'It's not supposed to happen. None of this is supposed to happen. We are supposed to have simple, boring lives like everyone else. It's not fair to experience tragedy. It's not right.' Frau Schneider looked so thin. Her lips wobbled even after she'd finished speaking. She stared at me in silence. I couldn't accept the intimacy; I had to look at the carpet. The pattern was abstract, cream on burgundy. Concentrate on the small things. I heard a tea cup jangling on a saucer, a wrist that was quivering, tears that were forming. The room was silent apart from muffled sobs and then the sound of a tissue being wiped across a face. I looked up. Frau Schneider wore a fake smile, her eyes glazed. 'I warned Bel about bicycling in such a big city like Birmingham with so many roads, so many motorways. I always worried about her.'

'I did too.' I sighed. 'But I knew it made her happy. She loved cycling. She made me buy a bike too. I hadn't cycled much since I was a kid. But I loved it.'

Frau Schneider didn't seem to be listening. She wanted to say or do something instead, move things forward somehow. This was a very 'Bel' trait. She spoke. 'I want to take you somewhere... after lunch.'

Once I was full of meat and potatoes, I helped her up. She put on her coat and I put on mine. We walked down the steps of her building and out into the sunlight. She linked her left arm through my right and guided me south through streets over which tall plattenbau blocks presided. The fences had holes in them, the pavements were a little cracked, but there was no rubbish around.

'What about your own parents? Peter and Alison, isn't it? Are they looking after you?'

'They're not around anymore, Frau Schneider. It's just me.'

'I should have known that, you should have told me. I'm sorry, Donald. I know what it's like... without Bel's father.' She looked at me now. 'You must call me whenever you need to. Berlin isn't so far away. It's just a short flight.'

The scenes we strolled through reminded me of the big estates in Birmingham: Castle Bromwich or Druids Heath. Bel never felt nervous when she stood in underpasses or before tower blocks in Birmingham. These estates in Berlin didn't seem as scary as those in Birmingham had been. They were quiet, and the people we passed all seemed well-behaved. We eventually arrived at something much scarier than an estate though – a compound whose cheap concrete banality spoke of a much bigger terror. The buildings enclosed a courtyard; they were all different heights and yet incredibly dull. Terror is shocking, but terror is also, evidently, a crashing bore, a dinner-party guest you don't want – even to make up the numbers. What was this place?

'The Stasi HQ,' said Frau Schneider. We stood, almost shaking, outside its entrance. 'I'm glad Bel went to England. This was not the sort of country I wanted her to grow up in. This was a place that lost its mind. And it lost its soul.' She seemed very frightened. 'You must excuse me, Donald. Once you have been inside Hohenschönhausen... well, once is one times too many. They broke my spirit. My optimism. People think of the DDR as a bit of a joke. The silly little cars and the nudism and the socialist brotherhood. But it was sinister. It was evil. Let me assure you of that. I managed to inoculate Bel against all that hate. But, Donald...' She turned to me. I squeezed her songbird arms and stared into haunted eyes. '…it came at such a cost. The time I wanted with her. My only child. So little time. And now it's all used up. Too soon. Just too soon.' I hugged Frau Schneider tightly. Then I looked into those eyes again. Suddenly they were Bel's eyes, the same colour and shape as Bel's eyes, the same kindness as Bel's eyes.

'Frau Schneider?'

'Yes, Donald?'

'Frau Schneider… would you like a beer?'

She smiled, wiping tears from her cheeks. We set off walking up Karl-Marx-Allee, which Frau Schneider told me had previously been called Stalinallee. Bel had expressed a particular distaste for the straight, wide avenue. I remember her saying. Now I realised that perhaps Berlin hid many ghosts for her, ghosts that she was as scared of as her mother was.

After two beers in a hipster bar on Alexanderplatz, a certain superficial jollity returned to Frau Schneider. I felt like a naughty schoolboy smoking in front of her, but today I offered her fags and she puffed away just like everyone else in the bar. I thought there was a smoking ban in Germany, but no one seemed to give two hoots. The bar had a retro aesthetic, such as it was, and as I casually scanned the posters around the room I suddenly thought I'd made an error. I realised many of them were regime propaganda pieces from the 1970s. Posters declaring *Berlin: DDR Hauptstadt* and showing a horrendously huge building which I assumed was the now-defunct Palace of the People, and the more easily recognisable Fernsehturm, which loomed right above us. TV was a cultural weapon in the Cold War; there was no getting away from the boastful monuments to it – like this one. Bel had taken me up the Fernsehturm the day before I proposed to her. She seemed more interested in the elaborate swoops of concrete at the tower's base. I wondered simply how it was possible to grow such a massive and obviously prick-inspired tower from nothing. Bel taught me its German nickname – the *Telespargel* or 'TV asparagus'. *Spargel* had become one of my favourite words, and I never missed an opportunity to order *Spargel* wherever I could. I felt pissed. I needed to get Frau Schneider away from her bad memories and from this weird world where totalitarianism could be ironically enjoyed by hipsters from a safe historical distance, where *Ostalgia* was – apparently – harmless.

'Frau Schneider, I'd like to take you somewhere too.'

After half an hour's drive, we got out of the taxi among some trees as the light was fading. A locked gate and a fence presented itself. 'We need to find a hole in the fence.' Frau Schneider looked shocked for a second, then that same flash of insouciance that Bel deployed so often made itself apparent on her mother's face. She wasn't scared. I helped her through a hole in the fence and she exchanged some pleasantries with a woman walking a dog, which seemed to put her at ease. We threaded through rubble and looped round the back of the derelict buildings. Frau Schneider chirruped away about taking Bel on outings when she was tiny, the same kind of meaningless chit-chat old women everywhere use. A way to keep hold of memories, to keep hold of sanity. I led her up some concrete stairs, and by the fifth floor she was clearly tiring.

'Not much further,' I promised. 'Hurry up or I'll have to carry you on my back.'

She seemed amused by this. We reached the top floor – at least, I thought it was the top floor. We walked out along a floor that used to be filled with American spies. We had to tread carefully, avoiding huge holes where the concrete had failed. At the edge, precipitous drops presented themselves on all sides. I realised our goal was higher still.

'Sorry, I forgot about this bit,' I said.

We had to climb a narrower stair core, up another four flights. But at the top we emerged onto a disc of floor with poles at its edge. An incredible cacophony of sound made it feel all the more surreal, a compete din as slices of plastic sheeting banged against the building's side. The plastic covered the golf-ball domes in which the listening equipment was stored. And out in the distance, towards the north-east, the lights of Berlin burned bright. But it could have been Birmingham; it could have been anywhere.

'This is incredible,' said Frau Schneider, hardly comprehending. 'I had no idea. What is it?'

'Teufelsberg. That's one bit of German I do remember.'

'The Devil's Mountain. Of course. I heard the stories of the rubble being stacked up. All of the rubble from the bombing made into a huge mountain by the *Trümmerfrauen*, the rubble women. But I never knew this crazy thing was on top of it. That's West Berlin though – a mystery to me.'

'It was the American listening station. I guess they were trying to listen to those Stasi bastards.' I put the word 'bastards' in here to try and placate Frau Schneider.

'They're all bastards,' she said. 'They're all men. Women wouldn't think this kind of thing up.'

'But the view?'

'Yes, it's worth it for the view. Totalitarianism and the Cold War did give us some great views. The Fernsehturm, and now this. Teufelsberg. Did Bel like it here?'

'That's why I've brought you here. She told me this was a favourite secret spot in the city.' I thought about the next bit for a second or two. 'She came to... parties here after the wall fell. Music parties.' She took a lot of drugs here on trips back from Birmingham to see friends and taste a more liberal nocturnal life in the newly unified city. 'She brought me here on that holiday we had. Remember when we came to see you?

I proposed to her in Hackescher Markt on that holiday. But she brought me here too and I thought it was incredible. I was scared as well though.' I really was. I remember thinking I was going to get beaten up by the security thugs who had arrived out of nowhere and looked displeased by our presence. Bel, in typical style, had shouted at them to get lost.

Frau Schneider continued to silently regard the view. Then she cleared her throat. 'I miss my daughter so much. I love her so much.' I began to cry as she finished speaking, and we both sat grieving quietly for a few minutes.

'You should come to Birmingham and see me, Frau Schneider. We're having a screening of the film, of *Ten Brutalist Buildings*, at my office, at the studios. You could come and watch it, meet everyone who knew Bel and loved her.'

'That's kind of you, Donald, but I'm feeling too old to travel these days. The last time, of course, for the funeral... I... it was...'

'We don't have to talk about that.'

Frau Schneider surveyed the scene. Her eye seemed drawn to something but I couldn't work out what.

'We have to be strong in Berlin. They've thrown so much at us. We all have to be so strong. But it's tiring. It's very tiring. Fighting is too much for me. I only want to be happy now. I don't know if that's possible.'

'It is. I've read so much about this place, and you have a spirit that must be unbreakable, really unbreakable.'

'They tried to break us. My God, they tried. Over and over again.' She paused. 'I think I brought Belinda up to be too tough, but you had to be tough here. You had to be single-minded to deal with the pressures placed on you. It was like carrying a huge weight around with you every day. When you went to the shops, to work, to see your friends. Always this weight on you. People said it lifted after the wall came down

302

but I'm not so sure. I still feel it weighing down on me, pushing me towards the ground. I just keep on pushing it back up.'

'Well that's exactly what you should be doing.'

She looked at her feet, like a moping child. 'No one cried in the DDR. It was weakness. I couldn't let anyone see me cry. I couldn't let Bel see me cry in particular, because I needed her to be tough enough to endure life – luckily the tides turned and she had hope, the hope of a free life. History was kind to her. But I had to show her how to be resilient. I learned to cry so silently. I trained myself to do it without making a sound. I could do it in the kitchen or out on the balcony or in our stupid Trabant. It steamed up so much, no one could see inside. I could sob without sniffing, without whimpering, without wailing. These days I have no more need to cry silently, but I still catch myself doing it and realise I am sitting there, not making a sound. Through the walls I hear rock music sometimes and those video games, but I can cry so silently that they'd never even know I was still there, still just sitting on my own in that chair.'

'Would you like a cigarette?'

'I'm an old woman. What harm is it going to do me?' She grinned, a big, soppy Schneider smile.

We sat down on the edge of the floor, smoking like a couple of teenagers, our legs dangling off the very edge of the building. Clouds rolled across our vista, the light rapidly fading. The few towers you could see rose into the sky, but I was struck by how vast and how flat and how bucolic Berlin appeared. A city of suburbs, just like Brum. In the very distance, in the direction of the Reichstag, I thought I could see a small white ball steadily rising and falling. It looked like it might be a hot-air balloon. It reached the top of its trajectory and then just fell back again. Then the process repeated. Again and again. It never got anywhere. Did it want to climb up to the stars, to break its leash? Did it want to rip out its anchor and make itself free? Or was it happy to just follow the rules? Bel made us watch a film once about a family who used a balloon to escape the East. They stitched it together themselves and they made a burner and a basket and they floated right up and over the border into West Germany. Where did ordinary people like that find such extraordinary courage? Being a hero isn't easy. We were so lucky in Britain that we hadn't been forced into a corner; we hadn't needed to make difficult decisions, choose sides. We just had simple choices. Meaningless choices: the supermarket with the orange bags or the one with the white bags? We forgot just how many choices we really had.

I looked across at Frau Schneider, her hand wobbling as she lifted the cigarette towards her mouth, inhaling slightly, clumsily. Her hair was grey and formed into a bun, and under her eyes she wore distinctive wrinkles which spoke of wisdom and experience. But in truth her skin looked surprisingly youthful. It was when she moved that I realised her age. She seemed frail on her feet. Those feet were tiny too – I looked at them swinging backwards and forwards in mid-air, at the white lace-up pumps she'd slid them into. Her dress was some kind of vintage 1960s number, covered in an elaborate, jaunty pattern of tropical fruit and birds. Quite a sight, in fact. Bel had told me that during the shortages all East German women had become expert seamstresses; they had to be. Communism couldn't keep up with consumer demand. Fashion was un-socialist. But there were hundreds of thousands of girls who just wanted to be like normal young women in other countries: to wear the latest skirts, to paint their face with make-up like film stars, to flirt with boys in discos. They just wanted to be normal, and they were trapped in this surreal world of want and authoritarianism where they had to sob in silence lest the Stasi get the idea that they were sick of the status quo and plotting a flight to the West.

'We went mad,' said Frau Schneider, unprompted. 'We all went mad. When this city was... cleaved in two, a madness descended. Nothing was real, nothing made sense, no one was happy. We were living in a world of fantasies and phantoms. The people at the top were psychopaths, the Stasi was run by people who weren't mentally right, the people themselves slowly lost their minds. I could feel myself losing my grip on reality. I just couldn't let her grow up here. I couldn't do that. She was indoctrinated enough in the state kindergarten system – they all were. I just couldn't let her live like this, in a cage. I had to set her free. Do you understand, Donald? I had to. I wonder if we'd have escaped if the wall had stayed up. I'd have found a way for her to. She was so lucky it came down when she was eighteen. I knew she was going to leave. I wanted her to. But I missed her so much it broke me. The whole situation tested everyone. We were all on the edge, always so anxious.'

My arms instinctively reached out to Frau Schneider and scooped her frail body towards mine. She probably thought there wasn't any madness in Birmingham, under its traffic islands and in its tower blocks. In me? Now wasn't the time for that chat though.

'Do you understand?' She sobbed and shook, and I stroked her hair as she rested her head on my chest. 'But I paid such a high price, Donald. Such a high price. I felt as if I'd lost her years ago. Seeing her so little, seeing you both so little. But I had to do it... for her.'

'I know. You did the right thing.'

A sparrow appeared from nowhere and landed on the floor, just three feet away from us. Its jittery movements were so rapid, so edgy, so precise. Its head jutted left and right as if aware of some constant threat, something preying on it at all times. It opened its beak, then flew off, out and away towards the middle of Berlin.

'She was pregnant.' I hadn't spoken those words out loud. No one knew. Words mean history is true. Saying something means an event actually happened, you didn't imagine it. If I didn't say it, it wasn't real. 'Bel was pregnant when she died. We didn't know if we ever could. I thought it was my fault, I had a... It was probably our last chance.'

Frau Schneider moved her head away from my chest and looked up at me. Her eyes showed that her soul had collapsed, and I guess mine had too. 'Oh my God,' she whispered. 'Donald...'

My room was little bigger than a closet. Hotel Bohm was, Kate told me when she was booking it for me, a 'hipster boutique kind of place' – and this meant that it was somewhere people *wanted* to stay. Because it was a 'hipster boutique kind of place', that meant the rooms could be very small and very claustrophobic. I found this odd, as Berlin is not a city where space is at a premium. There's so much room, in fact, that Berlin feels more like a country. It even gives sprawling Brum a run for its money.

But anyway, the room was Lilliputian. It was as if a divorcee needing a lodging on the fly had just come along and jammed all their stuff into a tiny space. The bed was shoved up onto a raised platform, and right beside it was a shower and a toilet in a small box. You had to duck to get into this quasi-bathroom. A solitary window looked out on the Prussian-style courtyard below.

It was too hot and I woke up in the night. I think I woke up. And put on the light...

Two figures were immediately illuminated.

'What the fuck are you two doing here?'

'Oh, don't mind us.'

'Yep, forget about us. We're not here.'

'You are here.'

'Rocaster and I were just in the area. Couldn't stop ourselves popping in. I mean, this really is a lesson in bad planning, isn't it?'

'Bad design.'

'Indeed.'

The pair of them were squashed up together on the wooden platform at the end of the bed. There was about eight inches between where the bed ended and the wall began, and they just sat there, looking about the room, cross-legged.

'This is getting ridiculous.'

'It's not ridiculous at all. On the contrary, it's rational for us to be here. It's rationality we seek!'

'I agree with Mr Benedetti. We're just trying to learn some lessons.'

'Why are you following me?'

'Following you? Are we following the chap, Rocaster? I don't believe we'd do that, would we?'

'Absolutely not.'

I was losing my temper, especially with Benedetti. He sat there, calm as a vicar, looking down his nose at me, while Rocaster held his hand up, apparently making mental measurements.

'You killed me last time I saw you. You pushed me off those fucking flats in Druids Heath! I don't want to die anymore. I want to live. For Bel. For Frau Schneider. For Kate. For Bob. For... me.'

'Kill you?' Benedetti scoffed. 'Bunkum. Why ever would we do something like that? What a ridiculous suggestion. Maybe it was a dream?'

'I can't take any more of this. I want you both to fuck off.'

Rocaster looked stung.

'We've been thinking,' said Benedetti. 'We've been thinking about those appalling… sick buckets, those glass cages they want to build once they've demolished the masterworks of our era. They're proposing a lot of filth where the best of, well, *our* modern Brummagem stood, our 1960s vision. They're knocking the important buildings down and putting up tat instead – glassy, plasticky garish apartment blocks and offices, cheap and nasty. Sullying the skyline. It simply won't do. Have you seen the plans, Donald?'

My mouth made an 'O' shape and was about to answer but didn't get a chance.

'Because I have, and let me tell you, they're not the kind of plans Rocaster and I would have worked up. Not in the least. They're really second-rate. And you know what you should be doing about that, Donald?'

My mouth made an 'O' shape and was about to answer but didn't get a chance.

'You should wait until they've built these horrible monstrosities and you should blow them to kingdom come! No use beating about the bush here, and no use being nostalgic. No one is going to save Brum's brutalist buildings now your wife isn't around to whip the buggers in power into shape. No one's listening. They're going to demolish the lot and put up some despicable flats for a load of terrible trainee accountants and solicitors where once we had these wonderful buildings for a new age. So blow them all up! That's the point I wanted to make.'

'That's the point we wanted to make,' added Rocaster, with a wink.

I sighed, lay back down in bed, slipped an eye mask on and pulled the covers around me. 'I want you both to just sit there

quietly in the corner. Don't make any noise. Stop inciting me
to commit criminal... acts.'

There was no response.

'Understood?'

Benedetti said, 'Of course, old chap. We'll just sit... be no
trouble at all.' Then after a silence of about thirty seconds he
started whistling the 'Colonel Bogey March'. I groaned and
rolled onto my side.

When I was a boy my dad gave me an atlas one Christmas so
that I could be just like him – a knowing navigator, a pin-
pointer of places, someone who'd do The Knowledge for fun.
A man of the world. The atlas was hard-backed and handsome,
so heavy I could hardly lift it. Instinctively, I thumbed straight
to Birmingham and I marvelled at the detail on the map of
the city, the names of the suburbs floating in the air and the
rivers and the railways. The roads were the most magical part
of all. So many of them. Some towns only had one going in
and one going out. Brum was a seething snake-pit of streets,
a spilled bowl of spaghetti, an unravelled ball of string. Roads
criss-crossed the city, boggling the mind. I asked Dad how he
could even remember where to go and he smiled one of those
secret smiles and tapped his nose with his right finger. I learned
later that his secret was his trusty pocket-sized A–Z, and grad-
ually this became my handbook too, my rules of Brum, my
companion on early expeditions round the city on my bike.
But this giant atlas was something else – a guide to the whole
world. The most important thing about the atlas was that, as
the scale went down, you could see how to get from city to
city, from country to country. You could see how close we
were. The city map pages isolated you in a way and made it
seem like each city was an island, somehow qualitatively dif-

ferent to every other city, when the truth was that there was a huge amount in common between those seemingly disparate conurbations.

Once I'd suitably eyed up Brum, I turned back one page and discovered a city I knew nothing about. Berlin. It looked similar to Birmingham. Though all the big cities in the atlas looked similar; they were just slightly different shapes – sometimes the sea ran up one side, or a river ran across the middle. But as well as a river, a thick black line sliced through my map of Berlin. I wondered what this strange scar running in a jagged line from top left to bottom right meant. I had to go and ask Dad. He sat me on his knee and explained as best he could.

A fiendish sun spat down on me as I strolled through the Tiergarten from Zoo Station. I stopped at a biergarten. The icy particles of pilsner bashed my brain and made me insensible. I thought about the German words I knew – how *biergarten* rhymed with *Tiergarten,* and I spoke some others out loud: '*Zurückbleiben bitte!*' I laughed a little. '*Brutalismus!*' A girl sitting next to me said '*Ja!*' and laughed to herself. Then I spoke more sadly. '*Zehn Brutalistische Bauwerke.*' Bel had given me a video that school children learned German with. I really enjoyed it. We watched it together, getting drunk. She offered to remove items of clothing every time I understood and spoke with a suitably Teutonic growl. She was harsh on me that night; I had to do it right for each item of clothing. I stumbled out of the biergarten, found my way past the horrendously phallic Victory Monument and pressed on towards the Interbau. I spied the array of apartment blocks rising from the green carpet of grass and bushes. I'd been here before.

35

Bel held up her left hand, and her engagement ring sparkled in the sunlight. She bit her lip as if she was embarrassed about smiling too much.

'I've never seen anyone this happy because of something I've done.'

'I love you, Donald. I love that you love me.'

'I bet you didn't see that coming last night.'

'Of course not! I thought we were just having dinner in some shitty tourist restaurant.'

'Unbelievable.' I tutted. 'But I had a plan.'

'Evidently.'

'How long had you been thinking about this?' She turned and opened her face to me, her eyes as wide as I'd ever seen them. 'Well?'

'A while. Was my timing right? I'm sure there's a very definite time in your country that you're supposed to propose at. No one's late?'

'Of course. You were late. Late like English trains. But I don't care.'

'Is it only English trains that are late?'

'German trains are late too. But I guess you invented them, so you win that. And you invented that magnetic levitation train.'

I laughed at the conversational sidestep, the little eccentric flight of fancy. 'What's that?'

'A train that floats on magnets. Incredible.' Bel looked lost in thoughts. 'It just... glides along. We really used to believe in the future. The first one was at Birmingham Airport. True story.'

'Where did it go?'

'From the terminal to the train station.'

'I've been on it then! I must have.'

'Good boy. And you know what else? Brum and Berlin have so much in common. Brum had the first ever maglev and we had the second ever.'

'Where did that one go?'

'From near Potsdamer Platz, down to Gleisdreieck Station. It was only needed because the wall cut a U-Bahn line in half. So when the wall came down and the U-Bahn lines were reconnected, pfff – it closed. It was supposed to be this futuristic technology that heralded some better world, but it hardly lasted any time at all. The quirks of life just snuffed it out.'

We came up Altonaer Strasse and suddenly there were muscular apartment blocks on each side of us. Beautiful beasts.

'Isn't it amazing? This is the Interbau. An architecture theme park. Some of the world's best designers, all of them allowed to build whatever they wanted, all for the people. Well, also to show that West Was Best. We Ossies had to live in plattenbau blocks that all looked the bloody same.'

The triangular legs on one block called out to me; the curved facade of another winked. Bel patiently explained who built what and why they were the shapes they were.

'This is from 1957. Same year as you, I think.'

'Steady on. Not quite; you know I'm a child of the Sixties.'

'But look at what they were trying to achieve. The best possible homes, the most stylish places, for ordinary people. All with landscaping, an architecture that was futuristic but not throwaway. A pat on the back for the city. An idea about creating a world that you could really live in. Everything a modern person could need. And it still looks good all these years later. Like you.'

'You are a great teacher.'

'*Danke schön.*'

We explored some more before eventually sitting down on the grass outside one of the blocks. We sat by the narrow face of the end of the block – which was coloured grey. It had two pairs of white box balconies protruding from the end, trying to escape from whatever lay within. I noticed the breeze gently fanning the blades of grass, making it look like we were boats on a green sea. The breeze blew Bel's hair out of place; strands danced around her face. She tilted her head down. Her hand smoothed the strands of hair out of her way. She caught my eye and grinned sheepishly.

Bel looked up at the grey wall with the white protrusions above us. '*Die Mauer im Kopf.*'

'The wall…?' I couldn't understand the rest.

'*Die Mauer im Kopf.* The Wall in the Head.'

'That's good. What a lyrical turn of phrase. What does it mean?'

She moved across me and rested her head in my lap, looking up at my face, her body stretched languorously. 'When the Berlin Wall came down, it only came down physically. It didn't come down mentally. The Easterners, my people' – she winked – 'they still saw the wall, felt the wall, were aware of the wall's power, its presence. It never disappeared for the people that still lived in Berlin; they still sense it. But the meaning has widened now. It explains those occasions where you feel held back by some kind of force, wherever you live. A wall in your head blocking you from doing something, an imaginary wall. I think there's something else too – because the walls around you become walls in your head, whatever kind of walls they are. It's not just the Berlin Wall – it could be your... your...'

'House walls?'

'Exactly.'

'Or your office walls?'

'See! You're getting it. All these walls are walls in your own head. The buildings, the cities even, that surround us, they affect us on a deep psychological level. We have walls in our heads. All of us. Now I don't think it always has to be in a bad way. There are lots of people who think architects are the worst enemy of the soul.'

'But you don't believe that.'

'No, I don't believe that. But I know buildings can have a profound influence on us, on the way we think and feel and behave. They can shape and mould us and affect our actions. And later on, when we think we're acting of our own free will, well, maybe all of us have a wall in the head. Maybe all of us are doing a particular thing because of all the time we spent in a particular building – those walls are making us happy or sad. If we make good buildings, maybe we make happy people. I hope so.'

'How's the wall in your head?'

A chuckle. 'I don't have one.'

'You have more than one! I knew it.'

'Not me. I knocked mine down – I moved away. And

besides, I've spent so much time learning about walls and being hemmed in by them that I have the power to get rid of them too.' She tapped her temple. 'With my mind. Isn't that cool?' Belinda blinked. 'I can't be constrained. You can't constrain me! Nobody can.'

'Do I have a wall in my head?'

'Of course you do. All English people do. You are a very… wary lot. Lots of fears and hang-ups. And you, sir, especially, have a wall in your head. All that time spent inside small rooms, surrounded by four walls, tapping away on a keyboard. It's made you into a monster.'

36

2008

Kreuzberg seemed eerily empty. What seemed like the entire surviving staff of Mids TV (minus the cook and the cleaner) had flown back to Brum on some plasticky budget airline 737. Some Turkish women were weighed down with groceries. Behind them, a murder of cackling hipsters smoked like pirates. Otherwise the streets were quiet, the sky seemed open – as if you could pole-vault up inside it.

I'd been drawn back once more to St Agnes Kirche, but not entirely by my own volition. Something was dragging me here. I didn't really want to be back. The shoot had been enough for me. Why couldn't I leave it at that? But I couldn't leave it at that; I was on my way again. To see more horror, to be more upset. I should have gone up the TV tower and just enjoyed the city views instead. The St Agnes campanile emerged from a side street. It grew like a fat, cuboid tree as I neared it. Inside, the space overawed me as it had done the first time I entered all those years ago. The room – the nave, I guess – felt oppressive in some sense, its walls blank and austere. Yet that plainness was oddly freeing – you could project whatever mental pictures you wanted onto those walls. It was dark, but when sunlight streamed in through the skylights (depending on the movement of the clouds) everything changed; the light jump-started the building. Bel continually told me that space, not a building itself, was the thing you should concentrate on. Space is hard to define. What does it feel like? You can't touch it. You can only sense it. The space here seemed like a portion too much. So much of it, I felt so small. I hadn't noticed any of this while I was getting married. The glasses of Sekt in the morning had played their cheeky little tune on my synapses, making everything bouncy and surreal; my mind was focussed not on a building that day but on a person. Bel had talked to me about the church, shown me round and discussed it all, but I was too excited to listen to what she was actually saying. I nodded in all the right places and *Genau*-ed and *Ja*-ed in the correct gaps. I never imagined that something like a wedding day could be such a joyous occasion – the ones I went to, where other couples tied the knot, were pretty prosaic affairs, essentially excuses for all-day drinking and pork pie consumption. They didn't feel romantic to me, they didn't seem important. It was all just... pleasant. But that's the strange power of love. An outsider can never grasp the delirium and despair, the secret passions and the hidden joys that couples succumb to. The intensity is so private, so hidden.

There were some pine chairs arranged in rows in the middle of the church. I sat on one for a while, concentrating on how the light got brighter and dimmer with the changing weather. I played out our wedding again in my mind, imagining how it would have looked from this vista, how Bel would have looked from here, beaming and beautiful in her dress, standing next to an Englishman in a dark suit. I heard the door creak open and some footsteps move in the direction of the bank of chairs.

I was aware that there was a woman diagonally behind me, over behind my left shoulder. I turned to look. She had honey-coloured hair. I'd had enough of being here. It wasn't helping.

When I walked out into the sunlight the woman followed me.

What she said amazed me.

'You wrote *Big Plans*, didn't you? That show was a big hit in Germany.' She spoke perfect English, but with an unmistake-able Teutonic twang.

'Was it?' Was it?

'It was.'

'It can't have been. It wasn't even shown in Bristol, let alone Berlin. I'm sorry, but have we met before? I swear I recognise you.'

'I'm from Birmingham too. Look for me in all the TV pro-grammes you wrote. I'm there, sometimes hiding, sometimes not. I've been in your dreams too. I'm in the novel.'

'What novel?'

'The novel that we're both in. I'm in the dreams you have in the novel we're both in, the one that's about to end.'

'This is crazy. Are you OK... in the head? Do you need some help?'

'Of course I'm OK. Look at me. Stop. Just look at me.'

She looked horribly familiar. 'I do recognise you from some-where. But who are you?'

'Do you have time for a cup of tea, Donald?'

'How do you know my name?'

'I just know it. Do you have time?'

'I do.'

'Let's take a stroll down to Tempelhof Airfield. I like it there. There's a little cafe – when we get there, I'll tell you about how things are.'

We made it to the cafe at Tempelhof, travelling pretty much

in silence. The old Nazi airport was like a time capsule. I was looking forward to hearing what she had to say but also worried that I'd just end up being led up the garden path by some old lady who needed a nurse more than she needed me. I bought a tea and went to find her but she'd gone. I wasn't surprised. I wondered if she was real. What she had said made no sense.

37

1999

The illuminated sign above the door said *SC NDALZ*. I could only assume the bulb on the first *A* had blown. Or maybe it was some kind of high-concept thing, a quirky sign for a quirky strip club. The building looked like it used to be a petrol station – brick, one storey tall. It sat, lonely, on a roundabout somewhere on the Birmingham Middle Ring Road. I was too drunk to notice exactly where when I fell out of the taxi and almost grazed my cheek on rough tarmac.

'It's your bloody stag do – get in that bloody door.' Bob lifted me up and shoved me through the door, slipping the bouncer a fiver in one motion, then beckoning for the others to follow us, whistling like a bellhop. The bouncer looked on, ambivalent.

'Perfect. This is a fucking stag do!' Bob grabbed my cheeks with a pair of greasy paws and gave me a kiss on the forehead. His breath wafted over me, hot and sour – chicken jalfrezi and pilau rice.

He'd booked us a table right by the stage. I sank into the

soft chair, the type you get in hotel receptions. In fact the place felt a lot like a hotel reception – the banks of easy chairs set around low tables, the boring bastards in suits looking sweaty and shifty, the crappy décor. It was darker than a hotel reception of course, and there was more chrome. Chrome was the international visual language of strip clubs; Bob had dragged me to enough around Birmingham (I'd say, in fact, *all* of them around Birmingham). Sitting down made me feel dizzy. I had to grab the arms of the chair to steady myself. The thumping soundtrack of Eurodisco added to the sense of dislocation I felt from my body and from the place. And yet, this was the most quintessential thing to do in Birmingham, a true city of white-collar sin (here sin comes served with a car park outside, naturally).

'Whiskies please.' Bob beamed at the waitress, charming her with twinkling eyes, totting up how many of us there were with the finger of his right hand. He needed to do it three times before he got to a number he was happy with. 'Eight please, love. And one for yourself.'

A girl in her early twenties, wearing a short dress, sidled up to the stage facing us, pouted artificially, and began to gyrate. Within the space of a few minutes she was wearing only a pair of knickers and heels.

The whiskies arrived and Bob handed them out. He chinked my glass. 'So how do you feel? You're not going to be a single bloke for much longer. Looking forward to getting that apron on and being moaned at?'

'I really, really am. I wouldn't do it for anyone else.'

'Yeah, Bel is the one for you, mate. She's a cracker. If I was younger…'

'Shut up.'

Bob leaned further over and whispered in my ear. 'These

bastards look like they're from some engineering firm, not a TV station. What the fuck did we bring them for?'

'That was your idea,' I bounced back.

He nodded and looked over at our motley crew.

Baxter sat completely still, transfixed by the girl on stage. Ralph Marks was next to him, fidgeting.

Some guy in a suit I didn't recognise bounded over, swaying from side to side, drink in hand, and started pointing at Ralph Marks. 'It's you! Off the telly! Ha! This is a better show though, isn't it?'

Ralph looked ashen and held his head in his hands.

The others were young writers and crew from *Welcome To The Masshouse*, all behaving like teenagers, pointing and smirking as if they'd never seen breasts before.

I looked into the girl's eyes. They looked familiar. I leaned over to Bob. 'Do we know her?'

'Doubt it, mate.'

I was drunk, but not so drunk that I couldn't recognise someone I knew. 'Seriously. I think we know her.'

She clamped her legs round a pole and span around it. Then she got on the ground in a kind of cat pose, on all fours. She crawled to the edge of the stage. Baxter was sweating; Bob was grinning. I leaned forward.

'Hi. Er, did you do work experience with us last month?'

The girl snapped out of her sexy stripper persona and turned back into a normal human. 'Oh my God! It's you lot from Mids TV!'

She jumped up from her previous stance on all fours, bounced onto the edge of the stage and perched there, leaning forward to chat. 'You're Don. I remember.'

'I knew I remembered you. Sophie?'

'Sally! Close though. Sorry, this is weird.' She made a gesture highlighting her breasts then reached for her bra in one move and put it back on. 'So what brings you fellas in here?' I could hardly hear her soft voice over the music.

'Oh, you know...'

Her smile seemed to say, 'I know. Because you're perverted sods.'

Instead she said this into my ear – like Bob had just done, but the words went in more smoothly: 'Wow. It's so noisy in here. Let's go outside for a smoke.' She darted behind a curtain and emerged fully clothed, then headed for the door.

I stood up and followed. Everyone on the table was regarding me with jealous eyes. I gave them a camp wave and followed Sally outside.

'Cigarette?'

'Yep.' I took one. She was shivering. 'Have my coat. You're freezing.' I handed it over and Sally wrapped it around herself demurely.

'Thanks,' she said softly.

'I do remember you, Don. You were very kind to me when I was doing that work experience on *Welcome To The Masshouse*. Not everyone was. Too many of your colleagues were mean. Or out to shag me. Or something.'

'I try. And I remember you came up with some really good ideas. What was it you were doing again? Media studies?'

'Exactly. Third-year student at Birmingham University. I only ever wanted to work in TV. It's my dream.'

'What else are you doing? Any more work experience?'

'We have a student TV station at the uni. Have you ever heard about that?'

'That does ring a bell actually. How does it work?'

'We're all just volunteers and we learn by doing, really. There are some techie guys, some journalism students, some designers and stuff, some presenters. I couldn't do that! Too shy.'

I coughed.

'I am shy.' She inhaled her cigarette flirtatiously. 'I just want to be a producer. Behind the camera. That's me.'

I looked up at the low brick building that was the strip club's home. Now it looked more like a former roadside eatery that used to have juvenile branding. I was suddenly reminded of family outings by car when I was young The music thudded out, just a dull *der der der der*. Flashing light escaped from the open toilet window and the blacked-out front door, in front of which were two wonky, rusted silver poles connected by a red velvet rope. 'So how did you end up here?'

'Have you got any idea how expensive uni is these days? Unfortunately my parents aren't nearly as rich or middle class as the mums and dads of most of the students I know. Well, in my case it's only really a mum now, so...'

'Is it... scary here? Is everyone OK?'

'It's fine. It's easy. I just switch off. I don't look at anyone's faces. I felt mortified when I realised it was you guys. I deliberately don't look at anyone.'

'What about being... you know... naked?'

'Who cares?' She looked me in the eyes as she smoked. The look lasted a second too long. I tried to be the sensible one.

'So I hope you're studying hard.'

Sally burst out laughing.

'What?'

'Why are you talking like a fucking dad would?'

'Because I should be one. I'm old enough.'

She looked at me again. Silence. Possibility.

'I need to go back in. The boss'll moan. But I'm finished at two-thirty. If you wanted to... continue this discussion? Back in Selly Oak maybe – over some rum and a spliff... in a cold house?' Sally looked up at me.

I paused with my mouth agape. 'It's my… stag night,' I said, looking at the floor. 'So, er…'

'Oh my God, I didn't realise! Well, erm… shit. In that case, I think… you should go and have some fun with your mates and erm… maybe we shouldn't continue this discussion…' She paused. '…tonight. But maybe some other time?' She looked around. 'Actually maybe not. Sorry. Sorry.'

'Don't be sorry.'

'I've got to go. It was lovely to chat, Donald. Have fun! But can you guys maybe… get a different dancer? I'm too embarrassed now.'

'Of course. I can't take much more of this place. I don't mean you. I just mean… you know. Not my scene. Take care.'

Sally turned back to give me one last look over her shoulder as she walked inside. Her face was impossible to read. She looked so young. What the fuck was someone like her doing here, surrounded by these debased examples of masculinity, these boys let loose for a night, these believers in the power of capital and the cock over the feelings of everyone and everything? And was I one of them?

I finished my cigarette, suddenly aware of the cold. Of my lack of coat. I didn't care about that. I needed a sit down. And some coffee. And something like an apple pie – maybe one of those six-packs of apple pies, each contained in their own individual metal case as if they'd just emerged from a doll's oven. This… petrol station would have sold pies like those, but instead it had turned into a fucking strip club. I stared over at the building, cursing it silently. The sign above the door stared back at me, flickering a little. Now it read *SC NDA Z*.

38

2008

Birmingham Airport late at night. Fat men in garish shirts, women with their arses hanging out of jeans. Everyone sun-tanned except for one or two businessmen in pressed shirts. Hardly anyone looked like they'd been on a work trip. Containers of fags and bottles of alcohol strained plastic bags.

'I'll come round and cook you something,' offered Kate on the phone as I was walking through Customs.

I said, 'Yes, if you bring wine too.'

She said, 'Deal.' We finished the call.

Just after I'd got home and dumped my suitcase on the bed, Kate came over and whipped up some kind of Vietnamese soup with prawns and chilli and noodles. My mouth was paint-strippered by the peppers and their devilish seeds. I enjoyed that bit.

'So what did you do for those two days after we all left Berlin?'

A chilli seed made me cough. 'I met Bel's mum.'

'How was she?'

'Sad.'

'I bet.'

'See anyone else?'

I lied. 'No one else.' But then if only I could see the blonde woman was it really a lie?

'Wish I could have kept you company.'

'Me too. You could have saved me from two days of currywurst.'

'Oh Don, I hope you ate something more than just currywurst every day.'

I looked at her.

'I've found you something. A present.' Kate slotted a video into the VHS and cuddled up close to me on the sofa.

Titles flashed up, the outline of the Midlands region morphing into a dartboard. A stern voiceover: *'It's the fourth of April, 1984. From the centre of the country, from the heart of your region... it's* Bullseye*! Tonight...'*

'Shit, not this one,' Kate fumbled over the machine. She ejected the tape and inserted another, flashing me a grin.

It whirred into action. The picture quality was appalling. But the title music was unmistakeable. I could recognise The Rationalists anywhere.

'Jesus! No way. Where did you find this?'

'Never you mind.'

'I thought they wiped all the tapes?'

'Well obviously they didn't wipe *all* the tapes, did they?'

'*Hail To The Brummies* still exists.'

'It does.'

'Wow. Kate...'

'Wanna watch it?'

'Go on then.'

*

[Title music – 'Hail To The Brummies!' by The Rationalists.]

[Aerial shot of Birmingham, the helicopter flying north from the city centre, cars and lights strung out along Corporation Street, then along the Aston Expressway. The music really supercharging the passion of this intro. Eventually the helicopter reaches Spaghetti Junction, the most Brummie place of all. Hairs on the necks of Birmingham natives will be standing up now. Over the top of this ant's nest comes the titles.]

Title card – Hail To The Brummies

[A Brummie voice speaks my words, my script.]

Voiceover: 'Motorway city, spaghetti city, canal city to rival Venice, car city, manufacturing city, city of culture, city of concrete, city of ideas, city of optimism, city of cynicism…'

[Cut to a hundred people outside the factories at Longbridge, speaking.]

'Hail To The Brummies!'

[Cut to a hundred people outside the university at Selly Oak, speaking.]

'Hail To The Brummies!'

[Cut to a hundred people outside the Town Hall in Chamberlain Square, speaking.]

'Hail To The Brummies!'

The Wall in the Head

[Cut to a hundred people outside Aston Hall, speaking.]

'Hail To The Brummies!'

[Then silence. Two narrative shots taking place at the same time, with cuts between them, like flipping back and forth between two really good programmes on two different channels. The first is a journey around the Inner Ring Road, a rear-facing camera strapped to the back of a car so you can see white lines dashing away, road being unfurled, office blocks appearing then shrinking, signs on the opposite carriageway directing drivers to Solihull... Coventry... Lichfield... Wolverhampton... Kenilworth... Bromsgrove... Redditch. The other narrative is a stationary camera in New Street with the Rotunda and the Bull Ring Centre in the background. The camera shows the faces of Brummies walking up and down the street. Oblivious poses, thoughtful expressions, fags in chops. It is a perfect one-two depiction of this fine city, and the two strands work so perfectly together, and in silence. Bob was right about the silence.]

[Cut to a music venue. Priory Square. It's empty and a band are about to play. The Rationalists. They start to play their song 'Outsiders' live, then the action moves to inner-city Brum. Shots of Sparkbrook: sweet shops, curry houses, fabric warehouses. Witton: young people listening to ghetto blasters, men eating patties in the street, laughing. Soho Road: market stalls, exotic vegetables, exotic places of worship. Digbeth: the inside of an Irish pub, singing, dancing. Hurst Street: an Oriental supermarket, a small church, two men holding hands and laughing...]

*

I was so incredibly chuffed about her finding *Hail To The*

Brummies – a programme I thought had been destroyed forever – that I went out to the shop in Moseley and bought some beers. Ayesha the checkout girl could tell that I was in a good mood when I got to her till.

I handed Kate a can when I got back and opened one for myself.

'Something really funny happened in Berlin,' I confessed, finally. 'This woman. There was this woman.'

'Christ, not ag—'

'No, no, no. She was in the church. In Kreuzberg, where Bel and I got married. And she knew me. She knew *Big Plans*. She said she lived in Brum; she said they showed *Big Plans* in Germany.'

'*Große Pläne!*'

'Ha, well yes, look, that's not the point.'

Kate snarled. '*Große!*'

'Come on. Anyway she said she knew me, she said she was in my dreams, she said she was in all of my programmes. We walked and we talked. She seemed real. We sat down in the old airport at Tempelhof where there's a little cafe and I went to buy her a mint tea and then... she just vanished.'

'Jesus, you do attract the nutters. So who was she? I thought you said you didn't see anyone else?'

'The woman from the idents. The woman from my dreams.'

'I need some weed if we're getting into this kind of territory.' Kate sighed, reaching for her mobile to text a drug dealer. Her voice sounded exhausted; her face looked drawn. 'Well... point her out to me.'

'OK, but we'll have to keep our eyes open.'

'How does she know who you are?'

'I have no idea.'

'Is she in *Hail To The Brummies*?'

'Who knows. We'll have to watch it again.'

'OK, sport.'

We chinked cans.

Kate went out for a cigarette.

I picked up the VHS Kate had accidentally put on earlier and rammed it into the machine.

Now it was time for *Bullseye*, the hard-hitting weekly current affairs show for the heart of the country.

*

'Now it's time for Bullseye, *the hard-hitting weekly current affairs show for the heart of the country!'*

[The titles burst to life: a blue background, the vaguely melon-shaped outline of the Midlands region drawn on a map in luminous yellow; it spins round a few times then rearranges itself via basic computer graphics to form the shape of a circle, then of a dartboard. Then, looking from a side angle, a spinning computerised dart drifts slowly across the screen towards the – now shown in profile – map, which again rapidly turns to face us, the dart flying away from us towards the board. It lands slap in the middle of the board. Random letters form into the word Birmingham and then into the word BULLSEYE.*]*

Ralph Marks: 'It's the fourth of April, 1984. From the centre of the country, from the heart of your region… it's Bullseye! *With me, Raaaalph Marks. Tonight… it's chocks away! For Birmingham's new airport! We look round the self-consciously space-age self-service lunch buffet… [cut to still picture of a mug of tea, beef stew and peas, and bread and butter on a beige plate, on a cream tray, on a red table], the high-tech architecture… [cut to still picture of a car park*

and crane], and the maglev technology that will be taking us from Birmingham to every city in Britain by the year 2000…!'

[Cut to still picture of a sign saying SORRY – MAGLEV IS STILL IN TESTING PHASE. PLEASE TAKE REPLACEMENT BUS TO BIRMINGHAM INTERNATIONAL STATION.*]*

*

I pressed the power button on the remote control.

Kate came back in from the garden. 'What are we going to do?'

'What do you mean? That's a big question. A Sunday night question.'

'I mean it. What are we going to do? We all know Mids is going to shit. How much longer it's going to last I don't know. The life is draining out of it – and the city.'

'Nah, it just seems that way. I think. There'll always be something. Right?'

'I'm not so sure. And anyway, spending too long in the same place is unhealthy.'

'But you're a Brummie.'

Kate smiled. 'So are you. I don't know. The world is so big. There's something… I don't know. Something that feels… draining here sometimes, a melancholy in the streets. Even your garden is depressing. I can hear those bloody trains going past, to somewhere more exciting. But I can't see them over the fence. They're taunting me.'

'You want to know where they're going?' I answered. 'Worcester. Great Malvern. Hereford. Are you still jealous?'

Kate flopped down on the sofa beside me. She rested her head on my shoulder and sighed. 'TV's for young people. I can't be bothered sometimes, with the competition and the long hours and the shit pay and the nights in motorway service station hotels, and the 4 a.m. filming starts. And is any of it worth anything? If we go for job interviews in London no one will have seen a single one of the programmes we made, Don, because no one at Mids has bothered crowbarring them onto the network schedules. It's such a waste.'

I lied: 'It's not a waste. We've done some good stuff. It's taught us things...'

'What has it taught us? We're just scratching the surface of all these different things – mocking them or else making them seem more noble than the reality of it ever was.' Kate drank some beer. 'What would you have been if you weren't a TV writer?'

'A proper writer? Or an explorer in a safari suit. You?'

'I wanted to ride horses. Or be a fashion designer.'

'This is last week?'

Kate exhaled. 'I think I'm a bit old for those little-girl maga-zine fantasy jobs. I'm basically a fucking PA, Don. I sort other people's mess out.'

'No, come on. You edit things. You book people. You run the show. You're almost a producer. You're a better producer than Bob!'

'So why don't I get the cash or respect Bob gets?' Kate sipped more beer. 'And why are there no men in Brum? No nice ones. I don't want any more fucking guys who love cars and football and know nothing about anything else.'

'That's everyone in this city discounted, I think.'

'Well exactly! It'd be different if I moved to London.'

I wanted to argue with Kate, but she was right. It would be different. We'd be nobodies from the regions. Rather than basically running an entire fading television channel together we'd just be some other schmucks working on some other show and living on some other council estate because it was the only place we could afford to rent. I looked around my front room. I didn't want to leave. I liked the big mirror slung over the fireplace. I liked the paintings Bel had put up – the abstracts and the psychedelic dot paintings from the 1960s. I liked the blue sofa. I liked the green carpet. I liked the door to the stairs which actually looked like a door to a cupboard.

'It's exhausting.' Kate rubbed her head against my chest. I sensed she was on the verge of tears. A long silence. 'I'm lonely, Don,' she said. The words sat awkwardly in the room, suspended in the air for all to see, written up in big capitals. Statements of intent, saying so much with so few letters. Words said in the English language but words not allowed in the English culture. I could feel Kate's heart vibrating in the silence, throbbing, embarrassed. Waiting. For me?

I stroked Kate's hair. Tears trickled down her right cheek, leaving slick trails which caught the light. It made me cry too. 'I'm just… really lonely.' I rubbed the moist lines on her cheeks with my thumb, erasing the emotion. Perhaps.

'I am too,' I said, softly. 'We all are… inside. We all are. Everyone I love has died – my wife, my parents… my fucking dog.' I heard a stifled giggle squeeze its way between Kate's sobs. 'You better not die too. Promise me?'

She rubbed a tissue against her nose. 'I promise.'

Something could have happened in that moment; it had once before – a very long time ago. But some moments sit so sweetly poised between happening and not happening, and this was a moment where nothing happened. We sat there for a while longer. Kate's breathing slowly returned to normal, and eventually she seemed less agitated. I put *Hail To The Brummies* back on, and we mocked it – picking out the people with the worst haircuts and the funniest clothes. Kate fished a small bar of dark chocolate out of her handbag, snapped it in two, and we ate it like grinning kids. She stared up at me as she sucked at the melted bar, and I leaned over to kiss her on the forehead.

'Remember Nottingham?'

I nodded. A banana grin lit up her face as she chewed on the chocolate and stared at the screen. Nottingham was a one-off though. A long time ago. A different lifetime.

TEN BRUTALIST BUILDINGS

By Belinda Schneider

Chapter Eleven

The final countdown: my beloved Brum

Birmingham confused me at the start. It teased me occasionally; mostly it seemed utterly indifferent to me. Was it even a city? Most of the places you went were just in the suburbs. The place where it felt least like Birmingham was in its core. In the main markets the shoppers talked in that delicious, sugary accent which I could spoon into my tea.

But I was soon hooked. And it wasn't just the accent that hooked me. When I was away from the centre, in these weird suburbs, the city was flighty and enigmatic. Roads stretching every bloody way, roads with two lanes, three lanes, four lanes. Rows of shops, sheds and small factories and lamp posts and fences and scrubby bits of park, and fire stations and railway stations and police stations and fried chicken shops and some clusters of tower blocks and some cul-de-sacs for the people who were better off. And this motley collection, repeated in different variants and different shapes and different colours and different quantities all over the city. This is what Birm-

ingham is. A road and a school and five cul-de-sacs of semis here; a warehouse, some terraced houses and a corner shop there. Infinite varieties of suburbia spread across heathland that sometimes pokes up and out at you. You know the heath is there because of these gentle contours – not flat, not hilly, in between. Gentle slopes and gradients a child would ski down.

Now you might think these suburbs could be in Manchester or Leeds or Sheffield or Southampton or Leicester or Bradford. But if you love something you listen to it, you look at it. Now look again at those Birmingham suburbs – spot the road names, the road signs, the bus stops, the 0121 phone numbers on the shop signs. Connoisseurs will recognise that there's something uniquely Brummie about the shape of these suburbs; there's certainly something uniquely Brummie about the scope of them (aside from London, these are the most sprawling suburbs you can find in Britain).

Why am I talking about suburbs now? I'll try to explain. I wasn't a fan of these suburbs when I first visited them. They seemed parochial. They are – in a way. I wanted the drama and excitement of streets in the sky, of city centres. I still do. But Brum is systematically knocking all of those streets in the sky down, knocking all its great city-centre brutes down. All of those sweet 1960s edifices are biting the dust. I should have known it would all end in tears: the city's motto is 'Forward'. So as Brum turns its city centre from a brutalist playground into a catwalk parade of skinny glass-clad supermodel blocks of apartments, how about – and I know this sounds crazy – looking to the suburbs?

I have this feeling that people might want to start reimagining the brutalist aesthetic and the brutalist ideology. But it isn't going to happen anywhere where the land value is so high that idiotic developers can plonk down a great glazed block of offices or shops. Maybe it's going to happen in the suburbs. Maybe people will club together

somehow – I'm putting my futureglasses on here – and realise bru-
talist villages at key points in these aching, yawning suburbs. Maybe
they'll build little connected blocks of flats, shops and services, schools
and anything else. And maybe the architects will want to design in
concrete, extrude the living fuck out of the stuff, craft these space-age
shapes to go with the exciting townscape that courts and mixed-use
buildings and walkways and balconies create. We can learn to live
together, right? We don't always want to have a semi-detached house
with a car in the driveway? Maybe there'll be more cycle lanes then
as well – so you don't have to risk life and limb when you're making
a right turn off the Bristol Road on your way home from the uni-
versity.

This is just an idea.

I think we need grand plans again. 'Plans' got a bad rap because
plans didn't always end with good results. Didn't always. But did
sometimes. They really did sometimes. So why can't we dream big
again, plan big again and build something exciting again? And do
these places have to become sad or dystopian? Absolutely not – they
can be extraordinary places for ordinary people: ordinary people like
you and me, leading ordinary, happy lives, and sometimes lives that
transcend the ordinary and become special. Brutalism can be a back-
ground for ordinariness or greatness. Seriously.

But that's probably never going to happen, is it? Not while we have
such dilettantes running the bloody show.

What I really wanted to say was more simple: Birmingham daz-
zled me. I feel like I'm saying goodbye to it for some reason, but that
won't ever happen. I love living in Brum and I will be here for the
rest of my life – however long that turns out to be. There's some-
thing about the place you live in, the place you love in, that draws
you in. Brum might be an eccentric – and occasionally unforgiving –

mistress, but I'm under its spell now. It doesn't try to trap you. I hate feeling trapped.

As for its architecture, well, the older you get the more you realise it's all a bloody big game, isn't it? Men build because of their dicks – what you end up with is mostly crap. But sometimes, just sometimes, there are these little periods where everything falls into place – like falling in love, really – where you get some great buildings appearing that aren't just giant cocks, but are actually something over and above that base need for spreading seed and constructing priapically. But Brum is a silly billy. It doesn't know what it's got; it never knows what it's got. It's a meat-and-potatoes town run by ex-businessmen and politicians that can't make it in London. How different it would be if it were run by artists and academics. But artists and academics have got better things to do than sit in meetings all day, drinking tea, filling in forms and going on trade visits to China. That kind of life suits a particular older chap. There's no taste at the top. I fully expect Brum to tear down all of its best buildings and be left with hardly anything of merit. That's already happening. All the great stuff from the 1960s and the 1970s will probably be gone by the time I am. Isn't that crazy? Buildings can last 1,000 years, and these won't make 100. But that's Brum. It's the kind of place that does that. Just like it ripped everything apart in the 1960s and started again. But that time, when it built everything back up it did so with pride and passion and a bloody belief in the future. A belief in itself. This time – well, you know. It'll be bland. It always is. I'm past caring in some ways. I used to get angry but I see now that it's just the great circle of life. Kids will pick up books in the twenty-second century and say, 'Wow, that was what the future was supposed to look like?' Because that was what the future was supposed to look like. Futuristic. What will the future look like instead? Bland. Controlled by technology and corporations. Safe – I hope. Clean and neat – probably. But nondescript.

Our kids will live in a world that hardly even demands their attention because their attention will be on other things, like screens and themselves. And I suspect they'll only come to the centre of Birmingham when it's dark, to drink or shop or hang out with their friends at night. They'll see lights but no sights.

And what will those young Brummies make of this rambling text? They'll say, 'She was being so bloody nostalgic, wasn't she?' And I am. Nostalgic for an era and an aesthetic, sure – whatcha gonna do about it?

But nostalgic for a city too, and that's the point; that's why – in a way – I don't care what Brum does to itself. Because the act of doing all that stuff is very Brummie. Birmingham just moves on, doing its own thing. Funny how somewhere at the middle of the country is not really at the centre of anything. In the middle but outside the mainstream – and that's why I like Birmingham. That's why I love Birmingham. It's an island; it's not in step. Its little quirks and nuances dazzle me. I feel like a lovestruck teenager when I think about it. I feel like a lovestruck teenager when I walk about in it. It's a mess, but it's my mess.

This is a dream:

I'm watching TV. That big bloody goofy M is spinning round. Round and round. What's powering it? Why does it never stop? It spins above an image of the skyline of Brum. Just round and round. I feel like I'm being hypnotised. But suddenly… it breaks free from its anchorage and moves upwards. Then it turns a little, shifts into a diagonal position, and starts to fly above the city like a spaceship or something, making this sickening 'GRNNNN' sound. I have no clue what's happening. I rub my eyes but it doesn't get rid of the scene. The M does a low fly over Brum and, out of nowhere, starts to fire lasers from its legs. The lasers hit the Rotunda, and the Rotunda bursts into flames. Incredible. Quick as a flash, without any warning, the M dives right out of the screen and starts flying round my living room. Then it disappears through the window and I hear some whooshing noises, followed by the sound of a laser being fired, then again, and again, and then the screams of women coupled with huge explosions. I run out of the house into the street to see huge plumes of grey smoke rising into the sky above St Mary's Church. Then flashes of ochre and red as laser beams coming from the vengeful giant M spew out and hit houses and people and blow them both to smithereens and Baxter is there and he shouts out to Belinda and she runs towards him and they are squatting down behind a gravestone and he has his hand on her cheek and now the noise is so loud and dust is in my nose and shit is this really happening or is...

'This one never changes, does it? Whadda place.' That was some serious mid-Atlantic drawling there. Did you hear it?

'I know. The good old Bride. Shit as ever. Still love it though. Closest boozer to my house as well.'

'Not true. In the taxi I saw some new upscale bar – what are they called now? Gastropubs? Yeah, one of those had opened up. Right on the crossroads in Moseley Village. Loads of wankers stood outside drinking cocktails.' Charlie sipped his pint of Birmingham Bitter.

'You know what? That's right. I just always ignore that one. I figure if I go in, I'll be charged more than my mortgage for a drink, and also... I'll become an arsehole.'

Charlie looked amused. 'Too late for that...'

'How's LA?'

'Whadda you think? Sunny. Girls. Food. No one drinks.

Paradise. In a way. You get lots done. When you're not in the car.'

'But I can think of somewhere else in the world it takes a bloody long time to drive from one end of to the other... somewhere else with a lot of roads and a lot of suburbs.'

Charlie seemed to like that. 'Good point. Maybe Brum should market itself as the British LA. So look, mate, I was thinking. As I'm back. Did Bel have a charity or anything she loved? We're doing this one-off show. In Priory Square.'

'Priory Square?'

'Yeah exactly, they're knocking it down too. Final show there. Not our *final* show, I mean the final show there – we'll be the last band to play that tatty venue. I thought we could, you know, say how much we missed her. Give ten grand to charity or something. Or more. Whatever you reckon really.'

'I remember seeing you lot there. A good few years ago.'

'Yeah, Bob was there, right? Rat-arsed as usual. And your wife. Looking hot. Whaddya know. I thought, "That's a fit bird." And then her fuckin' boyfriend walks in wearing a jumper. And I realised it was the *Hail To The Brummies* guy. The big-shot TV writer! Total loser though.'

'You remembered it right.' I sipped. 'Can you be a small shot?'

He laughed. 'So this new TV thing you're doing. You wanna use the music on that? Be my guest.'

'Yeah, that would be brilliant. I think it would be perfect to have "Elizabeth Anderson" as the closing titles music.'

'Tell me about the film. It's a documentary, right? About Brum?'

'Yeah, a documentary, but not just about Brum. Bel's book was called *Ten Brutalist Buildings*, and she looked at ten – or so, because she always managed to cram in more stuff that she loved – buildings and places. So we really tried to bring the book to life. To make it accessible to TV viewers, to teach people about that architecture that Bel loved – uncompromising, concrete…'

'Ugly? I love those ugly buildings, love 'em.'

'Yeah? Good. But she saw beauty in it. Even in the ugliness. It really came out in the book. I wanted to write a script for the film to do it justice. We went and filmed it in Leeds, Sheffield, London and Berlin. And in Brum of course.'

'Good old Brum. I honestly never thought people would be mourning all those freew— motorways, I mean. And parking structures, and all those 1960s blocks. I like 'em. But hey, what do I know? I just write about love.'

'So did Bel. In a different way, but still.'

'Good for her.'

'Good for her.' We chinked drinks.

'I'd love to see the film.'

'We're doing a screening. At the Mids building. It might be the last chance you get to go there. I keep hearing whispers they're knocking that down too. Maybe I'll get the chop one day soon. They've already let half the staff go.'

'No way? I think our first interview was there. On that fucking terrible lunchtime chat show. Remember it?'

I nodded.

'We were supposed to play during the closing titles. Of course, in those days they used backing tracks, and the dim bastards set off the backing track before we were even ready. It was a sodding disaster. We just stood there, looking around, while our bloody song played out. Compete bunch of jokers. It just seemed funnier to stand there doing nothing, to be honest. Not even to move. We all joked about it afterwards. The host went rhubarb!'

'Typical Mids.'

'So whaddya going to do? If they... ya know?' Charlie ran his index finger across his throat.

'I have absolutely no idea.' I drank. One gutsy draught. 'Move to LA and write screenplays?'

'Exactly. Come to LA! We can hang out. Write a film set in Brum. There haven't been any. Flog it in Hollywood to some movie exec.'

'Oh, there have. You just haven't seen them. And believe me, you don't want to.'

'Which?'

'I'll tell you some other time.'

'Let's go for a smoke.'

'Yup.'

As we stepped outside, a white van drove past with a huge poster attached to its side. It had a giant photo of a woman in lingerie, and the text read: *SCANDALZ Gentlemen's Club – Brum's sexiest nite out. Open every evening from 9 p.m. to 3 a.m. Come and get SCANDALOUZ with Brum's hottest girls.*

Charlie pointed at it. 'I wouldn't mind getting scandalouz.'

'You're not missing anything. Believe me.' I paused. Turned to Charlie. 'I always wanted to know...' I lit both our cigarettes.

'Yup?'

'"Elizabeth Anderson". What was the story? Your ex, right? That's what Bel reckoned.'

Charlie laughed. 'Mate, I'm going to have to let you down here. It's a band joke, I'm afraid. She's not real.'

'Really? But...'

'I know, in interviews and stuff... well, it's boring sometimes to justify everything. So I lied. Hands up. There is no Elizabeth Anderson. Never had my heart broke.' Charlie smoked. 'Though... there was a girl from Stirchley once. Worked weekends in a bakery in that shopping centre above New

Street Station. She was called… Tricia? Something like that. Or maybe Tina. But no Miss Anderson. Sorry.'

'Bel really thought she was real.' I shook my head. 'I mean, she really did.'

'Not everything's as real as you think it is. That's just the way it is. Surprises everywhere, my friend, surprises everywhere.'

'What are you up to later?'

'Seeing my parents. Mum's cooking up a roast. Can't wait. You can't get a Yorkshire pudding in LA, believe me.'

'I do.'

A woman in her forties emerged through the door and into the evening air, then casually asked Charlie for a light without really looking at him. But when she handed it back she looked up at him. And kept looking. 'Bloody hell. You're famous, aren't you?'

'We both are,' said Charlie, which I liked.

The woman didn't look at me though. 'You're in that band. I know… it's on the tip of my tongue. My husband loves you lot.' She reversed to the door, pulled it open and ostentatiously yelled inside so the entire Bride of Bescot could hear, 'OI, LAURIE. WHAT'S THAT BAND YOU LIKE, LOVE? COS THE SINGER'S OUT 'ERE. COME AND 'AVE A LOOK.' She came back over, index finger tapping her lips. Her face lit up in a moment of instant recognition. 'I know it! The Receptionists!'

*

[Presenter] '*Today on* The Obituary Show, *we look at the life of the writer and architecture lecturer Belinda Schneider, and the impact she had on the way we think about buildings – especially concrete ones from the 1960s. Schneider was born in communist East Berlin but adopted Birmingham as her home town after studying at the*

city's university. Schneider's degree was in architecture, but it was her writing that made her name, as the author Aliana Wills remembers.'

[Aliana Wills] 'I remember seeing Ten Brutalist Buildings in the bookshop in the small seaside town where I lived at the time. I bought it immediately and I adored it. I'd always loved architecture but I couldn't find writing that did it justice. It is after all a visual medium, yet one which is also about philosophy and ideas. But very few people seemed able to transmute any of that into writing that wasn't full of jargon. Belinda could do it though. It was amazing. Magical.'

[Presenter] 'Inspired by Belinda's book, Wills went on to write a novel which used brutalist architecture as its theme – a style of architecture which a lot of people in the 1980s and '90s had been wary of, or in some cases openly hostile to – as architect Djende Mariosco explains.'

[Djende Mariosco] 'Brutalism was a product of the 1950s and '60s, and the '70s. It was so closely tied up with the ideas from the time, ideas about utopia and social democracy and big bureaucracies and grandiosity and free-form sculpture, that it really aged quite badly – in some ways. Certainly the 1980s and '90s, and even the 2000s, were not a great time for the style and really not a great time for architecture either – this was when we were harking back with silly neo-Georgian houses and supermarkets shaped like barns and terrible business parks. Belinda's book marked a complete reappraisal of brutalism – a chance to look again at the best of it. And when we opened our eyes – when Belinda opened our eyes for us – we saw just how good this stuff could be, with its exuberant shapes and its merging of interior and exterior spaces. We began to see things we hadn't seen before. Certainly a lot of young architects I was at college with were dismissive of it; they saw it as "failed" and "eccentric". But a few of us wanted to challenge that and show how brutalism actually had a lot going for it, and Belinda's book provided a language for us to do that, for us to defend what we could see was good but other people perhaps couldn't.'

[Presenter] 'Belinda taught a module about brutalism to Birmingham's architecture students and lectured around the world, and it's something she enjoyed doing on top of her writing for architecture journals and magazines. She was known as a popular teacher and speaker, but it was her writing that was particularly praised, as Wills notes.'

[Aliana Wills] 'Belinda was a gifted writer because she was trying to show us something more than the cliched dystopian view of brutalism that had developed. That idea that you shot sci-fi or crime films around these buildings, that they were scary, that they were troubling, that they were inhuman. Belinda said, "Look again. Look at the utopian ideals, look at the avant-garde design. This is beautiful." She also encouraged readers to see buildings as places where things happen: nice things, romantic things even. She talked about her own experiences in these buildings, about sunny days and people having fun, about bringing up families and falling in love. I know, for example, that she met her husband outside Birmingham Central Library, which was probably her favourite building of all anyway, and because of that chance encounter, it became absolutely sacrosanct to her.'

[Presenter] 'Belinda did meet her husband, the writer Donald [tape is inaudible for a second here], outside the brutalist library in the centre of Birmingham. He wrote the scripts for little-known television shows produced in the Midlands TV region, like the game show I Love My Dog!, a sitcom set in a planners' office called Big Plans and a celebration of working-class culture called Hail To The Brummies. Belinda told Aliana Wills that Donald was filming for *a regional late-night comedy and variety series called* Welcome To The Masshouse *the day they first met.'*

[Aliana Wills] 'Belinda laughed about the fact Donald was dressed as — can you believe this — a chicken when they first met. He was a writer on this show, a kind of post-pub thing — only ever shown in the Midlands. He'd interviewed her for a skit on the programme, and he later went into the library to track her down. She said she found it hilarious to watch him from the balcony, walking up and down each floor, looking for her. Of course she was studying back then and he must have completely ruined her concentration that day. But anyway, they got on, he asked her out and she said yes, they fell in love, got married and lived together very happily in Birmingham.'

[Presenter] 'Another fan was the artist Marija Trajkovski, who was born in Macedonia.'

[Marija Trajkovski] 'Belinda's writing, it was something I cherished. My art is all about... responses to brutalism, and her writing was too. We were linked somehow, I felt.'

[Presenter] 'It was Belinda's warm personality that many people dwelt on. Marija Trajkovski:'

[Marija Trajkovski] 'She was wonderfully friendly when I met her, and she was a very kind person. I met her husband after she died, and he was the same, very warm-hearted, and personable. I think he loved her very much; he idolised her, in fact. A lot of us did. She was out of the ordinary, very talented. It's so sad that she's not here anymore. But her writing and her spirit will definitely live on, I think.'

[Presenter] 'Belinda Schneider was born on the eastern side of the Berlin Wall and, appropriately perhaps, reached her eighteenth birthday in the year the wall fell — 1989. She went straight to Birmingham to study, and fell in love with the city as well as the university, discovering an affection for many of Birmingham's maligned mega-

structures and 1960s planning – at the time that those things were falling from fashion. She returned to Berlin to marry Donald at St Agnes Kirche, Kreuzberg, which was itself an austere brutalist building. Her legacy is not just a book, but also a forthcoming television film, as sometime Mids TV producer, and now programme controller, Bob [inaudible section of tape here] explains.'

[Bob] 'Belinda was one in a million. I don't actually remember that first day me and Donald met her, but he does! Don and I worked on lots more programmes together – him writing the scripts and me presenting or producing, and Bel became a great friend. When I basically became the man in charge at Mids TV in Birmingham, which was due to everyone else having been laid off as much as anything, I commissioned a film where Belinda would talk about the buildings she'd written about in the book, about the Birmingham she loved and the brutalism she loved. It was all ready to go when tragedy struck, and well… well I'm just so pleased that Don agreed to write the new script, to continue Bel's legacy. I think the documentary we've produced posthumously stays true to Bel's wishes, and ultimately the most important thing about it is that it captures all these buildings she loved before many of them succumb to the wrecking ball. We'll all miss her horrendously, Don more than anyone, of course. But we've got to remember what an incredible talent she was. A real gem. I'll miss that German accent and that cheeky smile the most. She was too young. Too young. So much more to give.'

[Presenter] 'Belinda was a keen cyclist who navigated the legendarily car-filled roads of Birmingham with a confidence that not everyone could muster. But the traffic-choked streets of the Second City were eventually to prove her downfall. She was cycling from her home to Birmingham University when she was mown down by a truck making a left turn on a busy road. Belinda died instantly. But

it's not Belinda's death she'll be remembered for, it's her life – and particularly her contribution to architectural criticism.'

[Presenter] 'Belinda Schneider, who's died, aged 37.'

*

Bob gave me a bear hug, and as he did it he made a sort of 'Hurgh' noise.

'Bloody hell, watch my ribs!'

'Always complaining, you are.'

'What's the verdict?' I asked. My voice echoed around the empty bar, the only bit of Mids TV I'd really miss – the only bit anyone would really miss.

He looked at his feet. 'We've been shafted. It's over. I've walked straight up from New Street, got the train back as soon as he said his piece. Fucking headquarters. Fucking money-grabbing bastards. Fucking Mackenzie.' Bob's voice echoed around the bar. I noticed how grubby the windows had become, how some of the chairs had been knocked over, the stains on the carpets, the cigarette burns on the curtains, the smell.

'What did they say?'

'Mackenzie. He says it's just not sustainable anymore. Mids is *haemorrhaging* cash like a Villa striker in a strip club. Advertising is drying up, staff costs are unsustainable, viewing figures going down quicker than a barmaid on a first date, plus these buildings' – Bob hammered against the glass and it wobbled with a deep trembling timbre – 'are buggered. They need millions to do them up. They're as old as you, son; you can't get to that age and not need some TLC. Who said everyone wants to build but no one wants to maintain?'

'Vonnegut.'

'Right.'

'So it's over.'

'Finished.'

'What about us renting some other space, borrowing another studio for productions? Close the building – fair enough. But save the station?'

'That was never going to happen. You need a TV… centre. You need what's here: offices, studios, technical facilities, everything together. This was it. And that, I'm afraid, is that.'

'Fuck.'

'Exactly. *Ten Brutalist Buildings* is the final production. He's shutting everything down next month, flogging the station, and putting the entire site on the market. Probably be turned into flats, won't it? They turn everything into flats – sorry, "luxury urban apartments" – now. Fucking solicitors and accountants who work on Colmore Row fucking buying them no doubt so they can fucking do loads of fucking coke off a glass coffee table before they go to one of those new fucking trendy wankers' bars in the Jewellery Quarter.' Bob picked up one of the heavy-bottomed ashtrays shaped like 'M's from the table and sauntered over towards the bar, the ashtray swinging from his hand, turning his right arm into a demented pendulum.

'What say you and I take the lease on the bar and try to open it up as some kind of retro attraction? Posters of the stars of Mids TV from the 1970s on the wall, the great programmes we made.' He made a sarcastic 'Ha!' sound immediately after suggesting this.

He went behind the bar and I stood up to see what was going on. He smashed the ashtray down onto one of the locks keeping the fridges from being ransacked by alcoholic staff. He looked like a man who knew exactly what he was doing; the whole procedure was as casual as could be. He bent down then reappeared and walked back over carrying four bottles of lager.

He handed two to me and sat the other pair down on the table beside him. 'They've fucked us. It's happening to all regional TV. I know guys in Newcastle, Plymouth, Norwich – all the same story. No one gives a monkey's anymore. No one's making money anymore. Everything's a Londoner's game these days. That's it. They make everything down there, it makes more sense. Or buy it in from abroad. There's no more room for local programmes, things just for the Midlands, from the Midlands. From any region.'

'What about all the TV we made though? We slaved for them. Doesn't it mean anything? All that stuff we did on a shoestring.'

'That's the bloody problem, isn't it? It was all cheap shit.'

'I guess it was. With a few exceptions.'

'Hardly any. Obviously some of the stuff you did and some of the stuff I did.' Bob popped the cap and started drinking his beer. 'But even we made some shite. And as for everyone else... saints preserve us, there was some toss on the screens. And besides, people don't watch TV anymore. Or... well... not the kind of TV we made anyway.'

I exhaled.

Look at this place.' Bob looked around the room. 'Everything we built, everything we made. All gone to shit. What's the point?'

'It was good while it lasted.'

'It was fun, wasn't it? Maybe that was the point. The output may have mostly been crap, but it was a lark.' Bob snapped his fingers. 'Jesus!'

'What?'

'You'll see. Come with me.' Bob yanked my left arm.

'Alright, boss.'

'This way.' He frogmarched me towards the other end of the bar and finally fell on his knees, crawling along to the point where a brown and burgundy and white carpet ended and some wooden panelling began. We were about a foot from the floor-to-ceiling windows that ran the length of the bar. 'Yeah. Here… I think.' Bob reached into his jeans pocket and pulled out a prison warden's bunch of keys. 'Well, who cares now?' He made for a Swiss army knife, flipped open the blade and began to extravagantly slice at the carpet. 'Too blunt,' he moaned. He hacked out three sides of a square and began ripping it up. The carpet died with a hideous tearing sound, like a malfunctioning zip. 'Nah, must be…' He tried again, chopping out another square.

'Buried treasure?'

'Exactly.'

He ripped the square of carpet up and I saw a little white corner poking out.

'Here!'

Bob delicately grabbed the corner of paper with thumb and forefinger and began to tease it out from under the carpet. I could see now that it was a photograph, about A5 size. Bob pulled it out and blew on it. Then he presented it to me.

'Look how fucking young you look there. You clown.'

I smirked. 'Amazing.'

'Look at us. Look at you in that stupid chicken costume. Jesus, I wish you'd kept your fake head on for this photo, to be honest. Then I wouldn't have to see your ugly mug.'

'You look a lot less fat here. Less pasties back then, more five-a-side.'

'Same number of pasties, bit more footy, more fags.'

'Look at the library too – you can see it right behind us.'

'Fuck the library, look at those birds. That blonde one. And is that… is that…?'

'Bel. Yep. That's the day I met her.'

'Bugger me, of course it was.'

'Remember we were trying to find foreigners, asking them to do Brummie accents.'

'She was the type of foreigner you wanted to meet.'

'Rather than another bloody engineer from Dusseldorf, absolutely.'

'When the hell is this from?'

I turned the photo over. There was writing on the back. In my handwriting it said, *What a day to be alive. 16 June 1990. My heart was going like mad.* In Bob's handwriting it said, *You look like a dickhead mate.*

Bob ran his hand over the words as if he was trying to suck the meaning of them up through his fingers and into his soul. He looked up at me, like a puppy. I thought he was going to cry. 'Remember we got pissed and we decided to put this under the carpet, for a rainy day? Poked it right under using a brolly. One afternoon when we were supposed to be writing *Welcome To The Masshouse* in here. So we'd always have a part of us in the building – in our favourite bit of the building – forever.'

'And in case we got sacked.'

'Which was, of course, always quite a likely possibility back then.'

'It really was.'

I stared at the photograph. Bob had his arm round me, was grinning wildly; I was grinning too. And then the girls on either side of us, on benches, a long way behind us and right in front of the library. Bel on one side, the mystery one with blonde hair on the other. The one I'd bumped into in Berlin. The one who'd vanished as quickly as she'd appeared.

'We had some good times, didn't we? We really had some bloody good times.' Bob ran his hand through his hair and sighed. He looked defeated.

'We did. And now some of us are closer to death than others.' I smirked.

'Oi. Bring those beers over.' Bob flipped himself, slowly, heavily, off his knees and onto his arse. He backed into the window and fell hard against it.

I went to the toilet and then to fetch the bottles of lager from the table. When I got back Bob was asleep, slumped, drool running down his jowls. This leader, this inspiration, this guide to me. He belched but it didn't rouse him. I couldn't watch. I walked out of the bar and was struck by how empty, how quiet the whole sorry place was now. As if on autopilot, I strolled into the office tower and called a lift, but they all seemed to be broken. Maintenance was, apparently, already winding down. I climbed the stairs to the top of the building and walked out onto the roof. I stood there, out of breath, surveying Birmingham and wondering what else was about to be knocked down by the imbeciles running the city these days; people even worse than the clowns I satirised in *Big Plans* – because at least they had ideas, even if they were often the wrong ones. Today's city fathers are destroying at the same speed that the ones from the past were creating. Bel hated them. She could see her dream was dying. It was.

I peered over the edge, dared myself to lean out and see what I would feel. I didn't want to jump from here again. The sickness in my stomach confirmed that. Vertigo's normal service had been resumed. I wanted to live. At least, I wanted to live for the people who needed me. That was a start.

It suddenly became gusty; I felt a chill too. I heard the fire door, that familiar creaking and clanking. A black-clad human emerged and floated over. There was something spidery about the get-up: the bits of fabric billowing around, the black-cloth-clad limbs.

'What do you want? Why don't you speak to me?'

Baxter looked at me for ten minutes. Then he opened his mouth. One minute elapsed, and then he finally remarked, 'I had congress with Belinda, an affair.'

Er.

What.

The blood drained from me as I contemplated the seven words he'd just said. Could it be true? Jesus. I boiled. I fucking boiled. Then I coiled my right arm back. I hit Baxter with such force that he fell down to the ground in a pile of bones. He lay, propping on his arm on the roof, nose bleeding, rubbing his head. I crouched down. I looked him in the eyes.

'Is it true?'

'Yes.'

I pointed towards the edge, overcome with aggression, unnatural hatred. 'Well fucking jump off here then if it's true. Fucking jump.' Did I really mean it?

'I shall.'

Baxter struggled to haul himself up onto the lip of the wall that ran around the roof's edge. He dusted himself down. He coughed a little and calmly shuffled to the edge. 'I apologise, Donald.' I ran over towards the idiot and tried to grab him, to save him. He jumped off as my hands reached out. One clean manoeuvre. Cleaner than my try. I think... I think... I assumed there was some kind of forcefield. If it saved me it'd save him. No one could die jumping from up here to down there. Could they?

One.

Two.

Three.

Four. Pop, like a balloon bursting.

I bent over the safety rail. Shit. He looked like a swatted fly, a tiny black pinprick flattened out with bursts of ruby squeezed outward in three directions. Could have been me. Could have been me down there on the paving stones. But it wasn't.

'Oh… shit.'

I stood there, drinking that beer, grasping that bottle in a quivering hand, imagining my wife having sex with someone else. I thought I knew everything about Belinda, but clearly there was so much more to it, so much more to her, so much more going on. Maybe I'd never know the whole story. Belinda couldn't be boxed in – by the Berlin Wall, by Birmingham, by me. She had to escape. She had to choose her own path, make her own mistakes. It was as if everything had changed; everything I thought was there was not there. There's no narrative. I was right. Nothing makes sense. Nothing makes any sense anymore. Events aren't linked, people come and go, truths and half-truths ebb and flow, bits and pieces, ideas and regrets. There are no complete visions, no good stories, no perfect endings. I looked back over the edge. I thought long and hard about this. Thought about what had happened. Thought about what to do. I saw two paramedics rushing over to the swatted fly. Bystanders shouting, screaming.

'Fuck.'

TEN BRUTALIST BUILDINGS

By Belinda Schneider

Appendix – sort of

A guide to the buildings you've just read about

Most writers would put this in at the start, but I didn't want you to get bogged down in the boring details too early. I wanted you to get a feeling for these places, to see how emotions could mix with concrete before we got into too much of the serious stuff. I also wanted you to see how pieces can effortlessly slide into place – if something (a building, a painting, a book) is well-constructed and meaningful enough to do that without you even noticing how it's done that. Hopefully you've come to the realisation that we're dealing with an idea, an aesthetic, that's actually important. Uncommonly important. And in fact so important that it can and should be seen in hundreds of years' time as totemic of an age, as the totem of the post-war age of progress. Not just a concrete monstrosity. Not just an aberration. Not just a failed utopia. But a genuine attempt to reimagine and improve the cities of the world on a vast scale. Was it a success though? Well, again we come back to the human experience. I can't tell you what you feel, what to feel. But I can tell you that you must feel. That you must feel a building with your hand, that you must feel a building with your heart.

Our ten brutalist buildings:

1. Birmingham Central Library
Birmingham, England
Year built: 1974
A huge public library in my adopted home town. My husband said

that the first time he saw this library – on the day it opened in 1974 – he thought it was a spaceship that had landed in the middle of Birmingham. It was in this place I studied, in this place I met my husband. The library is part of a wider complex of shops, arcades, bridges and undercrofts in the middle of a roundabout evocatively named Paradise Circus.

Status: due to be closed and demolished.

2. Priory Square
Birmingham, England
1966

A complex in the shopping district of Birmingham on several levels, on a hill between Bull Street, Corporation Street and Dale End. Shops, an open-air market, bars and a huge music venue – all linked by stairs and bridges. Not as famous as the more widely remembered and regarded Bull Ring, but every bit as exciting. The complex had a second life from the early 1980s onwards as a haven for alternative culture. Its clothes shops catered to fans of goth, metal, then dance music. There were record shops. The music venue was the most important in the city from the 1980s to the 2000s, hosting an astonishing number of gigs by the best bands and DJs of the day.

Due to be demolished.

3. St Agnes Kirche
Berlin, Germany
1967

A stark church in Berlin's Kreuzberg where I married my husband. Look how little detailing there is. It's a powerful symbol of – to me – the unrelenting nature of religious adherence. It's now listed as a scheduled monument, and there are plans to turn it into an art gallery and cultural centre – the perfect way to treat it. Protected; cannot be demolished. Due to be reconfigured for a new use.

4. Eros House
London, England
1962
Built as offices first off, then it later became flats for the people of Catford. I love how the façade chimes different notes, with its window pieces popping in and out like piano keys. And I love the glazed staircase on the front. I found this little tic – this glazed staircase – on many more brutalist buildings I discovered later during my travels. This was the first time I saw that style, though. Now it's residential, and it doesn't seem in imminent danger of being knocked down, though it has had an odd re-clad job which has spoiled it a bit.

5, 6, 7. The three brutalist mega-villages:

Leeds University
Leeds, England
1963–78
A sprawling new campus for the students at Leeds University. The site drops off a cliff but the buildings keep flying through the sky so you can stay on the same level. The dramatic switches in levels, the bridges, the vast spaces – they're all quite profound. This complex includes the EC Stoner Building of classrooms, labs and offices; then there's the Roger Stevens Lecture Theatre building and the EC Boyle Library. The library was opened in 1975.
Listed, well looked after and still going strong today.

Thamesmead
London, England
1966–

A council estate so big that it resembles a new town. And it looks more like a town today because new building continues, so everything is from different periods. But the bit we're interested in is the southern portion of Thamesmead around South Mere Lake and along Yarnton Way. That was built from 1966 to roughly 1974. It consists of high tower blocks and medium-rise 'clusters' – courts of flats with walkways and paths threading through. There were also interesting shopping parades, a pub and a medical centre.

The site continues to be home to thousands of people – and more move in as new homes are built around the periphery of Thamesmead. But the pub, shopping parades and medical centre around South Mere Lake have been knocked down.

The Barbican
London, England
1965–82

One of the world's most impressive brutalist cities within a city, the Barbican is a huge complex in London's financial district that was bomb-damaged in World War II and rebuilt in this total style – not just a building but a whole space-age neighbourhood. There are blocks of medium-rise and high-rise flats, a school and a gallery, cinema and arts centre – everything raised up on a platform and free from traffic, with the cars in a tunnel below it. The water gardens in the middle give it an incredibly relaxing and quiet feel for such a central, highly urban location. If I could have lived anywhere in the world that wasn't the Birmingham suburb of Moseley – where my husband and I reside happily – then it

would have been here at the Barbican.
Listed, wildly popular and incredibly well janitored. This is bru-
talism that even the haters love.

8. Yorkshire Gazette Building
Leeds, England
1970
A headquarters for the local newspapers in Leeds – offices for
journalists and advertising departments, and a print room where
the papers were published. Interesting varieties of shapes built the
block up into a really engaging whole. The hexagon at the centre
catches your eye, as does the clock tower. The Inner Ring Road
flyover that shoots across a roundabout in front of the building
gives this whole ensemble a complete late-60s flourish. This was
what the future city was supposed to look like back then. Mighty
newspapers and TV stations of that era wanted to show a progres-
sive face with buildings like this.
The newspaper wants to move out and flatten the building.

9. Park Hill
Sheffield, England
1961
A snake. A snake for living in. Essentially one superblock of flats
that squiggles its way across a hill above Sheffield. The roof height
is the same, so the top bits are shorter and the bottom bits are much
more cliff-like. Corridors stretch along the whole thing, and there
are playgrounds, parkland, and pubs in the middle. A bridge, with
the graffiti Clare Middleton I Love You Will U Marry Me,
is my favourite bit of this place. It's the most sad, surprising and
romantic thing.
This is listed – but the renovation work is only really keeping the

shape of the building. Everything else will change. Council tenants kicked out. New facades. But at least it's not being knocked down, and at least it shows that brutalist buildings can be places that people want to live.

10. *Mids TV HQ*
Birmingham, England
1969

The HQ of the local television station for the Midlands of England (hence why the station is called Mids TV). There's a skinny concrete tower of offices, a fat squatting studio complex, and a bar with a long glazed run of windows. The bar overlooks a plaza, which is a teeming public space. Because it's television and it's glamorous, the whole complex feels alive and sprinkled with extra stardust. If you ever get a chance to get up to the top of the tower, you'll be rewarded with the most magnificent views of my adopted home town. You can make out all of Birmingham's best buildings from up here. You can look down on the Central Library, across at the BT Tower, over towards the Rotunda. And you can see all the roundabouts, roads and car parks working together in harmony. Cars gliding from place to place, people wandering through the busy streets.

'Cheese, that… Spanish ham, olives, breadsticks, crisps – salt 'n' vinegar, sour cream 'n' chive – sausage rolls, dips with vegetables.' Bob proudly read out the inventory of snacks. 'What a fucking wrap party this is going to be.' The last bit sounded sarcastic. It was so quiet. The Mids Bar had never felt like this for a wrap party. In years gone by the atmosphere was always, at the very least, rowdy.

People arrived in dribs and drabs, milling around in almost

total silence. They looked scared of the sausage rolls. 'They won't bite!' said Bob, noticing the same thing I did. I saw my neighbour Mrs Henderson gingerly go in for a try, and I waved at her. She waved back with the sausage roll held aloft like a pastry-coated trophy.

Bob, now back from his sojourn in the land of the sleeping giants, sighed and vanished, returning after five minutes with four bottles of red wine, adding them to the twelve already on the table.

'Where are they from?'

'Never you mind.' He tapped his nose. I wondered if he'd been secreting nicked bottles of wine from decades of previous wrap parties in a cupboard somewhere. He probably had something approaching a cellar now, and clearly there was no point in keeping them all anymore. I squinted at the bottles and saw that each had a different label, a different year. Each nicked, clearly, from a different event, a different bash to celebrate the completion of a different useless Mids TV production.

'Don't mind if I do,' said Kate, leaning over and casually filling a plastic pint cup almost to the brim with wine. She took a gulp. 'Jesus… is this from the 1970s?'

'You look nice,' I said.

'Thanks. Big occasion, isn't it? Though the vibe's a little bit…'

'Flat.'

'Yeah, that's the word I was looking for. Do you know all these people?' She looked around like a meerkat. 'There's some wedding crashers?'

'There's some security guards, I think, and the techie guys, cameraman and stuff. The cook from upstairs is somewhere as well, a couple of cleaners who asked what was going on and I told them to join us… oh, and few people from the university. And my neighbour. I don't know where everyone else is.

I invited Marija the artist; that writer I met at the Barbican, Aliana; Djende the architect...'

'Really? Well that's a fucking A-list party right there, isn't it? It's like Oscars night in here tonight.'

'Exactly like that. Give me some of that wine.'

'I wouldn't. Let's open another.'

'Is there even a bottle opener?'

'No, they're all screw-top.'

'Bob treats us too well.'

Kate smiled. 'Ooh, I forgot to say. Apparently someone just jumped off the tower. Suicide.'

I feigned surprise. 'Really?'

Kate munched on a crisp. 'Yeah, all I know is...'

Bob yelled, 'Kate, my love, can you come over here for a sec?' Kate made an exasperated face at me and went over to where Bob was fiddling with a shrink-wrapped pack of about a hundred napkins.

Janusz came over carrying a plate of Manchego slices. 'This cheese is good. Would you like some?'

'Thanks, mate,' I said, genuinely touched by his generosity. 'Top-up?' I picked up one of the bottles and blew the dust off it.

'It all tastes like shit, but yes, I will.'

'Donald, our waiter!' Shazia said, surprising me from the other direction. 'I'll have some of that wine if you're offering. And who's that guy in the leather jacket over there? The one who's in his fifties? The one who's looking at me.'

I span round. 'Oh, that's Charlie Sullivan from The Rationalists. They were Bel's favourite band. Brummie legends. Charlie! Come over here.'

'Got any smokes?' said Charlie when he arrived. 'I'm dying for one.'

We went out onto the plaza in front of the building and sparked up.

I caught sight of a woman in a summer dress approaching. She seemed to be looking straight into my eyes. At a distance of about thirty feet she shouted, 'Donald!'

'Who's this?' said Charlie.

'No idea.'

'Donald. You look just the same.'

'I'm sorry…'

'Sally. Remember me? From work experience.' She blushed. 'And, er…'

It took a while to register. 'Oh my God, yes!'

'I heard about your screening and…'

Charlie was smirking.

'Oh, this is Charlie.'

'I know. I love your band.'

'Thanks.' Still smirking.

'What a nice surprise for you to come and join us, Sally.'

'Well I wanted to. It sounds fab.'

'Can I ask how you heard about it?'

'On the TV grapevine.'

'Oh great, you're working in TV?'

'Yep, running my own production company in London. Just came up on the train. Thought I'd surprise you. Remember my work experience days here… student days in Brum! Crikey.'

'Amazing you run your own company now.'

'Hard work, let me tell you. Always looking for hires. We're very much in need of writers for a new topical weekly comedy show we're pitching to a couple of channels.' She winked at me.

'Is that so?'

'Maybe you can email me if you… hear of anyone good?' She handed me a business card.

'Come on in and have a drink with us.'

'Won't say no to that.'

'See you inside.'

Sally went through the doors. Charlie made a gesture with his hands as if he wanted me to explain more.

'What?'

'Who's that?'

'Someone I've not seen for… a few years.'

We went back inside and Charlie disappeared to go and chat up Shazia. I turned and saw a Chinese woman in her seventies holding a white cardboard box.

'Mrs Chu!'

'Mr Donald. I brought these.'

'Thanks for coming.' I couldn't remember inviting her. 'It's very kind of you to bring these…'

'Fortune cookies, Mr Donald.' She opened the box.

'Wow. I'll take one of these for later.'

After our little reception down in the bar we all filed up to the canteen. Bob sorted out the screen in the corner and turned down the lights.

I heard the door creak and turned to see Aliana Wills, Djende Mariosco and Marija Trajkovski tiptoeing in. Aliana glanced quizzically around the room and waved when she saw me, before making her mouth into one of those big 'O' shapes that represents the most distinctive part of the word 'sorry'. The three of them pulled up chairs at the back and sat down.

Bob rose to his feet and coughed. 'Thanks for coming. I'm not going to say very much today because… if I do, I think I might get a bit emotional, to be honest. I just wanted to say that you've all done a bloody incredible job on this film and that I think Belinda would be dead proud of us all for this.

We've tried to capture the essence of what she wanted to do – to show some love to these fucking great pieces of concrete. I still don't think I can see it myself, but I'd do anything for Bel. She knew best. Right, Don?' I nodded. 'We've created a piece of film here that no bloody idiot at the council or in our boss's offices can ever delete. This is a record, a memory, a tribute. To Bel and to her buildings. My biggest regret is that she couldn't be the one presenting this film, because she'd have been fucking great at it. And I think you'll agree that she was a lot better-looking than Baxter. Actually, on the subject of Baxter – where the hell is he? Has anyone seen him? The lazy sod could've at least turned up to see his own programme, for his own wrap party.' Cue some absent-minded glancing around and mumbling from audience members, as if Baxter was a set of lost keys hiding behind the sofa. I swallowed. My Adam's apple felt as big as a boulder. 'So enjoy it. And remember Bel.' As he hit the play button I glanced out of a window and noticed a police car pull up outside and two fresh-faced coppers jump out. 'Lights please, Shazia.'

We sat in silence to watch the final edit of *Ten Brutalist Buildings*. Fifty-seven minutes' worth. It was wonderful. Tender, poised, beautiful to look at, exactly what Bel would have made if she was able to. When it finished, Bob announced, coughing a little more, that this was to be the last programme that Mids TV would ever make. There were a few gasps, but to most of us it was no surprise at all. From now on, all content was to be bought in from London or the United States. The studios and the offices were to be knocked down. Kate corrected him and pointed out that *50 Years of Mids TV* was actually going to be the last official programme made, and he deferred to her. I asked if we could rewind and watch the closing montage sequence again. Bob nodded and rewound four minutes from the end.

The titles rolled up:

Written by Donald Fraser
From an idea by Belinda Schneider. Based on the book *Ten Brutalist Buildings* by Belinda Schneider
Presented by Baxter Turncastle
Production Manager Kate Crostley
Make-up Shazia Baqri
Transport logistics Janusz Wozniak
Camera James Ballard
Sound Bryan Johnson
Music by Charlie Sullivan & The Rationalists
Producer Bob Thorpe

And then the most incredible montage began again. Abstract shots of Belinda's most beloved buildings, moving images which showed spaces that were quite unexpected. I don't know how they did it, but the cameramen had captured everything without a single person spoiling the scenes. It was truly haunting. Low-angle shots, close-ups, pans, even some shots from above. Everything looked dreamy and dead. But then everything was dreamy and dead. An ending. Everyone wants beginnings, but endings are the parts that really get you in the gut. The inevitable, sad, inconclusive, messy, disappointing, lonely, overworked ending. I swallowed hard. The familiar sound of 'Elizabeth Anderson' began to soundtrack the images; the sadness of the pictures and the sadness of the song was too much. I looked at Kate. Tears streamed down her cheeks. I looked at everyone – most of them were upset too. There was only one shot with a person in it, and the one person in the shot was Belinda. It was a still from *Welcome To The Masshouse*, of her outside the Central Library, smiling. I pressed my fingers hard into my eyebrows and felt the life gushing out of me. Bob leaned over and hugged me. Underneath Belinda's youthful face, it simply said *(C) Mids TV MMVIII*. The tape ran out. The room remained completely still and completely quiet apart from some sobbing and sniffling coming from behind me.

Bob ruffled my hair, stood up, and said in a deep bellow, 'My round. Who's coming to the pub then?' And every single person got up.

Bob turned to me and whispered, 'Where the fuck's Baxter gone?'

I thought about Belinda and Baxter. It wasn't so much pain I felt as emptiness. It was too confusing to process. I shook my head and shrugged. 'Let's just go and get a pint.'

I felt hungry. I patted myself down and discovered a hard protuberance in my jeans pocket. 'The fortune cookie.' I snapped it open and wolfed it down in one. I unfurled the piece of paper. The message read, *We luv your TV shows!*

I must have looked puzzled. I heard some cackling and looked up to see Mrs Chu right in front of me. 'Turn it over, Mr Donald.'

On the other side, the piece of paper read, *Not really!*

'It's funny!' cried Mrs Chu, her eyes watering, happiness spreading across every wrinkle of her face. 'We take the piss out of you... but in a nice way.'

'You certainly did, Mrs Chu.'

39

2015

'I haven't seen you for a while.'

'I know, mate, I know.' I hugged Pete.

'Where've you been?' I asked.

'All around. You know. But I'm back here now. Back in Brum. It always drags you back. Somehow.'

'I know the feeling.'

The BT Tower loomed over us.

'Walk down the canal?' Pete offered. I nodded.

'So that TV programme you were making, the one about buildings. I watched it. Really enjoyed it actually. So did the wife.'

'Thanks for saying.'

'Your Belinda would have been very proud. I read on the Internet afterwards all about it. All about her book and stuff. I'll have to buy it.'

'She wasn't really *my* Belinda. She wasn't *anyone's*.' I felt sick. 'I'll lend you mine.'

'Oh, don't you worry about that. I'll order one online. Kids'll show me how. So I get the feeling you're after another favour.'

'I sort of am, actually. I had this feeling… you might be able to help me with something. Something a bit… well… I don't know quite how to put it.'

'Oh, you don't know how to put it? This sounds like it's gonna be interesting. Shall we go to the pub?'

'I think we should talk about this bit while we're walking, mate, but I promise I'll buy you a pint straight after for your efforts.'

Pete turned and beamed at me. 'You bloody better.'

I hesitated, bemused, unsure if I should continue. 'So I was thinking the other day – the times I've tried to get hold of you, when there was something like… a war on or something. You know. You weren't really around, were you?'

'Wasn't I?' Dramatically said.

'No. And it just occurred to me as well that I read some stuff, silly stuff really, about the BT Tower having all these tunnels, stores underneath. All kinds of top-secret stuff, high security. And also Bob once mentioned to me that if you wanted to go unnoticed then a uniform and a trade like the one you've got would be pretty much just the ticket. I mean, you've got a cover there, haven't you?'

Pete smirked as we walked. Silent.

'I knew I was on the right lines last night when I was think-ing about it. And don't worry, I haven't told a soul about this. I wouldn't ever tell anyone. It's just, I feel like there's a job I need to finish, I guess. Something really important that Bel would have wanted me to do.' I paused. 'Us to do. Pete. Mate?'

Pete inhaled. He looked both ways. There was no one around. He got out a cigarette and lit one up, then looked me straight in the eyes. 'What do you want blowing up?'

A smile spread over my face slowly, sheepishly. 'I fucking

knew it. I fucking knew it! You're in the Special Forces...
right?'

'Give yourself a pat on the back.' Pete paused and then made
a cycling gesture with his right hand. I got the hint.

'Yeah, so, I hadn't thought this far ahead. But really... yeah,
I want your help. I think I do. They're going to tear down Bel's
favourite buildings. The Central Library. Priory Square. And
the place where I used to work – the Mids TV HQ. All three.'

'Why?'

'Because they've got no fucking taste. They're monsters.
And they wanna make money.'

'Who?'

'Our esteemed city fathers. In their infinite wisdom, they
reckon Brum needs rid of the past, of anything from the 1960s,
from the '70s. Idiots.'

Pete chuckled.

'It's ridiculous really. Reading Bel's book, making this film
as a homage to her. We've been to London, Leeds, Sheffield,
Berlin – of course. They're knocking down some of the buildings Bel liked in those cities. It's just this stupid virus of destruc-
tion everywhere. But Brum is undoubtedly the worst of all
these cities – destroying *all* its brutalist buildings, *all* of its
links to the "Age of Progress", as Bel called it – the 1960s and
'70s, I mean, she meant. And they're replacing those buildings she loved with a load of shite. It's a big corporation in
charge – Aspiration Urban Existence Cocoons. They're going
to build these boring, soulless blocks of yuppie flats on top of
the ashes of Bel's top-three buildings. It's sacrilege. And the
names they're going to give these apartment blocks are beyond
belief: No. 1 The Books to replace the library, No. 1 The
Studios where Mids TV is, and No. 1 The Priories at Priory
Square. Just three glass towers, cheap and nasty, full of tiny
little flats that'll fleece young professionals who, quite under-

standably, want to live in the city centre. But it'll be a city centre without any bloody reason to visit. Mate, does that sound like the kind of Brum you want to live in?'

'Nope.'

'Do you wanna do something about it?'

'Nope.'

'That's not the right answer.'

'Why is Brum demolishing all this stuff if other cities aren't then?'

'Fuck knows. But I think you can take a guess from the city motto above the council HQ.'

'Forward.'

'Exactly. Forward.'

'So you want to stop them knocking all these brutalist buildings down?'

'It's too late for that. They're going to knock them down come hell or high water.'

'You want to blow up the council offices?'

'Jesus, I don't want to kill anyone.'

'Me neither. Not anymore.'

'I just want... I just want the story to end with a bang. That's all. No deaths. No one hurt. But rather than a depressing little whimper, I want Bel's story to end with a fucking bang. She'd have loved that. She'd have loved it like that. I know she would. A final tribute to her. On the day they open those bloody new apartment buildings, in a couple of years or whatever... so no rush... but – well, I want that first day to be the last day anyone will see them.'

Pete exhaled. 'Are you sure about this?'

I hesitated. 'I'm not sure... I think I am. Sometimes you have to stand up for what's right. Even if it means doing something wrong.'

Pete tossed the ciggie into the canal. The ripples from the

point of impact spread fast, wide. 'I'm not saying OK, because it is a crazy request. But I'll see what I can do. We've got time. Lots of time to think.' I saw his reflection in the dirty water. 'My dad was in the army. I remember he told me once about a plot, in 1974. Some of them were trying to drag him into this thing – it was a coup attempt. He said he told them to fuck off, to think about right and wrong. I remember his cheeks going red when he told me this tale.'

'I know exactly what you're talking about. My dad was fascinated with that plot. Thought we could have ended up with a crazy dictator like in South America. Maybe we nearly did.' A memory came to me. 'That was exactly one week after the library opened. That was when they were going to take over the country.'

Pete looked thoughtful. 'Everything's circular, I guess.'

'Hmmm. Maybe. Maybe not.'

Then he cracked a half smile. 'Now about that pint…'

Yellow dinosaurs with greedy mouths chomped into Birmingham Central Library. I'd survived but it had not. Its organs were visible in the wound of smashed concrete. I opened the pot containing dry ashes that were somehow once connected to my wife in a way that seems too abstract to comprehend now. I scattered half of them where the building was dying. They blew away in the breeze. I shook hands with the foreman and gave the white safety helmet back to him. I crossed the bridge that swooped over the traffic circling below on Paradise Circus and navigated Centenary Square, past the city's new library, which looked like an enormous Christmas decoration. The Mids TV HQ and studios were being knocked down too. More dinosaurs ate away at the structure. Everything was vanishing. Everything.

40

2019

Is this a dream?

Then I saw Pete. He was sitting on a bench, looking non-chalant. I turned round and time froze momentarily as I examined No. 1 The Studios. A monotonous new tower clad in glass and black plastic – shoebox-shaped, with dozens of odd protrusions up and down its facades like something approximating a pub game you play with stacked wooden bricks. The asymmetrical block was the worst kind of flimsy, flashy shite. Apparently this kind of architecture was what this kind of age was represented by. Bel had schooled me. I understood. This building said nothing of note. It meant nothing. It was all about making money for an elite. It was everything that Bel had railed against. It offended me because I knew it would have offended her. And because it occupied the site where our studios once sat. The studios weren't much and you probably don't remember them, but they were a part of my life.

This hideous skyscraper looked exactly like No. 1 The Books, with its even more moronic name, which sat 300 yards away over on the old Central Library site. The two were essentially the same building; the architects hadn't even bothered to make them distinguishable. All the flats had been sold in both blocks – many to foreign investors, some to British citizens in their forties and fifties augmenting their pensions. Most of the flats would then be rented out to Birmingham's young couples, master's students, office workers. 'Buy to let' had become a scourge. Over at No. 1 The Priories, it was the same story: same shit design, same sell-out. All three buildings were to be opened on the same day – today. 16 June 2019. A terrible trinity.

Pete rose. 'Just got the word back. All the buildings are emptied. I called in false fire alarms. Everyone's out. The ball's in your court...'

Suddenly, I was aware of a presence. From nowhere. I turned. It was her. A woman with honey hair stood next to me. 'I'm sorry I lost you in Berlin that time.' Hot breath in my ear. 'Now do it.' I turned and she had gone, but Rocaster and Benedetti appeared in her place, and they both nodded too. So I nodded at Pete. He raised his eyebrows and reached into his jacket pocket. Rocaster and Benedetti disappeared. Everything seemed so still and so calm for a few seconds. Then, suddenly, I felt a blast of heat like someone opening an oven door. A blinding white flash erupted in front of my eyes. I felt the earth contract and expand, tilt a little. I toppled sideways like a felled oak. Floored. A sound like a thunderclap cracked a mile into the sky. I lay there, blinking, looking up at the angry sky. I rolled onto my side. The faces of bystanders contorted in shock and wonderment – and fear. Rubble began raining down; dust billowed. A few seconds of silence, as if nothing had happened, as if time itself couldn't understand what had taken place on its watch. The peace, the lack of movement, the shock seemed to last for years. Then I heard the stomping boots clatter past me.

Then the alarms started wailing, wailing from every direction. No screams, thank God.

An Eastern European accent. 'Everyone is ok, yeah? What the fuck? Did you and the other two get out?'

'Yeah, everyone out, no problem. What the fuck? The entire building! Just come down!'

Men in overalls and blue hard hats just stood with hands on heads, surveying what used to be No. 1 The Studios, saying, 'What the fuck? What the fuck?'

Bob and Kate appeared from nowhere. Bob started laughing.

Pete was squatting, one knee on the ground, hand on head, unmoved, cool as a cucumber. Pressing a button.

Another flash, another enormous explosion from the direction of No. 1 The Books, where the Central Library used to bask. Not as loud. Still it thundered. Bob's laughs grew heartier now. Tears streamed down his face. Smoke rose up, turning day to night. When it cleared, all I could see was a gap on the horizon, a jigsaw piece removed, a tooth pulled, a slice of city given back to the sky, a blot on the landscape gone, a different view of the buildings beyond, an odd feeling, a sense of a job well done. I felt the tiles of Centenary Square hard on the back of my head.

Pete pressed again. One more huge bang in the distance, coming from the direction of No. 1 the Priories. Shock. Again, less loud than the first two. Too far away. Still demanding attention though. Then, my ears ringing, tinnitus squawking, like the sound of Mids TV after closedown. I put my hands on my temples and rubbed them, rubbed my eyes, my cheeks and my nose. Beamed. Laughed. Birds circled above, oblivious to the chaos, as smoke and dust wafted through the scene. Sirens sounded. Paused purgatory. Minutes stretching. Sickness simmering. Story ending. Bob and Kate peered down at me.

'Get up off the bloody ground,' said Bob, wearing a face like a Sunday-afternoon drunk, reaching down, his hands suddenly under my armpits. 'You silly sod.' I felt Kate's hand on my cheek. She stared into my eyes.

'Here's to life,' I coughed. The horizontals and the verticals mixed as I rose. I felt nauseous. I kept looking though. I kept looking. I always keep looking. I'll always keep looking.

Not The End

Unbound is the world's first crowdfunding publisher, established in 2011.

We believe that wonderful things can happen when you clear a path for people who share a passion. That's why we've built a platform that brings together readers and authors to crowdfund books they believe in – and give fresh ideas that don't fit the traditional mould the chance they deserve.

This book is in your hands because readers made it possible. Everyone who pledged their support is listed at the front of the book and below. Join them by visiting unbound.com and supporting a book today.

Iqbal Basi
John Boughton
Jon Bounds
Alan Clawley
Jane Clinton
James Drury
Peter Faulkner
Heide Goody
Una Haugh
Andy Howlett
Cassian Ledger

Emma Levine
Jamie Milton
Carlo Navato
Sarah Patmore
Penelope Rowland
Chris Sharratt
Jane Smith
Kat Squire
Josh Surtees
Hannah Whelan
Joseph Young